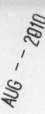

BACK ON MURDER

BACK ON MURDER

J. MARK BERTRAND

A ROLAND MARCH MYSTERY

BETHANYHOUSE
Minneapolis, Minnesota

Published by Bethany House Publishers
11400 Hampshire Avenue South
Bloomington, Minnesota 55438

Bethany House Publishers is a division of
Baker Publishing Group, Grand Rapids, Michigan.

Printed in the United States of America

Library of Congress Cataloging-in-Publication Data

Bertrand, J. Mark, 1970–
    Back on murder / J. Mark Bertrand.
        p.   cm. (A Roland March mystery)
    ISBN 978-0-7642-0637-5 (pbk.)
    1. Missing persons—Fiction. I. Title.
    PS3602.E7686B33   2010
    813'.6—dc22

                                                    2010005987

For Laurie,
witty and long-suffering,
a wellspring of creative inspiration

BACK ON MURDER

THE SUICIDE COP

PART 1

CHAPTER 1

I'm on the way out. They can all tell, which is why the crime scene technicians hardly acknowledge my presence, and my own colleagues do a double take whenever I speak. Like they're surprised to find me still here.

But I am here, staring down into the waxy face of a man who, with a change of wardrobe, could pass for a martyred saint.

It's all in the eyes. Rolling heavenward in agony, brows arched in acute pain. A pencil mustache clinging to the vaulted upper lip, blood seeping through the cracks between the teeth. The ink on his biceps. Blessed Virgins and barb-wired hearts and a haloed man with a cleft beard.

But instead of a volley of arrows or a vat of boiling oil, this one took a shotgun blast point-blank just under the rib cage, flaying his wife-beater and the chest cavity beneath. He fell backward onto the bed, arms out, bleeding out onto the dingy sheets.

Lorenz stands next to me, holding the victim's wallet. He slips the license out and whistles. "Our boy here is Octavio Morales."

He's speaking to the room, not me personally, but I answer anyway. "The money guy?"

"La Tercera Crips," he says, shuffling away.

I've never come across Morales before now, but his reputation precedes him. If you're short of cash in southwest Houston, and you don't mind the crippling interest rates or getting mixed up with the gangs, he's the man to see. Or was, anyway. Guys like him go hand in hand with the drug trade, greasing the skids of the underground economy.

"If this is Morales, then I guess the victims in the living room are his muscle?"

Nobody answers my question. Nobody even looks up.

Morales lies on the bed just inside the door, now blasted off its hinges by multiple shotgun volleys.

Down the hallway, another body is twisted across the bathroom threshold, clutching an empty chrome 9mm with the slide locked back. I step around him, avoiding the numbered evidence tags tented over his shell casings.

It's a hot day in Houston, with no air-conditioning in the house.

The hall opens into a living room packed with mismatched furniture—a green couch, a wooden rocker, two brown, pockmarked folding chairs—all oriented around a flat-screen television on a blond particleboard credenza against the far wall. Beer bottles lying in the corners. Boxes on the coffee table from Domino's and KFC.

This is where the shooting started. The couch cushions blossom white with gunshots, exposed foam bursting from the wounds. The floor is jigsawed with blackening stains. We've left our traces, too. Evidence markers, chalk lines. Imposing scientific regularity over the shell casings, the dropped firearms, the fallen bodies.

One on the couch, his underbelly chewed full of entry wounds. Another against the wall. His hand still clutching the automatic he never managed to jerk free of his waistband.

This was a one-sided fight. Whoever came through the front door polished these two pretty quick, then traded shots with the victim in the bathroom before advancing down the hall. Octavio Morales must have been the target. Maybe he'd tried to collect a debt from the wrong person. Only guys like this tend to be the perpetrators, not the victims.

"What do you think, March?"

I turn to find Captain Hedges at the front door, his white dress shirt translucent with sweat underneath his gray suit. He slips his Aviators off and tucks them into his breast pocket, leaving one of the curled earpieces to dangle free.

"You asking me?"

He looks around. "Is there another March in the room?"

So I'm the designated tour guide. I can't recall the last time Hedges spoke to me directly, so I'd better not complain. After soaking up some ambiance up front, I lead him down the hallway, back across the body hanging out of the bathroom.

"Looks like a hit on a local loan shark," I say. "A guy by the name of Octavio Morales. His body's in here."

When we enter the bedroom, activity halts. Lorenz and the other detectives perk up like hunting dogs, while the technicians pause over their spatter marks and surface dusting. Hedges acknowledges them all with a nod, then motions for me to continue. Before I can oblige, though, Lorenz is already cutting between us.

"I'm the lead on this," he says, ushering the captain toward the bed.

And just like that, I'm forgotten. According to my wife, when a woman reaches a certain age, she disappears. People stop noticing she's in the room. Not that this has ever happened to Charlotte, quite the reverse. But I'm beginning to understand the feeling. Beginning? Who am I kidding? I've been invisible for a long time.

I wouldn't even be here if it wasn't such a big event. An ordinary murder doesn't pull the crowds, but call in a houseful of dead gangbangers and every warm body on the sixth floor turns up. The call came in during a lull in my special duties, and I couldn't resist the itch. It's been a while since I've gotten to work a fresh murder scene.

"Looks like he was trying to hold the door shut," Lorenz is saying, miming the actions as he describes them. "They put some rounds on the door—*blam, blam*—and he goes reeling back. Drops his gun over there." He points out the Taurus 9mm on the carpet, a pimp special complete with gold trigger. "Then they kick the door in and light him up."

Lorenz stands over the corpse of Octavio Morales, wielding his air shotgun. He even works the pump, leaving out the sound effects this time. The gesture reminds me just how young this guy is to be in Homicide, how inexperienced.

While he's talking, I edge my way alongside the bed, putting some distance between myself and the group converging around the captain. This saves them the trouble of having to shove me aside.

The house is basically a squat. The property belongs to the bank, another foreclosure. There's no telling when Morales and his crew decided to move in, but they didn't exactly improve the place over time. The shiny brass headboard seems brand new, but the lumpy mattress is too big, drooping over the sides. And the bedding must have been salvaged from the dump. The sheets were rigid with filth long before Morales died there. My skin itches just looking at them.

I kneel and lift the sheets off the floor, peering underneath the bed. There's no point, really. The technicians have already been here. But I feel the need to look busy.

The window on the front wall casts sunlight under the far side of the bed. My eye goes to a dark line of filament silhouetted against the light, a length of cord hanging from the mattress frame. Probably nothing. But I circle around for a closer look, jostling Lorenz and a craggy-faced detective named Aguilar, who's busy explaining to the uninterested captain the significance of Morales's tats.

I crouch by the headboard, sunlight to my back, and start feeling underneath the frame for the hanging line. Once I find it—it feels like parachute cord—I trace the line back to the knot, then duck my head down for a look.

What I see stops my heart for a couple of beats. Maybe it's just the angle of my head. But the knot is secured around the mattress frame, and the end looks neatly severed with barely a hint of fraying. A fresh cut, made while the cord was drawn taut.

"Did anyone see this?" I ask.

When I glance up, nobody's looking my way. If they heard me, they're giving no sign. I scoot to the foot of the bed, running my hand over the frame. Sure enough, another knot. This time it's sliced close, leaving no dangling end. Returning to the other side, I push the sheets up and continue the search. My pulse hammering away so hard I can't believe no one else hears it. Two more knots, one at the foot of the bed, and another at the head.

I rise slowly, examining the mattress with new eyes.

Morales lies sprawled at the foot of the bed, legs off the side, arms thrown back. From above, the blood rises like a cloud, ascending several feet above his head. The pattern in the sticky sheets is not quite right.

"Sir."

I glance toward Hedges, who's nodding impatiently at Aguilar.

"Sir."

He turns to me, relieved at the interruption.

"What is it, Detective?"

Lorenz and Aguilar both turn with him, and so do the others. They blink at me, like I've just appeared out of nowhere. Even the technicians look up from their work.

"Come and see."

I get down on my knees, motioning him to follow. After a moment's hesitation, he does, careful not to get his pants dirty. I guide his hands to the knots, watching realization dawn on his face. We both cross to the opposite side of the bed, all eyes on us. He kneels without waiting for my encouragement. When his hand touches the dangling cord, he lets out a long sigh.

"Good work," he says.

Lorenz pushes his way forward. "What is it? What's under there?"

Hedges doesn't answer, and neither do I. As the detectives take turns under the bed, we exchange a glance. He looks at me in a way he hasn't for at least a year. Not since Wilcox left the unit. Even longer than that.

"When you're done here," he says under his breath, "I want you to swing by my office." Then, to the room at large: "I want a briefing in two hours. Lorenz, you better get on top of this. We'll need a blood expert to look at all this—assuming he hasn't already. And Lord help him if he already has and he missed this, that's all I can say."

And then he's gone, leaving the room deathly still in his wake.

The next moment, Lorenz has me by the sleeve, dragging me over to the corner. His voice barely a whisper. I half expect him to chew me out, so his real motive comes as a shock.

"I don't get it." He casts a glance over his shoulder, making sure no one's listening. "What's the deal with the rope?"

It takes me a second to find my voice. "They're restraints, Jerry. One at each corner, like somebody was tied spread-eagle to the bed. The blood on those sheets, it's probably from two victims. Morales and somebody the shooters took with them, after cutting her loose."

"Her?"

"Just a guess."

He takes all this onboard, then backs away, patting me on the front of the shoulder. But the pat feels like a push, too. As if he's distancing himself from me. Or from his own ignorance.

"All right," he says to the room. "Here's the situation."

Before he can launch into his speech, I'm out the door. One of the advantages of invisibility.

Outside, layers of garbage tamp down the knee-high grass out front, some bagged but most of it not: sun-bleached fast food packets, thirty-two ounce cups, empty twelve-pack beer boxes, all of it teeming with flies. The house is broad, one of the street's larger residences, complete with a double-wide carport and a driveway full of cracked concrete, rust stains, and a shiny black Escalade. The keys are probably still in Morales's pocket.

The perimeter line is being held by one Sergeant Nixon—Nix to his friends—a cop who can remember back far enough to the time when Texas produced lawmen instead of peace officers.

"Look who it is." He gives my shoulder a pat, but it's nothing like the heave-ho from Lorenz. "What are you doing at an honest-to-God murder scene? I thought you were putting in time with the cars-for-criminals team."

"I came out for old times' sake."

"Roland March," he says, looking me over. "The suicide cop."

"Don't remind me. Anybody talking around here? Neighbors witness anything?"

He glances up and down the street, like he's worried the nearby uniforms will overhear. "The lady down the way might be worth a talk. See the yellow house?"

"I think it's supposed to be white."

Nix isn't a fat man, but whenever he shrugs, his head retracts turtle-like, giving him a double chin. "We got a statement off her already, but she sure was talkative. If you're looking for the full canvassing experience, you might give her a try."

Ducking under the tape, I head for the yellow-white house. The neighborhood must have been nice once, before it was sandwiched in by apartment complexes. In southwest Houston, the complexes serve the same purpose as inner-city housing projects in other parts of the country. They're easy to secure, so gangs move in and start doing business. Colombian heroin and coke, Mexican meth, crack—it all comes through along the I-10 corridor, and the complexes serve as weigh stations.

A decade ago, there were places along here a patrol cruiser couldn't go without taking fire from one gang or another. We cracked down, and the dealers got the message. Now they stick to doing business. Everybody gets along, more or less, except for the ones in neighborhoods like this, where the trouble can't help but leak over. But there's a tension out on the streets, a lot of rumors about the Mexican cartels and the kind of trouble that might be around the corner.

I adjust the badge around my neck. Give the door a good knock.

When it opens, I'm greeted by a ripe young thing in her early twenties, bursting out of a tank top and pink shorts, pushing the door open with her foot. Glitter polish on the toenails, a flip-flop dangling. Her features are two sizes too big for her face. Huge eyes, a terrifyingly wide mouth marked out in brown liner.

I glance back at Nix, who's smiling at a cloud pattern overhead.

"Excuse me, but . . . I was wondering if I could ask you a couple of questions?"

"About that over there? I didn't see nothing."

"What about earlier?" I ask. "You notice them driving up in that SUV?"

"Last night you mean? I was out there in the yard. Octavio pulled up, and he had some others with him. Little Hector, I think, and someone else. They rolled down the window and whistled." If she was flattered by the attention, she gives no sign now. "They don't stay there or nothing like that. It's just their party pad."

"Did they have a woman with them?"

"People's always coming and going. I told the other policeman already."

"Well, thanks."

On the way to my car, I give Nix my best Clint Eastwood glare.

He smiles back at me. "Anytime, Detective."

I don't know which I prefer more, being ignored or jerked around.

In spite of my reptilian tolerance for heat, the air-conditioning back on the sixth floor feels great, especially given the white Freon my car's been spitting out in lieu of cool air. This is Homicide, the nerve center, humming as always with quiet intensity. The clack of keyboards is a constant, the hum of conversation. For the most part, though, the cubicles stand empty. Only a few detectives have trickled back in, filling mugs with coffee, combing the break room for anything not too stale, reviewing notes in anticipation of the big briefing.

We aren't what you'd expect. Watching television, you might think we're all scientists with guns, working our cases with calibrated precision. But we make mistakes just like anyone, and all that technical jargon can be a coping mechanism, an alternative to dark humor. Some guys like to crack jokes over the corpse, and others like to talk about castoff and trajectories and residue. We're only human, after all, and the job gets to us sometimes.

We aren't like the cops on cable, either. We aren't crooked. We aren't pushing drugs on the side, or even taking them. We're not functioning alcoholics. We don't take backhanders or use racial epithets or delight in parading our ignorance, even ironically. If anything, we pride ourselves on a certain professionalism, which means we won't beat you with a phone book or a rolled newspaper. We won't frame you, even if we know you did it.

We don't have our own reality show—a sore spot ever since the Dallas unit made its debut on *The First 48*—but if we did, they wouldn't have to edit out the violence, or even bleep that much of the language. For the most part, we're middle-aged and male, split pretty much down the middle between married and divorced. We dress like there's still a standard to keep up. And no matter who you are—a shirtless banger with enough ink on your skin to write a circuit court appeal or a corner skank in a skintight halter—we'll address you politely as sir or ma'am.

We are polite not because we are polite, but because we want to send you to Huntsville for the balance of your natural life, or even stick you with that needle of fate. And respect works. It's as good a way as any to send you down.

All of this is true about us. Except when it isn't. And when it isn't, all bets are off.

Don't mind my bluster, though. Like the sick jokes and the pseudo-science, it's just another way of coping. Because I'm on my way out, and realizing too late I don't want to go.

The man with all the power is Captain Drew Hedges, who sits behind glass walls and metal blinds, his door resolutely shut. In a department that's seen its share of shake-ups, Hedges has shown a knack for hanging on and, in spite of his better judgment, has a soft spot in his heart for others with the same knack, myself included. He doesn't just run the Homicide Division, he leads it, which means earning the respect of some notoriously independent-minded detectives.

I rap a knuckle against the wood, then wait. No sound from the other side. I try again. This time the door swings open.

Just inside, Lieutenant Bascombe stands with his hand on the knob, still listening to the captain's final instructions. I wait my turn. Bascombe is black, bald, and six foot four, an object lesson in intimidation. His eyes have as many signs for fury as the Eskimos have words for snow, and I've grown fluent over the years, having so often been on the receiving end of these glares. Now, fortunately, he doesn't even look my way.

"I'm not asking for perfection," the captain is saying, "but it wouldn't hurt to get some dictionaries in here. It may not seem like much, but I'm telling you, this is an embarrassment. We look like a bunch of illiterates here. Is that really the impression we want to make?"

Bascombe's nodding the whole time, trying to cut off the flow of words. I can tell he's heard enough, and if I've walked in on another lecture about the standard of spelling on reports coming out of Homicide, I can sympathize. Hedges can go from stone-cold cop one second to high school English teacher the next, and the latter incarnation is by far the more frightening.

"I'll take care of it," Bascombe says. Then, noticing me, he seizes on my presence as an excuse. "March's here to see you, sir. Let me get out of your way."

He pushes past, disappearing in the direction of his own, much smaller, office.

"Come on in," Hedges says. "Take a seat."

His jacket hangs on a rack in the corner, the sweat stains on his shirt all but dry. He's rolled his sleeves up like a man with hard labor on the agenda. I sink into one of the guest chairs, crossing my leg in an effort to look relaxed. His leathery, nut-brown face is so weatherworn that even a decade under the fluorescents hasn't raised a hint of pallor.

To look at him, you'd imagine that squint could see through any persona, plumb the depth of any lie. When I first joined the squad, I was in awe of those narrow-lidded, all-knowing eyes. But I've worked for him long enough now to realize that it's just an expression, no more indicative of insight than his starched shirts or his square, gunmetal glasses.

"You wanted to see me, sir?"

Instead of answering, he reaches behind him, pulling a book from a shelf bursting with color-coded ring binders. He slides it across the desk so I can see the cover. *The Kingwood Killing*. Brad Templeton's true-crime thriller. I feel a twitch under my eye.

He taps the book. "You ought to read it sometime."

"I don't have to read it. I lived it. Remember?"

"I remember. The question is, do you? The reason I wanted to talk to you is, that was good police work today."

"Thank you, sir."

"It's been a long time since I've seen that out of you."

How am I supposed to reply to that? Instead of answering, I give a noncommittal squirm. If I had my way, every copy of that book would be rounded up for incineration. It's like a yearbook photo, only worse. A reminder of someone I'd rather forget I ever was.

He sees me looking at the book and clears his throat. "Now, the fact of the matter is, you got lucky. Eventually somebody would have noticed those restraints. It just happened to be you. But I recall you used to be very lucky. You used to make your own luck. Question is, can you do it again?"

I'm getting tired of his rhetorical questions, but I don't show it. Instead, I force myself to nod. It isn't easy. My neck's as stiff as a corpse's in rigor.

"Sir, if you'd give me a chance, I think I could."

He shows me his open palms. "What did you have in mind?"

"Stop loaning me out for these special assignments. Put me back on the regular rotation. Let me work cases again. Hand the suicide cop mantle over to one of the younger guys."

His head shakes the whole time I'm talking. "You don't get it, Roland. I didn't give you these assignments. You earned them. You haven't been pulling your weight, so it was either that or cut you loose. And to be honest, that's what a lot of people have wanted me to do." His eyes flick toward the door, where Bascombe was standing a few moments before. I know the lieutenant doesn't have much love for me, but it's still a blow to realize he wants me out.

"I have a lot of experience, sir. I didn't discover those restraints by accident." His squint tightens, but I press on. "You've got Lorenz heading up that investigation, and you know it's too big a job. Coordinating something like that, it's a little more complicated than filling out a few reports and interviewing a couple of witnesses."

"You don't think he's up to it? That's too bad."

My throat dries out all the sudden. "Why's that?"

"Because I was thinking of putting you on the case with him."

"With him?" I ask. "How about putting me in charge?"

Hedges laughs. "I admire your nerve, March. But you've gotta be kidding. I mean, take a look out there." He jabs a finger at the blinds. "If I pulled a guy like Lorenz off the case and replaced him with you, I'd have a mutiny on my hands. In case you haven't noticed, your approval ratings in the bullpen are at an all-time low. Ever since Wilcox bailed—"

"But if I get results, people will have to respect that."

Whenever he has something to think over, Hedges temples his fingertips, resting his bottom lip on the steeple, bouncing his head slowly until a decision comes to him. He pauses, goes through the motions, and then sits up straight in his chair.

"Take it or leave it," he says. "You can work the case alongside Lorenz, with him as the lead, or you can keep doing what you've always done and see where it gets you. I'm sorry, Roland, but you're not in any position to bargain here. I'm throwing you a bone. You want it or not?"

I used to love this job, and there's a part of me that wants to love it again. That will take work, though. After a free fall like mine, you don't expect to summit all at once. This is a good offer. I'd be a fool not to take it.

"Well?" he asks.

Two things are holding me back. The first is Lorenz. Not his inexperience, which could be an advantage for me, but the fact that, in spite of his inexperience, he's made it so far up the ladder. The man is connected. He has friends everywhere. If he wants to, he can make my life difficult.

"I'd be working for Lorenz?"

"More or less," he says. "On this one case."

Then there's the second thing. "Would this mean I'm off the cars-for-criminals detail?"

"Well," he says, drawing the word out, widening his hands to show just how much distance he'd have to cross to pull something like that off. "When's your next show?"

"Tomorrow morning. The big Labor Day weekend haul. But to be honest, they're overstaffed as it is. They don't need me."

The hope in my voice must embarrass him, because suddenly he won't look me in the eye. "Listen, March. I can't get you out of it before tomorrow, but . . . let me have a talk with Rick Villanueva and see what I can do. You'll be off the hook by Monday morning, all right? Just one more thankless task and you can start working murders again."

"Just one more?"

He nods. "But keep in mind, this is something of a probation. If you don't pull your weight on the investigation, if Lorenz comes to me with a problem, well . . . my hands will be tied."

"I understand, sir. There won't be a problem."

"Make sure there isn't."

Outside, the detectives are gathering. The buzz of conversation dips as I open the door, then resumes once they realize it's just me. I pick my way through the crowd, looking for a spot on the periphery. As I walk, I feel eyes on me. Looking up, I see Lieutenant Bascombe sending one of his eloquent glares my way. Next to him, Lorenz practices his scowl. The lieutenant's lips move and Lorenz nods in reply. Whatever they're saying about me, I don't want to know.

But at least they can't ignore me anymore.

CHAPTER 2

Houston rain comes down like a jungle storm, hammering the windshield and the pavement all around. When the sky darkens and the black clouds pour out their wrath on the city, there's always this hope at the back of my mind that the temperature will drop. But the effect is closer to emptying water onto sauna rocks. The air thickens. An insinuating heat radiates from the ground, creeping between clothes and skin.

I wait the weather out, crouching behind the wheel. At the parking lot's edge, the George R. Brown Convention Center looms gray and ridiculous. Gray because its bright white walls suck up the surrounding gloom. Ridiculous because the building could pass for a grounded cruise ship, with red exhaust pipes trumpeting out of the roof. Blue metal latticework buttresses the eyesore.

Even my wife, Charlotte, who feels duty-bound to defend the city's architecture in all its particulars, throws the George R. Brown under the bus, calling it a cut-rate version of a really classy building in Paris whose name I can't pronounce.

Most weekends, the George R. Brown plays host to an assortment of gun shows and boat shows, bridal extravaganzas and expos, but today, in spite of the Labor Day weekend crush, a modest corner is set aside for the Houston Police Department, specifically Lieutenant Rick Villanueva and his intrepid band of media hounds. Of which I am one, for the time being.

Once the rain dies down to a drizzle, I shape a copy of the *Chronicle* into a makeshift umbrella and venture inside. No gun show today—we schedule our events so there's no overlap—but the off-roaders of Harris County have turned up in force to ogle a glistening assortment of all-terrain vehicles. We'll have a competing spectacle for them soon.

Our room is tucked into the far side of the building, down an escalator and through a wall of glass doors. I make my way through the roped stanchions, past a half-dozen signs flashing slogans like *Green Power* and *Hybrid Houston*, complete with a little icon marrying the old Rockets logo with a recycling triangle. A matching symbol adorns the knitted golf shirt I donned this morning for the final time. Burning it in my fire pit tonight will be a particular pleasure.

As soon as I enter, Rick Villanueva makes a beeline for me.

"You finally showed up," he says, flashing his superbly white and insincere grill. "After that call from Hedges, I was afraid you were going to ditch me."

"I am after today."

He glances around, making sure the other officers on the team are keeping busy. By my watch, we have half an hour before the doors open, but there's always a chance someone will arrive early. The prospect of a free car will motivate people like that, even if they're accustomed to waking up at the crack of noon most Saturdays.

"Are you sure this is what you want to do, Roland?"

"I'm a homicide detective. All this"—I gesture toward the stage up front, the revolving platform with the mint green Toyota Prius, the television cameras setting up in back—"it's not what I'm about."

The expression on Rick's face is boyish and grave. "We do important work on this detail, brother. We put bad guys back behind bars. If it wasn't succeeding, do you think they'd keep it going like this?"

The last thing I want to do is argue the point. Unlike most of my friends from the old days, Rick's still talking to me. But I'm not

in the mood to hear about how essential our little charade is to the
city's well-being.

"Do we have to get into this now, Rick?"

"When else are we gonna talk? You're unhappy, and the first I
hear about it is from Hedges. You were drowning and I threw you a
lifeline, buddy. This is the thanks I get?"

"It's not like that—"

"You're swimming with the sharks over there, Roland. Don't you
see that? The best thing you can do for yourself is get out of Homicide, and instead you're putting both feet back in. You really think
you're ready for that, after all you've been through?" He shakes his
head, answering the question for me. "If you do it, I guarantee they'll
bounce you out in six months. No, sooner than that."

"Rick—"

He raises his hands in surrender. "But hey, it's your call, man. Just
don't say I never warned you. And don't come crawling back."

I have something to say, but he's not interested. Before I can get
out a word, he's already backpedaling, already turning toward the
stage. He has sound checks to run, cues to go over, warrants to review.
The fact that he took time out to chastise me is a testament to how
hurt he must feel. These things get him plenty of press, but not much
respect within the department. If there's one thing he's touchy about,
it's that.

And here I am, his rehab project, throwing his kindness back in
his face. I don't feel proud or anything. But it had to be done.

Commensurate with the diminished expectations I came in under,
my role in the unfolding drama consists of watching. Rick dubbed
the job "troubleshooting," but a better description would be "trying
to look busy." I'm pretty good at it. Plenty of experience. Before our
guests start to arrive, I take up a position near the media pit, chatting with a couple of cameramen who've already been briefed on the
need for discretion. In theory I'd run interference if anyone actually
approached the crews, but in the five shows I've done, that's never

happened. Hardened criminals are as docile as anyone when there's a freebie at stake.

"This is my last one," I say to the cameramen.

"What's next for you, then?"

"Homicide. I'm back on murder."

They nod, clearly impressed. But why am I showing off for a couple of strangers like this? Why the need to distance myself from what's about to happen? It looks desperate. I wander away from them, hoping to minimize the temptation, and run straight into Sonia Decker.

I can't stand the woman, but she took a shine to me right from the start, spotting a fellow mid-forties burnout. Unlike me, Sonia's happy with how her career is going. She's the ideal government employee, content just punching the clock at day's end. Her wispy hair might be brown, might be blond. Under all that makeup, her skin might be good, might be bad. She touches too readily, knows nothing of personal space, and has a three-pack-a-day laugh.

"When I started with all this," she confides with a cynical sneer as close to a smile as I've ever seen on her, "it was all sweepstakes prizes and missing inheritances. You gotta hand it to Lieutenant Rick, he's got a sense of humor. I mean, all this green hybrid rubbish? It's priceless. So politically correct."

I give her a vague nod, hoping she'll go away.

"Just look at those suckers."

The first guests now shuffle inside, their dreamy eyes glued to the revolving Prius. Imagining themselves behind the wheel, or maybe driving the hybrid over to the nearest chop shop and cashing out. Either way, they're hooked.

"Something for nothing." She rubs her hands together. I've heard sandpaper that was smoother. "Not in this lifetime, my friends. Greed goeth before a fall."

I'm tempted to correct her quotation, but that sort of thing just encourages Sonia. Afraid of a five-minute digression on the precise wording of the King James Bible, I keep my mouth shut. Anyway, she may be wrong about the quote, but she's right about greed. That's the one lesson of my cars-for-criminals experience.

If they weren't blinded by greed, at least some of these baggy pants playas and buttoned-up cholos would take a look around. They'd start asking when random selection started favoring the predominantly male and predominantly minority population. When did chance suddenly take a turn in their favor?

They might wonder why so many of the giveaway program's green-shirted minions sport crew cuts and ex-military stares, why they look kind of familiar, a lot like the cops who busted them in the first place. They might even recognize a few of their fellow winners as former cellmates or street competitors. They might realize that what they have in common isn't that they're lucky but that they all have outstanding warrants.

But they don't. All they see—all they ever see—is the car.

"So I hear you're leaving us," Sonia says, and now I know why we accidentally crossed paths. I guess I was blinded, too.

"This is my last day. I'm back on the job now, working a real case. You hear about that house off West Bellfort full of dead LTC bangers?"

"Big loss," she sniffs. "That's yours, huh?"

"I'm working it."

She can't help noticing the way I hedged, which draws a sound from her lungs that might be a cough, might be a laugh. Pats me on the shoulder blade, nodding her head in an exaggerated way. "All I can say is, I wish you the best."

"Thanks," I say to her departing back.

The room starts filling up, then the lights dim. Onstage, a projection screen comes to life. A silver convertible—not a hybrid, but who's counting?—threads a series of alpine turns, then an artificially enhanced blonde in a sequined sheath prances around the parked vehicle, running her hands all over its curves.

Offstage to the right, a four-piece metal band lays down a thumping beat. They're off-duty vice cops who jam together on weekends, only too happy to provide entertainment at one of Lieutenant Rick's gigs. The crowd gets into it, clapping their hands, shouting encouragement to the on-screen blonde. Even in the dark room, a spotlight lingers on the Prius, a concrete image of the promise that brought them here.

As a testament to human gullibility, this show's tops. Watching it long enough could turn the right sort of man into a philosopher. Not me, though. All I get is depressed. I'd rather pluck these guys off the street one by one. Fair and square, without any subterfuge. Out there, I wouldn't pity them. I wouldn't feel sorry for the family members they dragged along, either.

Once we've checked everyone through, the video stops and Rick jogs out onstage like a motivational speaker, cupping a hand to his ear for more applause. His speech changes every time, depending on what we're supposedly giving away, but the essence is the same.

"It's time for Houston to get moving again," he says, "and you're gonna be part of the solution. On behalf of all my colleagues, I want to thank you for coming out. It's our pleasure to serve you in this way."

From the back of the room, a group of burly, mustached men in green polos let out a cheer, clapping their hands above their heads.

"Our pleasure!" someone hoots. The crowd applauds once more.

Part of the game for Rick is to work as many ironic digs into the speech as possible. Afterward, the team will celebrate each one with a clink of beer bottles. The joke hasn't been funny to me in a while.

It seems a couple of our guests feel the same way.

I spot their silhouettes against the stage lights, two men working their way toward the aisle, then navigating the darkness in search of an exit. A regular odd couple. One tall and broad, the other slight enough to pass for a kid. Maybe the impossibility of the giveaway suddenly dawned on them. More likely, they're heading for the restroom. Planning to snort one moment-heightening substance or another.

As they pass me, I follow. Time for some troubleshooting.

★

The side exit sign is illuminated by code. Once they find it, a ray of light shines in back of the room. By the time my hand touches the door I can see other officers heading my way, alerted by the flash. But I'm first in line.

Out in the corridor, there are two options. They can turn left and head toward the escalator, or take a right to the restrooms. I emerge into the brightness, blink my eyes a few times, then spot them huddled halfway to the exit, deep in conversation. As I approach, it's clear they're arguing about something.

"I told you—I seen him," the smaller one says. There's a sharp, panicked entreaty in his voice. He's in a black T-shirt and skinny black jeans, accentuating his diminutive stature. Olive-skinned. Unnaturally jet-black hair.

But it's the other guy I fixate on, because there's something familiar about him. A white tank clings to his lean, prison-built torso, hidden by the square overshirt hanging unbuttoned from his shoulders. Crisp denim and unlaced Timberlands. It's the face, though, the way he nods in comprehension as the smaller guy talks, pushing out his bottom lip. The white of teeth and eyes against his dark skin.

I know this man.

He looks up as I approach. The smaller one sputters into silence.

"Anything I can do to help, gentlemen?" I ask in my best approximation of a customer-service voice. "You're missing the best part."

"We're just about to leave," the smaller one says, jabbing his thumb toward the exit. "There's this dude I don't wanna run into—and anyway, this ain't my thing. I'm just here for the moral support."

The big guy holds him back. "Come on, man. Don't bail on me like this."

"Sir, you don't want to miss your turn. They'll be handing out keys in a minute."

He's clearly torn between his buddy and the free car, looking one way, then the other, rubbing a hand over his prickly face. Then his eyes fix on me. His expression starts to change. He raises an index finger, trying to place me.

Coleman, that's his name.

His eyes flare. "You're—"

A half-dozen officers suddenly file through the door, taking up positions all around us.

"Wait a second, here," he says, edging toward his companion and the faraway exit. His eyes dart around, looking for an opening.

Over my shoulder, the door swings shut with a *whoosh*. That's the signal. We converge on him all at once, the way we do, swarming a potential threat before it can develop. Coleman's still at the verbal stage, protesting as the illusion crashes down. No free car. No run of luck. No going home after this. By the time he gets physical, we've already cranked him around and pushed his face against the wall, pinning his arms back, securing his wrists with zip ties.

"This ain't right, now," he keeps saying. "This ain't right."

Meanwhile, his friend starts backing down the corridor, leaving Coleman to fend for himself. He turns to run, then sees another set of officers at the exit, cutting off his escape. That stops him. He leans against the wall, burying his face in his hands.

"It's me, Detective," Coleman says. "You know me."

My mental filing cabinet rattles, then the details flood back. Serving time for robbery up at Huntsville, Coleman found Jesus and started testifying against his former friends, including a trigger man I'd been trying to build a case against for months. My usual skepticism about jailhouse conversion was suspended, since for once the born-again felon followed up with some action. Last I'd heard, he'd gotten early release after a prosecutor and one of the prison chaplains went to bat for him with the parole board.

"I do know you," I tell him. "What are you doing here?"

He tries to gesture with his pinioned hands. "They said they givin' away cars in there!"

"Yeah, but not to just anyone. You don't get one of those invitations unless there's a warrant on you, Coleman."

His head droops, eyes closing in defeat. The officers around him exchange a look. Then he glances up with a pleading smile. "But, Mr. March, you gotta help me. It's true I messed up—"

"I thought you found Jesus, Coleman." I get a chuckle from the other cops, which is more gratifying than it should be.

"I found him," he says, "then I kinda lost him again. But I'm on the path now, sir, and this was just the thing I needed. This car, I mean. So I can drive myself to a job."

It's getting hard for the other cops not to laugh.

"There aren't any cars, boy," one of them says.

When this sinks in, Coleman's head drops again. He makes a keening sound and starts struggling to get free. We all press in, squeezing the fight out of him. The whole time I keep shushing him like a mother comforting her child. The less noise we make out here, the better.

The officers at the end of the corridor troop the smaller guy over to us, hands behind his back. He glares at me through wet-rimmed eyes. He can't be much older than twenty.

"What's your story?" I ask him.

"I ain't done nothing. I told you I just tagged along."

"He my ride," Coleman says, calm again.

One of the officers hands me the kid's wallet.

"Your name's Francisco Rios?"

"Frank," he says. "Can't you just let me go?"

"Anybody have the list?"

Almost before the words are out, someone hands me a copy of the guest list. There's a rugby scrimmage of officers in the corridor, and somehow I've taken the lead. It feels nice, I have to admit. I flip through the list. Francisco Rios isn't on it.

Checking my watch, I figure they're already processing people inside, calling manageable groups backstage while the loud music and the flashing video screen keep the rest entertained. Behind the curtain, we have a well-oiled assembly line that ends in a series of burglar-barred school buses out back. Until they're done, we don't want any distractions. It's probably best to sit on Coleman and Rios for the time being.

"Let's head down there," I say, pointing toward the restrooms.

Coleman follows passively—not that there's much choice the way we're frog-marching him—but Rios digs in his heels.

"I haven't done anything! You can't do this!"

I leave Coleman to help grapple with the kid. In spite of his size, he's got some fight in him. Somebody gets hold of his bound wrists, though, turning them into a rudder. Rios squeals and tries to twist free, but for all intents and purposes the struggle is over.

"Listen to me," he whispers. "Hey, man. Listen!"

"Will you shut up?"

"I gotta show you something, all right? Just let me show you."

He's nothing if not amusing. I signal a halt so we can hear what he's got to say.

"Look in my wallet," he tells me. "In the part with the money."

I break into a smile. "You trying to bribe me, Mr. Rios?"

"Just look. There's a card in there. Call that number, okay? Call it and he'll tell you to let me go."

We've got nothing better to do. I take a look, and sure enough there's a business card tucked behind a wad of crinkled Washingtons.

"Call him," Rios says.

The card is one of ours. I run my finger over the raised emblem. The name reads ANTONIO SALAZAR, a detective formerly assigned to the gang murder unit. Now he works on a bogus Homeland Security task force headed up by an old rival of mine. The less said about him, the better. But Salazar is all right. He's passed a few tips my way over the years, and I've returned the favor once or twice. There's a cellular number inked on the back.

I tap the card against my finger. "This is legit?"

Rios looks at me like I'm an idiot. "Just call."

"Give him to me," I say, grabbing his wrists. I pilot him down the hallway to the restroom door, kicking it open and shoving him through.

I park him against the sink, tell him to stay there. Then I flip my phone open and make the call.

It rings a couple of times, and then a groggy Salazar picks up. "What time is it?"

I check my watch. "Noonish. I didn't wake you up, did I?"

"Long night." He runs a tap, then makes a jowly sound like a dog shaking itself dry. "Anyway, March, to what do I owe the pleasure?"

"I've got a Hispanic male here, about a hundred and fifty soaking wet. Age—" I consult the license—"twenty-one. Name of Francisco Rios, goes by Frank. That ring any bells on your end?"

I hear a cigarette lighter flick to life, then a long exhale.

"Yeah," he says. "Frank's one of my irregulars."

In the old days, people used to say that whenever a trigger was pulled between the Loop and Beltway 8, Tony Salazar knew who was guilty before the bullet even struck. He had a knack for recruiting informants. Instead of investigating murders, he'd work the phones for half an hour and come back with a name. Usually the right one.

"So what do you want me to do? We rounded him up at the George R. Brown—"

"Cars-for-criminals?" He chuckles in a way I don't like. "I thought he was clean."

"I haven't run him, but he's not on our list."

Salazar starts making so much sound he could work as a foley artist for the movies. Bare feet slapping tile, newspaper wrinkling, even what I'm guessing is a half-empty coffee carafe being slotted back onto the burner. All the while he hums a frenetic tune, like he's sorting something out in his head, and having a hard time.

"Tony, you still there?"

"I'm thinking," he says. "The thing is, I need to talk to this guy."

"I can hold on to him." I glance at Rios, who's hanging on every word. An involuntary shiver runs through him.

"Really? I could be down there in, like, fifteen maybe thirty."

"Just meet us downtown," I say. "I'll have him transported and you can spring him when—"

"No, no, no. Don't worry about it."

"You sure? It's no trouble."

He rubs the stubble on his chin for me, so I can hear the friction. "Do me a favor, okay? Cut him loose and tell him to call me as soon as he's out. Put a scare in him, too. If my phone doesn't ring, I'm gonna look him up. You tell him that."

I palm the phone and repeat the message to Rios, whose relief quickly dissipates.

"Matter of fact," Salazar says into my hand, "go ahead and put him on the line."

I put the phone against the kid's ear. After a minute or so, the tinny rumble of Salazar's voice comes to a halt, and Rios lets out a subservient grunt. Remembering the fight he showed out in the corridor, though, I imagine this attitude won't last once the zip ties come off his wrists. If Salazar gets his call back, I'll be surprised.

Not my problem. I take the phone back, get through some final chitchat, then end the call.

"Turn around," I tell Rios, then I fish a lockback knife out of my pocket and slice the restraints off. "Next time, just so you know, don't flash the card in front of anybody. Pulling it out like that in front of Coleman, you basically blew your cover."

I slip Salazar's card back, then hand him the wallet.

As soon as we emerge into the corridor, Coleman proves the wisdom of my advice. He gets a funny look, seeing I've freed his buddy's hands, then his eyes follow the kid's progress, crazier with each step. When Rios passes him, he springs for the kid. It takes six men to hold him back.

"Frank!" he shouts. "Frank! Why they lettin' you go, man? Why? 'Cause you workin' for 'em, that it?"

Rios keeps walking, shows a little swagger.

"I'm tellin'! You hear me? I'm tellin', man! Everybody gonna know. You dead! You hear me? Frank! You dead!"

Sonia pops through the side door, a finger over her lips. "You wanna keep it quiet down there? We're trying to arrest some folks in here."

"You heard the lady," I tell Coleman. "Anyway, you've got your own problems to worry about."

The big man deflates as my reminder takes effect. He hangs between the officers, letting his weight drag him down. Finally they release him to the floor, where he curls up, ducking his head between his knees. From the jerk of his shoulders I think he's starting to cry.

That's the last thing I want to see. I head back to the door, where Sonia's waiting, and pause before going inside.

"It's just getting good in here," she whispers.

With a glance back at Coleman, I pull at my golf shirt, stripping it over my head while straightening the white tee underneath.

"You know what? I'm done."

I hand Sonia the shirt.

She hisses my name a few times, but like Rios I just keep walking. With a swagger in my step. It's nice to have some for a change.

CHAPTER 3

This is not my beautiful house. And this is not my beautiful wife. But with apologies to David Byrne, it is. And she is. But things aren't always what they seem.

The house is in the Heights, a creaky old thing from the late Victorian, lovingly restored over the course of the past fifteen years. I've forgotten more about dentil molding than I ever wanted to know, and can disassemble and oil a mortise lock blindfolded.

The wife, Charlotte, is in the wholly anachronistic kitchen, perched on a Carrera marble countertop, staring hard at her foggy reflection in the stainless refrigerator door. Like she's expecting it to wave.

"What's wrong now?" I ask.

Five minutes through the door and already I'm putting things badly. Adding that "now" like a barbed hook at the end of the question. Implying there's always something. But this time of year there is. Every September we become strangers again, Charlotte taking refuge in her prescriptions and me in the company of unfamiliar faces, blank canvasses of skin, out after dark, testing myself in a city that sweats all night. This distance is predictable. We anticipate its ebb and flow. But somehow knowing it will come never quite prepares us.

So I'm short with her, but the fact that she doesn't rise to the challenge—no flush on the ivory cheeks, no fire in her coal black gaze—means there really is something wrong. I go up to her, putting my hand on her denim-clad thigh.

"Charlotte? What's wrong, baby?"

She wipes her dry eyes with the back of her hand. Her way of letting me know that, while she isn't crying, she's considered the possibility.

"You have to talk to him." Her voice comes out in the quiet, measured flow characteristic of her ultimatums. A reasonable tone, but brittle as a sheet of ice over a running river. "If you don't do it, then I will." The surface cracks. "But it ought to be you, Roland, because you're the man here."

Charlotte walked down the aisle with an unspoken list of male responsibilities—pumping gas, putting out the garbage, going to the door when someone knocks—which has only expanded over time. The one thing not on the list, because she does it so much better than I do, is bringing home the bacon. She's so valuable to her law firm, she works the hours she wants, from wherever she wants, redlining contracts phrased in language so obscure that reading over her shoulder gives me headaches.

I flick a lock of chestnut hair behind her ear, letting my finger brush her cheekbone. She recoils ever so slightly.

"It's Tommy you're talking about?"

"Who else? This whole thing has gotten way out of hand."

My big plan for the evening looks hopeless all the sudden. Sharing my good news, dragging her to Bedford, the new restaurant she's been talking about, where I've already managed to secure last-minute reservations. Bringing her home, leading her upstairs and lighting a candle or two. After that, who knows? Ending up in bed these days requires ever-longer campaigns, and this one isn't off to the best of starts.

"Let's not talk about him," I say. "There's something I want to tell you."

She raises her eyebrows, incredulous. "You haven't even heard what happened today. I can't believe you're shutting me down like this, Roland. You've got to do something."

I sigh, then slink over to one of the matching barstools, hoisting myself into a listening posture. But Charlotte doesn't want a grudging audience. My gesture gets nothing out of her but a roll of the eyes.

"So what happened today?"

No response. She gives her rarely used mixer a pointed glance, anything not to make eye contact.

"I'm listening, baby. Tell me what happened."

Taking a deep breath, she launches in. "So I'm sipping my coffee out on the deck this morning, going over my mental checklist, all the things I had to get done today. And as I'm sitting there I notice a beer bottle on the ground. I start looking, and there's bottles all over—under the bushes, sitting next to the grill, tucked inside the planters. And cigarette butts, too. Everywhere."

"Tommy had a party, in other words."

"It must have been some kind of blowout, too."

"So you went up and talked to him?"

An imperceptible headshake. "That's your job. He won't listen to me. We already know that. But I will not be cleaning up after him."

I consult my watch. "I have something to—"

"I'm not finished," Charlotte says, blocking my words with a lazy swing of the arm. "So I'm about to come back inside, and I hear somebody on the garage stairs. His car wasn't in the driveway, but I thought maybe one of his friends had taken it. Hearing him coming, I decided to say something. How could I not?"

"Right."

"But it wasn't Tommy. It was this . . . girl. This half-dressed, sobbing, heartbreaking girl. She was clutching her purse to her chest, and the rest of her clothes . . ."

"Did she look—had she been abused?"

"I don't know what she'd been. I asked, and she said she couldn't remember. She just woke up on the couch, all alone. He left her."

"Is this his girlfriend, date at the party, something like that?"

"She wasn't in the mood for talking," she says. "I called him, obviously, and according to him, she's just some girl who came to the party and crashed afterwards. So I ask him what he's gonna do about it, and he says why would he do a thing? She can call someone for a ride. He acted like it was no big deal."

If we were talking about a normal person, I'd have a hard time believing this. But Tommy isn't normal by a long shot. During our early renovation work, we'd put in the garage apartment so we could redo the bathrooms without disrupting our lives. Then a couple of years ago, when Charlotte left her old firm, we decided to rent it out. Since Tommy was a grad student at Rice with his dad in the oil business, he seemed like a safe bet. That's not how it turned out, though.

"Tommy's in a tough spot," I say.

"You're defending him?"

"Not at all. I just think . . . Look, the boy's trying to find himself. Maybe he isn't doing a very good job, but deep down he's a decent kid."

"You didn't have to give that girl a ride back to her dorm, Roland. She didn't have any friends to come get her. Or she was too ashamed. So it was me, I took her home. She wouldn't even let me drop her at the building. I had to leave her in the parking lot outside." She grows silent, remembering the scene. "Anyway, I won't accept that kind of thing happening under our roof. I'm tired of it."

"I'll have a talk with him," I say. There's not going to be a romantic evening ahead. I've resigned myself to that.

"Talk? You're gonna talk to him? I don't want you to talk to him."

"I thought you did."

"I want him out of here, that's what I want. He packs his bags and goes. That's final. Tell him that."

"I'm not gonna tell him that," I say. "The boy pays his rent—"

"You mean his daddy does."

"Sure. Whoever. I'll have a talk with him and tell him to tone it down. No parties, no loud music, nobody coming and going."

"Roland, that girl could have been raped. I mean, she was really disoriented, like she'd been drugged or something. We can't do nothing."

The drug reference gets me thinking, but not about Rohypnol. I remember the sleeping pill prescription on Charlotte's nightstand. I wish she'd get rid of them, but it's a sensitive topic. Last night I was out past three trying to catch up with known associates of Octavio Morales. By the time I got home, the driveway was empty apart from Tommy's Audi coupe, and Charlotte was fast asleep. Could he really have thrown a party in the backyard without her knowing until the next morning? Even a couple of friends swilling beer in the moonlight?

"Those pills you've been taking—"

"I don't want to talk about that again." She jumps down from the counter, starts walking in her bouncy, equine way. Hair streaming in tendrils. Leaving me behind in disgust.

"Maybe we need to," I say, going after her. "Because if there really was a party"—she turns, shocked at my doubt—"and you slept through it, then I'm wondering if the pills are such a good idea."

"Why shouldn't I sleep?" She jabs her finger at my chest. "What would I have to be awake for in the first place? You weren't here. You never are. We're barely even a part of each other's lives anymore. And I ask you to do one little thing, just one thing, and you blow up on me like I'm some kind of drug addict."

"That's not what I said, baby."

"You think there's something wrong with me?" she says. "That I'm not right in the head?"

I start to reply, but we can't go there. We really can't. Not with our history. Not in September.

She's breathing heavily, nostrils flared, waiting for me to punch back, but when I don't she decides to keep going. "Don't you think you're missing the point? That girl this morning, she could have been a victim of sexual assault. Here. On our property. And all you care about is lecturing me about my pills? Have you ever stopped to ask yourself why I need pills to sleep at night? I bet you haven't, Roland, because there are some places you just don't want to go—you'd have to admit some things to yourself that wouldn't be too flattering."

She's right.

"What was her name, this girl?" I ask.

"I don't remember . . . I don't think she said."

"Did you take her to the hospital, Charlotte? Did you report the incident? Get a rape kit done? Anything?"

"Why are you being like this?"

"Why am I being like this? Baby, listen to yourself. You think there are things I don't want to admit to myself? Have you looked in the mirror lately?"

We're not yelling at each other. Not quite. But it's a hissing little knife fight of a conversation, no dodging or parrying, just attack, attack, attack. The kind of fight that makes her sick of the sight of me. The kind that leaves me baffled, wondering how we ended up like this. She's talking, saying something nasty, and I start watching the way her hands move, the way her eyes widen and narrow, the fine lines that bracket her mouth.

In a movie, I would take her in my arms, press my lips to hers, and after struggling a second she'd give in, flinging her limbs around me, running her fingers through my hair. And maybe I'd carry her upstairs and throw her onto the bed, and she'd pull at my tie and my shirt buttons like the whole argument was nothing but foreplay.

But that's not how it happens in the March household. She goes upstairs all right, but nobody carries her. I want to hit rewind, do the evening over, say all the right things. I want things to be easy between us again, open and natural, the way I remember us being. But I don't know how to get there, so I end up on the living room couch, basking in the light of the flat-screen television she's tastefully concealed in an antiqued armoire. Flipping channels, defiant, settling on the station most likely to irritate if she hears the sound through the ceiling.

Cable news. Charlotte watches Fox. I flip over to CNN.

Tommy needs dealing with, I know that. This is just the latest in a string of stunts. He seems to gravitate toward offenses I'll take lightly but Charlotte won't, though I doubt there's any calculation behind it. Just instinct.

But this is September so it's not about him anyway. It was that girl, whatever her name was. One of Charlotte's triggers. About the right age, too. Her protective instincts must have kicked in, and without any outlet she'd just stewed all day in her rage.

On the television screen, after a look at what the Gulf Coast is doing to gear up for hurricane season, there's a piece about the upcoming 9/11 anniversary. Already there's an underlying anxiety, a need to play up the *never forget* angle, but unlike the Holocaust, which gets similar treatment even though its absurd to think the deniers will ever get the upper hand, here the shrill solemnity seems almost necessary. As if we just might forget, or at least might stop talking about the tragedy for fear of being accused of using or politicizing it. Still, I don't want to watch. My finger trails to the channel selector.

But then a new segment begins, and a familiar face looks back at me.

She's cut her white hair short, and the camera flashes accentuate the pruning around her lips, but otherwise Lieutenant Wanda Mosser is unchanged since the days I worked Missing Persons under her tutelage. It was a brief stint, not my kind of thing, but I always respected the lady. She was straight out of the Ann Richards school of toughness, rising through the ranks at a time when, to hold her own, a woman had to be able to convince everyone she was the best man in the room.

"We're taking the case very seriously," she's saying to a press conference audience, obviously prerecorded. "We are following a number of leads at this time, and we encourage members of the public with any information that might help to please get in touch."

Boilerplate stuff, but Wanda delivers the lines with conviction. Curious, I watch a couple of former prosecutors-turned-commentators long enough to figure out why my old boss is on the tube. A teenage girl named Hannah Mayhew disappeared in northwest Houston. She left classes midday yesterday at Klein High and no one has seen her since.

Early this morning her abandoned car was discovered in the Willow-brook Mall parking lot, and now a major search is under way.

But why is this national news? The girl's only been gone a day and a half. Last week's big headline, the vanishing financial advisor Chad Macneil, a former Arthur Andersen accountant who'd gone out on his own after the Enron debacle, had consumed the local outlets without getting even a hint of national traction. The man absconded to Cancun and points southward, supposedly with a suitcase full of his clients' money. Macneil, one of those guys who sits on everybody's board, has a finger in everybody's pie, put a dent in some prominent bank accounts, but outside the Loop, nobody cared.

Now a missing Houston teen is big news? Kids run away all the time in this town. Finding the car might put a sinister spin on things, but as far as I can tell from the commentary, no one saw her being abducted or anything.

Then they flash a headshot of Hannah Mayhew on the screen. Everything becomes clear.

She's a beauty, haloed in golden hair with a dimpled smile that's gotten plenty of use. Her eyes are that crystalline ice-blue that catches light like a prism. The picture looks professional, the background taste-fully blurred, like it came straight out of·a modeling portfolio. Which is no surprise. She has the kind of face that gets photographed a lot.

You can't call yourself a jaded cop if you're not cynical about the different treatment an attractive white suburban blonde gets when she runs into trouble. Her story makes the front page, beams out into millions of living rooms, and strangers everywhere look upon her as their own. They worry, they agonize—and above all they love, projecting all their frustrated hopes onto this inscrutably attractive teen.

By losing track of their daughter, her parents have donated her to the public at large, and now she's everybody's missing kid.

I shake my head at it all. In my house off West Bellfort, sharing her deathbed with Octavio Morales, there'd been another girl. No one's interested in her. Not even the lab. When I called to request a rush on the blood work, hoping to get an ID on my absent victim, I got the usual answer. We'll get to it when we get to it. No cutting to the front of the line.

But Hannah Mayhew won't have to wait. They'll bump her right to the front. Because girls like her aren't supposed to disappear.

I can't watch anymore. I turn the television off and go upstairs to change, not even bothering to keep the noise down. By now, her pills downed with a glass of water, Charlotte's long past hearing.

There are closer bars and probably cooler ones, but the place I end up is the Paragon, where the waitresses wear layered tanks with plaid miniskirts and the crowd would rather drink than dance. Even on a Saturday night, even as Labor Day weekend kicks off, I can find a table in the back corner, far enough away from the speakers that the ice doesn't shake in my glass.

I cast a glance over the room, confirming Tommy's absence. Pearl Bar is his haunt these days, but I've caught him at the Paragon once or twice and had to leave. Nobody knows me here and I'd like to keep it that way.

A waitress named Marta flounces up, showing an inconceivable amount of tanned thigh. Acts like she's never seen me before, not realizing she actually has. She jots down my whiskey sour, which I have no intention of drinking, then shuffles bar-ward through the crowd, shaking schoolgirl pigtails that look anything but innocent. I watch her move even though I shouldn't.

She's a cute enough little thing, but she couldn't get famous just by vanishing.

"Excuse me. Are you using these?"

I turn to the table next to me, where a couple of women in low-cut tops are busy arranging extra chairs. One of them looms over me, a pink-skinned blonde with glitter on her eyelids, of indeterminate age, motioning to the unused seats around my table.

"Take them."

They all descend, dragging the chairs off just in time for another wave of girlfriends, who arrive with many air kisses and group hugs.

When Marta returns with my drink, she nods toward the packed table and asks if I want to move. I think about it, but decide to stay put. I don't plan on being here all that long. She gives me a suit-yourself shrug, then takes a deep breath before retrieving orders from the newcomers. I'm thinking girls' night doesn't generate the kind of tips for the leggy Marta that a table of men would.

I stare into the whiskey sour like it's a crystal ball, but it doesn't reveal anything. The glass sweats and eventually the ice shifts. My finger traces patterns in the condensation.

I've been coming to this place for years, going through the same ritual. The first time was October 6, 2001, and that night I made a big enough scene I had to wait awhile before showing my face again. Now I keep it discreet. Nobody needs to know why I'm here.

People stream past the table, some heading to the restrooms, others hunting the shadows for likely targets. As the crowd expands and contracts, the bartenders move with practiced grace. There's a guy at the bar I've seen before—not here, but out in the real world. He cranes his head subtly, taking in the room without seeming to. A white male, my age or a bit younger, with a hedge of black hair jutting forward like the figure on the prow of a ship. Probably someone I know from the job, another cop, judging from the never-off-duty vibe he's giving off. I lean sideways for a better look, but the crowd closes in.

For the rest of the night, the party at the next table bleeds girls. They peel off in packs of two or three, heading home or to other locations. As they go, their places are filled by empty shot glasses and slumped-over bodies. The glitter-eyed blonde starts scooting her chair closer to my side of the gap, sending sideways looks in my direction, keeping me here longer than I'd planned.

"Are you gonna drink that?" Marta says, appearing suddenly between the tables.

She gives off a self-assured vibe, but it's the kind of brittle hardness you always see in women who keep choosing the abusive boyfriends, or can't keep off the bottle or the needle. Deceptive strength, more protective coloring than character.

I glance at the melting lowball at my elbow, but don't answer. Reaching into my pocket, I peel off a twenty and toss it onto the table. It's a stupid gesture, the sort of thing that gets remembered. But I'm sympathetic to her type.

"All righty then," she says, swiping the twenty and running a towel over the place where it landed. She gives the girls next door a reproving glance. "Sorry, ladies, but I think I'm gonna have to cut you off."

The trio who remain howl in mock protest, then start giggling, proud to have downed enough liquor to warrant intervention. I slip away to the men's room, where I check the time and feel slightly appalled at the company I've kept.

In the mirror I find a hollow-cheeked man in need of a shave, wearing jeans too young for him and a T-shirt too tight, with a rumpled cotton blazer that might as well have been slept in. His nose is off-center, no upper lip to speak of, and his jaw is far from square. In fact, to my eyes, there's almost a rodent aspect to the face. I'm not sure even a daddy complex and a quart of tequila can explain the drunk girl's apparent interest.

As I'm drying my hands, the door swings open. Somebody stops on the threshold and does a one-eighty, disappearing from view. I only get a faint glimpse, but I think it's the familiar-looking cop from the bar. When I emerge, he's gone.

The table of party girls is empty, too, sparing me the indignity of having to slink past. At the bar, Marta tracks my departure. Leaving the twenty was a mistake.

Out in the parking lot, sweat rises on my forehead and in the small of my back. But I don't sweat in the heat all that much. This perspiration is psychological. Time to get home to my dead-to-the-world wife.

The pink-skinned blonde leans against the side of a red Jeep, stabbing at the lock with her keys. While I pause to watch, she gets down on one knee, eyeball to eyeball with the lock, slotting the key in with the care of a surgeon.

Later tonight, sitting in my driveway with the ignition off, I'll try to remember how I crossed the distance between us. Try to recreate the steps, and envision my hand seizing her bicep, jerking her up from the ground. I'll try to recall the instant before I pushed her, wondering what I was thinking to put so much force behind it.

And I'll try to forget, too. The sound of her body thumping against the Jeep, her choked-off yelping. The sight of the tears.

But now it all happens in a blur, and the next thing I know she's screaming and flailing blindly with her bangled arms.

"Are you crazy?" my voice is shouting. "I'm doing you a favor!" My hands shake her silly, leaving marks on the skin. "What's wrong with you, getting behind the wheel in your condition?"

She's not listening. She can't even hear me over her moaning. And then her face changes, her mouth forming an O, her veiny throat jutting like the neck of a teapot. I realize too late what's coming, and step back just as the first ropey torrent pours out, splashing down my pants leg and all over my shoes. She twists free, staggering toward the bar's door, her hand over her mouth. Another wave hits, bubbling through her clamped fingers. That image, caught in slow motion by the amber glare of a streetlight, sears me.

What have I done?

She disappears into the bar, and I head off shaking my damp leg. Disgusted with her and with myself. My car is parked on the other side of the lot. I get the door open just as the first patrons stream out of the Paragon, glancing left and right for the man who accosted the glitter-eyed girl.

I don't bother explaining. I couldn't if I tried. I just leave, knowing one thing for certain.

They won't let her drive home like that.

CHAPTER 4

About the paperwork. You spend the first hours and days waiting on reports—crime scene, autopsy, results of various tests both standard and specially requested—then suddenly, it all comes flooding in. And you go from not having enough information, building theories on hunches and the thinnest observations, to positively drowning in the stuff. Sifting the data for what's important, that's a skill not everyone possesses.

Take Lorenz, for instance. He sits in his cubicle, scanning an index finger back and forth over the page. I've been watching him for a solid minute. Every couple of seconds he licks his fingertip, turns the page, then nods slowly, as if he's assimilating an important bit of info. Problem is, assuming our boy Octavio died from the shotgun wounds to his gut, there's nothing in the standard tox screen that warrants assimilation.

"Something interesting?" I ask.

The funny thing is, he looks up in surprise. Like he didn't even realize I was watching. So the whole act was for no one's benefit, unless it's himself he's trying to convince.

I reach for the stack of paper at his elbow. "Mind if I—"

His forearm drops like a gate, blocking my reach. Nice. Lorenz had some muscle on him when he joined HPD, but somewhere along the line he reversed the balance between workouts and red-meat consumption. Now his blue blazer, which he keeps buttoned even when sitting, pulls at the belly and his shoulder pads ride up around his ears. On his lapel there are series of discolorations, spilled milk allowed to encrust, then brushed away without being cleaned. For a homicide detective, this verges on the slovenly.

"I'm kind of busy here, March. If you want to make yourself useful, why don't you start on those call-backs? A couple of tips came in over the weekend."

"I already looked. Nothing there. Can I just get the blood report? I want to see if there's an ID on the missing victim."

"If there even was one," he says, not budging. "Those ties could have been there forever, you know. There's nothing linking them to this particular incident, is there?"

"You mean it's just a big coincidence?" I stroke my chin in consideration. "That's a fascinating theory. Why don't you pursue that, and meanwhile I'm gonna stick to the more obvious explanations. Maybe we'll meet in the middle."

I'm baiting him, I admit. But to his credit Lorenz doesn't react. He just gives another of his slow, assimilating nods. Then he flips through his stack of reports, apparently hunting for the blood work. After reaching the bottom, he shrugs.

"Not here yet, I guess."

"Fine. Thanks for checking. I'm gonna call and see what the delay is."

As I turn, he grabs me by the sleeve. "Hold up a second. Have a seat."

I try leaning against the cubicle wall, but he shoves a chair my way and I finally relent. Once I'm seated, he leans forward and starts talking in a quiet, reasonable tone.

"Listen," he says. "I'm not an idiot. I know what's at stake here for you. You're thinking if you can make me look bad, the captain's gonna keep you around—"

"It's not about that."

"Let me finish. This is a big break for you, I get that. But I've been on Homicide for—what, a year?—so this is a big break for me, too. You're not the only one with something to prove. So we can do this one of two ways. You can back my play, in which case I'll be sure to throw some bones your way. Or you can turn this into a head-to-head match." He gives me his best psych-out stare. "In which case you'll lose."

"Really?"

"Yeah," he says. "Trust me. You won't even finish the game."

I vacate the chair, giving his oversized shoulder a friendly pat. "All right, then. Why don't we both just focus on the case? You do your thing and I'll do mine."

"That's not what I'm offering, March," he calls after me. "The deal is, we both do my thing. This is my investigation. Either we're clear on that, or we have a problem."

Halfway to my desk I offer an insincere wave. Reading you loud and clear. My brain says I should try keeping this idiot happy, but my gut wants to throw down. The thing about threats is, people make them out of fear. Either they don't have the power to follow through, or they don't want to use it. In this case, Lorenz probably could pull some strings, but he's smart enough to realize his position is only slightly less precarious than mine. At least I hope he is.

When I reach my desk, I notice Lieutenant Bascombe standing at his office door, peering over the cubicle walls. While I was watching my new partner, the lieutenant must have been keeping an eye on me. Having Lorenz for an adversary doesn't bother me—I'm not sure I'd want it any other way. But Bascombe's another story. Once he's sunk his teeth in, the man doesn't let go.

When your crime lab has had as much trouble as ours, popping in and out of the news, subject to independent investigation, with the

DNA section being shut down, opened, and shut down again, nothing is ever easy. I'm not surprised Lorenz doesn't have the blood report back yet. We send so much of the work out these days, it's hard to keep track of where it's gone, or what the status is.

But listen, this crime lab scandal has only been in the headlines for the past seven years or so. They're bound to get it sorted any day now. This is the fourth largest city in America we're talking about, not some backwater jurisdiction without two quarters to rub together.

So instead of making another pointless call to the HPD crime lab, I go to my work-around, dialing the county medical examiner's office. The music on the other end of the line is quite soothing. I could close my eyes and imagine I'm on an elevator.

"I'm sorry," a female voice cuts in. "Who were you holding for?"

"Bridger."

"He's in the lab, I'm afraid. Could I take a message?"

"I know he's in the lab. That's why I'm waiting. Tell him it's Roland March. He'll want to talk to me."

She thinks it over. "Please hold."

I might have stretched the truth a little saying Dr. Alan Bridger will want to talk to me. I'm pretty sure he won't. In the history of our friendship, I've done him exactly one favor, which he's returned a thousand times and counting. But it was a pretty big favor, introducing him to Charlotte's sister Ann. Plus I was the best man at the wedding.

When he comes on the line, eternal gratitude doesn't seem to be in the forefront of his mind.

"I'm not even going to say this had better be important, because I know it's not. So can you at least make it quick? The bodies don't autopsy themselves, you know."

"You're in a good mood," I say.

"That's why you called, to talk about my mood? I gotta go—"

"Hold on a second, Alan. I need a favor."

He coughs into my ear. "I'm sorry, could you repeat that? It almost sounded like you said you need a favor, and I know we already had this conversation."

"It's about some blood."

"You have your own people for that."

"Yeah, in theory we have our own people, but you're my work-around. And this is serious, Alan. I wouldn't have dragged you away from your thoracic cavities otherwise."

"What is it?" he asks, sounding unconvinced.

"That houseful of bodies from Friday. Octavio Morales, Hector Diaz—"

"Yeah, yeah, I know. I cut 'em for you. What more do you want? The reports are already out the door." He coughs again. "Wait a second. Are you working that?"

"Yes."

"An actual murder? I thought they only sent you out when a brother officer eats his gun."

"I'm off the odd jobs for now, and I'd like to keep it that way, all right? So you wanna help me out on this or not?"

He gives a theatrical sigh. "Not really. But go ahead anyway."

So I tell him about the bloodstained sheets underneath Octavio Morales, the ligatures tied to the mattress frame, and the obvious conclusion that someone was tied to that bed. If the second victim's blood can be distinguished, I need to know everything the sample can tell me, from type and gender to a possible identification.

"You're not asking for much," he says. "Seriously, though, can't your own people handle this?"

"Oh, they'll get to it just as soon as they can. But we're sending our DNA work out, and that's what this is going to take. We've got blood, but no body, and I think the whole key to this killing was that person tied to the bed. If I can identify her, that's the ball game."

"Her?"

"I'm assuming."

"Well, listen, I can't promise same-day service on the DNA front, but if you want me to expedite the basics, I can do that. That would tell you if you have another victim, give you gender and so on. Running the profile through CODIS, though, that'll take longer. But provided you can rush a sample over, I'll make sure it happens. All right?"

"Perfect, Alan. I'll bring it myself."

I thought taking Main the whole way would be clever, avoiding freeway traffic, but by the time I finally reach Holcombe I'm having second and third thoughts. The Harris County medical examiner is just a stone's throw from the Astrodome—assuming you have a good arm—but I can't seem to get there in the bumper-to-bumper.

If you'd told me at age twenty-one I'd spend a good portion of the next quarter century sitting in traffic listening to talk radio, I'm not sure I'd have had the strength of character not to drown myself in the toilet bowl. One of those phrases from Rick Villanueva's speech comes back to me. It's time for Houston to get moving again. When Bill White entered the mayor's office promising to do just that, I voted for the guy—and have twice more since then—never thinking this was more than a campaign promise. Nothing could get this city moving, unless you count a slow crawl.

During the news break, I turn up the radio volume.

"In the disappearance of northwest Houston teen Hannah Mayhew," the announcer says, "HPD officials announced today the formation of a new multi-agency task force to continue the search. A spokesman for the department refused to comment on rumors surfacing over the weekend that reported video footage of the teen's abduction in the parking lot of Willowbrook Mall."

Even though I work for HPD, just a couple of floors away from the center of gravity on the Mayhew case, this is the first I've heard about a task force. That's media pressure for you. Wanda's people, the ones with experience in these matters, haven't found the girl yet, so the powers that be decide to throw more manpower at the problem, confusing an already Byzantine jurisdictional map. A task force might sound good, but it just means more people to keep in the loop, more warm bodies without Missing Persons experience.

All the sudden I'm feeling grateful that my own missing

female—assuming there is one, and that she's in fact a she—doesn't merit as much public interest as the girl on the cable news. It's bad enough having to deal with Lorenz. And possibly Bascombe.

By the time I reach the ME's office, Rush Limbaugh is off the air and a new guy's repeating everything he just said. I switch the radio off, grab my sample, and hustle inside.

Bridger's lab is a lot nicer than the one I've just come from downtown, which always reminds me of a high school science classroom being run by student teachers. Here, everything is bright white and gleaming, an exemplar of sterile technology. None of the encrusted surfaces you see in our own lab, and none of the sexy mood lighting from TV. Every time I cross the threshold, a tremor of sci-fi excitement goes through me.

"You wait here," he says, pointing me into his office. He relieves me of the sample as we pass.

"You're gonna do it this minute? I want to watch if you are."

He pauses. "What part of 'wait here' didn't you get?"

Although he's my brother-in-law and I impose on him at will, Bridger can't help being intimidating. In his mid-fifties, handsome, with rimless eyeglasses and hair as white as his lab coat, there's something downright objective about the man, like whatever he says must be so. Which is why, when the district attorney's office has to put an expert on the stand, they always want it to be him. He speaks with the authority of science, even one-on-one.

So I kill some time flipping through this morning's *Chronicle*, the only piece of paper on Bridger's desk accessible to the layman. Not surprisingly, Hannah Mayhew's on the front cover, bottom fold, looking as blond and wholesome as she did on the flat screen. I dig for the sports section only to find it's missing. Someone must have snatched it, because Bridger's never taken much of an interest. I've had to explain to him twice who Yao Ming is.

As I'm shuffling through the pages, Sheryl Green pokes her head in. She stares at me like I'm a lab specimen, then she frowns.

"Where is he?" she asks, answering her own question by glancing back into the lab. "What is this, then, your break time?"

"He told me to wait."

I'm not sure if Dr. Green is Bridger's protégée these days or his chief rival, but I do know she's never cared much for me. Before my fall from grace, I camped out on Bridger's doorstep all the time, cadging for one favor or another. Sheryl reacted pretty much the way Jesus must have, arriving at the temple only to find money changers setting up shop. Lucky for me there were no whips handy.

With a sigh of resignation she drops a thin folder on Bridger's desk, taking the opportunity to glance over whatever paperwork happens to be faceup. Then she sees the *Chronicle* in my hand, her eyes tracking the headlines.

"Can you believe all that?"

I glance at the front, making sure it's Hannah Mayhew she means, then treat her to a commiserative headshake. "Yeah, I know."

"If that girl was black like me," she says, "or just ugly like you . . ."

"Tell me about it. That's why I'm here." I jab my thumb in Bridger's general direction. "I've got a bloodstain I'm pretty sure belongs to a female victim, from that shoot house off of West Bellfort? I can't even get anybody to look at it."

Not precisely true, but I don't often find common ground with this woman, so I'd like to make the most of it.

"That houseful of bodies?" she asks. "Four victims?"

"Possibly five. I think the guys who did the shooting took her with them."

Her eyes narrow. On the phone, Bridger hadn't seemed too impressed by the possibility, but Green is intrigued. I explain what I'm after from the test: confirmation of my hypothetical victim for starters, and eventually an ID.

"That's a long shot," she says. "Running a profile through CODIS would get you hits for known homicide victims, offenders, military, unidentified samples from other crime scenes, that kind of thing—"

"I know how it works."

"Then you know how unlikely it is you're gonna identify someone from the blood on those sheets. Unless you have something to compare it with."

What can I say? I answer with a shrug. "I've only got what I got."

"Then you don't have much."

Just as she turns to go, Bridger appears in the doorway. "You've got something, anyway."

He hands me a printout, which I spend all of two seconds examining. "How about an executive summary, Doc?"

"You have blood from a second victim on the sheets," he says, ticking the points off on his fingers. "Type O-positive, as opposed to Morales's much rarer B-neg. Your second victim is also female, as you suspected."

I feel like hugging the man, or at least pumping my fist in the air, but Green's presence coupled with Bridger's usual reserve precludes most anything beyond a smile.

"And there's more."

"More?"

"I told you not to expect same-day service, but—"

"You ran it through CODIS?"

He shrugs. "I got curious. Bad news is, you didn't get a hit. Whoever she is, she doesn't have a DNA sample in the system."

Green nods her head and gives me a told-you-so smile.

"You find something to match it against, Detective, and then you come back."

"Thanks," I say, and I really mean it. "That's exactly what I'm going to do."

Back in the parking lot, results in hand, I have no idea how to proceed. My initial hunch is confirmed, but then I never doubted there'd been a woman tied to that bed. All I know now that I didn't before is that I'm right. This will help me with Hedges, but it won't break the case, which is what I really need.

Instead of waiting until I get back downtown, I call in the results. Lorenz's number goes straight to voicemail, which is fine with me. I dial Bascombe and report directly to him.

"So that's that," he says.

"I guess so. It's more than we had this morning, anyway."

On the radio, a local call-in show is discussing nothing but Hannah Mayhew, alternating "oh, what a tragedy" with "why can't the police do more?" in perpetual rotation. A woman whose daughters attend Klein High calls in to let everyone know how devastated the students are. She's dismayed the kids are returning to class after the Labor Day holiday.

Then an anonymous caller who claims he's from the Harris County Sheriff's Department says this task force thing is only going to make matters worse. My sentiment exactly, but the rivalries being what they are, I find myself doubting when they come from a county deputy's lips.

"At this point," the host says, "Hannah's been missing for more than seventy-two hours. Since noon on Thursday. How likely is it now that she's gonna turn up safe?"

The supposed deputy clears his throat. "Well, I mean, stranger things have happened, but . . . If you ask me, it sure doesn't look hopeful."

I turn it off. Not because I disagree with his prognosis, which is only common sense, but because a light just went on in my head. Everyone's up in arms about this missing girl. And I've got a missing girl I'm looking for, too. With O-positive blood. Hannah Mayhew disappeared at midday Thursday. My shooting went down later that night.

Has the solution been staring me in the face? It's crazy, I know, but like the deputy said, stranger things have happened. And in a way, it's so obvious. How many girls go missing in one day, even in a city of millions? No one has reported my victim's disappearance, and that only strengthens the tie.

I'm afraid to say it aloud. Afraid to think it. But I'm going to have to when I get back to the office, because I'm starting to believe it's true. The girl tied to the bed, the one the shooters took after lighting up Morales and his crew.

It was Hannah Mayhew.

It had to be.

CHAPTER 5

I should know better. But listening with such rapt intensity, Lorenz fools me at first. As I show him the printout from Bridger, explaining the significance just in case, he nods in that odd way of his, like there's a neck spasm synchronized to his pulse.

"I know it's a stretch," I say, "but there are no coincidences."

Not that I believe this. My work is full of coincidences—people in the wrong place at the wrong time—but my need to persuade him overcomes all nuance. To pursue this line of inquiry without any hindrance, I have to convince him it's worth checking. At the same time, he needs to think it's a fool's errand, the perfect time-waster to keep me out of his way.

He examines a little chart on the page, bringing it close to his nose, then sets the printout to one side. The stacks of paper from this morning are neatly sorted into a series of piles, a sort that must have taken him all morning.

"Well?"

"Take a look at this," he says, handing me a folder from the top of the nearest mound. "I need you to follow up on it—" he consults his watch—"by the end of the shift today."

Inside the folder, there are several muddy faxes, half-page incident reports typed in capital letters.

"What about my lead?"

"The guy to talk to in Narcotics is Mitch Geiger. He's a friend of mine, does a lot of street-level intel. Rumor is, there's a crew that's been jacking stash houses on the southwest side. They don't report it, obviously, but we've been hearing things. I want you to follow up on the prior incidents, see if you can substantiate anything. Maybe there's a connection to the guys who hit our house."

I toss the folder on his desk. "You didn't answer my question."

"What question?"

"I'm going to follow up on the blood trail. Running the DNA profile turned up nothing, but if we can get a sample to compare with—from Hannah Mayhew's parents, for example—that will tell us whether there's a connection to pursue or not."

He nods, then hands back the folder. "That's what I want you working on, March. Geiger's expecting you. If you have a problem, take it up with Bascombe."

"What about the missing girl?"

"This is Homicide, not Missing Persons."

"We have a missing female victim, and they're missing a juvenile female. Her disappearance and our shooting took place on the same day. It's reasonable to assume—"

"Are you even listening to yourself, March? You think this girl from the news really ditched her classes, drove down to the ghetto, got herself tied down to a bed, then vanished after a crew came in and wiped out everybody else in the house? That's your theory? Trust me, I'm saving you a world of embarrassment here." He chuckles at the thought of this favor he's doing me. "You'd be a laughingstock, man. Just talk to Geiger, all right? I think all that time on the cars-for-criminals detail warped your instincts. The point here is to clear some murders, not get yourself on TV."

An hour ago I'd have put down money on the fact that nothing Lorenz could say had the power to sting. I would have been wrong.

Problem is, he's only saying what everyone else will be thinking. The lesson I learned putting in time with Villanueva is that the right kind of media attention makes careers. Hitching my wagon to Hannah Mayhew would represent the perfect application of the principle, assuming my hunch proved out. That's not my motive, but Lorenz won't be the last colleague to see it that way.

"I have to pursue this."

Again with the insufferable nod. "March, you gotta do what you gotta do. But so do I. You're either with me on this thing, or you're against me. And if you're against me, you're out. I'm not just blowing smoke here. Go ask Bascombe and you'll see."

"Fine."

I reach across him for the blood work, whipping the sheet within an inch of his nose. Just to be on the safe side, though, I keep the folder, too.

Bascombe's office, just a fraction of the size of Hedges's, is slotted into a row of glassed-in cubes along the back of the bullpen. On my way, I sense more than a few pairs of eyes tracking my progress. No one butted in on my conversation with Lorenz, but they all know what's going on. I can only guess where their sympathies lie. Lorenz has made a lot of buddies on the squad, but he's still pretty raw. My guess is, underneath the superficial bonhomie, my fellow detectives wouldn't be too sad to see him taken down a notch.

Plus, a few of them have been around long enough to remember what I was like in my prime. Their respect might not be what it once was, but all those years on top have to count for something.

Passing by a cubicle opening, I catch a flash of movement. I turn to find Mack Ordway beckoning me over. Before I teamed up with my ex-partner Wilcox, he and Ordway were the dynamic duo. Now, thanks to some health issues, Mack's mostly holding down a desk until retirement. Apart from a little water-cooler banter about the old days, we haven't had much contact since Wilcox left the fold.

"What are you trying to prove?" he whispers.

"Meaning what, Mack?"

He scratches his double chin. "I will lift up mine eyes to the lieutenant's office, from whence cometh his strength. The lieutenant is his shepherd, he shall not want."

"What is this, Sunday school?"

"Word of advice? You're not gonna score any points trying to make that kid look bad. He's on the fast track, no matter what. All you'll do is hurt yourself in the process."

"I'm just trying to do my job."

He shrugs. "Don't say I didn't warn you."

I thank him with a nod, then keep moving. He's not telling me anything I don't already know, but I guess his heart is in the right place.

Bascombe's door hangs open, as always. He never shuts it, never even lowers the blinds. Unlike the captain, he takes a hands-on approach, which means his office is a hive of activity. He's on the phone when I tap on the doorframe.

"One sec," he says.

I settle into a chair, using the time to flip through the incident reports in Lorenz's folder. They're mostly recaps of street intelligence. An informant complaining about supply problems driving up retail cost on the corners. Latin Kings issuing warnings after one of their packages gets jacked. A couple of Southwest cholos gunned down, supposedly in the aftermath of a rip-off. It's all pretty vague, which is to be expected. If there was anything solid, Lorenz wouldn't have passed all this paper my way.

Bascombe ends his call, prompting me with a palms-up shrug. "Now, what can I do for you?"

I slide the folder across the desk. "You seen this?"

"I'm the one who gave it to Lorenz in the first place," he says, not bothering to look inside. "But don't come to me about it—you need to talk to Geiger. He's got some kind of angle on this."

"I can do that," I say.

"Thank you, Detective. I appreciate your willingness to do your job. If there's nothing else I can help you with . . ." Bridger's printout shuts him up a second. He scrutinizes the results with a little smile.

"What do you want from me? Congratulations? Here you go, March. You were right. Good job, man. Way to deliver." An ironic handclap, one-two. "Now, was that good for you?"

"What I want is your permission to follow up a lead."

"My permission? You don't need it. I'm not gonna hold your hand on this thing."

"Lorenz wants me to follow up with Geiger, which comes from you. But I'd like to pursue something else in addition."

He hoists his eyebrows in mock surprise. "And what's that?"

Taking a deep breath, I launch into it, making my case as strongly as I can. Once he sees where I'm going, though, Bascombe starts shaking his head and shuts me up with a throat-slicing gesture.

"You wanna be assigned to the Mayhew task force, is that it? 'Cause I can make that happen right now." He reaches for the phone, then pauses. "Or, maybe you'd prefer to stay in Homicide instead? If that's your choice, then you better go talk to Geiger this minute. And if there are any headlines to grab in this case, believe me, you better not be the one I catch reaching for them."

"Is that what Hedges will say?"

"You wanna go ask him?" He smiles like he's starving and I'm his favorite dish.

The fact is, I don't. If Bascombe really wants me off the squad, I'm already pushing my luck too far. By giving me a shot, the captain put a wrench in the works, but he won't back me up the way Bascombe is backing Lorenz. So either I play their game or I'm out. Simple as that.

I can't bring myself to meet his eyes. "I'll go talk to Geiger."

But in the elevator I decide Geiger can wait a half hour. There's a stop to make on the way.

Missing Persons turns out to be a ghost town. I corner one of the civilian aides, asking to be pointed in Wanda Mosser's direction. She tells me the task force is operating out of the Northwest station, then starts rubbing her temples like they'll explode any moment. I thank her and turn to go.

"Hold on a second," she calls after me. "Cavallo's still here. You can talk to her."

I follow the direction indicated by her red fingernail, heading down a row of cubicles a bit more shabby and threadbare than our Homicide digs, though identical in principle. At the end of the row I discover a slender, dark-haired woman of about thirty, one long, pinstriped leg crossed over the other. The sleeves of her white blouse are rolled up, revealing sun-browned forearms and a diminutive silver diving watch on the left wrist. An engagement ring on the left hand, but no wedding band.

"I'm Roland March," I say, holding out a hand. "Homicide."

She looks up. "Theresa Cavallo." Her skin is cool to the touch.

I've never laid eyes on her before, or even heard the name, a testament to how out of touch I am. Because a woman like this gets talked about. I'm probably the last to find out about her. Large brown eyes, a sharp nose dusted with freckles, just a hint of makeup, and a slight dishevelment to her limply thick black hair. Letting the world know she can look like this without trying.

"You're working for Wanda?" I ask.

"Obviously." She motions lazily at the surroundings.

A knot forms in my throat. "I mean, on the task force."

"What have you got?" she asks. "I was just on my way out." She nods toward a black purse and a canvas messenger bag stacked side by side on her desk, a striped jacket nestled between them.

I'm not usually tongue-tied, but getting my hunch out proves surprisingly difficult. If I'd gotten Wanda face-to-face, there would have been no problem. If she laughed, I could take it in stride. But I don't want to look ridiculous in front of Cavallo, and the more I struggle for words, the more ridiculous I feel.

"What is it?" she asks with an impatient frown.

"Take a look at this," I manage, thrusting the printout from Bridger under her nose. "It's from the medical examiner's office."

"I can see that. So what?"

"This is going to take some explaining . . ."

She checks her watch. "I'll give you two minutes."

"Fine." I pull up a nearby chair, setting it just inside her cubicle. "That's a blood sample recovered from a house off West Bellfort. We got a call early Friday morning and found the house full of bodies. A Crip named Octavio Morales, if that name means anything to you."

She shakes her head.

"Anyway, under the bed we found parachute cord still attached. Somebody had sliced through the restraints, leaving the knots behind. Whoever was on that bed, the shooters took her with them."

"There was a woman tied to the bed?" Her eyebrows rise. "Was she sexually assaulted?"

I shrug. "Like I said, they took the body. Based on the amount of blood, I'd say she was seriously injured, or even deceased. But I'm just speculating about that."

Cavallo runs her fingers through her hair, shaking out the wavy mane. She has my attention. At her clavicle, a tiny silver cross catches the light.

"And you're telling me this why?"

"I'm looking for her. We didn't get a hit in the system, so her DNA's not on file."

For a moment she smiles with incomprehension. Then the bloom fades from her lips. "I see. And you think—what? That your missing body could be Hannah Mayhew?"

"It's worth a shot."

Cavallo laughs, showing off a pair of sharpish canines. "You've gotta be kidding."

"I realize it's a stretch—"

"A stretch? It's a hyperextension."

"I was hoping we could check our sample against one from your girl, or maybe the parents?"

"There's only the mother," she says. "Don't you watch the news? Her father died when she was a baby. Peter Mayhew? You don't remember him?"

"Should I?"

She shrugs. "Anyway, what am I supposed to do? Ask Donna if we can swab her mouth on the off chance her daughter was tied to a bed and gang-raped by a bunch of dead bangers? I'd just as soon not."

"I can appreciate that." I lean forward. "But before you say no, consider this. Your girl disappeared midday Thursday, right? Our shooting went down late Thursday, early Friday give or take."

"On the other side of town."

"Yes, but does that mean anything here? I can think of a thousand scenarios that would land a nice girl from the suburbs in a situation like this."

"But not this girl," she says. "You don't know her."

"Do you?"

"Not personally, no. But I've gotten to know Donna, the mother. She's quite a woman, I'll tell you that. If her daughter was mixed up in the kind of thing you're talking about, I think she'd know. And anyway, she's dealing with enough stress without putting something like this on her."

As she speaks, my eyes fix on the shape of her lips. This kind of sudden infatuation isn't common for me, but I'm having a hard time shaking off the feeling. Cavallo's my type, trim and striking and faintly exotic. A younger, taller version of Charlotte, without all the shared baggage. I inhale her perfume discreetly, then sit back, gazing at the sheerness of her blouse.

"I need your help," I say. "Call it a favor. I'll owe you. I can't do justice to my investigation without following up this lead. If it doesn't pan out, fine. At least we've ticked off that box. But if you don't help, I'll be honest, I won't be able to sleep at night. This is . . . important to me."

I shouldn't be pleading like this, exposing myself, but something about her seems to invite it.

"This is important to you," she repeats, glancing away. "What's important to me is not burdening this woman with more fear. She's living with the unthinkable as it is. I don't want to make her nightmares any worse than they already are."

"You don't have to tell her what it's for."

She thinks this over for a moment, resting her elbows on her knees, her mouth covered behind her long fingers. The engagement ring sparkles in my face.

"Look, here's the thing," she says finally. "The last couple of weeks, Hannah was getting calls from a certain number. And she called back a lot. The day she disappeared, she got a call at half past eleven. The problem is, the number belongs to a prepaid phone."

I nod in sympathy. Working murder, plenty of our leads dead-end at a prepaid number, enough to inspire legislation requiring IDs and tracking—not that it would help, given the ease with which a fake driver's license can be obtained. The things ought to be illegal.

"You know who uses those things?" I say. "Dealers, gang members, people who want to keep off the radar. If you ask me, that strengthens my case."

"Well, we already have a line on someone at her high school we think was making those calls. But you could be right. The point is, we've hit a wall. We're canvassing and re-canvassing neighborhoods, pulling in anybody who might have information, going over the Willowbrook Mall surveillance tapes with a fine-tooth comb. But I'm not sure it's getting us anywhere. Hence the task force. They're hoping to get a result by throwing more money and manpower at the problem."

"The same old story," I say. "Look, it sounds to me like you can justify pursuing something like this, whether it's a long shot or not. I used to work for Wanda. I know she won't stand in the way. She's played a few hunches in her time, too."

Again, she plunges into thought, knitting her eyebrows together in concentration. I'm tempted to say more, but I keep my mouth shut, letting her argue both sides in her head. It's not every day a stranger shows up trying to enlist you on his quixotic quest. The fact she's even halfway receptive bodes well.

"One condition," she says.

"Anything."

"You come with me. I'll introduce you to Donna, and if you still have the guts, I'll ask her for the swab. That way, no matter what happens, she'll know it's not coming from me."

Not what I was expecting. Not at all. But the prospect intrigues me. I'm not anxious to spend time with the frantic mother, but driving out to the suburbs in the presence of Theresa Cavallo seems like a worthwhile way to spend the rest of the afternoon. There's just one little problem.

"I need to make a phone call first," I say. Using her desk phone, I dial Narcotics and ask for Mitch Geiger. His number rings, then goes through to voicemail. I leave my name and my mobile number, asking him to call when he gets a chance.

When I hang up, Cavallo is already standing, slipping her jacket on. She's about five foot nine. Lean, but not skinny. She clips a holstered SIG Sauer just ahead of her hip. It disturbs the line of her jacket, but there's something about an attractive woman packing a gun. I've made the right call on this one.

"Are you driving?" I ask.

In answer, she dangles a set of keys.

CHAPTER 6

We battle the outbound traffic stacking up on I-45, then cut over on the Sam Houston Tollway to Stuebner Airline, crossing FM-1960 into a wooded, suburban terra incognita. My mental map of Houston grows sketchy this side of the tollway, but Cavallo navigates like a veteran, one hand on the wheel, the other perpetually in motion, punctuating her words. I like the way she talks, putting her whole body into it, like a sentence isn't really a sentence until it's acted out.

In forty-five minutes she's given me an overview of the entire case, and if I'd paid attention I'm sure it would have been edifying. But the way her watch slides down her wrist distracts me, and so does the movement of her leg as she accelerates and brakes. The shape of her ear, visible as she flicks her hair back. The vein in her throat that grows taut as she cuts off yet another inattentive soccer mom.

I let out a sigh.

"What?"

"I didn't say anything."

She eyeballs me a moment, then digs her phone out. After making a call, she tells me that instead of meeting Donna Mayhew at her home, we have to intercept her at church.

"Donna's camped out at her office there," she says. "It's easier to stay out of the media spotlight that way than going home."

"Why would she want to keep a low profile?" I ask, thinking the more attention her missing daughter's case gets, the better.

"She doesn't want to feed the frenzy. I'm not saying I agree with that decision, but the woman's had some experience in the public eye, so I have to respect it."

"What kind of experience?"

She looks at me with wide-eyed incredulity, like I've just admitted never having heard of the Rolling Stones or something. "Seriously? With her husband." Her voice jumps an octave. "The whole thing when he died? You really have no idea?"

"None."

So she tells me about Peter Mayhew, a local celebrity preacher from the early 1990s. After some kind of charismatic awakening, he abandoned his Baptist upbringing and founded a nondenominational church out in the Houston suburbs. It kept growing, along with his national status. In his early forties he married a woman half his age, fathered Hannah, and booked speaking engagements around the country.

"I heard him once," Cavallo says, "at a conference for teens my parents sent me to. He was really good. Very inspirational."

I'm not sure what to say to this, so I just nod.

Mayhew left for a South American tour, boarding a private plane chartered by his supporters. He never arrived. The plane's wreckage was recovered in the Gulf, but no bodies were found. Suddenly the story starts sounding familiar.

"So she's at this church?"

"She works there. In the women's ministry."

The familiar way she uses terms like that—women's ministry—and her teenage memory of hearing Peter Mayhew's inspirational message make me think that cross around her neck is more than decorative.

When she first mentioned the church, chalk white fluted columns came to mind, along with a needle-sharp steeple, stained glass and stone, like the one my mother dragged me to as a kid. Or maybe white clapboard. Cypress Community Church turns out to be nothing like that. We pull into the parking lot of what could pass for a junior college campus, a sea of blacktop with a ground-hugging brick and glass structure floating in the center. The electronic sign at the entrance alerts passing cars of next weekend's sermon series and an upcoming concert. Scrolling across the bottom is a reminder: PRAY FOR HANNAH'S SAFE RETURN.

"This is a church?" Along with the question, a dismissive laugh escapes my lips.

Cavallo tenses, but ignores my remark.

As we roll up, a red van with the church's name painted in white letters along the side pulls to a stop, the window sliding down. Behind the wheel, a heavyset man in sunglasses gives us his made-for-television smile. Cavallo asks about Donna Mayhew, and he directs her inside.

"Who was that guy?" I ask.

Cavallo shrugs. "Never seen him before. One of the staff, I guess. They have a lot of people working up here, and now a bunch of volunteers, too. The church is coordinating its own search, putting out flyers, going door to door. It's pretty impressive."

"Is that right?"

"Yes," she says. "It is."

Living in a city where the professional basketball team's former venue is now a megachurch, it shouldn't surprise me to find one of our many suburban congregations sprawling on such a massive scale. As we pass through one of a dozen glass double doors into the sub-zero entry, a vaulted shopping mall–style atrium hung with vibrantly colored banners, I'm slightly in awe. We pause at an unmanned information desk so Cavallo can conduct a quick orientation.

"The auditorium is through there," she says, pointing to the far side of the entry, where a dozen more double doors—made of wood this time—crouch under the dim mood lights. To reach them, you'd have to hike across a vast open space lit from above by skylights. "Off to the right, they have the classrooms and family life center." I nod appreciatively in the direction of a corridor wide enough to accommodate four lanes of traffic. "The offices are to the left, which is where we're going." A smaller hallway, barely big enough for a city bus, stretches off into the distance.

I start in that direction, but Cavallo puts a hand on my sleeve.

"Before we go any further," she says, "I want you to promise to be on your best behavior."

"What's that supposed to mean?"

"That crack you made earlier. The attitude. Whatever it might look like to you, this is a house of worship. You need to respect that. Or at least pretend like you do."

My enthusiasm for this woman is starting to wane, and I don't much appreciate the lecture. "I made one little remark. Don't you think you're blowing it out of proportion?"

"Just try and be sensitive, okay? This is a very . . . emotional situation, and you don't seem like you're in tune with that. You're a very detached sort of person."

"You say it like it's a bad thing." I crack a futile smile. "And besides, you barely know me."

"All I'm asking for is a little understanding."

My hands fly up in surrender. "Fine, you do all the talking. I'll work on my choirboy routine."

Satisfied, she leads the way down the left-hand corridor, heels clacking on the floor. I'm so disillusioned with her, I almost pass up the opportunity to study her from behind.

Almost.

Informing the loved ones of a homicide victim is hard enough, but at least there's a format to follow. People react in different ways, from unsettling stoicism to rage to something much worse, the kind of outright wailing despair that precludes all consolation. Still, the detective's script remains constant. We offer our condolences, even a shoulder to cry on, but make no mistake. We're here for information. We have a job to do.

In Cavallo's role, the dynamic is utterly different, because her appearance offers something a homicide detective's never does. Hope. It's no wonder she pauses at Donna Mayhew's door, working up the courage to knock.

"Come on in," a voice says from inside.

We enter a vanilla-scented, lamp-lit room with sponge-painted walls and fancy oversized couches upholstered in microsuede. The chair behind the desk is empty. Instead, Donna Mayhew sits in an armchair near the door, a mug of tea steaming in her hands.

"This is Roland March," Cavallo says. "He's another one of our detectives."

Not a homicide detective, because that would get things off on exactly the wrong foot.

She rises to greet us, her hands still simmering from the warm mug. If a police artist aged Hannah Mayhew's photo to show the most flattering outcome of an additional twenty years of life, the result would be standing before me. A compact, radiant woman, maybe five foot three, her beauty undimmed by her obvious stress, dressed in jeans and a frilly, netted top. Her thick blond hair pulled back into a ponytail, her face looking sober and scrubbed.

"Has something happened?" she asks.

Cavallo shakes her head. "Nothing like that."

Mrs. Mayhew presses a hand to her chest, deflating with relief. "You scared me on the phone. I've been trying to stay strong."

"I'm sorry." Cavallo touches the woman's elbow lightly. "Do you mind if we have a seat?"

"Not at all."

She motions us onto a nearby couch, resuming her place. On the coffee table between us, next to her tea, a fat Bible lies open, its crinkled pages bright from highlighting. A block of pink. A section of yellow. Tiny handwritten notes creeping into the margins.

That book, it gives a physical form to the woman's hopes. I can imagine her, stifling back the swirl of fear, forcing herself to focus on the words, reading and underlining anything significant, any stray phrase that can be interpreted as a message. I want to look away, but

I can't. Leaving the book open, it's like she's left herself sadly exposed. An image of my wife, Charlotte, flashes, one I long ago weighted and cast into the deepest waters of memory, only now it's slipped the chain and come back.

"Tell me what's happened?"

"I already have."

"I don't remember. Tell me again."

"I can't. I really can't."

Donna Mayhew notices me looking at her Bible. "I thought about canceling the study today, but to be honest I really needed it. Ironically, we're in the book of Job. 'The Lord gives and the Lord takes away. Blessed be the name of the Lord.' I'm trying to live that way, but you know, it isn't easy."

"No, it isn't," Cavallo says, giving her ring a nervous twist.

The two women share a look.

"You're doing everything you can," Mrs. Mayhew says.

Cavallo leans forward. "That's why I'm here. There's something I'd like to ask—"

Before she can finish, there's a knock at the half-open door. A man in his mid-twenties enters, stopping as soon as he catches sight of us. He mumbles an apology and turns to go, but Mrs. Mayhew calls him back.

"What is it, Carter?"

He looks like he's stepped out of a clothing catalog for the terminally hip. A line of fuzz under his bottom lip, his hair lovingly spiked, wearing expensively demolished black jeans and a brown Starbucks T-shirt stretched tight across Bally Fitness pecs. Only on closer inspection, as he advances tentatively into the room, the coffee-shill mermaid turns out to be a thorn-crowned Christ, extending his pierced hands, bracketed by the motto SACRIFICED FOR ME.

A piece of paper hangs limply from his hand.

"Is that the new one?" Mrs. Mayhew asks, taking it from him.

She inspects the page, then passes it to Cavallo. The familiar photo of Hannah, a toll-free tip number, a reward offer for information leading to her return. I wave away my opportunity for a closer look, so Cavallo hands the flyer back to the man. Before he can go, Mrs. Mayhew stops him again.

"Where are my manners? Detective Cavallo, this is our youth pastor, Carter Robb. He and Hannah are really close. Carter, this is the detective leading the investigation." She turns to me. "And I'm sorry but I've already forgotten your name."

"Roland March."

I stand, moving around the coffee table to shake the guy's hand. As strong as he looks, he has a weak handshake. I can feel him trembling. He won't make eye contact, either. The moment I let go of his hand, he backs out the door saying he has more copies to make.

I give Cavallo a quizzical look. "He seemed a little on edge."

Mrs. Mayhew smiles wanly. "We all are, Detective. This is especially hard on Carter because of their friendship. Hannah has been a real ally of his in the youth group since he first came here." The words are sympathetic, but there's something stiff about the delivery, running through the lines, not putting much feeling behind them. "It's hard on everyone, of course." She leans Cavallo's way. "Have you heard? They're trying to get me to go on TV."

"You should," I say. "It can't hurt."

Cavallo gives me a vigorous sandpapering with her glare, but I ignore her. Whether she wants to be in the public eye or not, what mother faced with the prospect of never seeing her daughter again raises scruples like this? She should be desperate to cooperate. Anything that helps the cause, no matter how peripherally, is worth a shot. I'm not about to say all this, but hopefully the way I'm looming over them, hands on hips, gets the gist across.

"Do you have children, Detective?" she asks.

I glance down. "No."

"My daughter, she grew up without her father. He died when she was still just a baby, so she only knows him through videotapes and other people's stories." Her eyes shine in the lamplight. "There was this thing she used to do. She'd come to me and say, 'Mama, I remembered something about Daddy.' And she'd tell some elaborate story about how she and her dad went to the park together, or ate their favorite ice cream, things like that. She'd remember the time he brought home a puppy. The most fanciful things—she has such an imagination—and then she'd say, 'You remember that, don't you, Mama?' or 'That really happened, didn't it?' Always wanting me to confirm the stories she made up, so they'd feel real."

"And did you?"

"Sometimes. The thing is, I was always afraid of what she might hear. When her daddy died, people told all kinds of stories. He was kind of famous in certain circles; he'd touched a lot of lives. Since his body was never found, there were people who said he wasn't really dead. Either he'd faked it to get out of some kind of financial trouble, or he'd gone undercover as part of his ministry."

"Undercover."

"Silly, I know. But there was a missionary to Bolivia, a really sweet man, a friend of Peter's from way back, and he came home on furlough and told me people down there had reported seeing Peter. He would turn up at evangelistic rallies, they said, and lay hands on people, healing them."

"Did you believe that?" I ask.

"My husband died. All the stories never changed that. But I lived in fear that Hannah would get hold of them somehow, and convince herself they were true."

"And this is why you don't want to do a press conference?"

"Not only this," she says. "But yes. I'll do anything to bring her back safely, Detective, but I won't turn her life into entertainment for strangers. Hannah has a right to privacy, don't you think? I don't want to give them more things to talk about on the news. I just want her back."

A woman after my own heart, I have to confess. Keep the media vultures on a starvation diet. But there's always a chance the added publicity will make a difference. Someone will remember seeing something. A witness will come forward. It happens all the time. In the same circumstances, I'd have to hold my nose and cooperate with the news cycle. Give it what it wants in hope that what I want will follow. Not that the world works that way.

As she listens, Cavallo's expression turns beatific with sympathy, only hardening when she accidently looks my way. There's more than just a feminine bond at work, but I can't quite put my finger on what's going on.

"Donna," she begins softly, "I have a favor to ask."

"What is it?"

"I'd like to get a DNA swab from you," Cavallo explains in her most soothing bedside manner. "It's not entirely routine"—a glance my way—"but in this case, it could help us with a particular line of inquiry."

Mrs. Mayhew stares down at her open Bible. "This line of inquiry. Is it something I don't want to know about?"

"I'll tell you if you do."

"But is it . . . ?"

"A very remote possibility," Cavallo says. "Just something we'd like to check off the list."

Donna Mayhew reaches forward, easing the book shut. "What do you need me to do?"

While Cavallo explains the process, producing the buccal swab kit from her bag, I wander back into the corridor to allow them some privacy. This woman still dreams of her daughter returning home safely, while I'm trying to establish the girl's a homicide victim. I'd rather not witness what I'm putting her through.

Across the hall, another door stands open. Glancing inside, I find Carter Robb sorting through boxed reams of paper, shifting the stacks on his desk, his back to the door. Unlike Mrs. Mayhew, he occupies a tiny, spartan office, almost entirely devoid of decoration apart from the cheap particleboard bookcases lining the walls, the shelves bowing from the weight of ragged, stringy hardcovers and creased paperbacks. The books seem at odds with his carefully ungroomed appearance. I wouldn't have figured him for a reader.

"Tell me something," I say, hoping he'll jump. He turns, holding his hands slightly out, like I've caught him in the act. "What exactly is a youth pastor?"

A slight smile. "Most days? A glorified baby-sitter."

He seems to expect me to laugh, but I make a point of keeping a straight face. "You want to elaborate on that a little?"

"Well, what I do is, I oversee the youth group. The teens, I mean. We have a service for them on Sunday nights, and some activities during the week, mostly after school."

"And Hannah's part of that?"

"Yeah," he says. "I mean, yes."

To his credit, he looks me straight in the eye. Set deep in that uncomplicated face, its perfect symmetry exuding all-American innocence, his gaze seems incongruous, darkened by an unearned seriousness, the sort brought on by books and too many grave conversations. This man, who has never killed and probably never even had to fight, whose only suffering up to now has been the failure to live up fully to all his grandiose teenage ambitions, somehow manages to project an old man's world-weariness, an acquaintance with pain that contradicts his unlined skin. The stress could do that, agonizing over the fate of his missing charge, but I get the feeling it's a preexisting condition.

"You two are pretty close, her mother says. Is that right? I was wondering if she ever said anything to you about gangs."

"About what?"

"La Tercera Crips," I say, flashing my best approximation of the appropriate sign. "A dude named Octavio Morales maybe?"

His mouth gapes open, but he doesn't answer. I might as well be speaking Greek. Or Sanskrit in his case, assuming they still teach Greek in seminary.

"I don't know what you're talking about," he says finally. "Hannah never mentioned anything like that, not to me."

"What did she talk about?"

Before he can answer, Cavallo's voice booms in my ear. "March, what's going on?" She dangles the bagged swab in the air, motioning for me to come along quietly, then gives the glorified baby-sitter a high-wattage smile. "Hi, Carter. We've got to get going. The flyers look great. You're doing a wonderful job. Just keep it up, okay?"

Robb looks from me to her in mild confusion, nodding in a bemused if baffled way. Before I can fire off another question, she starts pulling me down the corridor, a forced smile on her lips.

"What was that all about?" she whispers.

"There's something not right about that guy."

"The way you were eyeballing him, I'm not surprised. You can't run roughshod over these people. They're doing everything they can to help."

"You're telling me you didn't see that? The way he tensed up? I swear he was about to break into a sweat. And the mother, the way she talked about him, there was something she wasn't saying."

"Just keep walking," she says.

Once we get outside, basking in the orange sunset, she finally slows her pace. Unlike me, she's not impervious to the heat. She shucks off her jacket and pulls her blouse away from the small of her back. The way her heels snap out the cadence, I know she's telling me off in her head.

"At least you got what you wanted," she says.

Before I can answer, a couple of city cars roll up. In the passenger seat of the lead car, I recognize Wanda Mosser's snowy dome. She hops out, spry as ever, fixing me with her pearl gray smile.

"What's this man doing here?" she demands.

Cavallo rests a hand on her pistol's jutting handle. "Causing trouble, boss."

"I'm surprised he still knows how," Wanda says, pulling me to one side. Then, lowering her voice: "What's the deal, Roland? You looking for work or something?"

"Not me." I explain about the DNA swab and how Cavallo invited me along.

"Don't you have anything better to do?"

I glance at Cavallo, who dabs at her damp forehead with the back of her hand. "Not really."

"Ah." Wanda smiles shrewdly. "You did notice the engagement ring, didn't you?"

I nod.

"And the cross?"

I nod again.

"Roland," she says, shaking her head. "I never figured you for something like this. Aren't you happily married?"

Suddenly I do feel the heat. "I don't know what you mean."

"It's all right, Roland." She gives me a knowing smile. "We're all entitled to make fools of ourselves from time to time. But I have to tell you, you couldn't have picked a less likely candidate. Cavallo's straight as an arrow." She leans closer. "And to be honest, a little uptight."

I peel away. "Thanks for the warning."

We rejoin Cavallo and the other detectives milling around the newly arrived vehicles.

"What up?" Cavallo asks. "You need me to stay?"

Wanda shakes her head. "You better get this one back to the office. I'm just here for a chat with the mother. If I can, I'm going to get her on TV."

"Good luck."

The drive back into town proves awkward. Maybe Cavallo overheard some of what Wanda said, or at least picked up on the body language. If I could think of anything to say, I would. But my old boss was right. I've made a big fool of myself. In addition to pursuing this long shot of a hunch, ditching a perfectly reasonable assignment from my lieutenant, I've been as transparent about this newfound attraction as a fifteen-year-old boy.

I can sense a load of bad karma coming my way. To balance the accounts, I call Mitch Geiger again. I leave another message.

The moment I put my phone away, it starts to ring. The caller ID displays Lorenz's name.

"You're not going to answer that?" Cavallo asks.

"I better not. It could only mean trouble."

She sniffs. "Then I'm sorry for dragging you out here."

"What do you mean? I wanted to come. And listen, you can just give me the swab and I'll take it from here. I have a contact at the ME's office who can process it for me—"

"This isn't your case," she says quietly. "It's mine. I'll handle it from here."

I try arguing the point, but she's solid, and not going to be worn down. Whatever she heard or inferred, whatever thought process my interaction with Wanda set off, Cavallo's determined to have her way.

"I can get it done fast," I say.

She laughs. "Believe me, nobody has more priority right now than we do."

"So you'll follow up quick? I need the result as soon as possible."

She gives me a cloudy look, so cloudy I'm afraid to ask what's going on behind it. My phone starts ringing again.

I switch the ringer off.

CHAPTER 7

The back wall of Mitch Geiger's office features a network of stick-pinned mug shots and surveillance photos, some of them labeled and connected by lines but most marked with circles and question marks. Layered over them, frayed adhesive notes covered in ink. The display could be the work of an enterprising narcotics sergeant trying to map the local landscape. Then again, it could pass for evidence of a psychotic break, the kind of thing you find in the retrofitted garage of a perfectly average neighbor, along with the butcher knives and the stack of severed limbs.

Either way, it sparks my interest in Geiger. Unfortunately, he's not at home. Eight in the morning isn't the best time to find the narcs up and at it.

"You know where your sergeant is?" I ask a nearby stoner in a denim vest. If it weren't for the badge around his neck, I'd assume he escaped from lockup. He scratches his head something furious, then smiles behind his brush-like mustache. Even if he did know, he might not share. In my jacket and tie I'm obviously Homicide. We might as well be wearing gang colors. When you work murder, you assume everybody who doesn't wishes they could. We're the first string, and murder is the big show. But a certain type of police sees Narcotics in the same light. There's no accounting for taste.

For good measure I give Geiger's mobile number a ring before leaving. By now I could recite the man's recorded greeting from memory. No point in leaving another message. I've done what I can on this one for now.

En route to my desk I'm intercepted by a sullen twenty-year-old in tactical cargo pants and an HPD polo shirt, who waylays me just outside the elevator. He introduces himself as Edgar Castro from the crime lab, claiming to recognize me from the Morales scene, though I don't remember him.

"I've been trying to get through to Detective Lorenz," he says, "but he's not returning my calls."

As much as I sympathize after this morning's fruitless errand, there's a tribal imperative to observe. Crime-scene technicians can't expect to have homicide detectives at their beck and call. The food chain runs in the reverse direction.

"He's got his hands full at the moment," I say.

He brandishes a shiny-covered report. "So can I leave this with you, then?"

"You wanna tell me what it is?"

So he starts explaining, turning the pages as he goes. "It's actually pretty interesting. The victim in the hallway, the one sticking halfway out the bathroom? Hector Diaz—?"

"Little Hector," I say, remembering what the girl across the street had called him.

"Originally, we thought he must have been leaning through the door pretty far, because he was hit three times in the side. Right here." He uses his fingertips to indicate holes above his left kidney and between the ribs. "But I had a hard time making sense of that. I mean, if somebody's taking a shot at you, and you're returning fire, do you turn your flank toward them like that? For a right-hander like him, that's not the best use of cover."

I wonder if Castro's ever been in a firefight, or for that matter any kind of fight. Making best use of cover, that's a lesson they don't teach on the streets.

"So I went back to the scene," he says, "and took a harder look. The bathroom window is busted open—that's on the original report—but it looks like it happened a while back. No loose glass on the floor or anything like that. So nobody paid much mind. But when I went outside and started looking through the shrubs, I recovered a 9mm shell casing."

"Just the one?"

"Maybe the shooter collected the rest of his brass."

"So you're saying Little Hector was shot from outside?"

He nods. "What must have happened is, he was holding them off from the bathroom door, so they sent someone outside to . . . you know, flank his position." He makes a gun out of his fingers and jams it through an imaginary window. "That would make sense of the angles. He was crouched in the doorway, firing down the hall, when suddenly he starts taking fire from the window."

The report includes a three-dimensional computer rendering of the action, one stick figure outside the window with red lines streaming out of his stick pistol, intersecting the torso of another stick figure in the wire-frame doorway.

"That's a pretty sophisticated move, don't you think? For gang-bangers? The guy with the shotgun must have kept Diaz engaged while they sent the other one outside. That's fire and maneuver, isn't it? Basic tactics."

The cynic in me wants to squash Castro's enthusiasm, but the kid has a point. In a standoff like this, I'd expect the players to empty their clips and get out of there. Under fire, tunnel vision kicks in. Most people don't think much beyond the immediate threat. So if this crew managed to improvise on the go, I'm impressed.

Then again, they might have left a driver on the street, and maybe he noticed flashes in the bathroom window and went up to investigate, pumping a couple of rounds through the conveniently busted glass.

"I'll look this over," I tell him, tucking the report under my arm. "Good work, Castro."

He grins ear to ear, making me wonder how long ago his braces came off.

I catch up to Lorenz in Bascombe's office, and all at once I realize I've been outplayed. The two of them sit listening to a third man, hardly acknowledging my arrival. Ginger-haired, with deeply furrowed cheeks and a handlebar mustache, I'm betting this is the elusive Mitch Geiger. His voice trails off when he notices me. Bascombe snaps his head my way, hawkishly predatory.

"Just sit down and listen." He points with a talon-like finger.

I sink into a chair in the corner.

"Should I recap?" Geiger asks in a scratchy rumble of a voice.

After a nod from Bascombe, the narcotics sergeant repeats what I already know from the folder Lorenz passed along yesterday. There are rumors on the street about an independent crew hitting stash houses, disrupting the flow of product. Some of the gangs are using the hits as an excuse for drive-bys—not that they've ever needed one.

"But it's not about one gang putting pressure on another," Geiger says. "I've been mapping it all out, trying to connect the various dots. This crew is no respecter of persons. They're hitting everybody in Southwest, and not just the low-hanging fruit, either."

Lorenz leans forward, looking very serious. "Is there some kind of modus operandi with these guys? Something their jobs have in common?"

"Well . . ." Geiger draws the word out, glancing at Bascombe.

"Without examining the scenes," Bascombe says, "that's probably tough to determine. One question we need to ask, though, is whether they've killed anybody before now."

"From what I'm hearing out there, I'd have to say no. These sound like clean operations to me. In and out, just like that. Of course, assuming the same guys hit your scene, they might have run into unexpected trouble."

If Bascombe wants me to sit down and shut up, that's probably what I should do. But I just can't help jumping in. "There's a problem with what I'm hearing. Morales wasn't sitting on a stash. As far as I know, Morales handled the money, not the product."

"So maybe there was a brick of cash," Lorenz says.

"In that case, we should be hearing about it on the street." I look to Geiger. "Is that the story you're picking up out there?"

He glances sideways, gives me half a shrug. "Right now, we're not hearing much of anything." The words come reluctantly, like he's been warned in advance not to interact with me too much. The question is, was it Lorenz who gave the instructions or Bascombe? And did the orders include not returning my calls? Because this is feeling a lot like a setup.

"This isn't about a drug stash," I say, "and it's not about money. The girl on that bed, she's what it's about. She's why they were there."

"March," Bascombe snaps. "You wanna shut up a second?"

"Somebody has to say it."

"Well, you lost your chance. This was your job to do, but you didn't. So now I'm having to do it myself. Why don't you just sit there looking clueless. It's what you do best."

I should let it go, but I don't. "Either we can sit here trying to make a square peg fit a round hole, or we can start looking for a match to our female victim's blood sample. That's the lead we should be following."

Lorenz glares at me, bloated with contempt, while Geiger takes a sudden interest in the carpet. Bascombe, though, he's smiling, an unspoken thank-you on his face. He turns to the other two.

"Will you gentlemen excuse us a moment?"

They don't have to be asked twice. Once they're gone, Bascombe hops off the desk and pushes the door shut.

"You can't help shooting your mouth off."

"Hedges put me on the case," I say. "I'm going to work it. The politics mean nothing to me. I don't care if Lorenz likes me, or even if you do. There's a lead to follow and I'm going to follow it, no matter what you drop on my lap. You have to respect that."

"Respect?" he says, circling around the desk, slipping into his chair. "Oh, I do respect it, March. Now, I happen to know that after we talked yesterday, you went straight to Missing Persons, ignoring everything I said. I had to ask myself, Why would he do something like that? And all I could come up with was this: He really must believe in that connection. Crazy as it sounds, you're convinced the woman in that house is the girl from TV. You're so sure, you don't need any instructions from me, isn't that right?"

I shrug, not sure where he's going with this.

"So I give the whole situation some thought. And you know what I see? There's an opportunity here for a win-win."

"Meaning what?"

Nothing good, judging by all the teeth he's showing. After shuffling through the paper on his desk, he slides a document my way. The first thing I see is the captain's initials in the margin.

"Wanda Mosser has requested more manpower for her task force, March. First thing this morning I discussed it with the boss, and together we decided you'd be a good fit for her team. You've already shown such an interest in the case. And clearly"—he gestures toward the chair recently vacated by Lorenz—"you still haven't learned how to play well with others. You're an anchor as far as your partner's concerned, but Mosser will be happy to get an experienced homicide man such as yourself."

You have to admire the move. The lieutenant understands how the game is played. He wants to unload me, and by ditching Lorenz in favor of Theresa Cavallo yesterday afternoon, defying his instructions, I've given him the perfect opportunity. Such a little thing, but it was all he needed.

"I want to talk to the captain," I say.

He's so quick to agree I know there's no hope. Still, we troop over to Hedges's door, rapping softly until he invites us inside.

"It's you," he says, rising to his feet. "Off to your new assignment?"

"Sir, you told me I could work the case. That's what I've been doing. I don't want another special assignment. I'm tired of being farmed out like this. If you'd just let me get on with the job, like you said you would—"

"Listen, March. I have given you a shot, and from what Lieutenant Bascombe tells me, you haven't made the most of it. I told you to get along with Lorenz, but you can't seem to do that."

"What's more important, getting along or getting a result?"

He ignores the jab. "I'm also very concerned with your cavalier attitude toward the lieutenant's direction. He and Lorenz were relying on you to follow up with Narcotics—isn't that right, Lieutenant?—and instead you disappeared all day. I need my people to pull their own weight, March."

"Please," I say. "Reassign me, put me on another case, whatever. But don't loan me out again. That's all I ask."

Hedges glances down, embarrassed, and Bascombe shuffles his feet behind me, no doubt worried the captain will cave in.

"You did good work at the scene," Hedges concedes, "and I was really hoping it wouldn't be a fluke. But this idea of yours about Hannah Mayhew? That's guesswork, not police work."

"They're comparing the samples as we speak. If they don't match, fine. We can cross that one off. But if you get rid of me now and the samples do match, how's that gonna look?"

Hedges chuckles. "In that case, I'd feel pretty stupid. And if it happens, you can come on back. I'll owe you a big apology, and so will the lieutenant here—isn't that right?"

"That's right, sir," Bascombe says. I hear the smile in his voice.

"In the meantime," the captain says, "if this is the angle you've decided to pursue, I think it would be best to do it on Wanda Mosser's time, not mine."

"And she's agreed to that?" I ask, grasping at straws.

He answers me with a smile. "Everybody's off-loading their dead weight on Wanda. She'll be happy to see a familiar face. Especially one as motivated as you are. And I tell you what, if things work out over there, and you find at the end of her investigation that you're still feeling repentant, you come back to me and we'll talk."

"Let's talk now."

Coming around the desk, he starts patting me on the shoulder, easing me toward the door, where Bascombe, noticing my free side, starts patting that, too. The captain's happy to have one less problem to deal with, while the lieutenant can take pride in a well-executed maneuver. While Lorenz kept me pinned down, he went around the side and flanked me. But no, who am I kidding? I flanked myself.

So now I'm on the threshold, feeling like a paratrooper about to jump, knowing my chute was packed by people who don't care how hard I land.

So that's that.

I'm out.

CHAPTER 8

Free fall. There's something exciting about it, like finding out you have cancer and you'll be dead in six months. It's a bummer, sure, but liberating, too. All the things you were afraid to do back when there was too much to live for, suddenly they're fair game. I think about that scenario often, usually at night, with Charlotte sleeping at the far edge of the bed and the ceiling fan crawling through its circuit.

If you knew you were going to die, what would you do? Fight to hang on a few more months, or throw yourself into a task that really means something?

I dial Charlotte's number, expecting to find her at the computer in her home office, doing whatever it is corporate attorneys do. Instead, I hear footsteps on pavement and road noise in the background.

"Where are you?"

"Rice Village," she says. "I decided to do a little shopping."

"Good therapy, huh?" I glance at my watch. "Can we do lunch?"

"Is something wrong, Roland?" she asks with a note of concern.

"Kind of. I'll tell you when we meet."

She goes through her mental list of restaurants, cross-referencing whatever's nearest, finally suggesting Prego. The drive takes me fifteen minutes, then I burn another five navigating the warren of streets around Rice Village, trying to remember the exact location. By the time I park and walk inside, Charlotte's already secured a table and started scrutinizing the menu. She's always taken her food quite seriously. A couple of shopping bags are stacked at her feet.

"So why the midday rendezvous?" she asks. "It's been a long time since we've done something like this."

"You know about the missing girl, the one on television? Hannah Mayhew?"

"Vaguely."

"Well, they've put me on the task force."

She swishes the ice in her water glass. "Is that a good thing or a bad thing?"

"It's definitely not good."

The waiter comes and we order. I don't feel much like eating, but I get the lentil soup. Charlotte changes her mind a couple of times, finally landing on the grilled red snapper, joking that if I'm taking her to lunch for a change, she's going to get something expensive.

If we'd had this conversation the other night, instead of arguing over our tenant, the tone would have been quite different. That seems like a decade ago, but it was just Friday night. I blew my big break almost as soon as I got it, and over the stupidest thing. All I had to do was go to Geiger's office immediately, but instead I'd tagged along with Cavallo for no better reason than that she was easy on the eyes.

Not that I can tell Charlotte that. My account of the events is selective, but by the time I'm done she gets the point.

"So you've screwed up your last chance?"

"Pretty much."

She takes a bite of snapper, and I honestly can't tell if the contemplative look on her face has to do with my predicament or the taste of the food. I stare into my soup, moving the spoon in tiny circles.

"Roland," she says, "have you thought about chucking it in?"

"Retirement? I don't have the time in."

"No, not retirement. Just quitting. If they're not going to let you work Homicide, why don't you find something else? I mean, it's not like we're living off your salary or anything. Maybe it's time to make a course correction."

"Can we not talk about me quitting?"

"But if you're miserable with the job, I don't see why—"

"There's still a possibility," I say. "If I can connect the murders with this girl . . ."

"Roland, you know what I'd like? Just listen for a second. You've been thrashing around for a long time, like you've got some kind of clichéd inner demon. And we both know why. What I'd like is for you to let go. Leave the department. In fact, we could both get a fresh start. We could move somewhere else. We could sell the house and do some traveling—we always said we would someday. Why not do it now? What's the point of being unhappy? We have the money, Roland, so let's—"

It's a good thing I'm not hooked up to an EKG, or the whole restaurant would be deafened by the shrill, beeping pulse. As it is, my fist puts a decent bend in the handle of my spoon.

"We're not going to sell that house," I say, trying hard to keep my voice calm. "Never. And I'm not leaving the job. That's not why I wanted to talk."

"Then why did you?"

I drop the spoon in the bowl and sit back. Honestly, I don't have an answer. There was a reason, some deep and primal instinct that pushed me at a moment of crisis to reach out. But Charlotte and I, we don't function that way, not anymore. Especially not now.

"I just thought . . . I wanted to let you know what's going on."

"Great," she says. "Now I know."

She keeps eating, using her fork like a trident on the helpless fish, all joy in the process now gone. When the waiter swings by with offers of espresso and dessert, I shake my head and ask for the bill. Charlotte and I part ways on the sidewalk after a desultory kiss.

★

An hour later, on the far side of town, the wind blows Cavallo's twisted locks across her eyes. While she grapples with her hair, I flip through photos of Hannah Mayhew's abandoned car, a white Ford Focus hatchback. I match the painted lines in the photographs with the parking space divisions at my feet, working out the car's exact placement. A makeshift shrine by the nearest lamppost, wilting flowers, candles, and sun-baked greeting cards, helps to mark the spot.

As far as crime statistics are concerned, Willowbrook Mall ranks second in the city behind the notorious Greenspoint, mainly people breaking into parked cars or simply stealing them. Fortunately Hannah's Focus wasn't one of them, or we'd have even less to work with than we do. Along with the shots of the car, I have grainy stills from the video surveillance footage.

"Those haven't been released to the media," Cavallo says.

According to the time stamps, the Focus arrived at 12:58 p.m. Twelve minutes later, a gray shadow emerged from the driver's side— presumably Hannah, but the action transpired too far from the camera for decent coverage.

"While she was sitting there, she made a call from her mobile to the prepaid number. The connection lasted about thirty seconds. She was probably calling to say she'd arrived."

"And then the van pulls up?"

I flip to the next still, in which a white panel van blocks the view.

"One theory is, she got in the van. It was moving slow, and kind of stops right there, but you can't tell from the footage if she got in. A group of people passes by right then. She might have blended in with them and gone inside the mall." Cavallo fingers through my stack, sliding out another photo. "As they get closer, you can see one of the girls kind of looks like her. So that's another theory."

"Any footage from inside the mall?"

"Nothing we can confirm as her, no. You'd be surprised how many five-foot-four teenage blondes there are in the mall at any given time, and how hard it is to tell them apart on surveillance tape. She had a shiny pink purse, pretty distinctive, and we haven't spotted anything like that."

"No witnesses have come forward?"

She laughs. "Over fifty have. She was spotted in the parking lot, inside Macy's, Sephora, and Williams-Sonoma. She was all over the food court. Sometimes with other girls, sometimes alone. She was arguing with a boy—sometimes a white boy, sometimes Latino—and she was holding hands with at least two different guys."

"She got around."

"Yeah, you could say that. There was even a witness in the Abercrombie changing room who heard a girl crying in the next stall. She couldn't see this girl, but she's pretty sure it had to be Hannah Mayhew. They're all sure."

"And they just want to help. I know how it works."

Go to a neighborhood like the Third Ward, and no matter what happens—somebody can walk up to a dude in broad daylight and put a gun to his head—nobody sees anything. But out in the suburbs, everyone sees something. As they say, the crazies come out of the woodwork—only the crazies are normal enough. They're just starved for attention, captivated by their proximity to the girl on TV.

Not that they're making things up. I've interviewed witnesses before with impossible stories, the details obviously culled from news coverage, yet they were convinced what they said was true. Most could probably have passed a lie-detector test. No doubt at this very moment a young woman sits in front of the television in her Abercrombie T-shirt, convinced she was close enough to Hannah Mayhew to hear her weep.

"So you see where the manpower's going," Cavallo says. "We've got a small army checking out every delivery van and contractor in a ten-mile radius, and another one following up on every sighting that's been reported."

"What about her friends at school? Her church?"

"We got surveillance going on a kid at the school. Deals a little weed. Depending on who you ask, Hannah was either dating the boy or trying to convert him. His name is James Fontaine, and so far he's the likeliest suspect."

"You don't sound convinced."

"Honestly? I don't have a feeling one way or the other. Usually I do."

I hand the photos back, then walk a circle around the empty parking space, studying the pavement for I don't know what. The wind ripples my pant leg. Overhead, the clouds are black-rimmed and foreboding.

"Can I level with you?" I say. "There's only one thing I'm concerned about, and it's the DNA sample. If we get a match back on that, it blows this case wide open and puts me back where I belong—"

"And if it doesn't match?"

"It will. You may not have a feeling one way or the other, but I do. The girl on that bed was Hannah Mayhew. I don't know how she got there, but she did."

"You're convinced."

"Absolutely. So just tell me when to expect the answer."

She shrugs. "Maybe a day, maybe a week. How am I supposed to know?"

"You said you had juice."

"That doesn't mean your hunch goes to the top of my list. Like I said, I'm not convinced, so you can't expect me to put resources behind it, no matter how badly you want there to be a link."

My collar tightens around my neck. "If that's how you feel, I can go back to the ME myself and get it done. You should have let me do that in the first place."

"It's not your case."

"It's as much mine as yours now."

She crosses her arms. "No. It's not."

We head back to her car, neither of us very interested in continuing the conversation. Teaming us up was Wanda's idea. Maybe it was a favor to me—or maybe it was punishment, the hair of the dog, her way of teaching me a lesson.

She starts the engine, letting the air-conditioning blow, then turns in her seat.

"March, let's get something clear."

"All right," I say, not liking her tone or the intensity of her gaze.

"You see this?" She makes a fist of her left hand and brandishes the engagement ring. "You appreciate the significance?"

"Uh . . . yeah."

"It means that no matter what you and Wanda have cooked up between you, nothing's gonna happen. You understand that?"

"I'm a happily married man," I say.

Her eyes narrow in contempt.

"Look," I say. "You don't know me. All I care about is getting those results back. If you'd just make that happen, you could get rid of me a lot sooner."

She puts the car in gear. "Anyway. You're old enough to be my dad."

"What? No, I'm not." I punch the window button, then lean my head out to yell. "Thank you, Wanda, wherever you are."

Cavallo smiles, but just barely. When we hit FM-1960, I point right and she turns left.

"I need to get back," she says.

"Fine, but there's a lead I want to follow up while we're out here."

She sighs. "What?"

"That youth pastor from yesterday. I want to swing by and rattle his cage."

"There's no point."

"Just turn around, all right? Pretty please? You can drop me off. I'll hitch a ride back with some uniforms."

She glides into the left-turn lane, tapping her fingers on the wheel. When the light changes, she whips the front around late, giving the tires a squeal, then pours on the gas. The woman always drives like she's chasing someone. Or being chased.

★

Finding Carter Robb is easier said than done. His office at the church proves empty, and the number I worm out of the secretary goes straight to voicemail. According to Cavallo, who's decided to stick with me for the moment, he runs after-school programs on Tuesdays and Thursdays, trading slices of pizza for a captive audience to evangelize. But Hannah's disappearance trumps the usual schedule.

"All he does anymore is make copies of the flyer," the secretary says. "Then he posts them all over the place. Sometimes the youth group kids go with him."

"You have any idea where I could intercept him?"

She fingers the beads around her neck in thought. "His wife teaches at Cypress Christian School—no relation to the church. There's a coffee place across from there, Seattle Coffee. His home away from home, I think."

"I know where it is," Cavallo says.

This turns out to be only partly true, as she proves by hunting around for twenty minutes while I dig through the Key Map and try to navigate. When we finally locate the coffee shop, there's no sign of Robb, so I persuade Cavallo to take me to the school where his wife teaches. We page her from the office, then wait.

After a few minutes I check my watch.

"You're not like the other homicide detectives," Cavallo says.

"So you know a lot of them?"

She gives me a look like I'm an idiot. "They're mostly big talkers. Gift of the gab. But not you. You're more of a brooder, aren't you?"

"Maybe I've got more to brood about."

"I always expect them to be depressed," she says. "Doing that kind of work, seeing what they see. But I guess you develop an immunity. I don't think I could."

"You might surprise yourself someday."

Cavallo starts to reply, then looks past me. "Here she is."

Gina Robb can't be a day over twenty-five, but in her cardigan and cat-eye glasses she's serious enough for an elderly librarian. She's pinned a swag of dishwater blond hair back with a tortoiseshell barrette, exposing a swath of pale forehead. Under the cardigan, she wears a flower-print dress that flares at the hips, a self-consciously vintage look.

"You wanted to see me?" she asks, looking from one of us to the other, uncertain whom to address. "Are you from the police?"

I glance at my dangling shield. "How can you tell?"

She parries my attempt at humor with a grave frown. "Has something happened?"

"No, nothing like that," Cavallo says.

I would never have picked this girl as Robb's type. Proof, I suppose, that opposites attract, bookworms pairing off with jocks and vice versa. For some reason it makes him more interesting.

"We're trying to find your husband," I say. "Any idea where he might be?"

Her gray eyes flick toward the wall clock. "At church?"

"We checked. They said he might be out distributing flyers."

"I guess that's where he is then."

"We checked the coffee shop," Cavallo says. "They told us he hangs out there sometimes."

She nods. "Sometimes."

Either she's trying to make this hard, or she's genuinely baffled by our questions. "Would you mind giving him a call? Maybe he'll pick up if he sees it's you."

Her hands fret the hem of her cardigan. "We haven't dismissed class yet. I should really—"

"Please," Cavallo says. "Just humor him, ma'am."

She moves slower than a reluctant snail, but she does move, her hand sliding into the drooping cardigan pocket, returning with a tiny sliver of a phone, which she thumbs open without glancing down. She punches a speed-dial button and puts the phone to her ear.

"Baby?" she says. "I'm still at the school. Yeah. Listen, the police are here looking for you. I don't know . . . All right, here you go."

She hands me the phone.

"It's Roland March," I say. "We met yesterday. I was wondering if we could have a chat."

"Right." He sounds wary. "You want to meet at the church?"

For some reason I don't, and I tell him so. "How about I drop in wherever you are?"

"All right."

"You'll have to tell me where that is."

A long time passes. His wife looks up anxiously while Cavallo consults her watch.

"Mr. Robb?"

"I'm . . . I'm sitting in the van. Outside James Fontaine's house. Trying to work up enough nerve to go knock on the door."

I walk alongside the red church van, giving the roof a nice tap, then climb into the passenger seat. Robb doesn't even glance over. His eyes are fixed on the house across the street, a rather palatial brick mansion dating from the late seventies or early eighties with concrete lions on either side of the front steps. Not the crib I'd have expected for a Klein High weed dealer, but I can't think why not. Where else is he going to live? We're in the suburbs, after all.

I rap the plastic dash with my knuckle. "You really shouldn't be doing this. For one thing, you're not exactly keeping a low profile."

"I'm not really trying."

"For another thing—and I shouldn't even be mentioning this— we're already keeping an eye on this kid." I crank the rearview around, glancing back at Cavallo, who's still behind the wheel, leaving this one to me. "Putting up flyers is one thing. That's great. But conducting your own stakeout? Not so much."

"I'm not here to spy on him," he says. "I wanted to confront him."

"Won't he still be in school?"

He looks at me for the first time. "He's on suspension."

"Didn't the school year just begin? He didn't waste any time."

Robb wears cargo shorts today, along with Converse sneakers. His black T-shirt imitates the popular milk advertisements, but says GOT JESUS? instead. After meeting the wife, something tells me he chooses his wardrobe for ironic effect.

"Let me level with you," I say. "When I saw you yesterday, something didn't seem right. You were squirrelly. Like our being there made you nervous. So I started wondering what you'd have to be nervous about. Why don't you save me the trouble and just tell me?"

"I'm not nervous about anything."

"Really? 'Cause let me tell you something. What you're doing right here, it's abnormal. This is not how people react to situations like yours, not when they're on the level."

He runs a hand through his spiky hair. "How do they react?"

"Not like they're guilty."

"That's how you think I'm acting?"

"Am I wrong?"

He reaches out and straightens the rearview mirror, reclaiming the territory. "How am I supposed to answer a question like that?"

"You have a guilty conscience, Mr. Robb. I want to know why."

Human physiology is a funny thing. No matter how cool we think we're playing it, most of us don't have poker faces. Our tells can be ludicrously on target. Robb's a perfect example. His top lip clamps down over the bottom, forcing the tuft of hair on his chin to pop out like porcupine quills. He's literally biting down the words, and he has no idea.

"Come on," I say, jabbing his arm. "Just tell me what you're holding back. You'll feel better."

He turns toward the window, head shaking imperceptibly.

"You want to find this girl, right? So help me out. Don't hold anything back. It's not fair to Hannah."

He lets out a breath. "Hannah? You don't even know her."

"Then tell me about her, Carter. Fill me in."

His breathing comes hard and heavy, the muscles in his forearms flexing, struggling to hold himself together.

"Come on."

Then I hear it, the sound I love. The gasp of capitulation, a long exhale that leaves him smaller than before, hunched over and broken. In the interview room, this would be the moment the guys on the far side of the glass slap each other's backs. When they give that sigh, it means everything is about to come out all at once.

"This," he says, his voice quiet, "this is all my fault."

"Meaning what?"

"I encouraged her. I thought I was doing the right thing." There's a plea in his eyes. "You have to understand, when I first came to the church, nobody was on my side. What I found here wasn't at all what I expected. You've got this big, famous church—all my seminary friends, when they heard I was coming here, said I'd hit the big time. But what I discovered . . . It was all so comfortable. So complacent. The kids go to nice schools, they drive nice cars, they have nice lives to look forward to. It was all so nice."

"Nothing wrong with that," I say.

"Christianity, it's not about being nice. It's about sacrifice. All they wanted, though, was an ordained baby-sitter, like I said before."

"I thought you were trying to be funny."

"I was, but it's still true. The parents . . . The church, what they all wanted was some help with keeping the kids in line. Keeping them insulated. Sheltered and safe. 'You're young,' they'd tell me. 'The kids relate to you. They look up to you.' And they wanted me to use that to help them out, you know? Or they'd get me to lay down the law, then behind my back the parents and kids could bond by talking about how unreasonable I was. That kind of shocked me, but it happens."

As interesting as all this is, I don't need a lecture on how hard being a youth pastor is. "Can we steer this back to Hannah?"

"Like I said, Hannah was different. Her mom was, too, at first. They understood God didn't put us on this planet to be cozy and quiet. We have to be outward-focused. We have to be missional."

Cavallo would know what that means, but I don't—and I'd just as soon not find out. "Again, could we stick to the matter at hand?"

He stops me with a raised finger. "It's relevant. There was a sermon I did—I speak to the youth group on Sunday nights, I think I mentioned that. Anyway, you know the Narnia movies started coming out, and all the kids were eating that stuff up, so I did a talk about that line from C. S. Lewis—you know, about Aslan? 'He's not a safe lion, but he's a good one'?"

My eyes glaze over.

"Anyway," he says, realizing I'm not tracking, "the point is, God doesn't want us to be safe. He wants us to do good. There's a big difference."

"Right."

"So Hannah hears this, and it's like a light bulb goes on in her head. This was—what? Three years ago? She would have been, like, fourteen. But she really woke up and started living her faith."

I'm not looking for ancient history, but sometimes there's no choice. You have to let them tell the story in their own way.

"There was this girl," he says, "named Evey, short for Evangeline. She and her mom relocated here from New Orleans after Hurricane Katrina, and the kid was really messed up. Evey ran away from home, got into drugs and who knows what else. She was Hannah's age—but that's all they had in common. I don't know the whole history, but I think there'd been some kind of abuse, she'd been sexualized way too young and had this weird, kind of creepy maturity. The other kids in the youth group, they wouldn't go near her. I think they were afraid, and to be honest I was, too."

"But not Hannah?"

He shakes his head. "She befriended Evey, the way she did everyone. The same way she did him." He jabs his thumb at James Fontaine's house. "She didn't judge. She tried to show Christ's love to everyone, no matter how hard it was."

"So she struggled with this love thing? And confided in you?"

"Yeah," he says. "She grew up without a dad, you know, and I think I came along at a certain time in her life when she really needed one. A youth pastor's always acting in loco parentis, but it was more than that."

"You have any kids of your own?" I ask.

He shakes his head. "Not yet."

I'm not surprised. Telling other people's kids it's better to be good than safe is one thing. No matter how much you like them, or even feel responsible for them, they aren't yours. Losing them isn't always at the back of your mind. If Robb had a child, he might understand the attraction of keeping her "sheltered and safe." Parents want to raise future doctors and lawyers—above all, future candidates for happiness. They do not want to nurture martyrs, whatever the cause.

"You can ask a lot of people," I say, "but you can't expect them to sacrifice their own kid. You'll understand that when you have kids of your own."

"But that's exactly what Christianity is," he says, "a father sacrificing his son."

There's a flash of passion in his voice, transforming him for a moment, giving me a glimpse of what he might be like in action. I can see how the teens in his charge might be inspired, and why their parents might get a little nervous. It's one thing to talk the talk, but when you put your kid into someone else's hands, you've got to believe that underneath all the radical rhetoric, there's a check in place, some restraining impulse or inner voice to rein him in: *All this is great, and you need to hear it, but in real life, in the everyday world, you've got to look out for yourself.* Carter Robb doesn't seem to have that restraint, or if he does, he thinks rooting it out is an obligation of faith.

"And Donna," I ask, "did she encourage this bond between you and her daughter?"

"She thought it was great. Just like Hannah, she really got behind me. Considering what a great man her husband was, she could have let people at the church put her on a pedestal, but that's not her way. She works hard. She mentors women at the church. She's written books, you know. Quite a few of them. And speaks at women's conferences, that kind of thing. So when I came along, she said it was just what CCC needed."

"CCC?"

"Cypress Community Church." He smirks. "Sometimes we speak evangelicalese instead of English. Sorry about that . . . Where was I?"

"Donna supported you."

"Right. When I first got there, the youth group would have these annual retreats every summer. They'd pack up the vans and go to this adventure camp in Tennessee. Bungee jumping all day and preaching all night. It was a tradition. But I went to Pastor Mike—that's my boss, the associate pastor—and said, 'Hey, look. Instead of driving all the way to Tennessee, let's stay right here. There are ministry opportunities all over town, places where the kids can volunteer for a week and really advance the Kingdom.' He looked at me like I was crazy, but Donna got behind it. Without her, we'd still be wasting that week. Now we do inner-city mission work, help at shelters, that kind of thing."

"That's really great. But why did you say Hannah's disappearance was your fault?"

He takes a deep breath. "Because. She took it so seriously. I mean, she really got into the mission work. She'd take an interest in people, you know? Not safe people—and not necessarily good ones, either. Not that any of us are good, but you know what I mean. At school she started having some trouble. She was making friends with the wrong people—"

"Like the Fontaine kid?"

He nods. "And at the same time, she's a normal seventeen-year-old girl. She likes boys, she wants to date, and she has the usual confusing mix of adolescent emotions. Her mom had a hard time coping, and Hannah reacted by getting really secretive. Even with me."

"So she liked Fontaine?"

"I think so. And she also wanted to be a good witness, to be Christ in his life. I tried steering her away, tried to . . . you know, give her a reality check or something. But she couldn't understand what I was saying. All this time I'd been telling her one thing and suddenly I'm contradicting it all."

"Tell me about the relationship with him."

"I didn't know a thing about it until she got suspended last spring, that's how secretive she was."

This is the first I've heard of her suspension, but I try not to let on. "So what happened?"

He gives a disconsolate shrug. "All she'd tell me was they'd had an argument and he got really mad. The next day, there's a drug search at the school and they find a bag of pot in her locker."

So nice little Hannah Mayhew, the churchgoing wide-eyed innocent, was caught holding weed in her locker? That must have been awkward at home. Not that I'm surprised or anything. It's the sheltered kids who go wild.

"You're certain it wasn't hers?" I ask.

The question irritates him. "It wasn't. She said so and I believed her. Her mom, I don't know. After that, she had doubts about everything. About Hannah, about me, the whole direction of my ministry."

"What did she say?"

"She hasn't said anything." He rubs his eyes like he's suddenly tired. "But she doesn't have to. I know she blames me. And hey, maybe she's right. I came here so certain, so self-righteous, and now . . . I don't know what to think anymore."

His voice dies, his fervor ebbs away. He glances at the Fontaine house, shaking his head like he's not sure how he got here or what he intended to do. The conviction of a few moments ago is utterly gone now.

"That's all I've got," he says.

Everything he's said has the ring of truth about it, but as far as I can see, none of it advances the case. All he can give me is history. His awkwardness yesterday stemmed not from real guilt but from a false sense of responsibility, a dubious connection he's made between his Sunday school lectures and Hannah's ultimate fate. I'm disappointed, not because I expected a smoking gun from this guy but because I expected something and my instincts were off the mark. And I'm putting so much faith into those instincts right now that I don't like to see them fail.

I pat his shoulder. "Thanks for your cooperation." I should leave it there and go, but I get the urge to pass along some wisdom. "You know something? The one thing you can't control in life is the outcome. You do what seems right at the moment, and if it turns out wrong . . . well, that's out of your hands."

"It's in God's hands," he says.

"The point is, you shouldn't beat yourself up over this. And you shouldn't get in the way of the investigation, either. Leave Fontaine to us, okay? Put up all the flyers you want. Spend time with those students of yours—they probably need it right now. But let us take care of the rest."

"I have to do something," he says, running a palm along his leg. "I can't do nothing."

Sure, I can sympathize. I respect his urge. And I don't exactly agree with the platitudes I've just uttered, the boilerplate about letting the police handle everything. People expect too much from us sometimes. I'm not endorsing vigilantes or anything, but a little vigilance wouldn't be such a bad thing. In his position, I'd want to do something, too. But in my position, I'm expected to toe the line. And really, what can he do apart from posting his flyers and leading yet another fruitless search? I open the door and slip to the curb, turning to speak before slamming it shut.

"I'll tell you what you can do," I tell him. "Say a prayer."

The door snaps shut before he can get out a reply.

CHAPTER 9

Public is where you go to be alone. After my shift, instead of heading home to Charlotte for a reprise of our lunchtime grapple, the Paragon beckons with its promise of anonymity and thumping music. Though it's earlier than usual and a weekday to boot, the parking lot is filling up already. As the door flaps shut behind me, an icehouse chill descends, along with the soothing darkness. My eyes take forever to adjust.

When they do, I see Tommy threading his way between the tables, holding a longneck beer at shoulder level to avoid clipping the heads of any seated patrons.

"Hey, Mr. March, how's it going, man? Why don't you come join us at our table?"

He's filled a table with what I assume are students from one of the undergraduate courses he teaches while toiling away on his dissertation. A couple of guys in thick-rimmed glasses wearing fitted Western shirts, a girl in a long, crinkly skirt and engineer boots.

"You and me," I say, "we need to have a little talk. My wife told me about this girl who was up at your place, seemed kind of messed up. I didn't like hearing that."

"It was a one-time thing. You sure you won't join us?"

"No, thanks."

Instead of my usual table in back, which would put me in sight of Tommy's group, I slip around the front of the bar into a side room added in the most recent renovation to accommodate the Paragon's growing clientele. The ratio of speakers to square footage means the music is that much louder, but given a choice between deafness and another run-in with my tenant, I'll take the hearing loss.

The new location has an added advantage. No Marta. After the scene I made in the parking lot last time, I'd just as soon not run into the one person likely to remember me, thanks to that overgenerous tip. An unfamiliar plaid-skirted waitress comes by, taking my order without a glimmer of recognition.

So I've had my talk with Tommy. Maybe that brief exchange will suffice for Charlotte, if I can spin it right. But she'll want details, of course, which will mean explaining why I'm at the Paragon when the two of us have long since agreed I won't come here anymore. It's no good dwelling on things, she told me, back when she still had sympathy for my morbid obsession with the place.

When the waitress returns with my whiskey sour—I always order the same thing, and always do the same thing with it—I dig for my wallet, planning to settle up right away. With Tommy on the scene, I won't be nursing this one all night.

"You don't have to do that," she says, pointing across the bar to the main room. "A guy in there took care of it."

"You sure?"

She nods.

"All right then."

That idiot Tommy. Thanks to his father's deep pockets, he's never learned the value of money. I don't know if he's trying to impress me, or the kids at his table. Either way, it takes the shine off my evening. I push the drink away.

He's about the same age as Carter Robb. On the surface, they might not have much in common, but they both have kids looking to them for guidance. The burden seems to weigh more heavily on Robb than Tommy, though. It would be interesting to get the two of them in the same room. I imagine the tenant bending over backwards to deliver veiled insults, while the youth pastor, recognizing them for what they are, does his best to seem unruffled.

Staring into my drink, I recall Robb's wife. With her mannered wardrobe, Gina Robb wouldn't look out of place over at Tommy's table. I wonder what she would make of the guilt her husband's carrying. Maybe she feels it, too, the shipwreck of their shared idealism. What would have to happen for Tommy to feel that kind of guilt? Not a girl leaving his garage apartment the morning after, not very certain of what had happened to her. I'm not sure whether anything would.

I drop a couple of dollars on the table, about to get up.

Coming toward me, the man from the other night, the cop I couldn't quite place. The horn-like projection of black hair crowning his forehead, a more youthful style than his lined face will support. We make eye contact and he nods without smiling, pulling out a chair right across from me. He glances at my untouched drink.

"You don't remember me," he says.

"Should I?" I don't like the way he's drilling me with those eyes. I don't like that I can't see his hands under the table.

"We have some *friends* in common," he says, putting enough spin on the word that I know not to take it at face value.

Instead of facing me head-on, he cocks his chair, sitting sideways with his back to the wall so nobody can come up behind him. Keeping track of the other patrons from the corner of his eye. I was right the other night. This guy's one of us. A cop.

"You got a name?" I ask.

He nods. "Maybe it'll come to you."

My right hand leaves the table, resting on my thigh. Between the staring contest and his tight-lipped way of speaking, this is starting to feel like a high-noon standoff. Maybe that's what it is. He's got an advantage, thanks to the angle, since my gun side is facing him. In a draw I'd need to be quick.

The thing is, I am.

"If you're not going to introduce yourself, then I was just getting ready to go."

"You're not gonna say thanks?" he asks, nodding toward the drink. "Looks like you hardly touched it. Knowing your story, I think I can guess why."

"Knock yourself out. I'm going."

I rise quickly, giving the table a tap with my hip, the same way you'd finesse a pinball machine. The drink shakes, ice clinking on the glass, and the man grabs the table with both hands to steady it. He looks at me, then at his hands.

"Oh, I get it." He flattens them out. "You can sit back down. I don't have a problem with you, March. I'm here to do you a favor if you'd only let me."

"What kind of favor?"

"Have a seat," he says, tilting his chin. "I'll tell you all about it."

I turn my chair, sitting with my right hip away from him, my hand still resting on my thigh. "You can start with your name."

"Fine, fine." He reaches across the table. "Joe Thomson." I ignore the outstretched hand, so he pulls it back. "If you're not gonna drink this, mind if I do? You kind of stopped my heart for a minute there."

"Help yourself."

He sips the drink and makes a face. Down in the basement of my mental archive, I'm looking for a folder with Joe Thomson's name on it, coming up empty. The face is so familiar. He's one of those guys who was handsome once, but didn't age so well. Jet-black hair, blue eyes, and a kind of pucker to his mouth, like he's sucking an invisible cigar. The parchment lines on his skin look premature, due more to hard living than age.

When he puts the drink down, Thomson hunches forward and clasps his hands together like he has something to confide. He glances over his shoulder before speaking.

"I'm in a position to help you," he says. "Only you're gonna have to help me first."

"Don't take this wrong, Joe, but can I see some ID?"

"If that's what it takes." He smirks. "I'll reach slow so you don't jump to any conclusions."

True to his word, he edges a wallet out of his back pocket, sliding it across the table. I flip it open, a sergeant's badge catching the light, and match the photo to the face in front of me.

"You're looking a little beat down these days," I observe.

"Yeah, well." He takes the wallet back. "You would be, too."

"What are you offering me?"

"It's a two-way street. I need something from you first."

"What's that?"

His mouth opens, but he can't seem to form the words. He tries again, fails, then rubs his lips with the back of his hand, glancing away. A cough rumbles in his lungs. His cheeks color. The signs are pretty unmistakable. Thomson's embarrassed.

"Spit it out," I say.

He clears his throat, takes another sip. "What I'm looking for— and it's not negotiable—is a blanket immunity. The information I share, I want it in writing that nothing will come back to bite me. You understand? No prosecution, but on top of that, no trouble at work, either. I come out looking like a hero, or I don't take another step."

A tremor runs up my spine, but I try to look indifferent. "You've lost me, Joe. Are you saying you want to confess to a crime?"

His mouth twitches. "This isn't a confession, no."

"Why don't you give me an idea what we're talking about then."

"When I have something in writing, something I can take to an attorney and double-check, then we'll talk. Not before."

"You're a cop, Joe. You know it doesn't work that way."

"What I know is that sometimes, for the right people, that's exactly how it works."

"Let me put it another way. You're asking me to pull strings I don't have the juice to pull. If there's somebody in this department who can deliver what you're demanding, it isn't me."

"Wrong," he says, shaking his head. "You're the only one. You'll fight for it in a way nobody else will, because of who's involved."

My tremor turns into a vertebral earthquake. "Who is involved?"

He smiles. "Not yet, March. Here's what you need to do. Your ex-partner Wilcox, the one who's in Internal Affairs? He can deliver what I need. You go to him and explain, and he'll smooth the path. Those guys have a magic wand they wave to get the prosecutors to see things their way. Why are you laughing?"

I cover my mouth with my hand, shaking my head slowly. "You don't know Wilcox, do you? If it's a favor from him you want, then you've really come knocking on the wrong door."

"It's not me who wants it," he says. "It's you."

"That's my point. Wilcox is my ex-partner, the operative word being *ex.* That's Latin for 'no longer on speaking terms,' in case you didn't know."

"Whatever. Don't sell yourself short, March. You'll make it happen. Besides, this will work to his benefit, too. Tell him that. If he gives me what I want, he won't be working in Internal Affairs anymore. He'll be running it."

"That's a big promise," I say, wiping my damp palm on my thigh.

"And I can deliver."

He sounds confident, but as soon as the words are out, he turns to scan the room again, like he's expecting a knife in the ribs. When he looks back at me, there's a hunted look in his eyes, maybe a haunted one, too. I start wondering how much of this premature age he put on over the last few days.

"You make it hard for me to say no," I tell him. "But unless you're prepared to give me something, I can promise you I won't lift a finger. In case you hadn't noticed, I'm not real big on career advancement."

"All right," he says, leaning forward, sliding the drink aside. "I'm not giving you any names. This isn't even a preview. But that case you're working on, the Morales hit . . . ?"

"What about it?"

"What I have for you is gonna blow it wide open. I mean wide."

He pushes away from the table, takes another look around.

"As in what?" I ask.

He taps the table with his index finger. "As in shooters, March. Signed, sealed, and delivered."

And then he turns to go.

"How do I get in touch?" I call after him, trying to be heard over the music.

He pivots, putting a hand to his ear. I stick out my thumb and pinkie, jamming them phone-like to my head.

"You don't," he says. "I'll call you."

Nothing sinks in for the first minute or so. Then I feel a stupid grin on my lips. I wipe it with the back of my hand, but can't get rid of the smile. A blur of faces swirl around me. I want to kiss them all. I'm happy as a drunk, in love with the world, all the sappy clichés rolled up into one.

Cavallo can sit on that DNA test as long as she wants. Joe Thomson just threw me another lifeline. Last time this happened I screwed it up. But I won't make the same mistake twice.

I'm back in this thing.

Back to stay.

I put a few more dollars on the table for luck, then head for the door, still dizzy from the turn of events, gazing at life through a gauzy adrenaline-induced tunnel. Circling the bar, paying no attention to my surroundings, thanks to the thoughts blaring in my head, I come face-to-face with the waitress Marta. She stops short, almost ditching the tray of drinks in her hand. Her eyes light up with recognition.

I step around her, but not quickly enough.

"You," she says, grabbing my sleeve with her free hand.

I twist away. "Excuse me—"

"Wait just a second," she hisses, loud enough for people at the bar to turn.

Not wanting a scene, I'm torn. I can brave whatever she's about to say, or I can make a dash for the door. As tempting as retreat is, I'm in no mood to run.

She slides her tray onto the bar, then gets right up in my face. "I know what you did."

"What are you talking about?"

"You want me to say it in front of everybody?"

A couple of young men in striped, tall-collared shirts are watching, trying to decide whether they should take an interest or not. I've had crisis resolution drilled so deep into my psyche that my automatic impulse is to diffuse the tension. But I don't want to diffuse anything. There's a part of me that would like nothing better right now than a fight. I couldn't be beaten, not by anyone.

They step forward, shoulder to shoulder for support. To my surprise, Marta turns on them, freezing the men with her glare.

"Why don't you mind your own business?" she says, ticktocking her finger at them.

They shrug their way back to their drinks, pretending nothing's happened.

"And you," she says, back to me. "What gives you the right—?"

I whisk my jacket back just far enough for her to get a glimpse of badge and maybe a little gun just behind. It's a well-practiced gesture, perfect for shutting people up mid-sentence. On Marta it has a curious effect.

"You're a cop?" she asks, shaking her head. "And you think that means you can do anything you want? You can go up to random women and start pushing them around? For what?" She jabs her finger at my chest. "Because she wouldn't go home with you?"

"What's the problem, Marta?"

I find Tommy at my elbow. He takes her by the arm, nudging her back.

He's acting friendly, but Marta shuts down at the touch, suddenly petulant. "This is my problem."

"He's cool, though," Tommy says. "Hey, you don't want to make any trouble for him."

She pulls free, eyes on the floor. "That's exactly what I want."

"No, really, I'm serious. He's one of the good guys."

The men from the bar pause. One of the bartenders holds a mobile phone in his hand, his finger poised over the call button like he's going to detonate a bomb any second. I start going into resolution mode, flashing the badge, motioning for everybody to calm down.

Tommy's big smile starts working its magic, too. He puts an arm around Marta, easing her back, and sends some kind of invisible signal to the bartender, who takes his finger off the detonator button. The waitress tries to shrug free, but he holds her tight.

"Everything's cool, everybody," he says. "Hey, it's all right."

I owe him one, but instead of staying to chat about it, I take the opportunity to slip outside. The sun is gone without a trace, mosquitoes circling the lampposts overhead. Before I can make my escape, I hear footsteps behind me. Turning, I find Tommy and Marta, his restraining arm still around her.

She steps clear of him, standing halfway between us. "Why'd you rough that woman up? What kind of man thinks he can do that, badge or no badge?"

"You poured enough tequila down that woman's gullet to sink a whale. When I came out here, she was just about to get behind the wheel. She was going to drive in that condition. You understand what I'm saying? I didn't rough her up—I saved her life, and probably somebody else's, too. At the very least, she would have lost her license, spent some quality time behind bars."

"Oh," she says. "So you did her a favor. Now I get it." She plunges a hand into her tiny apron, pulling out a crushed twenty, waving it between her fingers. She balls the twenty in her fist and throws it to the ground, then turns on her heel to go.

Tommy stands there, eyes wide. "She's kinda loco, that girl. I think when she calms down, she'll be more understanding."

I take out my keys and unlock my car. "You really think I care?"

He laughs. "Deep down? Yeah, I think you really do."

CHAPTER 10

By the time I show up, the briefing's reached standing-room-only status, with plainclothes officers and uniforms from four or five different agencies shifting for elbow space along the back wall. Near the front, Cavallo motions for me, but I shake my head and find a hospitable notch between a couple of county constables and a Sheriff's Department detective with a tobacco-stained brush of a mustache. He wears a nickel-plated Government Model .45 on his hip, what we call a "barbeque gun" around here, for wearing to fancy shindigs. He looks lonesome without his Stetson.

There's a strange energy in the room, something I can't put my finger on. A lot of hard stares shooting back and forth. Something's happened, but I don't know what. I turn to ask the detective, but he just shrugs, mystified as me.

Scanning the brass at the far end of the room, I get a surprise. Next to Wanda, who stands out in any crowd on account of her snow white hair, Rick Villanueva sits reviewing a stack of documents in his lap, whispering the occasional question, like he's trying to get up to speed and only has half a minute to do it. This can't be good.

Wanda goes to the podium, tapping the mic a couple of times to get everyone's attention. Upwards of a hundred officers are packed into the cramped space, and it takes awhile for everyone to settle in.

"Before we get started," she says, "I'm sure you all saw the piece on Channel 13 last night."

A collective sigh goes up, along with some random profanity and a few choice words about Wayne Dolcefino, the investigative reporter.

"You see it?" I ask the sheriff's detective.

"At my watering hole of choice," he says, his breath smelling of stale coffee, "there are better things to look at than the idiot tube."

Wanda gives the microphone another series of taps, and Rick Villanueva eases out of his chair, standing at her elbow.

"The first thing I want to make clear," Wanda says, "is that whoever made those statements to the press, I'm going to find out. What we say in here has to remain confidential. Am I clear? There's a girl's life at stake, people. Never forget that. Secondly, Lieutenant Villanueva here is joining the task force as of now. From this moment forward, all information to the press—and I mean every single detail—will be going through him. No one talks to the media without his say-so. Understood?" A few heads nod. "Come on, people, I know it's early, but if you understand what I'm saying, raise your hand."

Hands go up across the room. I glance at my new buddy before hoisting mine. He shakes his head and does likewise. Everybody's craning around, like they expect to sniff out the leak here and now by spotting a telltale unraised hand.

"Okay, okay. You can put your hands down. Lieutenant, you have a few words you'd like to say?"

Rick, never at a loss for words, spends the next five minutes talking about his satisfaction in being asked to join the task force, and his determination to do everything in his power to turn this negative into a positive. While he's speechmaking, I quiz the constables for details about the news report. One of them, a thick-necked bulldog with a tight military crew cut, cups a hand to my ear and fills me in. The lead story on the Channel 13 news last night was about trouble inside the task force. No progress is being made in the hunt for Hannah Mayhew because of interagency rivalries and a general lack of organization. "Sources inside the investigation" were credited with the scoop.

After Rick starts repeating himself, Wanda squeezes back to the mic and starts going round robin through the room, soliciting verbal reports from the team checking out white vans, the canvass of Willowbrook witnesses, and the head of the surveillance squad keeping tabs on James Fontaine. He's a body-builder type in dark fatigues, more like a SWAT sniper than a binocular boy.

"Fontaine's movements are pretty regular," he says. "He hasn't led us anywhere."

No mention of Carter Robb's stakeout of the Fontaine house, or my curbside visit with him. I try to catch Cavallo's eye, making sure she picked up on that, but she's busy taking down notes. Though I'm tempted to raise my hand and ask a question, I decide to wait.

After the rest of the reports are made and new assignments handed out, Wanda wraps things up and dismisses everyone. The sheriff's detective shoulders past me.

"That was a whole lot of nothing," he says.

I decide to stay put, letting the room empty ahead of me. Rick Villanueva skirts the side wall. No one stops him to talk, so he makes good time. Before I can slip away, we're face-to-face.

"Funny seeing you here," he says. "I thought your days of exile had come to an end."

My smirk just amuses him more. "I could say the same thing about you, Rick. Are you, like, the new press secretary or something?"

"Not by choice." He leans in, lowering his voice. "To be honest, I'd rather be anywhere but here. In case you don't know it yet, this is a sinking ship. But the chief himself called me. He wants me on this thing to try and turn it around."

"With what, your winning smile?"

"Something like that," he says.

"Any idea who talked to Channel 13?"

He chuckles. "Between you and me? I'm thinking somebody at the Sheriff's Department. They're not too happy about HPD taking the lead on this."

"Aren't these jurisdictional things settled up front, though?"

"Sure," he says. "But that was before this was all over Fox and TruTV. Now people are thinking this case could make a few careers—and probably end some, too. If you want my advice, get out while you can."

I pat him on the arm. "Too late for me, pal."

"Yeah. Me, too."

After Villanueva pushes on, Cavallo comes down the center aisle with a file box balanced on her hip. I offer to take it, expecting her to put up a fight. Instead, she hands it over. It's heavy as bricks.

"All yours."

"What's in here?" I ask, peering through the gap in the lid.

"Witness interviews. All the kids we talked to at Klein High, all the kids from the Cypress youth group. That's our project for today, looking for new leads."

"Where do we start?"

She suppresses a yawn. "The nearest coffeepot."

Two styrofoam cups of scalding black brew later, we clear off space at the end of a long folding table, pull some chairs up, and divvy up the interview reports. I feel a little guilty for having slept last night, since Cavallo's bloodshot eyes and involuntary yawning fits make it clear she didn't.

"You okay?" I ask.

She moves a paper back and forth in front of her nose. "I can barely get my eyes to focus."

"You notice the surveillance report didn't mention anything about Robb, or us meeting him out in front of the Fontaine house?"

She silently peruses the form.

"You hear me?"

"I heard you," she says. "That was my doing, March. He asked if it was significant and I said no."

"Why would you do that?"

"It wasn't significant, was it?" She puts the report down and fingers the cross at her throat. "And anyway, I didn't want Wanda to start asking why we'd re-interviewed Robb. I figured the less said the better."

"For my benefit?" I ask. "Or his?"

"His? What are you talking about?"

"Nothing. Never mind." It was a stupid thing to say. I just thought that, she being one of them, a co-religionist, maybe she'd decided to cut the young minister some slack. "The thing we need to talk about is that DNA test. When are we going to get a result?"

She sighs. "You're a one-note, you know that? Do you have any idea the kind of grief I'd get if Wanda or anyone else found out we're pursuing this? I had to tap-dance around the whole swab thing already, and now she's giving me funny looks."

"Why keep it a secret?"

"I'm not," she says. "I'm just being discreet."

"But the test is being done, right? You took care of it? Cavallo, look me in the eye. You did take care of it, right?"

She looks at me, then blinks. "You know Sheryl Green at the medical examiner's office? She's doing it."

"Yeah, I know her."

Remembering Green's interest in the case, I'm somewhat reassured, but I'd still rather have Bridger involved. Maybe I'll call him and see if there's anything he can do to rush things along.

"By the way," I say, "I need to take a couple of hours today. Another angle to pursue."

She taps a finger on her stack of interviews. "This is the angle we're pursuing."

"I know that. How about one hour?"

"How about lunch, then. You can do whatever you want on your break, all right? Now, can we please get to it?"

Just twenty minutes into the reading, I find myself underlining typos. I guess serving under Captain Hedges has had an effect. The minutes drag by, which is fine with me. I'm in no hurry to talk to Wilcox. No hurry at all.

Stephen Wilcox is an Anglophile at heart, one of those guys who's traced his lineage back to some countryside castle, who can list a few centuries' worth of sovereigns in the order that they reigned, and wears tattersall and waxed cotton whenever the inhospitable Houston climate will allow. He tells me I'm paying, then says he'll meet me at the Black Labrador, our old stomping ground.

Given the distance, my lunch break is going to be a long one, meaning I'll have to face Cavallo's wrath. So be it.

Back in the day, Wilcox and I spent hours at the Black Lab, a Tudor-style pub on Montrose near Richmond, at the far end of a cobbled courtyard anchored by the ivy-clad Montrose Library, drinking in front of the unlit fireplace and watching the knee-socked waitresses scoot by. Once he even tried to coax me onto the giant chessboard they have on the front lawn to push the pieces around, but I drew the line at that. A cheeky snap of Charles and Di, severed down the middle, used to hang prominently up front, though it's been long since replaced by a reverential portrait of the dead princess.

I haven't been back since our split and I'm not looking forward to it. He's already installed at one of the creaky tables, his checked jacket draped over the back of his chair. Seeing him again in the flesh, a rush of feeling floods back. The long, thin Easter Island face with the jutting jaw and heavy-lidded eyes. The childhood scar bisecting the left eyebrow, the thinning blond hair buzzed short in an effort to conceal how much is gone. This was the one guy I could always trust. What happened with us?

"I ordered the mussels," he says.

An involuntary smile. "Thanks. I'll pass."

What happened was simple. Wilcox got tired of covering for my lapses. He got fed up with my indifference to the job. He cut me slack at first, saying he understood, saying he knew the kind of pain I must be in. But that sympathy could only last so long. When I was sloppy he'd tidy up, when I was indifferent, he'd make the extra effort. When I started making up my own rules, though, he drew the line. I remember him standing over me, one of my fictitious reports balled in his fist. *"What is this? What are you trying to do to me?"* And I remember staring back at him, unfazed: *"Do what you want. I don't care anymore."*

So what changed? It's hard to say. Was it as simple as seeing those severed cords hanging from the bed frame?

I don't need to look at the menu, but I do anyway just to have a prop in hand. The waitress comes over in a black tee and khaki skirt, her ribbed black socks pulled halfway over her knee. She tells me what's good, then shrugs when I order the unadventurous fish and chips.

"When in Rome," I say, glancing up at the timbered ceiling.

Wilcox doesn't smile. "You want to tell me what I'm doing here?"

"You chose the place."

"What I mean is, why is it that you can call out of the blue and I drop everything? That's what I don't understand. Does it make me a masochist?"

"You're getting a free meal out of it."

"We both know you owe me more than that."

There's a crack in the wooden table that suddenly takes on a fascinating aspect. I scratch at it with my nail, not wanting to see the expression on his face. "Listen, I wouldn't have called if it wasn't important."

"Important to you, you mean."

"And you."

He coughs into his hand. "Why do I doubt that?"

Driving over, I tried to tell myself his voice sounded pleasantly surprised over the phone. Maybe he'd even be happy to see me again. Wrong. I have no choice but to spit it out.

"What do you know about a guy named Joe Thomson?"

He ponders the question awhile. "Why are you asking?"

"He came to me with an offer."

I tell him the whole story, only leaving out the setting. He knows about the Paragon, and the last thing I need is a lecture. The further I get into the story, the more interested he becomes. His mussels arrive and he leaves them untouched, his eyes fixed on me.

"I said the odds were slim, but Thomson told me to come to you specifically. He said you'd be interested in what he had to tell. Was he right?"

Wilcox sniffs. "He wasn't wrong. I can't make any promises, Roland, but this is something my people would be very interested in. I'm not sure having you involved is going to work for us, though."

"It was me he came to. Take it or leave it."

"Setting that aside for a moment, are you telling me you don't know who this guy is?"

"He looked familiar."

"For a detective, you don't pay much attention, you know that?" He shakes his head, like he's remembering what it was about me he never liked. "Joe Thomson used to be one of the worst guys in the department, the kind the psych evaluations are supposed to weed out. We've got a thick file on him in IAD, full of excessive-force complaints going all the way back to his rookie days. Before I transferred, Internal Affairs was looking at him in connection with a couple of different cases. Planting evidence, making threats against fellow officers, we're talking a seriously bad dude."

"I got that vibe off him. But you said he 'used to be' bad?"

"Well," he says, dragging the word out. "About a year ago, he requested therapy. Of his own volition apparently. He patched things up with his ex-wife. They ended up getting remarried. As part of the therapy he started taking art classes—"

"Art classes?"

He rolls his eyes. "Yeah, I know. But I guess he really got into it. Does some kind of sculpting I guess. Anyway, we're talking about a pretty significant change in the guy."

I imagine a pottery wheel spinning a lump of wet clay in endless revolutions, my uninvited table guest of the night before hunched over, applying gritty fingers to the task of shaping. Or maybe taking a hammer and chisel to a block of marble, I don't know. For someone like me, a skeptic when it comes to the power of therapy, it's hard to credit the kind of transformation Wilcox describes. Cleaning up his act, reconciling with his estranged wife, and now coming clean about whatever corruption he's witnessed on the job. If only it were that easy to change course, to hit the reset button and become a good man again.

"What prompted this change of his?" I ask, suddenly thinking of Coleman, the supposed prison convert we rearrested at the George R. Brown. "Let me guess. Did he find Jesus?"

"You're not going to like this," he says, cracking a smile. "What changed Thomson was finding himself a new role model. Thomson left the gang unit and started working for Reg Keller."

Keller. Some messiah.

If I have a nemesis at HPD, it's Keller, the man who's been dogging my steps for the past fifteen years or more. I tried to bring him down once and failed miserably.

"The Homeland Security thing?" I ask, keeping my voice even.

He nods. "The Golden Parachute Brigade."

"So that's how he knew I'd be hooked: Keller's involved. You know, I was talking to one of Keller's guys the other day. Remember Tony Salazar?"

"Sure."

"One of his CIs wandered into our cars-for-criminals net."

"Salazar's on our radar screen, too. He paid cash for a nice boat a while back, and since he jumped to Keller's camp, he's been living way above his means."

"Well, I respect the guy personally. He's a sharp detective."

"Maybe," Wilcox says, meaning not so much. "But getting back to Thomson, I think Keller had a talk with the man. Told him to get his ducks in a row, that kind of thing. If you look at Keller's roster, you'd think he was running some kind of halfway house. He recruits the worst disciplinary cases, then turns them into model detectives."

"By pointing them to the real money?"

"Yes," he says. "That's my theory anyway. If I could prove it, I wouldn't be sitting here." He pauses. "I'll be right back, okay?"

He slides around the table and heads upstairs to the restroom. As soon as he goes, the waitress comes by to refill my water glass. I take a bite of fish, surprised that it's gone cold.

I met Reg Keller a long time ago, when we were both still in uniform. I was on patrol and he was an up-and-coming sergeant about to make the jump to plainclothes. We rode a shift together one night and something happened. He put me in a bad spot. It took a long time for me to work out the truth, not until I made detective myself. Once I did, though, I was at his throat, and for a while it looked like I'd nail him.

But I missed my chance.

My career rocketed into the stratosphere, burned bright a little while, then tumbled back to earth. My life in general went off the rails. Meanwhile, Keller racked up promotion after promotion, storing favors away for a rainy day, until he was too far up the line for a rank and filer like me to so much as touch.

Sometime after the Dubai Ports World scandal back in early 2006, when the administration tried to hand over American ports to foreign control, including stevedore operations at the Port of Houston, Keller somehow managed to get the green light on a special unit whose official remit was to assess security threats related to the port and Bush Intercontinental Airport. Even a longtime opponent like me had to admire his cunning. There were already a number of agencies doing the work, so Keller's team was superfluous from the start, but the assignment would look great on a résumé and no doubt lead to lucrative security work once he retired. Hence the nickname Golden Parachute Brigade. Nice work if you can get it.

"You look angry," Wilcox says, resuming his seat.

"I am angry. It's all coming back to me, the whole thing with Keller. You're telling me you can't touch a guy like that in IAD? Are they even trying?"

"I'm not going to comment on any ongoing investigations. But let me make something clear. For Thomson to get what he wants, this blanket immunity, we're going to need more from him than the shooters from your multiple murder. If he can give us something on Keller, on the other officers in the unit, then we can talk. You have a problem with that?"

Oh, I don't have a problem with that. I wouldn't have it any other way. Wilcox should know better than to even ask. Finding those shooters might be my lifeline back into Homicide, but bringing Keller down, that would be personal. Like I said, I have my reasons.

"You take care of things with the district attorney," I tell him, "and I'll make sure Thomson's ready to talk. And, Steve, we should move fast on this, all right?"

"I'll start making the calls the minute I leave."

I reach my hand across the table. "It's good to be working with you again."

He just looks at my hand, not wanting to take it. At the last second he changes his mind. We shake, and afterward we both look away in embarrassment.

"This doesn't change anything," he says.

"I know." I lay some cash on the table and get up. "But it will."

"March, wait."

I stop, but I don't sit back down.

"How's Charlotte doing?"

"Charlotte? She's fine."

"Things between you two, they're all right?"

"What is this, a counseling session? If I want therapy, I'll sign up for an art class, okay?"

He holds his hands up in surrender. "I'm just asking, man. I know it's tough, this time of year. Tell her I said hello."

But he's not just asking. I know Wilcox. I understand the way his mind works. He's sensed something in me, but can't put his finger on exactly what, so he's rooting around a little to see if he can work it out. Judging from the look on his face, he thinks he has.

CHAPTER 11

Apologies for my late lunch turn out to be unnecessary by the time I catch up to Cavallo, who's packed the witness statements up tight and transferred the box to the trunk of her city car. I reach her in the parking lot just as she's about to leave the station without me. If it were directed at me, the look in her eye would give me pause, but she hardly acknowledges my arrival.

"What's up?" I ask.

She gazes into the sky, brushing the hair back from her face. "Oh, I don't know. It's just that as of this morning, we had no developments on the Fontaine front, and now all the sudden the order comes down to snatch him. Apparently he just made a buy."

"Stupid kid," I say. "We're making the arrest?"

"The Sheriff's Department's going to do the heavy lifting, leaving us to ask the questions. Are you up to it? Only it's not like we have anything on him. The kid deals some weed, he knows our missing juvenile—that's about it."

"If we catch him dirty, that'll give us some leverage."

She shakes her head. "Not enough. All this investigation needs him to do is lead us to Hannah. If he can't do that, he's a waste of time.

But if he can, do you really think he'll cop to a kidnapping charge to get out of possession with intent?"

"You have a point," I say. "But still, how else would you expect them to play it? If surveillance really caught the kid making a buy, it's not like we can pass up the chance to apply the thumbscrews, is it?"

"We could play that card anytime. Doing it now reeks of desperation, if you ask me. But Wanda won't listen. After this morning, she's operating on the news cycle."

We climb into the car, slamming doors and snapping seat belts into place, then she reverses out of the parking space, cranking the wheel sharply. The tires kick up loose gravel as we bounce onto the road, cutting in front of oncoming traffic. Next time I'll volunteer to drive. Cavallo has a knack for channeling emotion into the gears, and as often as I dream about it and wake up sweating, I'd just as soon not die in a car crash.

"It's all spinning out of control," she says.

"The case or the car?"

She ignores my attempt at humor. Frustration comes off her in waves. I suspect that what isn't released through her cathartic high-wire driving can only come out by talking. She's not the type to hit or break things, which is too bad considering how calming violence can be.

"Once a case gets traction in the media," I say, hoping to get her talking, "you can only work it the right way as long as you keep getting results. As soon as you hit a wall, the daily pressure from upstairs to provide new sound bites overrules everything else. It's not Wanda's fault—"

"So have you heard the latest?" She wrenches the steering wheel with white-knuckled intensity, like she's thinking about snapping it off. "They're trying to persuade Donna Mayhew to go on TV alongside the chief. They want to get her on *Larry King Live*."

"How does she feel about that?"

"I'd ask her, March, if I could get her to pick up the phone."

"Ah," I say.

"Ah, what?"

"That's why you're so worked up. You have a special bond with that woman, and you don't like anybody interfering."

She stomps the accelerator like it's my face. "Of course I have a bond with her. Who wouldn't? Doesn't your heart go out to her in a situation like this, with her daughter gone and—"

"Of course." I cut her off, not wanting to dig too deeply into my heart and what it goes out to. "But you've been very protective of her." I tighten my grip on the door handle. "Of them."

"Them? Who do you mean by them?"

"The church people. The mother, yes, but Carter Robb, too. You know. Your fellow travelers, so to speak."

She makes no reply at first, letting her lead foot do the talking. I hunker down into my seat, trying not to think about air bags and side impacts and trauma to the head. I was lucky to avoid a chewing out for my late return. I should have left well enough alone.

"March," she says.

The silence was too good to last.

"Do you have some kind of issue with me?"

"Issue?" I ask. "What kind of issue would I have?"

"You keep needling me all the time, like I've done something to you. But apart from bending over backwards to do you a favor, and then taking responsibility for you when your friends in Homicide gave you the boot, I can't think of what you're holding against me."

She drifts in and out of the lane as she talks, while I do my best not to flinch.

"Seriously? Listen, Cavallo, I think you might be projecting your frustrations about the case onto me—"

"What was that quip about my 'fellow travelers' then?"

"I just meant . . . you know. That cross you wear."

She fingers the necklace, then lets it drop. "What do you believe, March? About God, the universe and everything?"

"You're asking me this for real?" I should keep my mouth shut. "All right, I'll play along. About God, I guess it depends on what kind of mood I'm in. Sometimes he exists, sometimes he doesn't, and when he does sometimes I'm all right with that, and sometimes I want to give him a good kicking."

She flinches and I know I should really stop. But I'm on a roll.

"The universe? It's pretty screwed up, if you ask me. The world is on its last legs, people are pretty much rotten, and happiness is just an illusion, a kind of opiate—but it's not actual happiness that keeps us going, it's the promise of getting a fix later on in the soon-to-be perfect future, which makes it that much more desperate when you think about it . . . Not that I often do."

There's more. Something underneath the words, unspoken, for me unspeakable, an article of faith I can never doubt. What I believe in is evil. Its existence and power, the way it grows like mold on every surface, teeming beneath the walls, as insinuating as the Gulf Coast heat. It has a grip on all of us. It has its claws in me.

"Fascinating," she says. "And what do I believe?"

"You?" I shrug, exhausted from my bout of self-expression. "How should I know? Why don't you tell me?"

"Don't you know already?"

"I can guess."

"Well if you don't know, and you haven't asked, then why don't you stop making assumptions? And while you're at it, you can stop with the little digs you're always making, because I've had it up to here and the last thing I need on top of everything else is your constant annoying buzz in my ear. All right?"

"Sure thing."

Now I'm the one who needs to hit something. As much as I'd like to, at least with words, all the lines that come to mind are variations on the same bitter theme: it's your fault I'm here in the first place. And why is it her fault? Because given the choice, I decided to spend the afternoon with her rather than do my job. What can I say? It made sense at the time.

But I can already hear her retort—how is that my fault?—and of course she'd be right. Not only that, but in making the argument

I'd reveal something more pathetic about myself than my half-baked views on God and the universe.

My loneliness.

"That's all you have to say?" she asks.

I nod. "That's it. Or do you want me to apologize? I'm sorry for goading you. Won't let it happen again."

"Are you mocking me?"

"I'm just trying not to annoy you."

"Well," she says, "you could sure use the practice."

The drunk girl at the Paragon comes back to me, the one with the glittering eyelids. Marta said she had bruises all over, like she'd been slapped around. But I didn't do that, did I? The truth is, I can't remember exactly what I did, or most of what I said. It was like someone else was doing it through me. I don't know what happened. Like one of our notorious inner-city witnesses, I didn't see nothing.

My first glimpse of James Fontaine inspires some hope. He looks ready to crack. The Harris County Sheriff's Department team, a bunch of armed linebackers with shaved heads and mirrored sunglasses, nudges his black BMW X3 to the curb near the intersection of West Little York and Antoine, maybe a mile away from the Northwest Freeway. Our car is near the back of the convoy, tagging behind the surveillance truck.

They drag him out of the driver's seat, bend him over the hood, then do a quick search of the vehicle, going straight for the back compartment, where they find a vinyl flight bag with a Puma logo, right where they knew it would be. A squat surveillance officer in baggy jeans records everything with a handheld video camera.

We thread our way through the flashing lights, coming alongside the X3. When he sees us, one of the deputies hands the bag to Cavallo, who's just pulled on a pair of gloves. She plops it on the hood across from Fontaine, slowly fingering the zipper.

James Fontaine is a lanky black kid of about seventeen, handsome in a boyish way, wearing a G-Unit polo that's actually been pressed—the creases are still visible down the length of the sleeves. He looks about as thug as a clean-cut suburbanite whose knowledge of the street comes mainly from the media can. Now that he's in custody, he makes no pretense to being a hard man. His eyes alternate between watching Cavallo unzip the bag and clamping tight in prayer, like he's trying to make the contents miraculously disappear.

Watching him sweat, a thought occurs to me. If he's just made a buy, then he had no idea he was under surveillance, which means he hasn't intentionally been avoiding the secret location where he's stashed Hannah Mayhew. The odds that this kid has her locked up somewhere are thin to none. But maybe he knows something that can help.

Cavallo peers inside the bag. "Wow, James. I guess you just re-upped, huh? You must have quite a little operation going."

I lean over for a look. Inside, a one-pound brick of what I'm guessing is Mexican schwag. Not the finest herb, but given the quantity there's going to be no trouble calling this possession with intent to distribute.

I lean over the hood to get him eye level. "Partner, you just stepped in it."

"That's not mine," he says halfheartedly.

"So your fingerprints aren't going to be all over it?" I point to the cameraman, who waves at Fontaine. "This gentleman here with the camera has been watching your every move. That means we've got every step of the process, from the time you picked up the bag and put it in your hatchback to right now."

He drops his head and starts sniffling. When he lifts it, sure enough there are tears streaking his cheeks. "Aw, come on, man," he says, begging with his eyes. "You gotta be kidding me. It's just weed, that's all it is. It's like, what, a misdemeanor, right? You don't gotta call out the SWAT team and everything on account of something like this."

Cavallo dumps the brick onto the hood. "We're talking about a pound here, James, not a gram. That's possession with intent. You divide this up into ounces and hand it out to your little dealin' friends, is that it?"

"Look at that brown brick weed," I say, nudging the plastic-wrapped packages. "I wouldn't make brownies out of that. It's a shame to go down for such low-quality product."

The insult dries his tears a little. He's about to protest when one of the Sheriff's Department men takes his arm. "Come on, G-Unit. Let's read you your rights."

They Mirandize the kid, then put him in the back of a cruiser to sweat. Once he's stowed away, we all gather for an impromptu powwow around the BMW's hood, everybody looking to Cavallo for direction.

"This isn't about building a case," she says. "The clock is ticking, and if that boy knows anything we need to get it out of him fast. If that means he walks on the drug charge, are any of us going to lose sleep over that?"

Headshaking all around. If there are any qualms in the group, they go unexpressed. Cavallo notices the surveillance guy's camera.

"That thing's not on, is it?" she asks.

Everybody laughs.

"Okay, so let's get him into an interview room and see what happens."

As the team packs up, I wander over to the unit where Fontaine sits. He leans his shoulder against the rolled-down window, sipping air through an inch-wide gap in the glass.

"You all right back there?"

"It's pretty hot."

"Yeah," I say. "It'll only get worse."

The Northwest interview room is surprisingly spacious and well appointed. The table has all four legs, the chairs match, and the stains on the floor look dry and non-toxic. There's even cold air blowing from the registers overhead. Fontaine slumps forward, his head resting on the table. We observe from the room next door, where the video feed is channeled onto a monitor. Lieutenant Mosser sits just to the side, where she can study the image closely, while Villanueva stands in the back corner, arms folded, signaling his unwillingness to get in the way.

"He's not sleeping, is he?" Wanda asks.

Cavallo leans closer. "Sounds like he's crying."

There's an old saw about the interview room: Whoever sleeps while he's waiting for the detectives is obviously guilty; only the innocent are plagued by fears. I don't put much stock in that kind of thing. Leave people in a bare room for long enough and they'll do all kinds of strange things.

"What do you think this kid can give us?" I ask.

Wanda studies me a moment. "That's what you're going to find out, Roland. You think you can handle that?"

"Never mind him," Cavallo says, taking my arm. "Come on."

When we pop open the interview room door, Fontaine gives us an apprehensive smile. Cavallo takes the seat across from him, and I sit on the corner, cheating my chair over a bit so that I'm technically on his side. He isn't sure which one of us to face, so he splits the difference.

We begin with small talk, Cavallo asking about his nice car, what his parents do for a living, how he likes school and what he thinks about his classes. His recent suspension for drug possession is glossed over—only happy or neutral topics for now. Hannah Mayhew isn't mentioned. His answers are tentative at first, but the more questions she pitches across the plate, the more he loosens up and enjoys hitting them. This isn't so bad, he's probably thinking. He might just get through this.

"You seem like a smart guy," Cavallo says, getting him to nod along in agreement. "You've got a lot going for you. It's a shame to see you in a situation like this, James. We'd rather be going after the real baddies, you know. Not giving guys like you a hard time."

"That's all right," he says, perversely apologetic. "You gotta do your job. I understand."

"Maybe you could help us, James. And maybe we could then help you. Are you nervous, James?"

He nods.

"I'd be worried, too, if I was in your shoes. Buying bricks like that, you know what it tells me? You've got more money than sense.

And you know something, Texas is not exactly lenient when it comes to drug sentencing."

Fontaine mumbles something.

"What was that?"

"I'm a minor."

"In the eyes of the Penal Code, you're an adult."

"Welcome to Texas," I say.

Cavallo smiles. "Problem is, if you're slinging that stuff at Klein, you're probably looking at a penalty enhancement, too, for distributing near a school."

"To actual minors," I add.

"Exactly. This is bad news, James. For one thing, say goodbye to that nice Beemer of yours."

I nod in agreement. "That'll be seized for sure."

"You can do that?" he asks.

"Sure we can. Or . . ."

"Or what?"

"Or we can work together on something," she says. "Like I told you, if you help us, maybe we can help you, too. How does that sound?"

His eyes widen. "Help you with what?"

Cavallo leans forward, ready to make her pitch. "The thing is, James, we're willing to deal, but first we need to know if you have anything worthwhile. If there are any open cases you can help us with."

And just like that, he rolls over. I wish I could credit our interrogation skills, but James Fontaine would have cracked for anyone.

"You want the names?" he asks. " 'Cause I can give you some names. The dude I bought it off of, my connection, I can give you him. And the ones at school that actually do the dealin'? I can give you those, too. Me, I'm more like what you'd call a middleman, you know? The real bad guys, like what you want, I can give you some of those."

Cavallo takes everything down, the various names and nicknames, the way he breaks the brick down, who it goes to, the number he calls when he wants some more. He knows other dealers, too, and where they get their supply. By the time he's done, he's leaning over the table helping with the spelling of names, saying who to underline and who to cross out. He's almost exhilarated, working with the cops, thinking his problems are about to go away.

I can't help feeling sorry for the kid.

"All of this, James," Cavallo says, tearing the page off her note-pad. "It's worthless. It's nothing." She balls the page up and tosses it over her shoulder.

Fontaine's jaw drops in shock. He glances to me for help as if to say, Look what she just did. I shrug. You asked for it, son.

"There's something else I want you to help us with," she continues, ignoring his devastated look. "You know that girl who disappeared, the one from your school?"

His right eyelid starts to flutter. Cavallo and I exchange a look. This kind of nervous tick is what we're after. Now that we've chatted awhile, getting a baseline feel for how Fontaine behaves normally, the signs of stress that erupt under questioning will serve us as guides.

"What's that girl's name?" I ask, as if I can't quite think of it.

Fontaine blinks harder, then wipes his hand over his face.

"Come on, James," Cavallo says. "You know her, don't you?"

"You mean Hannah?"

"That's right. Tell me about Hannah."

He shrugs. "Tell you what?"

"For one thing, how do you know her?"

"From school."

"Are you two friends?"

"No, we ain't friends." He expels a puff of air. "Not hardly, not no more."

"Why is that?" I ask.

"On account of what she done to my car, her and that other girl."

Not the answer I was expecting. "And what was that?" I ask.

"Busted the windows out," he says, swinging an imaginary bat through the air. "Keyed up the side."

"When did this happen?"

He hears the skepticism in my voice and rolls his eyes. "You the police, man. Look it up."

Cavallo jumps in. "You reported it?"

"Of course we reported it," he snaps. "You gotta report it for the insurance. And we told them who done it, too, but that didn't matter obviously. They didn't do nothing about it, did they?"

Cavallo scribbles a note, then tears the sheet off her notepad, walking it out the door. While she's gone, I give Fontaine a stern but paternal look.

"Hannah seems like a nice girl," I say. "Why would she do something like that to your ride?"

The question makes him thoughtful. Sometimes a pause is strategic, buying time to invent an answer, but the way he starts rubbing his neck and studying the suspended ceiling tiles, I'm guessing he's never stopped to wonder about this.

"She is a nice girl," he admits with a nod. "In her own way. I liked her at first. I mean, she's pretty fine looking, right? And underneath all that Jesus talk, she could be pretty cool sometimes."

"You liked her."

He shrugs. "She was all right. But all that religion and stuff—it's fine for some people, don't get me wrong, I'm not judgin' or nothing—but it gets old, you know what I mean? Feeling like you the pet project, always needin' to be dragged into church. And then she got all, like, clingy, you know?"

Cavallo reenters, pausing on the threshold. She has a new stack of papers in her hand. When she sits, she starts shuffling through them. "James, I have a question about your phone. The one we found you with, that's with Cingular, right?"

"Yeah."

"But you have another phone, don't you?"

"I got my home phone."

"Another mobile phone, I mean. What's the number to that?"

He glances at me, confused. "What she talking about?"

"Your other phone," I say.

"You already got my phone. I don't got another one."

Cavallo shakes her head. "You don't conduct business on that phone, do you? The one your parents pay the bill for?"

"I'm seventeen," he says. "I don't conduct no business."

She reaches down to the floor and starts unfolding the pile of notes he gave her a few minutes ago. "This looks like a business to me. What were you doing last Thursday?"

"I don't remember. Why?"

She sits back. "You're not being very cooperative, James."

"What you want me to say? I don't remember what I was doing. Probably nothing, since they suspended me from school."

"Let's talk about the car," I say, breaking up the rhythm. "You never did tell me why she'd do something like that."

He turns his chair so he's facing me, ignoring Cavallo across the table. "Prob'ly 'cause of the weed they found in her locker."

"So that was yours?"

"I didn't put it there, if that's what you mean."

Cavallo taps her pen on the table. "Why'd she think you did?"

He turns toward her. "Like I said, she was interfering with my game. I was, like, 'you need to back off,' and she was all uppity about it, you know, so we ended up having some words. That's it, just words. And she was all crying and everything, and saying how she cared about me." When he says *cared*, his shoulders tighten. "She was living some kind of fantasy in her head, I guess, thinking there was something more between us than there was."

"Did you ever go out on a date?"

He laughs. "Man, she wears one of them rings—what's it called? A promise ring?" He shakes his head. "Shawty's saving herself, you know? Why would I take a girl like that out? Nothing in it for me."

"You're a class act," Cavallo says.

He smiles her way. I liked him better when he was crying.

"So you told her to back off," I say, "and suddenly some dope turns up in her locker. She assumes you put it there to get her in trouble, so she trashes your car?"

"Her and that other one. The Katrina girl."

"Katrina who?" Cavallo asks, making a note.

He scrunches his face up in contempt. "No, not Katrina who. That New Orleans girl that was Hannah's friend." He edges toward me, man to man. "Talk about messed up. It's that girl you need to be talking to, if you wanna know what happened. She was the instigator."

Cavallo's pen is still poised. "This girl have a name?"

He shrugs. "She got one. Don't mean I remember it."

"Evey?" I ask.

His eyes light up. "That's the one. Talk to her. She's one of those people seems normal, then all the sudden they just freak out on you. I told Hannah she needed to get clear of that one, but the girl don't listen to me."

Cavallo stands. "Let's take a break."

When it came to ratting out his friends, Fontaine seemed only too helpful, but on the subject of Hannah Mayhew, his answers strike me as evasive and confused. Not that I think he strangled her and buried her in his backyard, or has her locked up in his bedroom closet. Now more than ever, I'm convinced she ended up in that West Bellfort house, bleeding out on the dirty bed. Only I don't know how she got there. If Fontaine had picked up his brick from some Crips, we'd have a direct link, but he went to the wrong neighborhood, Latin King territory if it was anyone's at all.

And what was really between them? He speaks so cavalierly about her, denying any attraction on his part, but then he turns around and warns her about the people she hangs with? I can't help thinking there was more to their relationship than he wants to let on. Out of pride, maybe, assuming it's not plain fear. Not wanting to get mixed up any deeper than he already is.

In the monitoring room, Wanda Mosser sits watching him on the screen. She looks up at us, clearly disappointed. Villanueva's corner now stands empty.

"We need to call the question," she says. "Ask him point-blank where Hannah Mayhew is."

I shake my head. "It's not him. He wouldn't be talking if it was."

"Do it anyway."

Cavallo gives her the nod, then turns to me. "Who's the Katrina girl he's talking about?"

"Someone Robb mentioned. Evey something, short for Evangeline, like in the poem." She looks at me blankly, but I decide now's not the time to astonish her with my knowledge of Longfellow. "We'll need to follow that up."

She hands me some printouts on the vandalism. Sure enough, the incident was reported. Fontaine's father, a Hewlett-Packard employee, even retained a lawyer and managed to get a restraining order against Hannah Mayhew, preventing her from approaching either the family home or James personally.

"So not only have we failed to recover our victim," Cavallo says, "or seize her kidnapper for that matter, but we've turned up a little dirt to tarnish her name."

"You think this might be why Donna's reluctant to go on television? The drug suspension, the restraining order, that's a lot of dirty laundry to put out there."

Wanda interrupts with a long sigh. "Mama's tired, boys and girls. And if that kid walks out of here without giving us our missing girl, that means our only real lead isn't a lead anymore. Then I'll be real tired, and when I'm tired I get irritable."

"Should we beat him with a hose until he talks?"

"Don't put ideas in my head, March. Just go in there and ride him until he either coughs something up or has a nervous breakdown."

"He's just a kid," I say.

"A kid who slings dope. I couldn't care less about his feelings."

"It's not his feelings I'm worried about. It's his rights."

"Look, he's not going to jail for dealing, so he's in no position to complain. If he knew he was walking on that one, I'm sure he'd thank us. I just want to find this girl and get the chief off my back, okay?"

"Where is Hannah Mayhew?"

"You gonna keep asking, and I'm gonna keep telling you I don't know where she is. How many times I gotta say it? I. Don't. Know."

"James," Cavallo says. "Where is she?"

His eyes roll for the hundredth time. I feel like rolling mine, too.

"Did you kill her?"

"No." All trace of shock or indignation long since gone.

"Did you have someone kill her?"

He smiles wearily. "One of my *posse*?" He makes air quotes with his fingers. "No."

"Is she still alive, James?"

"How. Should. I. Know?"

The door opens and Wanda signals for us to come outside. As soon as it shuts, she starts shaking her head.

"What?" Cavallo asks.

"It's on the news."

"What is?"

"That we have him," Wanda says. "They're reporting right now that we have a juvenile suspect in custody."

"You gotta be kidding me."

"No," she says. "I just got off the phone with Villanueva, who's been trying to get them to stall the story. Too late. They're talking about it right now on TruTV."

I shake my head. "Beautiful. So we haven't fixed our leak."

"What's the plan?" Cavallo asks.

"The plan?" Wanda presses her fingertips to her temples. "I'm gonna start by shooting myself, and if that doesn't work, I'm gonna shoot myself again."

The two women head down the hallway, conferring on strategy, leaving me to wander back into the monitoring room. On the screen,

Fontaine wipes his palms on his jeans, then scrutinizes his fingers, peeling at some loose skin around the nails.

I need to talk to Carter Robb again so I can track down this girl Evey and see what she has to say. And it's time to call Bridger, too. I've waited long enough for my DNA results.

Fontaine looks up at the camera. He shakes his head, then rests it on the table again, settling in for another long wait.

CHAPTER 12

As the elder sister, Charlotte grew up with competing and possibly counterbalancing senses of both entitlement and obligation, feeling she had a place in the world but also a set of duties, often unpleasant, to go along with it. Her younger sister, Ann, inherited a finely tuned sense of proportional justice, probably stemming from a childhood concern that everyone, herself in particular, receive a fair share. It's probably too simplistic to trace their many differences in temperament and politics back to birth order, but I find myself doing it anyway.

Both sisters went into law, but Charlotte gravitated toward high-paying corporate work, scratching her civic itch with occasional involvement in the Harris County Republican Party. Ann, on the other hand, works mainly on death-row appeals, believing that while there might be guilty people behind bars, it's a safe bet none of them received fair trials.

Even over dinner, the types persist. Charlotte, the gracious hostess, reigns over a plentiful table, while Ann subtly annoys her, double-checking that each of us gets the same amount of food and drink. Afterward, when Charlotte takes charge of clearing the dishes, Ann tries to press all of us into duty. Failing that, she insists on helping her sister in the kitchen, leaving Bridger with me.

"So I hear you got pulled into that task force," he says. "How's that going?"

"It would be better if you expedited those test results I've been waiting on."

His eyebrows rise. "What results?"

"You said I'd need a sample to compare, so I found one—Hannah Mayhew's mother. I think she's the girl missing from the Morales scene. Now we're waiting on you guys to say whether I'm right. Sheryl Green has the samples in her lab apparently."

"Really," he says. "That's news to me."

"If you could light a fire under her, I'd appreciate it."

He gives a noncommittal nod. "I'll look into it."

I'd like to get more out of him, but Ann saunters into the dining room with coffee, followed by Charlotte, who looks lovely in a white linen blouse and mustard tan trousers, her lipstick freshly reapplied. I pause to admire her.

To say the years have been kind to my wife, at least physically, is an understatement. As time passes and her contemporaries either go to seed or under the knife, she only improves, still as thin and leggy as the day we married, the patina of fine lines on her face never detracting from its essentially placid symmetry. Looking at her now, the thought that my eyes could stray even for a moment seems ridiculous. A show of ingratitude toward God or the cosmos, whoever arranges such things.

In contrast, Ann sips her coffee with a harried, squinched look, like she's worried or anticipating a blow. I wonder if this is general agitation, or the result of words that passed between the sisters while they were busy in the kitchen.

"So," Ann says, adding more cream to her cup. "Alan says you're assigned to the Hannah Mayhew task force. Is that right, Roland?"

I nod.

To my left, I see Charlotte tense up. Her unspoken rule about no work at the dinner table is being violated by a longtime offender.

"How are you dealing with it?" Ann asks.

"I've been trying to get a little help from the ME's office."

Alan smiles distantly. "I told you I'd check into it."

"That's not what I mean, though," Ann says. "How are you dealing? I mean, a case like that, and you of all people . . ."

Charlotte's spoon hits her saucer. "What is that supposed to mean?"

"You know—"

"No, I don't know. Why should Roland have to *deal* with anything? He's a professional, Ann. This is what he does. You don't ask Alan how he deals with having to cut people up."

"That's not what I'm saying—" Ann begins.

"It's all right," I say, holding up my hands. "I'm doing fine. I'd rather be back in Homicide, and if some tests come through, I should be back there soon. In the meantime, I'm just keeping my nose clean and trying to avoid the cameras."

"I can't believe all the interest in this thing," Alan says.

"They're trying to get the mother to go on *Larry King*."

A little shiver runs through Charlotte, who folds her arms tightly. "That's awful. The way they make such a spectacle of people's pain."

"But if it helps find the girl," Ann says.

I shake my head. "It won't. That's not what it's about. There's always the chance, I guess, but the real motive is to get in front of the story, so it's not about Channel 13 raking the department over the coals again. But maybe I'm just cynical."

Charlotte pushes away from the table. "I don't want to talk about it anymore."

She slips through the kitchen and keeps going. Ann gives me a guilty look, then goes after her, leaving me and Bridger to stare into our coffee.

"Let's go out back," I suggest.

The balmy night envelops us, the stars hidden behind muddy

clouds that give even the moon a soft-focus halo. I cast a glance toward the detached garage and the side stairs ascending to Tommy's apartment, then lead Bridger off the deck and across the yard. We stand just outside the pillars of light shining through the back windows, where he can smoke his obligatory postprandial cigarette without Ann telling him off.

"I'm thinking about quitting," he says, fitting the cigarette between his lips, firing the tip with a shiny Zippo.

"You should."

"That's easy for you to say." He exhales into the darkness. "You're an all or nothing kind of guy when it comes to vice. No moderation."

"Are you moderating your smoking?" I ask.

"Considering it, anyway."

Unseen in the surrounding bushes, cicadas chirp and mosquitoes buzz, forcing us to occasionally shrug them off. Across the fence, the neighbors are grilling outside, scenting the air with barbeque.

"Are you 'dealing' all right?" he asks.

"I'm better than all right." I tell him about the approach from Joe Thomson, with its promise not only to shed light on the Morales killing but also to shovel some dirt over what will hopefully turn out to be Reg Keller's professional coffin.

"You've got a lot of irons in the fire. Hope you don't get burned."

"Yeah, yeah. If you could come through on that victim identification and Thomson gives up the names of the shooters, then everything will turn around for me."

"Everything?" he asks, jabbing his cigarette toward the house. "You and Charlotte seem a little on edge. Are things okay with you two?"

I sniff the air. "They've been better, I admit. But I'm working on that, too."

He gives me a sideways look. "You mean you're considering it."

"More or less. It's that time of year."

He nods. "You've got something special, Roland. I mean that. After all you've been through together, I'd hate to see it go off the rails."

"It won't."

"You don't sound too sure."

"It won't," I repeat.

He rubs out his cigarette, half-smoked, and we head back inside. At the doorway he gives me a pat on the back, a gesture of solidarity, maybe sympathy. We find Ann sitting on the couch with the television on, volume low. A yearbook photo of James Fontaine is on-screen, cutting quickly to a mid-forties African-American couple standing in the driveway of what turns out to be the Fontaine home. I can see one of the concrete lions at the edge of the frame. The man is talking about how outraged he is by the behavior of the local police.

"Where's Charlotte?" I ask.

Ann clicks the tube off. "She had a headache, so I gave her some aspirin and put her to bed."

Bridger gives me a second pat. I could go the rest of my life without another one.

I see them out on my own, then climb the stairs, finding Charlotte in front of the bathroom mirror in a camisole and socks, brushing her teeth with excessive vigor. Her eyes follow my reflection a moment before drifting away.

Gina Robb comes to the door in a T-shirt and shorts, the cat-eye glasses the only reminder of her eccentric appearance the first time we met. Behind her, blue light flickers across an overstuffed couch and a shadowy hallway leads deeper into the apartment.

"I'm sorry it's so late. With a job like mine, you work odd hours."

She ushers me inside, frets over the best place for me to sit, then decides the vinyl armchair is the only choice. Once I'm settled, she goes to the kitchenette to pour coffee, which I don't have the heart to refuse.

"It's hazelnut," she says, handing me the mug.

They live on the second floor of a gated apartment complex across from Willowbrook Mall. The spot where Hannah Mayhew's car was found is just about visible from their tiny balcony. The furniture has a haphazard hand-me-down quality, and apart from a clock over the breakfast nook, the walls are unadorned. The television is flanked by bookshelves filled with crimped paperbacks and DVDs.

Robb appears at the mouth of the hallway, also in shorts and T-shirt, toweling his hair dry. He pours himself coffee and sits on the big couch, then changes his mind and scoots closer toward me.

"Just taking a quick shower," he says.

Gina flips on a lamp, then feels along the cushions until she finds the TV remote, switching the set off. She sits on the edge of the couch, hands clasped over white knees that seem never to have been touched by sun.

"Is it all right if I stay?" she asks.

I shrug. "Fine with me. You heard we pulled in James Fontaine today? He mentioned an incident we hadn't heard anything about. Did you know he accused Hannah of vandalizing his car back in late February?"

They exchange looks, then Robb gives an awkward nod. "Donna didn't mention that?"

"Nobody did. You want to clue me in?"

He takes a deep breath. "After the drugs were found in Hannah's locker, she told everyone they weren't hers. But she wouldn't point the finger at anyone, either."

"Why not?"

"She'd told Fontaine how Jesus suffered unjustly for the sins of others, so how does she turn around and complain for suffering unjustly herself?"

"She said that?"

"Not in so many words. But I think that's what she thought. Because she wouldn't talk, Donna felt like she had no choice but to ground her. It would have looked strange otherwise, nothing happening when her daughter's suspended for marijuana possession."

I can't help smiling at the irony. If Hannah really kept her mouth shut for Fontaine's sake, she showed him more loyalty than he'd extended to any of his friends in the interview room.

"It looked strange anyway," Gina says. "Punishing her made her look guilty."

He nods. "But I can understand how Donna felt. Hannah did, too. But there was one thing Donna didn't consider, which was that Evey was leaving to go back to New Orleans. Her mom had tried making a go of things here, but ultimately she missed her home. So we'd planned this big goodbye party, which Hannah now couldn't attend. It was a big deal, because like I told you before, Hannah was pretty much the only friend Evey had."

His wife nods. "She was a tough girl to love."

"So what happened?" I ask.

"Evey left the party and drove to Hannah's house, talked her into going out, and somehow the two of them ended up at James Fontaine's."

"They keyed his car up?"

"Well," he says. "There are two versions of the story."

Gina puts her coffee mug on the low table in front of the couch. "I talked to Hannah the next morning, and she wouldn't say what exactly went down. The impression I got, though, was that Evey did all the damage. She was paying the boy back."

"For planting the drugs?"

"Yes, that," she says. "Also for breaking Hannah's heart."

Next to her, Robb shifts nervously.

"It's true," she insists.

"I know," he says, "but—"

"But nothing. Hannah had a crush on that boy." She looks to me for support. "You don't always choose which direction your heart goes. She knew he was bad news, and I don't think she ever would have compromised herself . . ."

"Of course not," he says.

"Even so, as smart as she is, she's just seventeen. I told her, 'You know you can't save his soul just to make him safe to date,' and she said she realized that. But in her heart, I don't think she did. So when he pushed her away—and I mean really pushed—it hurt her. And that's why Evey did what she did, because Hannah was the one person who understood her."

Robb nods the whole time, but I can tell there's something in this he doesn't agree with, not entirely. "What you have to understand about Hannah is, she's friendly with everybody, but only made friends with a few. And when she makes a friend, she holds on tenaciously, whether it's good for her or not. She's very open emotionally, like a child almost. And Evey responded to that, in a protective sort of way."

"You said there were two versions of what happened?"

"Evey left before anyone could get her side," Robb says. "But some of the girls in the youth group told me Evey liked Fontaine, too, and it was her not him who put the drugs in Hannah's locker. According to them, Evey was going to run away with the drug dealer, and to stop her, Hannah busted up his car."

Gina shakes her head. "Those girls are thirteen. They don't know what they're talking about."

"There could be a kernel of truth, though—"

She dismisses the idea with a wave of the hand. "They're in my class," she explains, "so I have a pretty good idea how reliable they are. I guess the point is, rumors were flying, and the only person who could have told us what happened was Evey, who'd already gone."

"Where exactly?" I ask.

"Back to New Orleans," Robb says. "I'm not sure where. They were trying to buy a house, I think, but I don't know whether they did. The insurance payout from the old one wasn't much, but Mrs. Dyer was a nurse, so she might have saved something while they were here."

Gina frowns. "Nurses don't make that much."

"You have a number where I can reach them?"

Robb's cheeks color. "I don't know that we do."

"We haven't heard from them in ages," Gina says.

Robb gives me a pained look, then shrugs. He'd been so proud of Hannah for befriending the girl, prompted by his encouragement, but he hadn't bothered to keep in touch himself. Reading my mind, he nods slowly.

"I feel bad about it," he says. "Hypocritical. But with everything going on, I have to be honest, the Dyers leaving was a bit of a relief. I kept telling myself to follow up, but I never did."

"Would anybody at the church have a contact number?"

"I don't know. I could check around."

"I'd appreciate that. One more thing. Fontaine said Evey—it's Evey Dyer, right?—he said she would kind of explode on people. Is that right?"

Gina nods. "She did it with me once." She takes a sip of coffee, gulps hard. "It was kind of scary to be honest. The girl had a mouth on her, but it was more than that. I don't know if Carter told you, but she's had a tough life. Spent time on the street as a runaway, did things I don't even like to think about. I found her in the women's restroom up at the church one Sunday and she was just bawling. I don't know why, or what had happened, but I went to put an arm around her and she just flipped out. She started pushing me back and screaming and her hair was flying everywhere. And the things she was saying . . ." She shudders. "Finally she pushed me so hard I fell back into one of the toilet stalls."

Robb listens silently, hands over his mouth.

"Then, as quick as it started, it all went away. She helped me up and kept apologizing and she was begging me not to tell anyone." She glances at her husband. "Besides him, I didn't."

"Was she ever like that with Hannah?" I ask.

She shrugs.

"They had a strange bond," Robb says. "Evey told Hannah a lot of things about herself she wouldn't share with anyone else. Most of what we know, really, comes secondhand from Hannah. Like I said, when she and her mom moved back, I was relieved. After Gina told me what had happened in the restroom, I was always afraid of a repeat."

According to the breakfast nook clock, it's edging close to midnight. I've imposed long enough, especially considering how easily this could have been handled by phone. Still, in person there are nuances you miss over the line. And it's not like I was going to get any sleep.

"Last thing," I say. "You don't happen to have a photograph of Evangeline Dyer, do you? Maybe the two of them together?"

They glance at each other, then shrug.

"No problem. I'll check the computer. Sounds like this girl might have a record."

As I descend the stairs outside, Robb comes out of the apartment alone, trailing after me, calling in a hushed voice.

"What's the problem?" I ask.

"What I said the other day? I was serious. I need to do something. There has to be some way I can help."

"You're doing plenty. I don't know what more to tell you."

"I could track the Dyers down for you," he says. "Or that picture you wanted? I could ask around and find one. Maybe I could talk to people again, see if they'd open up to me in a way they wouldn't with the police."

He looks to me for agreement, with a desperate eagerness that's a little appalling, unaware that not only is he asking me for something I don't have the power to grant but he's also conforming to a stereotype well known to law enforcement: the guilty helper. When a civilian suddenly offers up his services, you always take a harder look at him, because more than likely he's involved—or so the thinking goes. I think I know what motivates Robb, though. Not his involvement, but his lack of it, for he's convinced if only he'd invested more of himself before the fact, none of this would have happened.

"I appreciate your feelings, Mr. Robb, but—"

"Anything," he says.

I stroke my chin, buying time, wracking my brain for a non-binding exit strategy. "If you can track down a number for the Dyers in New Orleans, that would be fine. And if you want to talk to the kids in your youth group, see if anything else comes up, go right ahead. But beyond that—"

"Thank you." He grips my hand and gives it a shake. "I'm grateful, really. I'll do whatever I can and get back to you. And if you think of anything else, just let me know."

"I'll do that," I say, slipping away, making a beeline for my parked car before he can offer up additional thanks.

The next morning I roll over to find Charlotte's side of the bed empty. The slight dimple in the mattress is still warm. I throw on some clothes and pad down the stairs. She's in the kitchen, fully dressed, gazing out the window over the sink.

I kiss her warm cheek, then brush the hair from her neck. "You all right? You're up early."

"Just thinking," she says.

I open the refrigerator, pour out the last of the orange juice, splashing half of it into a second cup, which I place in her waiting hand.

"I'd like things to be how they were," she says. "No, that's not right. I want them to be how they should be. In the future, I mean."

"Okay." I'm a little baffled.

"Ann said something last night. When we were doing the dishes. She said we didn't seem happy anymore. Do you think that's true?"

"I don't know," I say. "I don't think so."

"You're lying. I can tell, you know. My husband's a detective."

"Things can be like they were—"

"They'll never be like they were," she says. "I know that. I'm not naive. But I want them to be good again. All right?"

I down the orange juice, lower the glass. "I want that, too."

Upstairs, my mobile phone starts to ring. I should honor the moment by letting it go, but the moment's already as good as it can get. I kiss her on the juice-dampened lips and rush the stairs two at a time. The phone flashes on the nightstand charger.

"Hello?"

"March, it's Wilcox. Good news."

"I have the go-ahead to approach Thomson?"

"So long as he's willing to give us everything, we're prepared to work with him on the rest."

"He wants it in writing."

"Should I fax it over, or do you want to swing by?"

"I'd better come by. The fewer people who know, the better."

When I head back downstairs to tell Charlotte, she's standing in the open back door, arms crossed, glaring up at the apartment over the garage. I come up behind her, resting my cheek against her neck. At the top of the stairs, I catch sight of a girl in a crop top and tight jeans just disappearing into the apartment.

"You've got to take care of that, too," she says.

"I did have a talk with him."

"A talk's not enough." She turns, puts her hands around my waist. "He's got to go. It's past the point of talking. Just get him out."

My hand rests on the small of her back and I inhale the scent of her hair.

"I'll do what I can," I say. "Whatever you want."

CHAPTER 13

Instead of heading straight out to the Northwest, business as usual, waiting for Thomson to get back in touch, I make an unscheduled visit downtown, breezing through Homicide on the pretense of having left some files in my desk. Lorenz gives me the cold shoulder, as expected, but Bascombe proves surprisingly cordial, stopping me outside his office to ask how the task force is going and whether I'm fitting in all right. Now that I'm no longer his problem, I guess the lieutenant wants me to see he's not carrying any grudges. Neither should I, the implication seems to be.

"Any breaks on the Morales case?" I ask.

He gives his head a wary shake, like he suspects a trick question. "There's a cool breeze blowing over that one, I'm afraid."

"I'm sorry to hear that."

We stand there a moment, pondering the way a live case can suddenly flash-freeze, all the leads going cold at once. In this instance, with so many bodies and so much physical evidence, it's hard to believe the line's already gone dead, even for Lorenz. Strangely, I feel no satisfaction. If my test results come back positive and Thomson really can put the shooters in the frame, the fact that Lorenz got nowhere will only make my victory that much sweeter. Still, there are so many contingencies, so much that could go wrong. I can't gloat for fear of jinxing my chance.

"You hear anything about your DNA test?" he asks.

"Not yet."

He rubs his chin thoughtfully. "You still think there's a connection?" He doesn't sound quite as skeptical as when they gave me the boot. Maybe he's realizing he backed the wrong detective.

"It's hard to say." I turn to go. "We should know soon enough."

The files are in my desk drawer. I tuck them under my arm, aware of Bascombe hovering nearby, watching my every move.

"If you do get back a positive match," he calls after me, "I'd appreciate a heads-up."

"Sure thing." I slip down the aisle toward the exit, giving a little over-the-shoulder wave of acknowledgment. When I glance back, he's still watching, and I notice Lorenz's head poking above the cubicle wall.

The sign next to the door reads COMPREHENSIVE RISK ASSESSMENT, not Golden Parachute Brigade, but the matching, nick-free furniture and the glossy new computer screens let me know I have arrived in the right place. The suite is compact, just a bullpen flanked by half a dozen enclosed offices, quiet enough that I can hear the rush of air through the registers overhead. A civilian secretary seated near the entrance behind a low-walled cubicle motions for me to halt.

"Can I help you, sir?"

"I'm here to see Tony Salazar."

She unclips her telephone earpiece and saunters over to one of the offices, tapping lightly on the closed door. After a pause, she opens it and leans inside. My story is simple: since I did Salazar a favor over the weekend, cutting loose one of his confidential informants, he now owes me one. I've come to see whether his ears on the street have heard anything about the Morales shooting. If in the course of this errand I happen to run across Joe Thomson, so be it. The meeting will have occurred by chance, and he'll know without my having to say anything that the arrangements he requested have been made.

After a hushed conversation, the secretary returns to her desk, nodding for me to advance. Salazar meets me at the door, enclosing my offered hand in his thick boxing glove of a fist. He's short but powerfully built, with tight dark curls and a nose that either came out flat or was beaten into that shape long ago. To accommodate his broad shoulders, he's had to buy a white button-down that billows out around the waist, making his legs look disproportionately small.

He pulls me over the threshold, snapping the door shut behind me. My disappointment must show, but he misinterprets the reason.

"The boss is in," he says with a shrug. "You two aren't exactly the best of friends."

It's flattering to know that after all these years, Keller still keeps our rivalry alive on his end, long after it has stopped making sense for him to perceive me as a threat. The closed door means Thomson won't be able to pass by and notice me, but in a small way Salazar's reason for shutting it makes up for that. Once I'm done, I will just have to make a point of lingering.

"So to what do I owe the pleasure?" he asks, hoisting himself up onto the edge of his desk. Like the area outside, the office is nicely furnished, though a bit on the bare side. Apart from a couple of photos on the credenza, the contents are impersonal to the point of being generic. Whatever work the team actually does, it seems to leave little trace.

"I'm here for a favor."

He points to his head, then shrugs. "Well, duh. I guess I now owe you one, don't I? You know that Rios kid never called me."

"I had a feeling he might not. Trouble there?"

"Nothing I can't handle," he says. "What can I do for you?"

"You know Octavio Morales got himself killed? I was wondering whether, with all your gangland connections, you'd heard any rumors about that."

"Lorenz caught that one, I heard."

"Yeah," I say. "I was working it, too, then they pulled me off."

He smiles. "And you want to show him up, is that it?"

"Pretty much."

He drums his fingers on the desk in thought. "I do owe you," he concedes. "The fact is, I haven't heard anything, and now that I'm on this detail, I haven't really kept up with my network, apart from the odd informant like that guy the other day. Obviously, I haven't even kept up with him. But if you want, I guess I could make a couple of calls and see what comes up."

"I'd appreciate it."

"All right then." He smacks his hands together, rubbing the palms, then hops off the desk. "Anything drops, I'll let you know."

He's anxious for me to go, and since I can't think of any excuse that would stall him awhile longer, I oblige. The moment I'm out the door, though, the office next to his opens. Thinking it might be Thomson's, I pause. Salazar puts a hand on my back, urging me along, but I slip his grasp, pretending something's just occurred to me.

"What?" he says under his breath.

I smack my forehead, buying a few seconds.

From the open door, Reg Keller emerges. He takes one step outside, then freezes, drawing in breath like he's just stepped on something. His flame-blue glare zeroes in on my shoes, as if he somehow recognizes them as mine, then slowly works its way upward, taking me in inch by inch.

"Sorry, boss," Salazar says.

Keller makes no reply. He's an inch or so taller than me, menacingly fit, with a shaved head and a tight row of clenched teeth. He wears his stiff navy suit like a uniform, shirt crisp with starch, tie knotted just so, knife-edge creases everywhere you look. As much as I hate the man, there was a time I admired him, and coming face-to-face like this it's hard to keep myself from reflexively cowering. In a dream, now would be the time to throw my punch, but in the flesh I find there's more flight in me than fight.

He plants his hands on his hips, leaning forward aggressively, a vein going rigid in his neck. "You want to tell me what he's doing here?"

Salazar sputters, hands spread.

"Instead of just standing there, maybe you should do something about it."

With surprising power, Salazar takes me by the elbow, pulling me back. I dig in at first, but he shoulders me along.

"Come on, man," he whispers.

The secretary stands, one hand to her chest, shrugging emphatically in Keller's direction, her chin ducked as though worried he might be able to hit her from across the room.

As Salazar bunches me through the door, I glance back at Keller, who still hasn't budged an inch. His cheeks flush with outrage, nostrils flaring, and at that moment it wouldn't surprise me if he charged. A note of protest sounds at the back of my mind. What have I ever done to him? What's he got to complain about? He should be the one they're afraid of. They should pack him out the door.

Then I'm in the hallway and the door swings shut. The last thing I see is the apologetic wince on Salazar's lips.

The whole exercise was pointless. If Thomson was there, I didn't see him and he didn't see me. I shouldn't have wasted my time. All the old feelings come rushing back, the vengeful drives I surrendered back when it seemed there was no hope of ever fulfilling them. My leg rears back of its own accord, and it's all I can do to keep from kicking the shut door.

But I don't. That would only make a bad situation worse. And besides, the visit isn't a total loss. They're going to be talking about it for a while in there. Maybe Thomson, if he wasn't already lurking behind a closed door, will hear about the incident, and realize it's time to get in touch.

Sergeant Nixon settles behind the wheel of his cruiser, giving me a sideways glance. "Don't get the wrong idea, Detective. It's not a taxi service I'm running here. But you used to be one of my boys, so that entitles you to some special treatment."

"Thanks, Nix," I say. "I appreciate this."

The last time I saw him was at the Morales scene, when he sent me on the wild goose chase across the street, interviewing the hot Latina who'd witnessed nothing much. Before that, we've bumped into each other a few times, him always making a point of addressing me by my rank, the way a proud father would. I started out under Nix, driving one of his patrol cars, and while we hadn't formed anything like a special bond, I have a few fond memories of his sarcastic lectures and crass practical jokes.

Seeing him in the car pool, already feeling a bit nostalgic after my run-in with Keller, I decided to hitch a ride. Northwest was far out of his way, but he told me to hop in regardless.

"You remember Reg Keller?" I ask.

He snorts. "He always thought he was something, didn't he?"

"Still does."

"I take it you two haven't made peace yet? That's what I figured. I wish you could have brought him down, Detective. He was ripe for it back then, but I'm afraid you done missed your chance."

I'm tempted to contradict him, but I don't.

Nix is one of the few people who knows the story about my beef with Keller. When Big Reg showed up in Central, he was already larger than life, with a ready-made entourage of corner-cutting patrol officers fawning on his every utterance. I was one of them, or at least I wanted to be. For the longest time, Keller shut me out, treating me like the unimaginative, by-the-book stuffed shirt I was afraid I really was. I'd see the guys he took under his wing, strutting around like they were God's gift to law enforcement, and I wanted nothing more than to be one of them.

Noticing this, Nix took me aside for a heart-to-heart, telling me I was lucky Keller hadn't taken a shine to me. The guys he groomed had one thing in common: a moral flaw. The way Nix put it, they'd rather have the gun than the badge.

"You warned me about him," I say. "All those years ago."

"Did I?" He rubs his mustache, a little pleased with himself. "Did it do any good?"

"Not really."

Everybody knew Keller was moving up the chain, sloughing off the uniform to get a shiny new detective's shield. Rumors circulated, as they always do. He'd be taking some cronies along with him. This was the time to get yourself on Big Reg's radar screen. So one night as we're tooling up for patrol, I go up and tell him he can ride shotgun with me, assuming he wants to. I can't remember the exact words, but it came out like a challenge and that kind of bravado appealed to Big Reg. Before I knew it, we were on the street. I finally had my chance to prove myself.

Nix must be remembering, too, because he sighs against the driver's side window. We're taking I-10 through the middle of town, hooking up to the Loop and then heading up the Northwest Freeway.

"I should have listened," I say.

He just grunts.

Near the end of the shift, desperate to impress, I floored it over to a convenience store robbery in progress called in by an employee hidden in the back room. As we rolled up, Keller press-checked his grandfathered Government Model in the passenger seat, confirming the round in the chamber. I popped the thumb break on my SIG Sauer, leaving it holstered for the moment.

Two men burst through the glass doors. The one up front saw us and stopped short, but the second one ducked around him, breaking off to the right. Keller went after him, shouting. The first guy, meanwhile, leveled his pistol right at me.

The distance was about thirty feet, but I recognized his weapon. I'd worked all through school at my uncle's gun shop off of Richmond, selling handguns and hustling on the indoor range, priding myself on the knowledge thus acquired. He was pointing a nickel-plated Browning BDA at me, or possibly a Beretta Model 84—essentially the same thing, though they tended to be blued. The fact I had time to register this is a testament to how everything slows down under stress. I noticed the gun, then a split-second later noticed the plume of fire coming from the muzzle.

I didn't take evasive action. I didn't move for cover. I just stood there flatfooted and let the bullets whiz by. When he ran, I was still standing there, my hand on my holstered side arm.

It was the first time anyone had ever shot at me. I couldn't quite believe it.

Keller's kid had bolted, but I could still hear him shouting around the side of the building. I started off after mine.

He skimmed his way along a chain-link fence, then ducked down a driveway running parallel to a self-storage unit whose bright lights made him impossible to miss. I had my gun out now, but without closing the distance there wasn't much hope of actually hitting him. So I poured on some speed. By the time he reached the end of the road, where the light suddenly dropped off, he was winded and staggering. I brought my pistol up and started yelling for him to freeze.

Instead, he turned on me.

I thought I saw the gun barrel shining through the shadows. I put two rounds into him, my gun bucking in my hands.

He stood on tiptoes a moment, then sank to one knee. By the time I reached him, he was facedown on the cracked concrete, breathing hard, moaning.

Keller drove up with the second kid in the back of the cruiser. He told me to holster my gun, then rolled my perp over to check on him. I'd have sworn both rounds hit center of mass, but in fact he'd only been hit once, the projectile ripping a superficial channel through the fleshy part of his side, then smashing into his bicep just above the elbow.

"He's gonna be fine," Big Reg said. "But, son, we seem to have a problem."

Namely, there was a wounded perp on the ground, but no nickel-plated automatic. Stand-up guy that he was, Big Reg doubled back along the route we'd just run, searching the uncut grass along the chain-link fence for any sign of a discarded piece. He came back shaking his head, telling me not to worry, though, because he'd back my story. The guy had taken a couple of shots at me, there was no disputing that. Later, it turned out Keller didn't have to back me: the video-surveillance cameras took care of that.

Still, I was grateful.

Six months later, once Big Reg had disappeared into the detective bureau, word trickled down that he'd had to gun down a dealer who came after him off duty. Feeling a bond after the way he'd helped me through my own shooting, I made a point of dropping in as a show of support. Talking to the other narcotics detectives, I learned something significant. The thug who'd stepped up to Keller was brandishing a nickel-plated Browning BDA.

He hadn't missed the discarded weapon. He'd pocketed it for use later on. Which meant his latest shooting was dirty.

"You know," I tell Nix as we emerge onto 290, "if you'd helped me out a little when Keller planted that piece, we wouldn't be having this conversation."

"Right," he says. "Because we wouldn't be with the department anymore. I'm all in favor of settling scores, but not at the expense of the job." He gives his badge a pat, reassuring himself it's still in place.

He's probably right. I could've made trouble for Keller, but not enough for it to matter. People would have closed ranks, because that's what you do when a brother officer is challenged. None of us knows when he'll be forced into the same situation, making a mistake that needs covering.

"I'll tell you one thing," he says. "If you're gonna slip a knife into somebody's back—whether they deserve it or not—you gotta make sure you sneak up on them first. Get my drift?"

Yeah, I do. And showing up in Keller's office, putting myself front and center like that, it probably wasn't the best move. Maybe Nix already heard the news and is letting me know. If he's just spouting random advice, it's pretty good advice.

From now on, I'd better start listening.

For the second time I show up at task force headquarters late, with no explanation, and for the second time Cavallo chooses not to call me on it. She eyes me silently as I approach, then slides a stack of interview forms across the table, picking up where we left off before. I recap my late-night visit to the Robbs', giving her the various accounts of the vandalism incident.

Yawning, she digs through her box of files, pulling a couple of sheets out. I skim them quickly. The thirteen-year-old youth group girls Gina Robb said were in her class gave statements to the police early on, including the accusation that Hannah had bashed up the car of an unnamed boyfriend of Evangeline Dyer.

"How does stuff like this get missed?" I slap the pages down.

She shrugs. "Information overload. Nobody knows it's important at the time. And anyway, is it important? If it's true Hannah keyed his car, then I guess that gives him some kind of motive—but I thought you'd already ruled Fontaine out."

"Maybe. But we should at least follow up on Evey Dyer, get her side of things. If she was such a good friend of Hannah's, no matter how they left things, she might be able to tell us something useful."

"Anything's worth a try." She throws her hands up in frustration.

"What's wrong?"

"Nothing." She brushes her hair back. "Everything."

I remember Bascombe's words about the Morales case. A cool breeze blowing. The same thing's happening here, and Cavallo's not taking it well. The reason professionals don't invest too much of them-selves in a case like this is that it's almost certain to end badly. But of course professionals do it all the time, because they're human like anyone else. Cavallo lets out a sigh, then rubs her eyes until she can't rub anymore. She starts back on the interview forms, making me wonder if she's more human than most.

"So you want me to follow up on the Dyer girl?" I ask.

"Knock yourself out."

After an hour of hunting and pecking on the computer keyboard, I decide to take a shortcut around my technological limitations, placing a long distance call to Detective Eugene Fontenot, a New Orleans homicide detective who helped me out years ago on my most celebrated case, the Fauk stabbing, which was the basis for Brad Templeton's book *The Kingwood Killing*. We had a good laugh about that, Gene and I, when he stayed at my place after Hurricane Katrina blew his house down. Like Evangeline Dyer's mother, he'd toyed with the idea of a new life in Texas before NOPD reeled him back.

"Don't you people have such a thing as databases out there in Texas?" he asks. "I'm lucky you didn't talk me into staying."

"There's nothing like the human touch, Gene. Besides, I heard you'd gotten fat and could use some exercise."

Over the line I hear him patting his belly. "My ex-wife been talkin' again?"

He asks about Charlotte, then gives me an update on his leisure time, which seems mainly to be taken up by fishing. Finally, I get his attention by explaining the link between the favor I'm asking for and the case that's on every television screen.

"This is connected to that girl?" he says, wonder in his voice.

"The one you'd be locating is supposed to be her best friend."

Fontenot hums a tune, thinking things over. "For you, I wouldn't lift a finger. You've never brought me anything but trouble. Still, I've got kids of my own, and if one of them went missing, I'd want anybody who could lift a finger to do it."

"That's noble of you, Gene."

"I'm a noble sort of man."

"Not according to your ex-wife, you're not."

He laughs with me a little, then at me, and then hangs up the phone. Cavallo, who's been making an effort not to pay attention—or at least, not to seem to be—can't help looking up with an inquisitive lift of the eyebrows.

"Gene Fontenot," I explain.

"That name sounds familiar," she says. Reaching under the table, she digs through her shoulder bag for a couple of seconds, then produces a dog-eared copy of *The Kingwood Killing*. "I've been reading up on you, March."

I snatch the book away, flipping absently through the pages. "I wish you wouldn't."

"Not everybody around here has a book written about them."

"It's not about me." I hand it back to her. "Trust me, when you're at your prime, the last thing you want is for someone to capture it like that. You'll always be reminded of what you used to be."

She fingers the book contemplatively, then stashes it away. She has questions to ask, I can tell, but I'm not in the mood to answer them. With Evey Dyer taken care of for the moment, I still have Thomson to worry about. I excuse myself from the table and go in search of a telephone directory.

I wait until the shift ends, then call from behind the wheel of my car. A woman's voice answers.

"Is Joe there?"

"No, I'm sorry. Can I take a message?"

"Is this his wife?"

A pause. "Yes, it is."

So what Wilcox said is true. He really has put his marriage back together. The same woman who divorced him is now waiting at home by the phone. I can't quite fathom how a life so shattered can be put back together like that, but remembering Charlotte's words this morning, the idea gives me hope.

"Do you know where I can reach him?" I ask.

"Ah . . . can I ask who's calling?"

"Just a friend."

She's about to hang up, and for some reason I don't want her to. I have this crazy notion all the sudden that she can tell me something.

"I didn't catch your name," I say.

"Stephanie."

"Hi, Stephanie. Listen. I heard Joe's taken up sculpting?"

She clears her throat. "Yeah . . ."

I can tell from her tone that she's a little perplexed by my call. Nix's words about sneaking up come to mind. Time to end this.

"Never mind," I say. "I was just thinking . . . Anyway, it's great that you two are back together. It's great about the . . . art."

"Thanks."

After I hang up, a strange laugh echoes in the car. It's me, only I can't think what's so funny all the sudden. Maybe it's the desperation of my phone call, trying the guy at home instead of waiting for him to touch base. Now that I've put in an appearance at the office and chatted with his wife, Thomson's bound to come out of the woodwork. When he does, I'll tell him what Wilcox said. Putting the Morales case down is all well and good, but there are bigger fish to fry. If he wants the written assurances I collected from Internal Affairs, he's got to give me nothing less than Reg Keller.

Perhaps the reason I'm laughing is because, for the first time, I'm starting to believe Thomson will actually be able to deliver.

CHAPTER 14

Working cases from behind a desk, while some might consider it an art form, requiring as it does the carefully orchestrated ferrying of witnesses back and forth, the adept use of fax and phone—not to mention a comfortable chair with adjustable lumbar support—has never been my style. Task force headquarters is starting to resemble a teenager's bedroom, paperwork and debris stacking up on every available surface, including a tower of mostly empty pizza boxes from I don't know when. Cavallo and I have staked out a corner, but even here the chairs aren't comfortable and the white noise of nonstop conversation grows increasingly difficult to tune out.

I'm ready to get out on the street, to go anywhere for almost any reason, but my partner seems glued to the interviews. She hunches over her dwindling stack, head propped on hand, her face veiled behind a curtain of hair. She stares at the page, but I'm pretty sure her eyes don't move.

"Cavallo," I say. "Are you even reading those things?"

She flips the page, ignoring me.

"Let's get out of here."

"And go where?"

"How about the school?" I throw it out there, a random sugges-
tion, the first thing that comes to mind. "We could re-interview some
of these people. Instead of just rereading the original notes."

"Something's here," she says. "We just need to keep looking."

"No, what we need is to shake things up."

She leans back in her chair, throwing her arms into a leonine
stretch. "What we need," she says, "is more coffee. It's your turn."

At the far end of what we're jokingly calling the catering table, two
chrome vats of lukewarm coffee beckon, the constantly diminishing
regular and the untouched decaf. While decanting the leaded version
into Cavallo's styrofoam cup, I glance through the open door of Wanda
Mosser's temporary office, a converted conference room. She and Villanueva watch Nancy Grace on a portable television, volume muted,
while a series of angry voices on the other side of the speakerphone
carry on an indecipherable argument.

Noticing me, Wanda slips out for a refill, not mentioning her
departure to the superiors downtown. Behind her, Villanueva mimes
a cup with one hand, pointing with the other for emphasis. I give him
a nod and pull a fresh foam vessel from the nearby stack.

"How's it going, cowboy?" Wanda asks.

"I'm gonna hang myself if I don't get out of here soon. My new
partner thinks they're handing out toy surprises for whoever gets
through the most paperwork."

She laughs. "I told you she was uptight. And those interviews
aren't the only thing she's been reading."

"You mean *The Kingwood Killing*? I already know."

"She was asking me all kinds of questions this morning."

"Spare me," I say. "Though come to think of it, I'd rather she
ask you than me."

I refill her cup, then hand it over along with the one for Villanueva,
who still listens silently to the squawking phone. Before I can make
good my escape, though, she steps closer.

"You know something, Roland? It's nice to see you putting your
heart into the work again."

"Is that what I'm doing?"

"Looks that way to me."

She goes back to her crisis management meeting, leaving me to ponder her words. If this is my heart in the work, I have to admit it doesn't feel much different. Rather than an increase of passion, or a single-minded focus, what I'm left with is more frustration spread thin along a wider front. The Morales killing, Hannah Mayhew, Thomson's pending defection, all of it promising enough, but so far nothing has actually delivered. Charlotte's unexpected announcement yesterday morning, her declared aims for our future relationship, pending apparently on a solution to the tenant crisis—a problem which, after Tommy's assist at the Paragon the other night, I'm reluctant to even address. No, if this is my heart in the work, I'd just as soon keep it out.

Cavallo accepts her coffee in both hands, as if they need warming in spite of the temperature outside, which is threatening to creep into the lower nineties, with a heaping side order of humidity. She sips while giving me an interested look, like her off-duty reading is coming back to her.

"March," she says, "can I ask you something?"

I fumble for a response, but then the ringing in my pocket saves me. With an apologetic shrug, I flip the phone open and press it to my ear.

"Detective March," I say.

"You the one assigned to Octavio Morales?" The words are precise, though heavily accented, a male speaker probably in his twenties, I'm guessing.

"That's right."

"I got some information for you, okay?"

"May I ask who's speaking?"

My tone arouses Cavallo's interest. She puts her cup down and leans forward, eyebrows raised. I motion for a pen.

"You want the information or not?" he asks.

"Go ahead. I'm just getting something to write with."

He gives me an address on Fondren not far from the Sharpstown Plaza shopping center. "I'll be on the side of the road with a red bandanna. You pick me up. And come alone or I'll just walk, okay?"

"When?" I ask.

"Now, dude." Then he abruptly hangs up.

Cavallo asks for the incoming number, then walks it over to one of the support staffers to run a computer search, which comes back with the news that my caller used a public phone at Sharpstown Mall.

"The phones still work there?"

She smirks. "Anyway, this sounds kind of cloak-and-dagger."

"I called in a favor yesterday hoping for some street-level intel, and I guess it paid off."

Frankly, I wasn't expecting Salazar to follow through on his promise, not after the awkward confrontation with his boss. Wilcox hadn't seemed very impressed with him, but it looks like Salazar is a stand-up guy after all.

"Are you really going to meet this informant alone?" Cavallo asks. "Don't you have protocols for this kind of thing in Homicide?"

"I'm not in Homicide," I say.

"Maybe I should tag along."

Eager as she sounds, the last thing I want is Cavallo's company on this errand. The drive to Sharpstown would give her plenty of time to ask whatever questions her reading *The Kingwood Killing* has raised. I hate that book. I'd only agreed to be interviewed as a favor to Brad Templeton, a former *Houston Post* reporter turned true-crime writer, never realizing he'd turn the case into a lurid movie-of-the-week thriller, complete with me in the role of hero, something I've been trying to live down ever since.

"You know, I think those interviews need another going over."

"What, I'm not good enough backup for you?" She frowns. "Should I mention this to Wanda, considering it has absolutely nothing to do with the case?"

"I think it does," I say. "And when those test results come back, you'll think so, too. In the meantime, I have a friend down there who can lend me a hand. Ever heard of Sergeant Ed Nixon?"

As I gather my things and prepare to go, Cavallo stands there, arms crossed, like a disappointed mother watching as her teen gets ready to run away. But to her credit, she doesn't tattle to Wanda or even wag a finger at me as I leave. Pulling out of the parking lot, I check the rearview to be sure she's not following. She isn't. Cavallo knows better. She's probably back at her interviews, hoping that on the next read-through the words on the page will change.

Sharpstown Plaza, just across Bellaire from Sharpstown Mall, boasts a strip of mostly vacated retail spaces and an empty swath of yellow-lined parking reminiscent of the oil bust back in the eighties, which left so much real estate unoccupied. They used to say back then that the difference between a Texas oilman and a pigeon was that one of them could still put a deposit on a Mercedes.

Although the signs are now gone, I can still tell from the color-coded facades which chains used to operate here—pretty much the same ones that operate everywhere else. I pass by on the Southwest Freeway feeder, taking a right on Fondren as directed.

I caught Nix at the end of his shift, after he'd changed into street clothes and squirted on cologne. He was happy enough to check out an unmarked car and tag along, and now he's keeping way back, just in case.

Coasting by the Wendy's on the right, I spot my red bandanna. Five foot seven or eight, in wide black shorts with white stitching and a loose-fitting Rockets jersey, the bandanna cinched tight over his forehead, covering his eyebrows but leaving his scalp exposed. He sees me rolling up and snaps his phone shut, slipping it into a bottomless pants pocket.

He opens the passenger door, slips inside. "Keep driving, homes."

"Yo, ese, you got a name or what?"

He brushes me forward, not looking too impressed by my mastery of the lingo. "Just move, okay? We can't be talking right here."

I let my foot off the brake and coast back onto Fondren. He smells of fast food and stale cigarettes. A hairline goatee rims his mouth, and he has an ominous teardrop tattoo under his eye. I get a strange vibe off the guy, but people who can name names in a murder are a different breed, and strange is the only vibe they give off. At Bellaire he motions for a left, and then another left onto Osage, into a shady residential block full of low-slung ranch houses, their backyards divided by pickets of sun-grayed fencing.

"Park under one of these trees," he says, pointing to a row of oaks overhanging the street.

I slide the gearshift into park, then turn in my seat. "So what do you know about Octavio Morales?"

He answers with the flash of a hand, his half-formed fist snapping against my jaw, knocking me back against the driver's side door. I wince, my teeth rattled. His other hand comes up, and I see a glint of metal. The notched round cylinder of a J-frame revolver. He punches forward with the muzzle at my belly.

I go for his wrist, seizing the bone just in time to push the muzzle wide. The hammer drops and the cabin fills with smoke, like a bomb's gone off. All I can hear is silence, but my eardrums throb.

I jerk his gun hand forward, blading my body to get my right arm between him and the revolver. He buries his hand in my hair, ripping backward.

Another concussion and this time the driver's window shatters. Glass everywhere, and I'm choking on the cordite-filled air.

I trap his gun hand against the steering wheel, setting the horn off. It blares, but I hear the sound as if it's coming from over the horizon. I cock my right arm back, smashing my elbow into his face. His chin snaps back, so I pound him again. And again.

His fist tightens around my hair, pulling hard, but I barely feel the pain. My elbow rams back at him over and over, until I feel his grip on the revolver loosen. He shrinks back, letting the gun drop, then fumbles for the door handle.

I catch a handful of jersey as he goes, but he twists free and starts running down the sidewalk.

Then I'm outside, leaning into the crook of the open door, the front sight of my pistol lining up over his shrinking silhouette. I'm breathing too hard to take the shot.

My hearing fades back in with a distant screech of tires somewhere behind me. I turn, ready to unload on Nix, who should have rolled up with lights flashing at the first shot.

Instead, a massive red Ford pickup speeds down Osage, the tinted passenger window sliding down. I can't make out the driver until he's on top of me, at which point his face is hidden behind a sawn-off double-barrel shotgun.

I drop to the pavement. A hurricane of buckshot blasts through the half-open window, showering me with glass.

The truck screeches off, accelerating toward my would-be assassin, who crouches winded on the sidewalk. Looking down at my pistol, I find the hammer back and smoke rising from the muzzle. On the ground around me, a half-dozen silver shell casings, even though I don't remember pulling the trigger.

When I try to stand, a knife-like burn runs through my left thigh. My pant leg is damp with blood, but I can't find a hole, just black wetness and the smoky char of a contact wound. Up ahead, the truck's passenger door opens and the man climbs in. I raise my pistol one-handed, take a breath, and almost pull the trigger. But I don't, not wanting to miss and send a stray round flying.

As the truck moves away, laying down more rubber, I slump halfway into the driver's seat, dropping the cocked hammer with the thumb release. On the floor beneath the brake, the shiny revolver lies smoking, flecks of blood on the metal.

Sergeant Nixon's unmarked car pulls alongside.

"Did something just go down?" he calls out.

"Yeah," I say, holding my sticky fingers up for inspection. "I just got shot in the leg. But don't worry, the shooter got away."

Nix looks at me like I haven't answered him. Maybe I haven't. All the sudden I have this incredible urge to lie down. I set my pistol on the floor mat and stretch out, staring up at the car's ceiling. Somebody's in the vehicle with me, making this high-pitched animal whimper. I glance between the seats, but there's no one in back. It must be me.

In the back of the ambulance I inspect my new wool cutoffs, the left leg shorn to reveal a crisscross of white bandages. The paramedic, looking pleased with his work, gives my knee a slap. Thanks to the pain medication, I barely feel it.

"You're lucky it caught the meaty part," he says, talking loudly in deference to my temporary hearing loss.

"I feel lucky." I lift my leg to inspect the underside. "Are you saying I have fat thighs?"

He chuckles, climbing out of the ambulance. Down on the pavement, Nix looks haggard under questioning from Captain Hedges, who, in spite of having farmed me out, responded with admirable speed when the news reached downtown. We don't take an officer-related shooting lightly around here, even when it happens to an officer we've thought about shooting a couple of times ourselves. Mosser is out there, too, and so is Cavallo, who keeps sending told-you-so glares in my direction.

Bascombe hops up onto the fender, then slides alongside the stretcher for a look.

"You want to tell me what happened?"

"Come again?"

He repeats himself, dialing up the volume.

"What I really want," I tell him, "is to eat. I'm starving."

"You can eat at the hospital. But seriously, if this guy drew down on you without no warning, then—"

"No hospitals," I say, shaking my head. "Look, you've got his description and his prints will be all over that revolver. I didn't get the license plate of the truck, but I'm thinking you'll be able to recognize it from the bullet holes. When you catch the guy, you can ask him what he was thinking. Me, I don't know."

"We are gonna find him," he says. "That's a promise."

"I know we are."

He looks at the bandages awhile, shaking his head. "And that's everything?"

"Why wouldn't it be?"

"All right," he says, scooting his way back to the ground.

In fact, it's almost everything. I left out only the part about my visit yesterday to Tony Salazar. That is one angle I intend to follow up personally.

Despite my protests, the paramedics insist on transporting me to Herman, where Charlotte turns up in an understandably apoplectic state. Cavallo, perhaps motivated by some instinctive revenge impulse, takes her aside, and instead of glossing over the details, fleshes them out one by one, making sure no aspect of the life-or-death struggle escapes Charlotte's notice. From my bed I can hear them out in the hallway, and every so often one or the other will glance inside, Charlotte's nose and mouth hidden behind her hands, Cavallo shaking her head at me.

The doctors troop in and out, displaying about as much sensitivity as homicide detectives hovering over a headless corpse. One of them, a youngish Indian with a posh English accent, assures me that in spite of the superficial nature of the wound, it'll make for a nasty scar, as if he can already imagine me showing it off years from now, telling the story to my nonexistent grandkids.

"Can I please just go?"

Half a dozen different medical personnel answer in the affirmative over the course of a couple of hours, but there's always another doctor to see, another bout of bedside manner to endure, until I start to feel like an animal in a zoo. Finally, a thick-waisted nurse comes in, her every movement calibrated to communicate how unimpressed she is by my suffering—after all, her frown seems to say, they get plenty of real gunshot wounds here. I'll have to do better next time if I want to be taken seriously.

"You're ready to go," she says, and this time she really means it.

Charlotte, who's been sitting quietly at the foot of the bed most of this time, rises to her feet. As I put weight on my injured leg, she rushes forward.

"Are you all right to walk?"

"Of course," I say, trying not to wince at the jab of pain.

Out in the hallway, Cavallo leans against a wall checking messages on her phone.

"I'm fine," I tell her. "I'll see you tomorrow."

"Your next appointment's waiting." She nods down the corridor toward a couple of guys in nice suits. IAD and the District Attorney's office. Standard procedure after a shooting. "And when they're done with you, you've got a few days off, March. Don't even think of coming back."

Charlotte coils her arm around mine. "He won't."

On the way home, Charlotte swings by Whole Foods, leaving me in the car while she picks up all my favorites, which means nothing but ice cream and white chocolate until the weekend, possibly fried chicken and barbeque, too. She makes me wait in the car with the engine running.

"Keep the doors locked," she says, like she's afraid someone might come along and snatch me.

I sit fiddling with the radio for a while, avoiding anything that promises to develop into a news update. Two meteorologists are arguing on an AM call-in show about the severity of a hurricane building out in the Caribbean, so I let them talk. My hearing seems back to normal, but I snap my fingers a few times just to be sure.

As I'm waiting, a squeaky shopping cart rumbles past. I crane my neck around to watch. Last time I found myself sitting in a car, somebody tried to kill me. It seems like a long time ago, but it was only a few hours. The sun is just now setting on the near-fatal day.

My phone rings. Checking the display, I see it's Bridger.

"You heard, huh?"

"Everything's all right?"

"Don't worry," I say, "I won't need you to do my autopsy for a while yet."

"Actually, I think Dr. Green has first dibs."

"That's comforting."

"Listen," he says. "Are you sitting down? I have the results of that DNA test for you."

My back straightens and I press the phone tight against my ear. "Go ahead."

"Sheryl did the comparison, but I went in and double-checked, just to be certain. We worked up the swab from the mother, got a profile, then made the comparison with the samples taken from the sheets at your crime scene."

"I understand the process, Alan. What did you get back?"

"The results are pretty conclusive . . ."

"You're killing me here, man, and I was already in some pain. Just tell me. Is the girl missing from my scene a match for Hannah Mayhew?"

He lets out a long sigh. "No, Roland. It's not a match. Not even close, I'm afraid."

The driver's door opens and Charlotte leans in, asking me to reach over and pop the hatchback button. She turns, then does a double take, leaning further into the car.

"Roland, what's wrong? What are you doing?"

Her eyes are wide with alarm. I glance down. My free hand is clutched around my bandaged thigh, squeezing hard enough to make the blood seep. I don't feel pain, though.

"Bridger," I say into the phone, "I've gotta go now. Thanks for letting me know."

I close the phone and toss it onto the dashboard while Charlotte leans over my leg, clamping a hand over her mouth.

So that's it. My long shot proved too long. Of course it did. A coincidence like that, how did I ever convince myself it might pan out? I'm a fool. They all knew it. Hedges and Bascombe with their convulsive back-patting, the long-suffering Cavallo indulging my idiotic whim. It would have made for such a neat, simple conclusion, but then there are no simple conclusions or neat ones, either. I want to hit something, even shoot something—only I've done that already today, and it didn't seem to help.

Charlotte loads the groceries, then studies me for signs of collapse.

"You are all right, aren't you, Roland?"

"I'm fine."

If I were the sort of man to learn from his mistakes, I would be fine. I could go home with my beautiful wife and let her prop my leg up and proceed to baby me, passing the next couple of days in a well-earned anesthetized haze. Then I'd go back to the job practically a hero, having fought off single-handed a pair of stone-cold killers, no doubt gang muscle, hardcore enforcers.

Instead, as Charlotte drives quietly toward our neighborhood, as the sun's orange hues deepen and the first fat drops of rain break across the windshield, I steel myself for a nighttime errand. Once she's satisfied that I've been squared away in front of the television, confident enough for a glass of water and a couple of sleeping pills, I'll dress quickly and limp out to the car, keeping a rendezvous with my last hope.

Joe Thomson, if he's going to drop in on me, won't do it at my house. He'll be waiting at the Paragon for me to show. And after today, there's not a chance I'll disappoint him.

The girl tied to the bed and Hannah Mayhew are not one and the same. But Thomson's still dangling the names of the shooters. My path back into Homicide just contracted into the tightest of crawl spaces, but it's still there. And no matter what it takes, I intend to squeeze through.

CHAPTER 15

I wait, alone at a table, quite still in spite of the movement all around. For ten minutes. For sixty. For half as much again, until the ice in my untouched glass is down to a pair of floating lozenges, murkily transparent. I wait as the crowd ebbs and wanes, as the music changes and the lights dim. The second hand on my watch crawls by, but I'm done with checking it.

Either he'll come or he won't.

If he doesn't, then I'll make it my business first thing in the morning to track him down. Regardless of my enforced leave, ignoring all the hoops still left to jump through after a good shooting, I will make Joe Thomson my focus, my case, my mission in life. If he doesn't come to me, then I will go to him.

The bartender's playing one trance anthem after another, the rapid pulse insinuating itself into my leg, which doesn't seem to know the difference between superficial and serious wounds, judging by the throb no quantity of prescription tablets seems to dissolve. No sign tonight of the waitress Marta, sparing me any potential drama. There's only so much I can take in the space of a single day.

All the televisions overhead are showing silent baseball highlights, except for the small flat-screen just over the bar, where the close-captioned news is running. My eye, drawn to the screen, anticipates the familiar images of Hannah Mayhew, her Ford Focus, the seventies Greenwood Forest mock-Tudor she and her mother call home. Or a clip from one of the local interviews Donna Mayhew finally submitted to—not Larry King, not yet, but she's finally doing her duty to the public, to all those strangers out there acting, as Carter Robb said, in loco parentis, at least as far as the grieving is concerned.

But they don't appear. Instead, the usual montage of men in dark suits lit by camera flashes making carefully worded statements to the press, interspersed with the occasional defendant trying to shield his face from the lens as he's hustled up the courthouse steps. Maybe people have grown tired of Hannah, or at least need a break.

I think about her mother, remembering clenched hands over the crinkly, highlighted pages of her Bible. The physical manifestation of her hopes. Then I ponder my own recently dashed hope, the link between her daughter and the girl tied to Octavio Morales's bed. Given the nature of my work, it's not the first time my hopes have run perversely counter to the dictates of human decency. Donna Mayhew wants more than anything to see a living, breathing girl walk through the door—a miracle, more or less, under the circumstances—while I wanted nothing less than to establish Hannah's death, to match her up to the unknown woman who suffered and probably died in our West Bellfort kill house.

She wants her daughter back, and what I wanted was essentially to take Hannah from her. To make her fit into my rubric, the missing puzzle piece. In that sense I'm no better than the rubbernecking voyeurs tuning in for the latest Hannah updates. Probably worse.

"You of all people"—that's what Ann said at the dinner table. The words take on a special potency, imposing themselves like a mantra onto the haze of music, the noise of the people all around. You of all people, she'd said, as if they—the powers that be—ought to know better than to put me, me of all people, in a spot like this.

Me of all people. They should know better. Or maybe I should know better.

The sudden buzzing in my leg, which I first interpret as an alarming new symptom of the gunshot wound, turns out to be my ringing phone. Even next to my ear I can barely hear it, so I tell the caller to hold on, flick a couple of bills on the table, and head outside.

"Thomson?" I ask.

The caller fumbles his words. "Is this Roland March?"

"Yes."

"Oh, good, I thought I got the wrong number there for a second. Hey, Roland, it's just me. I heard about what happened today, man, and I just wanted to check you were all right."

I struggle to place the voice, then it comes to me. Brad Templeton. I haven't heard from him in more than a year, not since he realized my string of special assignments weren't going to yield new book ideas.

"Brad," I say, "it was nothing."

"Getting shot is not nothing."

Standing outside the Paragon weighing the relative seriousness of gunshot wounds is not my idea of a good time.

"You've caught me at an awkward moment," I tell him. "But I appreciate the concern."

"Listen, I was wondering . . . they'll have you riding the desk now, right? Taking a few days off? It's just, I was kind of hoping you and me could have a talk about this thing you've been working on, the Hannah Mayhew case."

"Why, are you planning to write another book?"

"The thought had occurred to me. So when I heard what happened today, then found out you'd been assigned to the task force, it seemed like a natural—"

"The thing is, I've spent the last five years living down *The Kingwood Killing.* Not to mention I haven't exactly solved this thing. As far as Hannah Mayhew is concerned, there may never be a solution, though don't quote me on that."

"I hear you, but look . . . could we at least talk? There is some interest in this thing. I've already spoken to my editor about it, and her ears definitely perked up."

It's hard to say no to Brad, mainly because of the relationship that developed during the book research. He was part of the family for a while, back when there was a gap to be filled, awkward silences that needed exactly his brand of unselfconscious banter to alleviate the strain. Even the things I take issue with in his book resulted from a kind of hero worship that, at the moment I was its focus, was profoundly gratifying. He'd reacted to our time together the way reflexively leftist journalists in the Iraqi desert responded to being embedded with troops, sloughing off whatever preconceived notions he'd had about law enforcement—and as a result "holding his manhood cheap," a quote from Shakespeare he kept repeating until I asked him please not to anymore.

I had no idea what the result of that idolization would look like on the page. The Roland March who dominates *The Kingwood Killing* goes through all the usual routines, but they're described as if he invented them personally, and had mastered every one. Especially the one chapter, which I've never been able to reread, in which the intrepid March, cruising at high speed along the Atchafalaya River Basin, induces the confession of wife-murderer Donald Fauk, using his own tears of grief as a pry bar into the killer's soul. Distorted by his awe, Brad got all the details right, and at the same time utterly wrong.

"Look," he says, probing my long silence for an opening. "I know you had mixed feelings about the book. I can respect that. But let's at least talk, all right? For old times' sake, if nothing else?"

"This isn't the right moment."

"Sure, I understand. I just wanted to see if you were okay. But maybe tomorrow I could give you a call? I could swing by your place, or maybe we could meet up for coffee . . . ?"

Maybe I'm just getting rid of him, or maybe I really will answer his call tomorrow and meet him somewhere. Right now, I really don't know. I just want to get him off the phone. So I say fine, give me a ring, I'll look forward to it, then hang up before he has a chance to form an opinion one way or another on my sincerity.

The biggest issue is Thomson, who hasn't put in an appearance. I don't know where the man lives, and even if I did, I've already done enough on that front. He'll make contact when he's ready, and so long as he doesn't wait too long, I can be patient. At least that's what I'm telling myself. We'll see whether it turns out to be true. In the meantime, a thought occurs to me, a little visit I need to make, paid best at the dead of night.

In addition to the nice boat Wilcox told me about, which must be housed on the water somewhere since I see no signs of it now, Tony Salazar owns a quaint mid-century ranch house in Bellaire, with a close-cropped yard edged in solar-powered night-lights. Behind the picture window, a silver arc lamp illuminates a small swath of interior space, a tulip table and some glowing plastic chairs, everything precisely arranged as if for a photo shoot.

From my position down the street, the more telling details are only visible through my field glasses. Motion-sensitive area lights. Discreet video cameras mounted under the roof on one end of the house and the carport on the other. The fastidious little show house is not exactly a fortress, but Salazar has taken the usual precautions to ensure any guests, though uninvited, can never arrive unexpected.

"Is this really such a good idea?" Cavallo asks.

"You keep saying that. It's almost like you don't trust me."

"Bingo."

She didn't appreciate the one o'clock wake-up call. But after some coaxing she emerged from her apartment complex near Alabama and Kirby, dressed head to toe in black and gray, like she couldn't see a way for the evening to end apart from breaking and entering.

Wilcox, equally unimpressed by the late hour, nevertheless coughed up the necessary information. In addition to the address, he volunteered the fact that Salazar lived alone, had paid cash for extensive remodeling to his pad, and owned a restored Chevy Corvair—presumably the tarp-draped form under the carport—and an extended-cab Ford pickup, of which there is currently no sign. I didn't ask Wilcox why he had these details handy, and he didn't ask why I wanted them.

"So the plan is what?" Cavallo asks. "To knock on his front door and punch him in the nose?"

"No, Detective. I'm guessing from the absence of light inside and the empty stall under the carport that nobody's home."

"People turn off the lights when they go to bed," she says. "You'd know that if you ever gave it a try."

"You're welcome to knock on the door if you want."

The fact is, I don't have a plan. I just want to see where the man lives, and to let him know that I know. I've already played the voice-mail from Salazar to Cavallo. He must have left it while I was still at the hospital, though I didn't think to check until I left the Paragon, already determined to reach out and touch him.

"I heard what happened, man, and I just wanted you to know, whoever this dude was you met with, he was no informant of mine. In case you're thinking I might know him or something. Yeah, I know I said I'd help you out and all, but after you left . . . I don't know, it just kinda slipped my mind. So I never even . . . Well, anyway, I hope you're doing okay, man. You can call me if you need to, but . . . Anyway."

Funny thing is, if he hadn't called, I might have given him the benefit of the doubt. As bad as it looked, as much as it looked like a setup, me getting a call from a would-be informant the day after I request an assist from Salazar, coincidences do happen. But for him to phone in with an alibi first thing, covering himself in case I shot my mouth off, all that does is solidify my suspicion. Wilcox tipped me that the guy was dirty. I should have believed him.

"With guys like this," I can hear myself telling Cavallo, "you can't let things go unanswered. You have to look them in the eye, let them know that you know."

"Is that really smart?"

"Maybe not, but you still have to do it. They have to realize that coming after you is gonna cost them something."

She processes the information, nodding slowly. "So what's this going to cost Salazar? You can't beat him down if he's not at home."

"I'm not so sure I could beat him down if he was. He's built like a welterweight and looks like he can take a few punches. And anyway, when a man tries to have you killed, you don't put up your dukes and slug it out. This problem requires some lateral thinking."

I lift the field glasses again. They're nothing fancy—my budget doesn't stretch to night-vision gear—just a pair of beat-up binoculars I keep in my scene bag just in case. Looking the property over, I run a few scenarios through my head. That picture window is crying out for a rock through the center, but minor vandalism won't make my point. Something major would. He's bound to have a grill out back, some accelerants handy, and I'll bet his house, having been built in the heyday, is chock-full of asbestos. The idea of Salazar coming home to a bonfire. That starts to feel like retributive justice.

"Just so you know," Cavallo says, "I'm not going to sit here and be a party to anything illegal. If that's what you're thinking, you don't know me too well."

"The man did try to have me killed. An eye for an eye, doesn't the Bible say something like that?"

Her smirk, glimpsed in the golden streetlight, mingles frustration and amusement. "Well, if you want me to hold him down while you put a round through his leg, okay. But I draw the line at damage to property."

I consider this. "Maybe he has a cherished pet in there."

"March."

I hand her the binoculars. "Any ideas?"

She studies the scene awhile, then lowers the glasses. Her head cocks slightly. "You know, if Hannah were here, I think I know what she'd do."

"Or her friend," I say, cracking a smile.

The nice thing about being a cop for so long—or, depending on your perspective, the unfortunate, morally dubious, unconscionable thing—is that not only do you get to meet the worst sort of people but some of them end up being, if not friends, at least fond acquaintances. If Salazar can send a couple of gangbangers out with instructions to punch my ticket, I have to know somebody who could even the score up a little.

"I'll bet that car over there means a lot to him," I say.

"Well, I was joking about smashing up the car."

"There's a guy I know . . ."

"March, really. I'm not going to sit here and be a party to anything—"

"Why'd you come if you're not going to help?"

"I am here to help, to help prevent you from doing something stupid. If you really think Salazar tried to put a hit out on you, then a little property damage isn't going to make any difference. You have to report it, that's all you can do. This isn't some macho high school testosterone contest. It's serious."

"So I do nothing? I don't think I can just do nothing."

"Here's what you do," she says, turning in her seat. "Look at me, March. This is the plan. If you want to get him, then wait for those test results, and if they link Hannah to that house—"

I open the door, easing my leg out. "I already have the results."

"And?" She rattles her hands in the air, like she's shaking a tight-lipped kid. "And?"

"And nothing." I step outside, pushing the door shut.

Cavallo jumps out after me, rounding the hood, and we stomp off in the general direction of Salazar's house. Moving down the sidewalk, we set off one motion detector after another, lighting our way in stages.

"Whatever you're thinking of doing, it won't solve anything," she says. "I understand now. This is your anger talking. You wanted there to be a connection and there isn't. But taking it out on a house or a car, that's not the way to cope. You'll make trouble for yourself, and it won't help anyone."

"It'll help me."

"Will it really? March, look at me. Will it really help?"

She grabs my arm and pulls. I could twist free. I could whip my arm away and start running—limping, anyway—but I know she's right about this.

"I want to hurt him," I say. "I want to hurt them all."

She stares at me, breathing hard, moving her hand in a calming but tentative way, as if she's working herself up to touch something that might scald.

"Let's get out of here," she says.

"Not yet."

I walk up the driveway, bending over to catch the bottom of the tarp, pulling it free to reveal a shiny patch of red metal. I hike the crackling fabric all the way to the windshield, then flick the wiper up.

"What are you doing?"

From my wallet I slip out a business card, tucking it under the wiper. Then I slide the tarp back in place, giving the hood a tap. I pause to eyeball the video camera. I don't know whether the feed goes to tape, but if it does, I want there to be no mistake.

After dropping Cavallo off, I head home, pulling up the driveway at a little past three. On the way to the back door, my foot hits something round and glassy, sending it spinning across the concrete. A beer bottle by the sound. I glance up at the garage apartment entrance, but there's no crack of light under the door.

Charlotte's asleep in bed, the covers pooled at her knees as if, feeling warm, she's unconsciously kicked them down. I undress quietly and slip beside her. Overhead, the fan turns, lulling me to sleep.

I dream about Hannah Mayhew. She's younger than her picture, a little girl, walking around our kitchen like she owns the place. Charlotte pours a glass of milk, makes her sit at the breakfast table, ruffling her hair with exaggerated tenderness. I pause in the doorway, frozen by the pretty scene.

"You're here," I say. They both look up at me in surprise. "They told me . . . never mind what they told me."

And she gets up, bouncing toward me, bare feet slapping the tile. "What did they tell you about me, Daddy? What did they say?"

The phone starts ringing. I open my eyes. The nightstand clock says four hours have passed and there's a faint brightness behind the closed window shades. I reach for the sound, miss, then try again. I can't quite find the handset. The next ring prompts Charlotte to vault over me, elbow digging into my side. She grabs the phone and presses it into my hand before remembering my injuries.

"Sorry," she whispers.

I push a bunch of buttons but with no effect, then open my eyes wider to locate the right one. Is this Templeton calling at this hour? If so, I'll wring his neck. On the other end of the line, though, a serious-sounding Captain Hedges starts asking questions about my fitness.

"You looked all right yesterday, all things considered."

"I'm fine, sir."

"The thing is, something's come up. I know I shouldn't be doing this, and you're entitled to a little time after what happened yesterday—not to mention the strings I'd have to pull to get you cleared for work this soon. But under the circumstances, and knowing how the task force assignment wasn't what you wanted . . . I know you're looking for a way back into the squad, so—"

"Yes," I say, sitting up straight. "Whatever it is, yes."

"You haven't even heard what I'd like you to do."

"I don't need to, sir. I want back in."

"It's not exactly what you're looking for," he says. "I know you're tired of these peripheral assignments, but—"

How much clearer can I be? "I'll do it, sir."

He exhales long and hard, either relieved or despondent, I can't tell which. "Before you say yes, I need you to know it's a suicide, March."

"Ah."

"I know you don't like the nickname, and I can't argue with you that the assignment was originally not, well, not very complimentary. But if you're serious about getting back in . . ."

"I am serious. And no I don't like the name, but I realize somebody's got to do it. We owe something to our people, even when they . . ."

My voice trails off. When somebody takes a shot at one of us, like what happened yesterday, it doesn't matter if you like the guy or not, if you think he's a solid officer or a lightweight, crooked or straight. When they come after one of us, they come after us all. We hit back quick, and we hit back hard. Because that kind of thing, it could happen to any of us.

When one of us tops himself, though, when a sworn officer sticks a service piece under his chin and lets off a live round, then suddenly we're all tongue-tied and bashful. It has to be handled, and as with the other, quick and hard is the only way. But woe to the detective who pulls the duty. He'll get no sympathy or slack. Because this kind of thing, we have to believe, it could never happen to us. We could never sink so low as to eat a bullet. Nobody wants to get close to that.

So it falls to one man, typically the lowest, which over the past few years, ever since I fell off the captain's good books, has been me. Roland March, the suicide cop. If you wear a badge in the city of Houston and decide to put a gun to your head, the first face you'd see, assuming you could ever open your eyes again, would be mine.

I ease my legs onto the floor, running my hand over the now-familiar bandage. My holstered pistol sits inside the half-open nightstand drawer.

"Where do you need me?" I ask.

"Good," he says. "Thanks. I really mean it. The body's in a truck parked over on Wayside, close to where it crosses Harrisburg."

"Near Buffalo Bayou?"

"Sort of. There's a bunch of warehouses. Looks like he just pulled over to the side of the road and did it right there. There happens to be a fairly decent golf course not far down the road—I don't know if you play, but . . ."

I'm not sure what to say to that, so I don't say a word.

"I could send a car by for you, if that would be easier."

"No, just give me the address and I'll find it."

I jot down the specifics on the pad next to the phone stand, then go over the obvious details. Patrol has already sealed off the road, redirecting traffic, and the crime scene unit is en route. Even an obvious suicide gets the full treatment. This one sounds pretty straightforward.

Officers on the scene say gunshot wound to the head, he's holding what appears to be his duty weapon, empty bottles kicking around in the foot well.

"All right," I tell him. "I'm on my way. Just one thing."

"What's that?"

"Who is it? Anybody I know?"

It never has been. I've shepherded half a dozen of these things through the process, never anybody I'd worked with or even knew by sight. We're a big department, so there's nothing strange in that.

"You might know this guy," Hedges says. "A narcotics detective, or used to be. Guy by the name of Joseph Thomson—ring any bells?"

"Joe Thomson?"

A pause. "So you did know him. I'm sorry to hear that. Does it change anything?" He listens for an answer, but on my end nothing comes. "March?"

"I'll handle it, sir. This one's mine."

WHILE WE WERE YET

PART 2

SINNERS

CHAPTER 16

The corpse of Octavio Morales, with its mask of beatific agony, had put me in mind of some martyred Spanish saint, but Joe Thomson's puckered wince is more pedestrian, the look of a man who's just smashed his thumb with a hammer, or remembered an errand he'd promised then failed to perform. Rimmed in black, the contact wound over his right ear raised a blood stamp roughly conforming to the muzzle of a SIG Sauer P229, the same as the service pistol he still clutches in his right hand. The cavernous exit, blasting out the top left side of the head, sprayed wet tissue over the interior windows, the projectile embedding itself in the door pillar. We have a neat, self-contained scene, one that tells a straightforward, though tragic story.

"What were you thinking?" I ask under my breath, peering at him, willing the lips to move, but of course that's not going to happen. To my shame, in spite of the spectacle of a man's death—a man I had met and spoken with, a man whose life I knew a little about—my thoughts are entirely focused on the loss Thomson's death represents to me. No shooters named in the Morales case, no damning testimony against Reg Keller or Tony Salazar. The fact that my captain sees this as an avenue toward redemption doesn't comfort me much, since I'd been planning to return in triumph, thoroughly vindicated, and not as a kneeling supplicant.

The smell of burnt gunpowder is still strong, in spite of the open driver's side door and the post-rain mist. My nostrils twitch, and the sound of the revolver going off in my lap fills my head. A sympathetic ache in my thigh reminds me, that could be you. I step back, glancing at the droplets clinging like dew to the exterior of Thomson's vehicle, a several-year-old blue GMC Yukon.

"Good to see you again, sir."

At my elbow, an eager kid in the garb of a crime-scene investigator smiles at me, giving no sign of being affected by the scene. I nod.

"Remember me?" he says. "Edgar Castro. We talked about that other case . . . ?"

"Right. Castro. I remember. Let's get to work here, okay?"

Overhead, a muddy gray sky threatens a repeat of the shower I drove over in. In spite of the sticky air, the first responder, a squared-away young patrolman named Nguyen, still wears a dripping poncho over his uniform. After Castro's eagerness, I appreciate the businesslike demeanor of Nguyen. I take him to one side and let him rattle off his satisfyingly precise report. He responded to a call from dispatch at 6:04 a.m., arriving at the scene seven minutes later, where he secured the victim's vehicle and did a preliminary interview of the security guard who called in the shooting.

"His name is Wendell Cropper," he says, nodding toward a uniformed security guard having a smoke just outside the perimeter tape. "First thing out of his mouth is, he used to be on HPD back in the mid-nineties, which is funny because he should have known better than to disturb the scene."

"What did he do?"

Nguyen makes a pistol out of his fingers. "He opened the door and uncocked the pistol, then pushed the victim's finger out of the trigger guard. Said he was afraid it might go off again. Then he shut the door and called us."

"The car door was unlocked?"

Nguyen nods.

"Okay, I want to have a talk with Mr. Cropper."

The security guard flicks his cigarette away at my approach. I lift the tape, letting him duck underneath. He's about my age, mid-forties, with a lean, smooth face and thick black eyebrows knitted together in the middle. Pale skin, but a charcoal shadow of beard in need of shaving. His uniform consists of fatigue pants and a short-sleeved shirt with epaulets and his name embroidered over the pocket.

"What exactly is it that you secure?" I ask.

He points with two fingers, like he's still holding the cigarette between them, sweeping a row of gray corrugated buildings behind the tall hurricane fence.

"I got these warehouses here, and then some others a street over, which is where my security office is. About four in the morning, while I was doing a foot patrol, I heard what sounded like a gunshot off in the distance. I couldn't tell where it come from, so I just noted the time—4:14 a.m.—and went on with my route."

"You didn't call it in?"

"I wasn't a hundred percent sure," he says. "Plus, I know you boys got better ways to occupy your time than hunting down random gunshots in the night." He alternates between crossing his arms and resting his hands on his hips, unable to find a comfortable posture. "In hindsight, I guess that's what I should've done, but the rain started up and, honestly, I started second-guessing myself."

An hour later, though, he'd hopped behind the wheel of his truck and done another circuit, finding Thomson's Yukon.

"From the exhaust I could tell the engine was running, so I got out and walked up alongside. Soon as I flashed my light on the window, I knew something was wrong." He gives an exaggerated gulp. "All that blood and brain on the glass."

He's apologetic about interfering, but says he'd heard a story before he left the police department of somebody taking a bullet at a crime scene because a cocked pistol hadn't been rendered safe. He reached in without thinking and uncocked Thomson's gun.

"Why'd you leave HPD, Mr. Cropper?"

The question prompts some thinking on his part, but after I remind him how easily these things can be checked, he admits the department cut him loose.

"I had a whole series of problems," he says with a bashful smile completely at odds with his rough appearance. "The main thing was, I didn't like all the reports, so I'd kinda forget to do them, you know? This work here, it's much more suited to my temperament." He pronounces the word as *temper mint*. "I don't mind the hours or the solitude."

When police officers daydream about bagging the job for some high-paying private sector security gig, this isn't what they typically have in mind. Consulting on matters of security is where the money is. Actually securing things? Not so lucrative. Cropper's a type I've encountered before, desperate to be part of the real action in spite of his reluctance to admit disappointment with the turn his career's taken. In that light, his behavior makes sense. He didn't think we'd be irritated at his tampering with the suicide weapon so much as grateful that he'd prevented the dead man's punching an officer's ticket from the grave.

As I'm conducting the preliminary interviews, detectives start trickling onto the scene. Mack Ordway rambles up with grim-faced determination, followed by Hedges and Bascombe, who apparently shared a car. Aguilar arrives with a few others, and a while later, bringing up the rear, Lorenz reports in. He walks toward Bascombe, but when he gets close, the lieutenant moves my way.

"You up to this, March?" he asks.

"A suicide? I think so. Don't forget, I've had a lot of experience."

He nods. "Then maybe it's time to get the canvass going. Put some of these detectives to work."

Across the street from the warehouses, a scrawny hedge of pines screens a residential neighborhood lit by amber streetlights, the mist forming haloes around their bulbs. I gather up the detectives, give them a rundown on the situation, and make the canvass assignments. As I speak, eyes cut frequently to Bascombe as if saying, Is this for real? We're taking orders from this guy? The lieutenant ignores them. Before we break up, Hedges offers a few words.

"I don't have to tell you men, but this was one of our own. Let's get the job done, all right? Quick and thorough."

The sky rumbles and we all gaze upward, as if it might have something to say. It doesn't, so the team breaks up, heading into the gray morning on a perfunctory hunt.

Edgar Castro comes up to me, a plastic evidence bag dangling from his hand. Inside, a mobile phone buzzes silently, the screen illuminated. The name on the display reads STEF. Bascombe reaches for the bag, quizzing me with a raised brow.

"The wife," I say.

He draws his hand back. "Ah. We better get the notification taken care of."

"You want to come along?"

From the way he recoiled from the ringing phone, I already know the answer. But Bascombe surprises me by saying yes. He notifies the captain, then motions to my car. "You drive."

Stephanie Thomson comes to the door with dried mascara on her cheeks, wearing an oversized men's button-up shirt and a pair of loose-fitting cotton shorts. She's younger than I expected, more Cavallo's generation than mine and Thomson's, pretty but with the lined, hollow-cheeked look that comes from hard drinking. Her nose and the rim of her eyes shine pink. In her tight-packed fist, a puff of damp Kleenex juts from between the knuckles. Bascombe shows his badge and makes the introductions, setting off more tears.

"It's all right," I say, putting an arm over her shoulders, guiding her to a brown recliner in the apartment's open living room. Of course it's not all right. It's terrible and will only get worse. But

I speak the words out of reflex, prompted by emotional muscle memory. When people cry, you tell them not to. The first impulse is to take the pain away, because if you don't, how can you give any comfort?

Bascombe crouches wide-legged at the edge of the sofa, leaning toward her with his hands intensely clasped. He looks like he's about to break the news, but no words come out of his mouth. I kneel beside the recliner, taking her hand.

"I have something to tell you, Stephanie—"

"Is it Joe?" she asks, nodding her head over and over. "It's Joe, isn't it? I've been trying to call him all night, and he never answers. I knew something was wrong, I just knew. Is he . . . ?"

"He's dead," I say. No use in dragging it out. "His body was discovered earlier this morning. He was sitting behind the wheel of his vehicle, pulled over on the side of the road. He had his pistol in his hand, and a gunshot wound to the head."

Her tear ducts open up, expelling a river of glistening salt, an impossible current pulsing out in silence. Shaking from the shoulders down through to the knees, an involuntary tremor, reminding me of a marble column under earthquake pressure, the dusty cracking that presages impending collapse.

"He shot himself," she says, nodding violently, so certain. "He did that to himself."

"We're still conducting our investigation, but—"

"How could he . . . ?" Her mouth widens, like she's trying to swallow something too large. "He did that to himself?"

Suddenly she's slamming her fists against the armrests, kicking her legs, screaming in unintelligible, angry spasms. Bascombe springs forward, pinning her arms like he thinks she's having a seizure. I stand back and let him do it. After a few moments she goes limp in his arms and starts crying again. I go into the kitchen and look for a glass, pouring water I found in the refrigerator door. When I return, putting the glass on the table beside her, she's clotting her tears with a fistful of tissue. Bascombe is back on the couch, looking ready to pounce at a moment's notice.

"I know this is hard, but I do need to ask some questions. And we'd like to take a look around, too, if that's all right. It's standard in a case like this."

"Did he leave a note?" she asks, her voice weak.

"Not that we know of. I was thinking he might have left you a voicemail message?"

She shakes her head. "I've been checking my cell and the home number, thinking maybe . . . but there's nothing."

I hand her the water glass, which she examines with a bleak stare. Instead of hammering her with questions right away, I ask permission to take a look around. She consents with a flick of the hand. The lieutenant sticks to the couch, motioning me to go ahead. As I walk down the hallway toward the bedroom, I can hear him speaking softly to her.

The apartment is small but quite nice, recent construction with a hardwood entry, slate-colored tile on the kitchen floor, granite counters and stainless sinks, completely at odds with the couple's furniture, which I'm guessing is a mix of family hand-me-downs and big-box economy buys selected with an eye to comfort, not looks. The kind of place Charlotte would turn her nose up at, but exactly what I'd expect, given what I know about the Thomsons' history. I'm guessing this is where Stephanie landed after the divorce, and Joe moved some of his things in when they remarried.

At the back of the hallway there's a bedroom and bath on one side and a small home office on the other. I step into the office, noting a dusty-screened computer and a stack of printouts which turn out to be real estate listings annotated in loopy, feminine handwriting. In the corner, a half-open closet door beckons. Behind a series of Men's Wearhouse suits, mostly black and blue solids, I find several rifle cases. Inside one, a padded plastic case, I find a bolt-action hunting rifle with a scope. The next contains a flat-top AR-15 carbine with a telescoping stock and a nice ACOG sight on the rail. The third case is a short nylon number with narrow pouches on the side for extra magazines. About the right size for a SWAT-style 9mm submachine gun, but I can tell from its slack droop that the case is empty. I unzip it anyway just to be sure.

Across the hall, I note the rumpled bedcovers, the framed wedding and honeymoon photos on the dresser—dating back maybe five years at most, making the original marriage more recent than I'd supposed— and a tangle of dirty clothes on the floor. On Thomson's nightstand, there's a stack of paperback books, including a new-looking copy of *The Kingwood Killing* with a bookmark halfway through. Inside the cover, a receipt from Murder by the Book, a local independent on Bissonnet specializing in all books crime-related, dated last Saturday, the day after I joined the Morales investigation. So Thomson was doing his homework. Inside the nightstand drawer, a loaded .357 Magnum snub nose, one of those weightless titanium numbers that's easy to carry and excruciating to shoot, fitted with a Crimson Trace laser grip.

As I close the drawer, Bascombe leans into the bedroom, waving his phone. "Can you sit with her, March? I've got to take this outside."

He exits the apartment, leaving me alone with Stephanie Thomson. She slumps sideways in the recliner, exhausted, quiet apart from the occasional sniffle. I know from experience she's not done crying. It'll come in waves, interrupted by surprising, clearheaded stillness, a constant ebb and flow between mind and heart.

"Has Joe been depressed recently?" I ask.

"Not the past couple of days. But before that, yeah. For the past week, it was like living with the old Joe. The bad one. We only got back together a few months ago, and he seemed like a changed man—the one I married, instead of the one I divorced."

"He'd taken up art, I hear."

She gives me a long look. "He'd taken up something, anyway."

"What do you mean?"

She shakes her head. "It doesn't matter now."

"Please," I say. "The more information I have about his state of mind, the better."

She wipes her eyes, gives her nose a hard rub, sitting up straight in the recliner. "Then here's the story, for better or worse. Just recently something changed, and the old Joe was back. He said he wasn't drinking, but I knew better. He has this duffel bag he carries his gear in, and I looked inside and found something."

"What was that?"

"A soft white cellophane-wrapped package. I don't know what it was, but it looked like drugs to me. Cocaine, whatever. I don't have any firsthand experience of that stuff. But I figured he was using again."

"Did you confront him?"

"Not about that."

"But you did confront him about something?"

She nods, then coughs back a fresh flow of tears. "You mentioned the art. Well, it was a therapist who put him up to that, before we got back together, and he really took it seriously. Rented a studio at this place over in Montrose, and he'd spend hours over there, sometimes all night, working on his sculpture." Her mouth wrinkles at the corner. "I know nothing about art of course, but it wasn't anything I'd call artistic, just globs of clay and all these faces that looked like they could've been made by a kid. I mean, the man can't draw a picture to save his life, so I don't know what kind of artist he could really be." She pauses, thinking over the words. "But it made him happy, so . . ."

"You were saying you'd confronted him?"

Again with the nods. "Like I said, he reverted back to his old self, and the way he was when I left him, and that first time the problem wasn't just the substance abuse. It was the other women. Don't get me wrong, when I married him I already knew he was a bit of a stray dog, you know? But that was then. I expected him to put that stuff behind him, and when he didn't, that was it for me. I couldn't trust him. So my first thought when all this happened was, he's seeing somebody. And there's this cute little thing down at the studio, the girl who rented the space across from his."

"You thought they were having an affair?"

"An affair?" She smiles at the quaint term. "You could say that, I guess. But when I brought it up, he denied everything. He said it was just trouble at work. And I . . . it sounds crazy, but I wanted to believe him. I wanted more than anything to be wrong because what we had, I didn't want to lose it again. You can't possibly understand how special he was to me, all the plans we had, the way we could be together."

She doesn't cry or convulse with grief. She's talking about him now like he's ancient history, like the news of his death came to her years before.

"You said the past couple of days, things were back to normal?"

"Yeah," she says, wrapping her arms around herself. She looks down, noticing the shirt she's wearing, pulling the fabric up for inspection. She sniffs the sleeve, then lets out a small but terrible sigh, smelling his scent and realizing how soon it will fade.

The conventional wisdom is, when a suicide makes his final decision, a sense of peace follows. He loses interest in the everyday world, and as a result becomes capable of beautiful gestures. Taciturn men suddenly confess to acquaintances how much their casual encounters have really meant over the years. Treasured objects are given away as the suicide divests himself of things which now mean nothing.

Stephanie Thomson's description of her husband's rebound doesn't quite fit the pattern. After a dry spell, they'd been "intimate" again—her word—and he'd apologized for being distant. Things would be better from now on, he said. They were even looking for a house.

"But I knew it couldn't last."

"Why not?" I ask.

"I got a phone call," she says. "A really strange one, out of the blue. Some guy acting all friendly, asking questions about Joe, saying he wanted to get in touch with him. It was trouble, I could feel it. There was something creepy about him."

"Did he give you a name?"

She shrugs. "If he did, I don't remember. I got scared, though, thinking maybe it was connected to the drugs in his bag or something."

The truth dawns on me. "This call, did you tell Joe about it?"

"No," she says. "I called Tony and he said he would take care of everything. He told me not to worry."

"Tony?" My pulse races. "You mean Antonio Salazar?"

She nods calmly, the most natural thing in the world. "They work together on the same squad. They've been friends for years. Tony's always looked after Joe. Even in the bad days, he tried to get me to stick it out for Joe's sake, that's the kind of friend he is. This . . . this is going to just devastate him."

I sit back on the couch, suddenly weary. So the day after I visit Salazar's office, hoping to touch base with Thomson, Stephanie calls Salazar, telling him about my conversation with her. The next day, some random Latino banger dangling information on my case tries to punch holes in me. And early the next morning, Joe Thomson is dead, apparently by his own hand.

She sits there glumly in her chair, shaking her head at the pain her husband's death will cause Tony Salazar, and I want to grab her by the shoulders and shake her. I want to slap the frown off her face. You did this. It was you. He's dead because of you. But I might as well slap myself. It's not Stephanie Thomson's fault. What she did made perfect sense, just trying to protect her man against himself. I'm the idiot. Yet again. If I'd just been patient, everything would have turned out right. If I'd let Thomson come to me, given him time to be discreet. Instead, desperate to make something happen, I'd blundered into the lair of Keller and Salazar, fatally tipping my hand.

I hadn't just missed my last chance. I'd gotten him killed.

Stephanie hands over the keys to Thomson's studio, along with the address and a hand-drawn map, just as her sister arrives, prompting a new outpouring of grief. I find Bascombe outside on the landing, sheltering from a percussive bout of rain.

"Give me sunshine any day," he says.

In the car, I can tell he's got something on his mind, but asking what would be the equivalent of sticking my finger in a trap. No thanks. I'd like to go straight over to the studio—given how clean the apartment was, I can't help thinking the studio is where Thomson kept his personal files, and maybe that duffel bag his wife mentioned—only the first order of business is unloading the lieutenant. I don't want him over my shoulder for every step of the investigation.

At this point, Thomson's suicide looks perfectly straightforward. If I suggest otherwise to Bascombe or anyone else before I can actually prove it, the only thing I can be sure of is my removal from the case. Once I'm alone, the first order of business will be a call to Wilcox. The longer I can keep him quiet, the more likely it'll be to make headway.

"So what did she have to say?" Bascombe asks.

I give him a rundown, omitting my call and the note now residing in my pocket. I also downplay the studio, omitting reference to the keys now in my possession.

"He had cocaine in his bag?"

"It might have been coke. She couldn't be sure."

"How much?"

"One package, she said."

The news makes him restless. He shifts in the seat, fiddles with the air-conditioning vents, raps his knuckles in rhythm against the window. Whatever information he's holding, it's clearly dying to get out.

"What?" I ask, knowing I'll regret it.

He jumps on the question. "That call I just took? That was from a friend of mine over in IAD. You know what he told me?"

My heart takes a break, leaving the blood to settle in my veins. Yes, I know what he told you. He said I'd been wrangling for a deal, using my ex-partner as a go-between, trying to get a blanket immunity to open Thomson's lips. He said whatever was going on here, I'm hip-deep in it and the first thing for the lieutenant to do is pull me off the case.

But Bascombe volunteers nothing. He wants me to earn it.

"What did he tell you, sir?"

"That our victim has been the subject of a number of internal investigations, including an incident a couple of years ago when some evidence went missing from a drug bust. He was dirty, in other words. And when I told the captain, he called up Thomson's boss, Big Reg Keller, and you know what he said?"

"Tell me."

"He said the other officers in the unit had been concerned about Thomson. He was a loose cannon apparently, and was suspected of having a substance problem."

Sure he was. Keller is wasting no time insulating himself, doing the necessary damage control, just as Salazar had done when he called me after my own shooting, making sure I couldn't connect the dots between my request for help and the subsequent attack.

"Does that sit right with you?" Bascombe asks.

"Sit right? In what sense?"

"In the sense that when a brother officer eats his gun, you don't trash his memory."

"The blue wall of silence, you mean?"

"Common decency. What good does it do anybody for them to say he had a drug problem, or was a dirty cop or whatever? Whether it's true or not, the man's dead. He shot himself, right? So if he deserves anything, it's pity. Instead, his own people are throwing him under the bus, when they ought to be sticking up for him."

This isn't what I expected from Bascombe, not by a long shot. The problem is, when you've singled someone out as a nemesis, it's hard to get an accurate read on character. The lieutenant, since I know he's never much cared for me, has always lacked psychological depth. He's a one-note, a foot soldier in the anti-March crusade, without any nuance necessary. Suddenly I find myself agreeing with his instinct, if not his reasoning. Like Wilcox, whose move to Internal Affairs simply externalized a cherished principle, I think the dirty cops should go down. But then I know firsthand what it's like to suffer for their benefit. If a cop snorts white lady from the evidence locker, plants a drop piece on an unarmed suspect, or takes money on the side for looking the other way, I don't think a self-inflicted bullet to the brain should whitewash the record.

Call me naive, but I still subscribe to the "few bad apples" theory. We might be cut from the same cloth as the people we lock up, we might have a tendency to jackknife our relationships or channel the violent impulses that go hand in hand with what we witness into unprofitable avenues, but for the most part, we're clean. Not squeaky clean, because no one is, but relatively unspotted. Because we didn't get into this for the cheap thrill of packing a gun, or to work out our inferiority complexes, or because we couldn't find a better line of work. Carter Robb has it right, in a way. We could have kept things safe, chosen decent occupations that make for polite dinner conversation, better pay and better hours and a far reduced probability of being shot or beat down. But we didn't choose to be the safe guys. We chose to be the good guys, hard as that is when the world is bad.

And maybe Thomson was bad; maybe he was the sort like Wilcox said who should have been screened out by the personality tests. Even so, the man had changed. He'd changed enough to get his wife back. Enough to turn on his former friends. He'd changed enough that they had to put a bullet in him, which in my book made him one of us, not them.

The dates aren't lost on me, either. The change in Thomson, his dark relapse, dates back a week or so, roughly the same time as the Octavio Morales death. That's what shook Thomson up. That's what made him seek me out. Something happened in that house. Either he was there or he found out about it secondhand. Whatever it was, he couldn't live with it. Thinking of that girl tied to the bed, her blood on the sheets, her body now missing, I can imagine what was eating away at him, because it's eating away at me, too.

Does Bascombe see any of this? Is he giving me some kind of unspoken license? That's what I can't figure out.

"What are you saying?" I ask him. "That I should take a harder look at his unit?"

He shakes his head, waves a dismissive hand, his eyes scrunching up at the excess of my misreading. "No, man, that's not what I'm saying.

But if you ask me, when you talk to his colleagues—as you no doubt will under the circumstances—nobody on my squad is gonna be upset if you omit the common courtesies, if you know what I mean."

"Yessir," I say, almost liking the guy. "I think I do."

CHAPTER 17

Bridger waits for me back at the scene, standing aloof from the circle of detectives who've gathered post-canvass to compare notes. In my absence, he's gotten Thomson's body bagged and on the stretcher, ready for transport. As I slip under the perimeter tape, all eyes turn. I can see from the glum expression on Ordway's face and the way Aguilar keeps checking his watch that the canvass hasn't gone well, so I skip it for now and head straight to the pathologist.

"I'll have the details once the autopsy's done," Bridger says, "but my preliminary conclusion, big surprise, is that he died from a gunshot wound to the head."

"Self-inflicted?"

A cautious nod. "Seems consistent. Clearly a contact wound. Your forensics people can connect the dots once they check the bullet recovered in the door pillar against the ballistics of his side arm. What I see here is consistent with the time the security guard claims to have heard the shot, but if that changes, I'll let you know."

"We'll need a really thorough tox screen. Alcohol, drugs. Cocaine has been mentioned as a possibility, so I'd like to check for that."

He gives me a perfunctory nod, not needing to be told how to do the job. I tell him anyway, just to be thorough. Then, after getting him to commit to a quick autopsy, I let him get on with it, turning my attention to the impatient detectives.

"Nobody saw anything," Ordway says with a shrug.

Lorenz adjusts the sunglasses on the bridge of his nose. "They didn't hear nothing, either. No gunshot, no nothing. So no help fixing the time."

I glance through the tree line at the gray fences and low black roofs. Given the distance and the early morning storm, it's not surprising we don't have any witnesses from the neighborhood. Still, it was worth a shot.

"Here's what I'm wondering," Ordway says, picking up on the conversation I'd interrupted with my arrival. "Why'd he choose this exact spot to punch out? Say you were gearing up for your final sayonara—is this where you'd do it?"

Aguilar rubs his nose. "I'd do it in the bathtub."

"The bathtub?" Lorenz says, looking over his sunglasses. "Seriously? Then don't expect us to respond to that scene—"

"What?"

"—unless you promise to keep your clothes on."

Ordway chuckles. "Me? I've actually given this some thought, boys. At my age, you do. When my time comes, I'm taking the elevator to the top of the Transco Tower—"

"It's not called that anymore," Lorenz says.

"The Transco Tower," Ordway insists. "And when I get there, I'm gonna leap off into the air and see if I can land right in the middle of the Water Wall, right there on the steps where they take all the wedding pictures. Splat." He smacks his hands together and gives us a demented grin. "People would be talking about that forever."

Aguilar scrunches his nose up in thought. "From the Tower to the Water Wall? I don't think you could make it that far, not as fat as you are."

"But if I did," Ordway says, "people would talk about it."

I put a hand on his shoulder. "As interesting as this is, guys, there's only one death we need to worry about here—"

"No, but think of it," Ordway says. "Why did he do it here? There's gotta be a reason. It could be anything, I guess. Maybe he grew up in one of those houses over there, or maybe he was on his way somewhere important and decided to pull over and get it done with."

Lorenz gives a dismissive snort. "Or it has nothing to do with the place. He's drinking, he's depressed, whatever, and so he's just driving around aimlessly. What matters isn't where he's going on the road; it's where he's going in his head. And when he gets there"—he points a finger at his temple, cocks his thumb back—"*pop*. End of story."

I leave them to theorize in peace.

The captain has long since departed the scene, so I offer Bascombe, who's conferring with the crime-scene technicians, a ride back downtown. He declines, saying he'll tag along with one of the guys and leave me to it. I'm relieved. I need some time alone to think through my plan of attack. Since they were close colleagues, I'll have to talk with both Keller and Salazar, but before I do that, I want some kind of leverage. Otherwise they're going to give me the same story they previewed for the captain.

There are only two places I think of to get what I need. Bridger's autopsy findings, which at the most optimistic estimate won't be available until late in the day, and Thomson's art studio. If he had anything worth hiding, maybe that's where he'd have left it. The keys rattle in my pocket, begging to be used.

And then Brad Templeton calls. I'd forgotten all about my commitment to him, and my first impulse is to dodge. But the man's a bloodhound in his own right, and it's just possible I can put him to work. Like I said, I don't think everything should be left to the police. Sometimes a private citizen needs to step up.

"What do you know about an HPD officer named Reginald Keller? He runs some kind of Homeland Security–related squad downtown."

"Never heard of him," Templeton says. "Should I have?"

"I want you to do me a favor, Brad. Take a look at this guy and see what you find. My contact in Internal Affairs leads me to believe he's the subject of ongoing investigations, which means there's a story there for you."

"Not the one I'm after, though."

"Think of it as something extra. My captain's put me back to work, so there's nothing I can do for you at the moment on the other thing—"

"You're off the task force?"

"I'm keeping a hand in," I say, not wanting him to wriggle off the hook. "Do this for me and you'll not only get the IAD story but I'll give you what you need on Hannah Mayhew, too. It's a twofer. You can't beat that."

The wheels are turning on Templeton's end of the line and I know better than to keep talking. After some audible groans and sighs, he finally relents. I repeat Keller's name and give him Salazar, too, along with everything I know about Comprehensive Risk Assessment. By the time he's finished writing, there's an energetic note in his voice.

"You're gonna follow up on this, right?" I ask.

I hear his pen rat-tat-tatting against the receiver. "You take care of me, man, and I'll take care of you."

"Deal."

On the way over, I try Cavallo's phone, hoping to make my apologies for ditching the task force. Not that I'd had a choice, not really, but I didn't want her thinking I was ungrateful, especially for the good advice last night.

It's not Cavallo I'm abandoning, though. It's Hannah.

Detectives are reassigned all the time. I took a shot at the Mayhew case and struck out. I did what I could for the girl, and now it's up to Cavallo. That's the logic, anyway. Only this isn't about logic. I'm turning my back on the girl. Moving on. Like it never mattered in the first place. Like it was just another job. The phone rings, Cavallo doesn't answer, and in my mind the luminescent face of Hannah Mayhew starts to dim.

I leave a message and hang up.

The address is on Morgan Street, a couple of blocks north of Westheimer between Montrose and Bagby, a tight-packed warren of blocks where newly built modernist houses and condos sit cheek by jowl with run-down duplexes and wood-paneled apartment blocks. The sidewalks disappear and reappear, some patches of road pristine and others as fissured as a polar ice cap of concrete. Hipsters and homeless mingle on the block, shiny Volvos and Mini Coopers parallel parking alongside aging rust buckets.

The place I'm looking for is a two-story redbrick affair with tattered awnings over the ground-floor windows. Seventy-five years ago it could have been a factory or a warehouse, but now it has that long-abandoned look, with grass growing up through the sidewalks and the wood-trimmed window splintered with rot. The signs of occupation are slight, the sort of markers left by squatters rather than developers. The original front door, approached by a short flight of cracked steps, has been replaced by a glass commercial entrance with hand-painted lettering announcing the MORGAN ST. CAFÉ & ART COLLECTIVE. Near the handle, a series of adhesive credit cards assure the cash-strapped of a ready welcome, and a taped-in sign indicates free Wi-Fi.

Inside, the impression is better. Glossy concrete floors, zinc-topped café tables and aluminum chairs giving off a dull sheen under the track lights. The corners house overstuffed leather chairs, most of them occupied, and a series of rickety bookshelves bursting with fat paperbacks. As I make my way to the counter, a tooled mahogany buttress reclaimed from some old building—possibly this one—repurposed without being restored, no doubt intentionally, several students glance up from their laptops, making me as the Man.

A large square table, another refugee from bygone days, hosts a half-dozen middle-aged ladies crowned in various stages of blond, each of them clutching a copy of the same book. They pause in mid-discussion, turning to watch me pass. Judging by the volume of ink on skin, the multiple piercings, they're doing their best to keep up with their daughters.

Over the counter, the menu's inscribed in chalk on four large blackboards suspended from the rafters. I missed my morning coffee, so the first order of business is testing the house blend. The girl on duty is short and lithe, upholstered in nubby fabric from the developing world, dreadlocks tied back, a stack of tribal bangles protecting her wrists. But her glasses say ARMANI on the side.

The coffee is better than good. After two gulps I'm seeing the world with new eyes. My elbow on the counter, I scan the room, realizing I'm one of only three men present. Everyone else is female and white, affecting an affluent version of grunge. The girl behind the counter hovers a few feet off, seeming uncertain how to deal with my lingering presence.

"You have some studios here, is that right?"

She raises a pierced eyebrow, like she wasn't expecting someone in a jacket and tie to know about the studio space, or even art in general.

"Umm," she says. "Yeah." Her ringed thumb indicates a set of double doors to the right of the counter. They're painted the same matte black as the walls, so they blend in nicely apart from the crack of light running between them. "There aren't any shows or anything today, though. And the studios are actually private."

"Nothing is actually private." I slide a card across the counter, then finish the last of the coffee.

She holds the card close, staring at the words through her designer glasses. It's a while before she processes the significance.

"You're a cop?"

"I'm a homicide detective." I dangle the keys to Thomson's studio, a long silver door key and a shorter brass one that looks like it might fit a padlock. "I need to take a look inside."

"My manager's not here," she says.

"That's okay. As you can see, I have the keys."

"Well, but . . . I mean, don't you need a search warrant?"

I lean across the counter, making eye contact. "Not actually."

The double doors swing open at the first push. As I pass through, I half expect her to rush after me, but mine are the only footsteps along the tiled floor. The featureless hallway turns right, then dead-ends at a locked door. This is where the building renovation seems to have ended. Through the glass panel over the lock I see a long corridor of raw sheetrock lit by a string of exposed bulbs, the walls pierced by a series of garage-style openings sealed off by the same segmented metal pull-downs that secure self-storage units, each with a shiny padlock at its base.

The silver key opens the door. The pull-downs are numbered sequentially, but only some of them are labeled. Near the end of the corridor, one of the doors is slightly raised and I can hear music playing on the other side. Sarah McLachlan. That one I steer clear of. I check the names on the other doors for Thomson's, but he isn't listed, which means I have to go one by one, testing the brass key in every padlock.

I'm a quarter of the way down when the music stops and the raised door rattlesnakes toward the ceiling. A small black-haired woman peers out, wiping her hands on a pair of paint-mottled jeans.

"Can I help you?" she asks.

"Sure." I cast a hopeless glance along the corridor. "You wouldn't happen to know which one of these belongs to Joe Thomson?"

She leans against the doorframe, crossing her arms skeptically. "Joe's not here. Nobody is but me."

"I know he's not here," I say, walking toward her. "I'm not looking for him, just his studio."

Her eyes dart to my hand, where the keys glisten. She's in her twenties, attractive in a candid, wide-eyed way, her hair wrapped in some kind of scarf, maybe to keep it clear of the paint. The baggy plaid shirt and loose-fitting jeans give her a squared-off look, hiding any figure she might have. Her feet, mostly concealed under a puddle of denim, appear to be bare.

"Are you a friend of his?" she asks.

I hand her one of my cards, giving her a moment to look it over. "Could you point me to the right door, please, ma'am?"

"I don't understand," she says, still looking at the card.

"A little help here is all I'm asking for."

"I mean, what do the police want with Joe? Has he done something? He's such a nice guy, always helpful. He's, like, my art buddy. I can't believe he'd do anything . . ."

Her reaction doesn't seem right. There's nothing strange about one cop showing up on another's doorstep, no reason to assume there's any guilt involved. Unless.

"Ma'am," I say. "You realize Joe's a cop, right?"

She blinks. "What do you—? No, I didn't realize. How could he . . . I mean, we shared a . . . No, never mind what we shared. He's a cop? Joe? You're not making this up?"

"He was."

"Was? He's not anymore?"

"No," I say. "He's not anymore. Now, can you tell me which door is his?"

She holds the card in both hands, thumbs squeezing it into a parabola. Without speaking, she nods toward the lockup directly across from hers. I stoop to the ground, fitting the lock inside, twisting until the hook unclasps. The lock fits tightly. Once I work it free, the door springs up a couple of feet, then sinks several inches. I give the handle a good yank, lifting the metal skin clear.

"The switch is on the wall," she says.

I flick the lights on. Thomson's studio is narrow, not more than twelve feet across, but it's almost twice that length. One wall is covered in shallow gunmetal shelving units that hold, in addition to a few cardboard boxes, an inventory of crude busts executed in plaster, clay, and in a few cases stone. Vaguely human heads on rustic pedestals, mostly looking—intentionally or not—like victims of blunt force trauma, with swollen lips and cratered eye sockets and half-formed ears. I stand there looking at them, uncertain what I'm seeing.

"Joe's heads."

I turn. "We haven't been introduced. I'm Roland March."

"My name's Jill," she says. "Jill Fanning?" Turning the name up at the end like it's a question. Either she isn't sure who she is, or she thinks maybe I will have heard of her.

"These heads, that's what he made?"

There must be thirty of them at least, lined up with methodical precision like cans on the grocery store shelf. On its own, I doubt any of them would be that remarkable, but it's another story taken together. A kind of primitive power resides in their collective stare. This was therapeutic? Somehow I doubt it. Not so much the work of a man chasing away his demons as courting them, but then I'm no critic of art.

Turning from the sculpted glare, I take in the rest of the studio. The opposite wall houses a series of tables—folding metal jobs with dust-covered tops, a couple of tall, narrow wood platforms straight from the planting shed, some boards propped between sawhorses. Chisels and hammers of various sizes litter the surfaces, along with awls, files, and a rust-red saw.

A couple of scrap-metal sentinels stand in back, figures composed haphazardly of random parts. The welding gear sits in the corner. As I approach to inspect it, Jill Fanning gives one of the iron figures a tap with her knuckle, sending a vibration through its limbs.

"He's been experimenting with this stuff recently. It's nice to see him branching out."

On one of the tables I find a black sketchbook underneath a smooth kidney-shaped rock. The pages are filled with portraits—creaky, literal-minded, two-dimensional sketches that hover somewhere in the gray zone between folk art and simple inability. The pictures are all of the same woman, round-faced with flowing black hair, full lips and closed eyes. If the misshapen heads elicit revulsion, these earnest attempts at photo-realism induce pity. I turn the book so Ms. Fanning can have a look.

"I've never seen these before," she says, taking the sketchbook in hand, flipping the pages slowly. She bites her lip.

"I think they're meant to be you."

She laughs. "I doubt that." Then, frowning. "They don't look like me, do they?"

I answer with a noncommittal shrug. But yes, they do. Stephanie Thomson's suspicions come to mind, the fear that her husband had gotten involved with one of his fellow artists. Maybe there was more truth to this than she realized.

"How often would you say Joe was down here?" I ask, glancing into a couple of boxes on a nearby shelf, which contain mostly clay-covered books and abandoned tools.

She's still transfixed by the sketches. "I don't know. Maybe once or twice a week. I've been here constantly—I've got a show coming up—and I'll typically see him early in the morning, sometimes late at night. He's unpredictable, I guess you could say. The way it seems to work for him is, he gets this inspiration and rushes over here to do something about it."

"Always the same inspiration, it looks like." I pick up one of the heads. It's surprisingly light. Plaster dust transfers to my hands.

"He's one of those people who can't get it to come out right. So he keeps doing it, different variations, like he's obsessed, you know? There's a shape in his mind, a certain face, and he keeps trying to capture it again and again."

She closes the sketchbook and returns it to the table, putting the rock back on top. The halting repetition of her own face on the page has given her pause. I can see the wheels turning as she realizes the implications of her own words. Hers was one of the shapes in his mind, the latest obsession. Before letting her leave, I ask all the usual questions, but she can't say whether Joe seemed depressed or not, whether he'd been behaving differently.

"Had he given away any prized possessions?"

"No," she says, then pauses. "When he was up here a couple of days ago, I did hear him talking to Vance—that's the guy next door—asking him to hold on to a box of stuff. He said he didn't have room for it."

Glancing along the shelves, I find that a little hard to believe.

"He gave it to this Vance individual, and not you?"

"We weren't that close." Her eyes cut to the sketchbook. "Really."

"You have a number for this guy?"

She crosses the hallway, retrieving a BlackBerry from her purse, scrolling through the numbers to find the right one. I copy Vance's information into my notepad, then thank her. As she leaves, I have the feeling she hasn't told me everything. I get that a lot, and sometimes it's hard to know whether what's being held back is important or not. One thing I'm fairly certain about. When Jill Fanning said she was not close to Joe, that was a lie.

I leave a message for Vance, asking him to get in touch as soon as possible, then try Cavallo's number again. She doesn't pick up, so I call the station, which routes me over to the task force desk, where a secretary asks me to hold. A few minutes later, Wanda's voice comes on the line.

"Theresa isn't here," she says. "She took a personal day."

"Oh. Well, I guess you heard about my new assignment?"

"Congratulations. I can tell you, your friend Lieutenant Rick is green with envy. He's been scampering all over the place looking for a way off this sinking ship." She frames the observation as an ironic joke, but her tone is pure bitter. "I just spent the last half hour listening to him argue why, in spite of being here to handle the media, it shouldn't be him in front of the camera. He's afraid having his face associated with this would tank his career."

I'm not sure what to say to that. There's a reason why I've never had the urge to chase after rank. Listening to the resignation in her voice, I feel guilty for abandoning her team, even if it was at my captain's request. Guilty but also relieved, which makes me feel even worse.

"I'll talk to her later," I say, hanging up.

Downtown, back at my own desk, I start working my way through Thomson's personal effects, broken down into a series of inventoried evidence bags. Most of these things I examined quickly at the scene, but I have some time to kill before heading over to see the medical examiner, so I might as well use it.

I locate the bag containing Thomson's phone, then limber up my writing hand for some extensive transcription. We have software to do all this, but call me old-fashioned. I like to do some jobs myself. Every call he placed, every call he received, every call he missed, I record them all. Then I work my way through his programmed numbers, seeing what I can find. Jill Fanning is there, though no calls have been recently placed to her or received from her. There's no listing for Vance, but the number she gave me is on the list of placed calls two days back.

This morning's incoming calls are all from Stephanie. Just after midnight, though, he received one from Reg Keller's home, and then he placed one to a number I recognize, Tony Salazar's mobile phone.

On the back of the phone there's a peephole camera. I thumb my way through the menu layers, then find Joe Thomson's stored photos. They're the usual jagged, low-quality images, random photos of the skyline, of himself, of the world viewed from behind his steering wheel. There's one of Stephanie grilling in the backyard, her moving hand blurring her face. Nothing surprising.

The last picture on the roll is the exception.

It's worse than the others, taken in dim light, the face not much more than a white smudge framed in black, the features vague. The torso, equally washed out, cropped halfway down the chest. If I hadn't seen the sketches, if I hadn't just come from meeting Jill Fanning in the flesh, I'm not sure I could have made the identification. All I could have told from the picture is that the woman's eyes were closed, and she was undressed.

But since I did just see the sketches and meet Ms. Fanning in the flesh, since I heard her tell me the two of them weren't close and recognized it immediately as a lie, I don't have much trouble imagining who this woman is, or what it means that Joe Thomson carried around a photo of her in the nude. His wife's suspicions are more than confirmed. I'll have to have another talk with the woman now.

Remembering Stephanie, though, my thumb hovers over the erase button. Bascombe had a point earlier. The man killed himself. You don't have to trash his memory. Ignorance being bliss, it might be better for his wife to go on thinking she was wrong, that there was nothing between Thomson and this other woman. I can spare her this much with the push of a button.

But like I said, I don't have the whitewash gene. Part of me wants to cover for him—not so much for his sake as for hers—but I know deep down that the unvarnished truth is better than even a well-meaning deception. I'm not here to pretty things up, to give Stephanie Thomson or anyone else a reassuring vision of the world as she thinks it is. All I have to do is uncover the way things really are. I didn't make them that way, and I don't have the power to change them. Even if it's tempting to think I do.

My thumb moves away from the button and I turn the phone off. Maybe she'll find the photo once his effects are released, and maybe she won't. That's not my decision to make.

The autopsy is why I'm the designated suicide cop, simple as that. Nobody wants to see a fellow officer on the slab, whether you knew him or not. Hedges could spread the burden around, but he chooses to let it rest on his least favorite, no doubt thinking this will motivate better performance. In my case, it only seems to make things worse.

Bridger waits until my arrival to begin work, starting with some observations about the state of the body and the visible wounds. By the time we reach the Y-incision, I've tuned out, retreating a few steps, letting the soft-focus blinkers fall over my eyes. Organs are transferred to various stainless-steel vessels for weighing, samples are taken. The process is methodical, one I've witnessed so many times over the years I have actually lost count, something I never would have imagined when I first joined the unit.

Toxicology results don't come back overnight. The preliminary reports on the Morales shooting were exceptional, not just for their superfluousness but for their speed. As much as I'd like to know by tomorrow morning whether Thomson was coked up when he pulled the trigger—assuming he pulled it—I don't make a fuss when Bridger says "as soon as possible." There's no doubt, after all, about the cause of death.

He follows me outside after stripping down to his scrubs. Out on the curb, we watch the thunderheads roll by and Bridger lights up a cigarette, quickly generating a cloud cover of his own. We're silent awhile, because we have to be. Jaded as we are under the professional veneer, the fact is we've just finished cutting someone up, and that's not the best way to initiate conversation.

Bridger stubs the butt out in an ashtray near the side exit, then returns to the vigil.

"There's a storm coming," he says. "That's what they're saying on the news."

I glance at the sky. "Looks like."

We fall silent again. I can sense him working up to something.

"I know you pretty well," he says.

I nod in agreement.

"There's nothing on the scene to suggest he didn't kill himself?"

I shake my head.

"But you don't think he did it."

"No, I don't."

He ponders this, scrubbing his sole against the pavement. "All right, well here's something. It isn't much, but since you're thinking along these lines . . ."

My ears perk up. "What have you got?"

"The trajectory of the bullet. The entrance is low, right by the ear, and the exit is high, almost the top of the head. So the gun would have been held like this." He puts his index finger against his temple, adjusting the angle to roughly forty-five degrees. "If you wanted to be sure, though, you wouldn't hold the gun at an angle like that. You'd be afraid of ending up a vegetable instead of dead."

"If you put the muzzle right under your chin and fire straight up, you're good to go."

"Right," he says, adjusting his finger accordingly. "That's what I'd expect. Or maybe you'd hold it sideways right at the center of the head, so you know the bullet's going straight through."

"So it doesn't look consistent with a self-inflicted wound?"

He shakes his head. "I'm not saying that, Roland. His hand might have slipped, he might have been distraught—I can think of a thousand reasons why he'd end up doing it this way. But there's just that little twinge of doubt, you know? Because I'm not seeing exactly what I'd expect."

The problem is, a medical examiner's gut feelings are no more admissible than a detective's. If the shooting doesn't sit right with Bridger, all I can take from that is encouragement. And I need more. A shared hunch isn't the leverage I need in the interview room with Keller and Salazar. Unfortunately, when it comes to the pathology, it looks like that's all I'm going to get.

CHAPTER 18

It's not my house. Better not be. But the closer I get, the louder the music—the peculiar thump and whine of the dirty South. And the cars get thicker, too, lining the curb on either side of the street.

Rolling up to my driveway, I find a Toyota SUV squatting halfway over the line, with a queue of others sitting bumper-to-bumper all the way up to the garage. The windows of Tommy's apartment glow orange, silhouettes grinding in and out of view.

As I sit there, foot on the brake, a group of young men in jeans and V-neck shirts thread their way toward the back, hoisting twelve-packs of Shiner and Lone Star to keep from clipping an antenna or side-view mirror. The one bringing up the rear pauses, cups a hand to his mouth, and howls into the night "Whoooo-hoo," already lit up from the previous stop on their evening crawl.

A fantasy reel flickers to life in my mind: I'm dragging Tommy down the apartment steps by the scruff of the neck, kneeling him down on the curb, dispatching him execution-style. But violence isn't the answer. Except when it is.

Down at the end of the street I find a parking spot, then double back along the sidewalk. The neighbors have taken refuge behind closed drapes and lowered blinds, but my house emits no light.

I let myself in the front door. Inside, the only illumination comes through the back windows, a grid of shadows with the occasional figure ducking past. The only sound is the muffled music and the vibration of hundred-year-old glass in the windowpanes. Otherwise, the house is so still it could pass for abandoned.

I head to the back, lifting a shade with my finger. The yard is empty, but a crowd of people congregates on the stairs, most sitting while a few cling to the railing, trying to pick their way to the top. I count fifteen, maybe sixteen heads, and I'm guessing there are as many more again packed into the small apartment.

Another reel: the wooden stairs collapsing under the weight, Tommy teetering on the threshold to keep his balance, arms wind-milling through the air, then falling with a gasp onto the jagged tip of a two-by-four.

I told him to keep things low-key. I told him there would be trouble.

"Satisfied?"

Her voice makes me jump. Behind me, veiled by the dark, Charlotte sits gargoyle-like in a wing chair, her feet on the cushion, knees drawn up to her chin.

"I didn't see you there."

She keeps very still. "You said you were going to have a talk with him. You promised to at least do that."

"I did," I say. "I told you that."

"It wasn't enough." Her voice rises. "It obviously wasn't enough."

"I guess not. And you've been sitting here all this time? In the dark? You should have at least called me, babe—"

"And said what?" She throws up her hands, but without much force in the gesture, weary of repeating the complaint. "Anyway, there's no telling where you'd be this time of night. No, wait." A stiff laugh escapes her lips. "You'd be where you always are. Even though you promised me you wouldn't go there anymore."

"Charlotte—"

"I'm tired," she says. "Tired of what's going on under my nose. Tired of every conversation turning into some kind of argument."

The fight goes out of her, and in the gloom I can see her gazing at me, her bottom lip in a swollen pout. That gesture strips years off her. I feel my heart moving in my chest.

"So am I." I perch on the edge of the sofa, stretching my arm toward her, resting a hand on her knee. "I have a blind spot when it comes to that kid. I know that."

She covers my hand with hers. "You identify with him."

"It's not that."

"Roland, it is. Trust me, I know you." She rubs at my knuckle with her thumb, smiling in the darkness. "You cut him slack because you've been cut so much slack yourself. Do unto others, you think. You have this crazy take on the Golden Rule."

"Is that such a bad thing?"

"No, honey, it's not. But you do it because you're afraid."

"Of what?" I ask.

"Of the world coming down on you. It's like he's your good luck charm or something. So long as you let him run wild, you can run wild, too."

I squeeze her knee, then slip my hand away. "I'm not running wild. And I don't identify with that slacker, either. And to prove it, I'll go talk to him now. I'll throw them all out."

"My hero," she says with a girlish laugh, not even a hint of irony. Then she uncoils and puts her arms around me, pulling us close. "It's the right thing to do. And don't worry about the consequences."

"I'll go right now."

She draws my head down, hands warm on my cheeks, anointing my forehead with a kiss.

I throw the back door open, pound my way across the deck. Seeing me coming, the more perceptive people on the stairs realize the party's over. They stand and make way for my ascent, slipping down the driveway once I pass them. Near the top, a shaggy-haired boy squints appraisingly at me, blowing smoke through his pursed lips. He starts to gesture toward me with the lit cigarette, starts to open his mouth to speak. I swipe the cancer stick out of his grasp, sending it somersaulting into the night, then shoulder him out of the way.

The apartment door hangs wide. I give it a kick anyway, to get people's attention. The furniture's shoved into the corners to accommodate more people, all of them youngish, probably a mix of college kids and Tommy's fellow grad student instructors. And strangers, too, I bet.

"Tommy!"

Heads turn, couples break up, but my tenant is nowhere to be seen. I squeeze through the door to the bedroom, but he isn't in there. I head for the narrow galley kitchen.

"Tommy!"

In the kitchen, sitting on the counter with her feet propped on the opposite cabinet, the waitress from the Paragon. Marta. She sips from a red plastic cup, gazing absently through the arrow-slit window. The others packed into the kitchen file out at my appearing. She glances over, recognizes me, and chucks her cup into the sink.

"What is this?" she says. "Police harassment?"

"Where's Tommy?"

"He left not long after I showed up. Didn't want to talk, I guess. But listen, you should leave him alone. He hasn't done anything."

"He's done this," I say, sweeping my hand inadvertently against the refrigerator. I try again, motioning carefully at the party still ebbing along over my shoulder.

"So what?"

"So I told him not to."

"What does it matter to the police if he invites some people over?"

"It matters to me," I say. "I live here."

She cocks her head, then smiles wryly. "This is your place? You're the landlord? So that's how he knows you." Her eyes roll. "Now it all starts to make sense."

I don't have time for this. There's a neck to wring. But there aren't many places to hide in here, so I suspect she's right about Tommy taking a hike. Who throws a party and then leaves? The more I think about it, the more my tenant fits the bill.

"Your wife is nice," Marta says.

"My wife?"

"The lady who lives here—she's your wife, isn't she?"

I nod. "How do you know her?"

"I met her," she says. "When I was here before. She gave me a ride home."

"That was you?" I ask, leaning against the cabinet across from her, arms crossed, not exactly blocking the exit but fencing her in a bit.

She glances out the window again, nodding.

"Charlotte, my wife . . . she was worried about you."

There's something false about her sudden laugh. "About me?"

"You were in quite a state, she said. She even thought maybe something happened to you, that you'd been drugged or something."

Her bravado is gone, and in spite of the heavy eyeliner and tight-fitting top, she seems quite childlike and small, almost virginal. And she's lost all ability to meet my gaze. Still, her voice keeps its hardness, projecting world-weary scorn.

"I was just a little out of it from the night before."

"Are you and Tommy friends or something?"

"Do I look like any of these people are my friends? I just know him from the bar. A bunch of them come in and, I don't know, I just thought it might be fun. See how the other half parties, you know? Personally, I didn't bother finishing school, and if you ask me, I didn't miss anything. From what I see here"—she nods toward the living area—"I'd say I didn't miss nothing at all."

"How old are you, Marta?"

"Old enough."

"Twenty-one, at least?"

She rolls her eyes again. "Well, duh. You know where I work."

"Charlotte said that when she drove you home, she dropped you at a dorm. If you're not in school, why do you live in the dorms?"

"I don't," she says. "That's just where I left my car."

"She also said you couldn't remember who you came with."

"Not their names."

"Is that a common thing for you, memory loss?"

She glares are me. "I'm not good with names, okay? That doesn't mean anything. Look, I said your wife was nice to me. I wasn't trying to make a big thing out of it."

"Sorry," I say. "I'm just concerned. Because if something did happen to you—"

"Then what?"

"Then I'd have to do something about it."

The words come out, they float between us in the air, unseen but making their presence felt. Why am I worried? The memory of Charlotte's distress, perhaps. The sudden though incomplete vulnerability Marta's shown, or my earlier hunch that her hardness concealed a penchant for abuse. Or maybe it's all the missing girls at the back of my mind, blending together, seeping out as a general concern for young femininity. Hannah Mayhew, the nation's absent daughter, and the nameless one I tried to make her into—not even a woman, just a pattern of blood on the sheets.

And behind them all, the girl who's always absent but always threatening to make herself tangible, always visible in hints and traces in the face and shape of every woman I see of a certain age. The one I won't talk about, because Charlotte's right about the futility of revisiting the past.

"You're kind of nice," Marta says, "in a weird sort of way."

"Not really. Not once you get to know me."

"Tommy says you are."

He has his reasons. And maybe Charlotte sees them more clearly than I do. I've been shielding him without realizing why, afraid that a reckoning of any kind could start off a chain reaction, forcing everything into the light. As a consequence, a girl like this, motivated by God knows what undefined ambition, some desire to belong, could come under my roof and suffer—what? Nothing, she says, and I want to believe her. I want to believe I don't deserve a reckoning on her account.

"You're young," I tell her. "I don't know what happened to you the other night, if anything did. But your life . . . it should be a lot more than this. I'm just saying, don't waste it."

She hops off the counter, heading slowly toward the living room. "I'm not looking for a surrogate daddy," she says, "but if I was . . ."

A surrogate daddy. And what is Tommy to me? An adopted son?

"Get out of here. I'm gonna be rude to some people. You don't want to see me when I get rude."

"You forget," she says. "I already have."

Tommy's party ends not with a whimper but a bang, the sound of me snapping the door shut behind the last of his friends. I follow them down the stairs, herding the pack, channeling people into their cars and then tapping the roofs until they pull away. The final car reverses down the drive with me trailing the bumper, hands on my hips, badge and holstered gun gleaming in the headlights. If Tommy gets it into his head to throw another shindig, I have a feeling not too many of these folks will see fit to attend.

Once they're gone, I camp out on the front steps for a little while on the off chance my tenant will return. But I figure he's been tipped off and decided to spend the rest of the night on somebody's couch. Back inside, Charlotte greets me at the door. I start to say something, but she pushes her lips against mine.

"You did it," she says. "Time for your reward."

"You were right," I say.

"Don't sound so surprised. Now come on."

I let her take my hand and lead me up the back stairs. All is not right in my world, but one small corner is about to get noticeably better.

It's Marta at the breakfast table this time, looking just like she did a few hours ago. She sinks a spoon into her cereal, letting milk drip over the side, and Charlotte gazes at her fondly, stroking her hair. They show no surprise when I appear at the door. They both smile at me, both with the same smile, bearing a resemblance to each other that they don't in real life.

"I'm all grown up," Marta says, holding her spoon up like an exclamation mark.

Then the kitchen door starts rattling over her shoulder. A knock so loud it sends tremors through the floorboards. They turn, eyes wide, Marta dropping the spoon into the bowl, Charlotte covering her mouth with her hand.

"Don't let him in," Marta pleads.

"Let who in?" My legs take me forward. My hand goes to the doorknob.

"Please don't do it! Please, please, please!"

"Don't be afraid," I say.

"Roland." Charlotte's voice. "Roland, wake up."

My eyes blink open. I turn toward her. "What?"

"Someone's pounding on the door."

"For real?"

And then I hear it. The nightstand clock reads just past six. I roll out of bed, pulling my pants on, sliding my pistol from the holster. An overreaction, maybe, but it's underreacting that gets people killed. At the bedroom door I pause and turn. Charlotte's crouched at the bedside, feeling around for her discarded clothes.

The back door rattles on its hinges. Whoever's doing the knocking, he's hitting wood, not glass, otherwise there'd be shards all across the kitchen floor. I don't open it. I don't slit the shades for a peek. Instead, I go to the window overlooking the deck, which affords a flanking view of the back door. Tommy's my prime suspect, and I'm considering putting a round into him. Nothing fatal, just a nick in the thigh. I know firsthand how annoying those can be.

When I part the shades for a look, it isn't Tommy at all. I pad into the kitchen, tuck my SIG into the snack drawer, then unbolt the lock.

Wilcox glares at me, nodding slowly. "I should have known."

"Known what?" I ask. Then, when he doesn't answer: "I meant to call you."

I beckon him over the threshold, motioning in the direction of the breakfast table, but he doesn't budge an inch. He wears a gray suit and regimental tie. Already, there are sweat stains on his white, spread-collared shirt.

"I didn't come here to chat," he says. "But I heard about your new case. I want you to tell me one thing—and you'd better not lie to me, because I'll know if you do. Tell me you didn't have anything to do with Joe Thomson's death."

"What?" I take a step back. "Is that what you came here for?"

"I know you didn't pull the trigger, Roland. That's not what I'm saying. But are you working some kind of angle here, using me to do it? All that work I did with the DA, and suddenly the guy tops himself. And who do they put in charge of the investigation but you? Questions are going to be asked. It's already happening. Just so you know, I won't be covering for you."

"I have no idea what you mean," I say.

"Tell me you didn't have anything to do with it."

"I didn't."

"It was just a coincidence. The guy's cracking up, he's feeling guilty about turning on his friends, and in a fit of despair he dumps one in the brainpan. Happens all the time."

"He didn't just shoot himself."

"No? Then what?"

"What do you think?"

He runs the back of his hand over his forehead, mopping the sweat. "I think that if you're trying to play me here, if this is some kind of windup so you can settle the score with Reg Keller—"

"They did it," I say. "I can't prove that yet, but we both know it's true. He was going to roll over on them, so they staged his death. What else could it be?"

"Yeah, but how would they find out? You think he told them?"

"I don't know," I say.

I'm not going to tell him about my call to Stephanie Thomson and how she tipped Salazar off. The thing about Wilcox is, he likes everything to be neat. Even at our best, my unpredictability could make him nervous. Pulling over on the highway and switching a digital recorder on so Donald Fauk could do his patriotic duty by confessing to his wife's murder—that had made his skin crawl. He'd have kept Fauk quiet until we could hustle him into an interview room, everything tidy and squared away.

But I knew, in spite of everything I was going through at that moment, a much worse ordeal than a superficial gunshot, a pain I would have endured a thousand gunshots to forgo, I knew that it was now or never with Fauk, whether the confession was orthodox or not.

"You're upset," I tell him. "I get that. But you haven't done anything wrong here, and neither have I. They're the ones who did this, and they're going to pay for it. Just stick with me, all right?"

"I'm not lifting a finger for you."

"Fine," I say, shrugging off the hurt. And it does hurt to hear him speaking this way. "You don't have to do a thing. I don't want you to do a thing, if you get my drift. The thing I specifically don't want you to do is tell my captain—or anybody else, for that matter—about the deal we had in place for Thomson. They'll pull me off the investigation if they find out."

Finally, he steps into the house, a bum-rush over the threshold, getting right up in my face, jamming his finger into my chest.

"You think I can keep that quiet? They're gonna find out, my friend. Bascombe already talked to a guy in my office."

I shake my head. "He only knows about the past. Not this. And I'm not asking for a cover-up here. Just keep your own mouth shut, okay? Buy me some time, at least."

His finger rears back for another peck, then pauses in the air. His eyes drift over my shoulder. I turn to find Charlotte there, wearing my shirt from last night. Her legs look pale in the morning sun. Her eyes blink.

"Stephen," she says, doing another button up. "What are you doing here so early? What are you doing here at all? I haven't seen you in . . . forever."

He drops his eyes and backs off, mumbling excuses on his way out the door.

"Don't leave on my account," she says.

He turns his back on us and goes, not even bothering to shut the door. I hear his shoes tapping the concrete, then his car door slamming and the engine turning over.

"What was that all about?"

I shut the door, turning the dead bolt. "Work."

While she kicks off breakfast, I go upstairs, running my head under the shower and then dressing quickly, collecting my keys and wallet, my empty holster, my newly charged phone. Coffee is on the table when I return, and so is my pistol.

"I found that in the drawer," Charlotte says, buttering some toast.

I eat fast, but not fast enough. Just as I'm leaving, my phone starts to ring.

"Who is it?" she asks.

"I don't recognize the number."

She walks toward me. "If it's somebody with information wanting to meet up face-to-face, I'm not letting you out that door."

"Don't worry."

The voice on the other end of the line crackles with nerves, but after a sentence or two I realize it's the overeager crime-scene tech, Edgar Castro.

"It's a little early, Edgar."

"Is it? I've been up all night."

"Are you going to tell me why, or do I have to guess?"

He clears his throat before continuing. "The thing is, I'm getting static here from my boss, like they don't want me to make a big deal out of this. And maybe it's nothing, but . . ."

"Maybe what's nothing?"

"It's kind of complicated," he says. "But I thought you'd want to know."

"Know what?"

"It'd be easier to show you than try to explain."

"Show me what?"

"Could you come down to the lab?"

I sigh, rolling my eyes for Charlotte's benefit. She rolls hers back for mine.

"Half an hour," I say to Castro.

"Excellent," he replies. I imagine him on the other end of the line, pumping his fist in triumph. Whatever has got him so worked up, it better have the same effect on me.

CHAPTER 19

The moment the gun is in his hand, Edgar Castro's eyes light up. He uses a serrated folding knife to remove the plastic tie running through the barrel, then eyeballs the breech to make sure there's not a round in the chamber. When he passes it across the desk, I can sense his reluctance to let go. After double-checking for safety, I release the slide. It slams shut with a familiar metallic snap.

"Everything look right to you?" he asks.

I give the pistol a closer inspection. The blued finish is worn down on the edges, probably from holster wear, and the plastic factory grips have been replaced by checkered cocobolo. Along the front strap, a strip of skateboard tape provides tacky traction. The barrel is stamped .40 s&w, the cartridge our service pistols are chambered for. Thanks to my time clerking in the gun shop as a young man, I have an abiding awe for the trusty .45, but over the years I've come to respect the smaller, hotter .40. Apart from the fancy hardwood, this gun is a tool, plain and simple, the same as the one I carry every day.

"The tape's a little ghetto," I say, "but otherwise it looks fine."

Castro's little corner of csu is dark, packed with computer screens, lit by arc lamps, littered with a recycler's dream supply of empty Dr.

Pepper cans. The workspace, wiped clean apart from the pile of plastic evidence bags, was created by fitting a tabletop over a shoulder-to-shoulder rank of filing cabinets. He scrounged a desk from somewhere, too, a castoff from the dark days before the current cubicle system was installed.

He fishes a loaded magazine from a separate evidence bag, sliding it over.

"This stuff's all been checked for prints already?"

He nods. "It's cool. Now, does that look right?"

The magazine's weight feels good in my hand. I press down on the uppermost cartridge with my thumb, testing the spring's resistance.

"I don't get what you're asking," I say. "If there's something wrong here, you're going to have to point it out."

He takes pistol and magazine back, inserts one into the other, then works the slide.

"Is that really necessary?" Even though the muzzle is safely aimed at the ground, I wince a little. Castro doesn't inspire gun-handling confidence. He seems just the sort for an accidental discharge. Fortunately, the other technicians seem to give him a wide berth. The only other occupant of this particular room—calling it a lab would only dignify what looks like an oversized storage closet for high-tech equipment—vacated as soon as I showed up.

He drops the magazine and ejects the chambered round. It flips through the air, thumping to rest on the gray carpet.

"Just what you'd expect, right?" he says, setting the weapon down between us. "Now take a look at this."

The next item on his show-and-tell list is a double magazine carrier, nice tan leather from Milt Sparks, the sort of thing you clip to your belt to keep spare ammunition handy. Thomson seems to have been a man after my own heart, judging from the grips and gun leather, splashing out for the good stuff.

"Nice," I say. "So what?"

"Look at the magazines."

With a sigh I withdraw the mags. They look the same as the other one. I thumb down the top round again, letting it spring back. Then the difference registers. The shape of the cartridges. Instead of the long, flat plane of a .40 caliber round, these are bottlenecked at the point where the bullet fits into the brass to accommodate a smaller projectile. I slide a round out, inspecting the bottom.

"These are .357 SIG," I say.

"Exactly. And they're both the same. Now, the spent brass recovered inside Thomson's vehicle was .40 caliber, and so are the rounds in the clip we found inside the gun. We dug the bullet out of the door pillar, and it's .40 caliber, too, and a match for the barrel. So the fatal round was fired through that barrel, from that magazine. Everything is how it should be."

"Except this." I tap the .357 SIG round against the desk.

"Right. So my question is, why was Thomson carrying one kind of ammo on his belt and another kind in his gun? You can load .357s into the same magazine as a .40, but have you ever tried firing one from a .40 caliber pistol? A little hint: don't even try it. So either this guy Thomson was monumentally brain dead—I mean, really—or he didn't pay much attention to detail. Or . . ."

"Or what?" I ask, though I already know where he's going.

Castro picks up the gun and fieldstrips it, removing the entire slide assembly, then pulling the barrel out. He holds it up to his eye like a telescope.

"This is the barrel that fired the bullet that killed Detective Thomson," he says, "but does that mean this is the gun?" He taps the pile of disassembled metal. "Not necessarily. You know what happened when the .357 SIG round first came out? A lot of guys believed the hype, so they went out and bought drop-in barrels to convert their .40s into .357s. It's as simple as fieldstripping the piece and putting a differ-ent barrel inside. Like this." He opens a drawer, removing a silvered drop-in barrel, which he fits into the slide assembly, putting the pistol back together. When he's done, he racks the slide a few times. "Now, if you stick one of Thomson's spare mags in, this baby's good to go. That's really all it takes."

He blossoms his hands like a magician, then sits back looking very satisfied. The theory forming in my head goes something like this. Someone in the passenger seat pulls a gun, pressing it against Thomson's head. Pulling the trigger creates a contact wound, but to make the ballistics look right, the killer has to improvise. And it could only be improvisation. If he'd planned ahead, he might have found a way to cover his tracks better, but in the moment he just has to make do. He's shot Thomson—now what? So he switches barrels between his own pistol and Thomson's. Meaning the killer was armed with a SIG Sauer P229, as well. One of us, more than likely.

"So let me get this straight," I say. "You think someone shot Thomson, then fieldstripped both the murder weapon and Thomson's gun, swapping the barrels and the magazines? Only why would he switch mags?"

Castro shrugs. "Maybe he's doing it, and he realizes there's a difference in the bullets. He wouldn't be able to chamber a .357 round in a .40 caliber barrel, so that might be what tipped him off. He tries it, gets a jam, and has to switch the mags."

"Then why leave Thomson's spares behind?"

"He doesn't see them," he says. "Detective Thomson's sitting down. He was wearing the mag carrier behind his left hip, so they'd be on the opposite side." He pats his left hip. "Plus everything's happening so fast. The perp messed up, basically."

"Any prints on the barrel? What about the rounds in the magazine?"

He shakes his head. "There he didn't mess up. They were wiped clean. Which is strange when you think about it. Those rounds should have prints all over them, right?"

"Mine would."

I go through the motions in my mind, stripping the guns, changing the barrels, sorting out the ammunition. It's complicated, but under stress someone familiar both with handguns and forensics could make it happen. And missing the extra magazines would be an easy mistake. The scene would have been dark, he'd be pumping with adrenaline, a dead man on the seat next to him, the rain hammering on the roof. There's a problem, though.

"Maybe Thomson was absentminded. Maybe he forgot he'd loaded those mags with .357 SIG rounds."

"And he wiped his own prints off the barrel and cartridges?"

"I hear you," I say. "I think you're on to something, Castro, but you have to admit it's thin."

"Circumstantial, I know. But here's another piece of circumstantial evidence. The trajectory of the bullet? If Detective Thomson really shot himself, he held the gun at a strange angle—"

"That's what Dr. Bridger said."

"Look at this."

He produces a plastic-bound report just like the one he gave me on the Morales shooting, flipping to another one of his 3-D reconstructions. This one has two panels. In the first, a crash-test dummy representing Thomson holds a pistol to his head, canting the gun at a forty-five degree angle. A red line from the barrel penetrates his head, continuing up through the roof of the vehicle.

"That's not right, is it?" he says. "The bullet didn't go out the roof. It was in the door pillar. But if he was sitting upright, the trajectory would have sent it through the ceiling. So he was leaning toward the door, like this." He points to the second panel, where the dummy rests his head against the pillar. Now the red line is flat, running side to side, and the head is at an angle. "But why would he do that? It's a strange way to shoot yourself, isn't it?"

Yes, it is. But it makes perfect sense if someone else was in the car. The shooter drew on Thomson, punching the pistol forward into the side of his head. It struck him, pushing his skull against the door pillar, and then the shooter fired.

"You mind?" I ask, snatching the empty pistol.

Not only does Castro not mind my putting the gun to his head, he's eager to arrange things just so. We set our chairs side by side against the wall, then he sits down and drapes his hands over an imaginary steering wheel. I get beside him, my finger away from the trigger, and slow-motion Thomson's pistol through the air, from my lap to a point just above his ear. As soon as it touches, he slides toward the wall. When his head taps sheetrock, the angle of the gun is pretty much straight.

"It works." I put the weapon down. I let out a sigh. "So that's what happened."

The sudden grin on Castro's face, like I've just awarded him an A+ on his class project, reminds me again how green the kid is. Green or not, though, he's sharp. And if there were a mirror in the room, it wouldn't surprise me to see an equally stupid-looking grin on my own face, because my excitement has to be on par with his, if not higher.

"Good work, Castro. Really. Now, I'm going to have to ask you to do me a favor, and it won't be easy for you. This information? We need to keep it between the two of us right now."

His smile fades. "But why?"

"Think about it. If your theory is right, this wasn't a premeditated thing. Something happened and the killer decided there was no other choice. He pulled his gun and fired."

"And?"

"And it just so happened his gun matched Thomson's. So does mine, Castro. So does yours. You see what I'm saying?"

"Anybody could have a SIG Sauer."

"Sure they could," I say. "But we both know that's not the deal here, right? For the time being, I need this to look like a suicide investigation, and if you shoot your mouth off about this theory, the wrong people are going to find out I'm on to them. So for now, can we keep it between the two of us?"

"I already told the other guys," he says quietly.

"But they didn't listen, did they? Let's leave it at that."

The struggle on his face lasts a second or two, then he nods with resignation. Playing along means no immediate recognition for his work, but since his colleagues aren't backing him, there's not much risk of professional trouble. This way, at least, he can feel like he's in the know, keeping secrets for the detective in charge.

"Okay," he says, sticking a hand out. "Deal."

There's no way he'll let me go without a handshake, so I give in. His palms are damp and warm. I wait until I'm safely hidden behind the elevator door to wipe mine dry.

Get a cop to open up about his personal frustrations, and once you get past the office politics, the slow advancement, and the various fractures in the justice system, he might, assuming he's the philosophical type, start talking about the gap between knowledge and proof. I've been cut by both sides of the blade, knowing things I couldn't prove and proving things I didn't really believe. The idea that there's any connection between what we believe and what we can prove goes out the door early, at least it does if you're paying attention.

I've sent men to prison with no idea whether they did the crime or not. The case was there, so I made it. The ultimate decision belongs to the judge or jury, something I took comfort in once, though not so much anymore. If we had to know—really know—what happened, no one would ever go to jail. Fortunately, you can prove things in court that you can never truly know.

By the same token, you can know things that can't ever be proven. And that knowledge often has a certainty to it that the evidential sort never does. There are these unproven things about which I have a quasi-religious certainty, things I would act on more readily than anything I could support with mere evidence. I can't explain this exactly, but anyone who has trodden long enough on the line between fact and truth will tell you the same.

Or not. I can only speak for myself.

When I try imagining Keller's hand on the murder weapon—or Salazar's, which is easier somehow—the mental image is absurd, almost laughable. Even so, it's my new article of faith. Castro's hunches fit in with Bridger's qualm, but it can all be explained away. Everything can. Only I know what these men are capable of. I bear the marks on my flesh.

It's not enough. It won't convince Hedges or Bascombe. It won't satisfy Wilcox. And if I go to any of them, I'll tip my hand. That's why Castro has to keep quiet. That's why I have to tread very carefully, planning my next moves for maximum effect.

Back at my desk, I put in another call to Cavallo. She hasn't returned yesterday's call, and I'm beginning to think she never will. She's probably relieved to see the back of me. Vance, the man who's supposedly holding a box from Thomson, hasn't called me, either. That's the lead I want to follow up, and it's as simple as feeding his phone number into the computer.

While I'm copying down the contact info on Mr. Vance Balinski, a Caucasian male aged thirty-four years, residing in an Uptown condo with a ten-year-old Mercedes coupe registered to his name, Detective Aguilar appears at my elbow, black eyes sparkling in his lobster-red face, a photo lineup clutched in his hands. Thanks to his gang experience, he caught my shooting, and now he perches on my desk and hums a little fanfare.

"What're you so chipper about?"

He hands over the lineup, along with a well-chewed ballpoint pen. "You know the drill."

Right away, I recognize the shooter. Looking at his mug shot, I'm surprised my guard wasn't up from the get-go. A tough customer with the faraway stare of a man who'd gut you just to see whether his knife was sharp.

Aguilar nudges my chair with his foot. "You see him here or not?"

I circle the right man and hand the page back.

He nods in satisfaction, humming another bar. "Dude's name is Rafael Ortiz, an enforcer for LTC. Which means the cholos in the house with Morales were his boys." He gives me one of his unreadable stares. "Any reason they'd want to clip you?"

"Something to do with the case, I assume. Beats me what it is."

We commune silently, aware that I've only stated the obvious. Then he starts humming again, like a man whose case is down. He folds the sheet and tucks it into his jacket. "You won't have to worry about this Ortiz, anyway."

"Why?" I ask. "You haven't picked him up already, have you?"

"As we speak, he's cooling on a slab at the morgue. Most of him is, anyway."

"He's dead?" It doesn't make sense. I replay the shooting in my mind. He put a round in my door, then another in my leg, and I touched up his dental work with my elbow, but nothing rough enough to put him in the ground. Plus, it was after I shot up the truck that he hopped inside, so my bullets didn't do the work. I can't figure it out. "It wasn't . . . I mean, I didn't do it, did I?"

He gets a kick out of this and slaps my arm in appreciation. "Did you put a shotgun in his mouth and pull the trigger?" He flattens his hands against his head, then pops them sideways, the same gesture he might use to exaggerate the size of a fish he'd caught, only in this context it's meant to be an exploding cranium. "No? Then you can rest easy, March. It wasn't you."

"The individual driving the truck," I say. "He had a shotgun."

"Yeah, I know."

As he leaves, patting the lineup in his jacket pocket, I sink back into my chair, wallowing in bewilderment. Not that I'm going to lose much sleep over the buckshot decapitation of a man who tried to make Charlotte a widow. Still, I'd like to know who did the business. And why.

"I'm not avoiding you," Cavallo says. "Believe it or not, there's all this work they want me to do. It didn't stop just because you left."

"Wanda said you took a personal day."

"I was sick. I think this case is giving me an ulcer."

There's more to it than that, I have no doubt, but I don't want to press her. Her voice sounds scratchy, like she's been yelling at someone. I don't want to make her yell. I want her happy. She doesn't know it yet, but she's an integral part of my master plan.

"Listen," I say, "Theresa . . ." If she objects to my use of her first name, she doesn't verbalize it. "There's a favor I need to ask you."

"Fire away. But just so you know, the answer's gonna be negative."

"In that case, I'm not going to say it over the phone. Mind if I drop in on you?"

A long pause. "Is it really that important?"

"Life or death."

"Right. Well, I'm up at Northwest. Lunch is on you. And the answer's still going to be no."

"See you in twenty."

As soon as I hang up, I grab my jacket and take the elevator down, moving on autopilot through the car pool. After lunch I'm going to drop in on Vance Balinski in person and find out why he hasn't gotten back in touch. First, though, I need to convince Cavallo to do a little moonlighting.

The car *clunk-clunk*s along the Pierce Elevated, static coming in loud and clear over the radio. My phone starts to ring.

"March."

"What do you want?"

I notice a silver Impala on my tail, edging closer, the driver's bald dome visible, a phone pressed to his ear.

Keller.

"You wanna pull over a minute?" he says. "I'd like to talk face-to-face."

I give my car a little gas. "No, thanks. I'll be in touch to arrange an interview in due course."

"An interview?"

"You worked closely with my victim. Standard procedure."

He sighs. In the rearview I can see him kneading his brow. "They've still got you working the suicides. If I'd have remembered that . . ."

"What?" I ask. You wouldn't have shot Thomson? You would've made it look gang-related, like my attempted murder, instead of staging a suicide?

"Nothing. Pull over. I want to talk."

We race past the I-10 exit, switching lanes to avoid a stack-up on the far left. Everything slows down, lights are flashing, shattered glass kicks out across the interstate. A pickup with a dislocated fender hugs the concrete median, and up ahead a little Honda looks like somebody set off a grenade in the trunk.

"Nasty," Keller says.

I hang up the phone. A second later he calls back.

"What's the problem, March? You were only too happy to barge in on me the other day. Now you're running scared. You got a problem with me or something?" Baiting me. He's too far back for me to make out his expression, but I can imagine the sneer on his lips. "The thing is, I've been hearing these rumors about you. They're saying it won't be long before you're out on your ear. Bouncing from one detail to another, that's what they call terminal velocity. Means you're about to hit the ground. Hard. I'd hate to see that happen to a guy of your caliber, March."

"Really."

"I was thinking . . ." He chuckles. "I've got an opening on my team . . ."

I push the end button. We're coming up on Cavalcade. Near the exit he moves to the right and puts his blinker on. I watch his car until it disappears down the ramp. Just as I begin to breathe easy, the phone rings again.

"One more thing," he says. "If you don't want the job, there's no hard feelings."

"I'm not even going to dignify that with a response."

"Fine. Tell that pretty wife of yours I said hello."

This time it's Keller who hangs up, leaving me to contemplate the fact that Cavalcade will take him to Studewood, five minutes away from my house. He wouldn't be stupid enough to go there. But then, I wouldn't have thought he was stupid enough to kill a cop, either.

CHAPTER 20

Thanks to Keller's veiled threat, I turn up late to my lunch with Cavallo. While evicting the tenant might not rank high on my list of marital duties, protecting my wife does, even though I'm pretty certain the man's just yanking my chain. I find Charlotte upstairs in her office, drinking cold coffee and staring at a column of text on her computer screen. Moving closer, I can read the lines, a stack of *whereas, whereas, whereas* down the left-hand margin, waiting for her to come up with the wording of each petition.

"You wanna trade jobs?" she asks.

"No thanks. I prefer getting shot."

She blinks affectionately. "What are you doing home?"

I make up some excuse about forgetting something, then head out the door, casting a glance up and down the street. No sign of Keller, of course, and no sign of Tommy's car, either, which is a shame. As much trouble as he is, I wouldn't mind him being nearby right about now. Still, there's no danger. Keller's just pushing my buttons.

Cavallo chooses the 59 Diner across from Willowbrook Mall, triggering my speech about eating at chain restaurants when there are perfectly good hole-in-the-wall establishments nearby.

"Not out here," she says. "And anyway, at least it's a local chain."

In my book, the 59 Diner actually located on Highway 59 makes perfect sense, and has the added benefit of being a little broken down and slightly greasy. The slicked-up suburban version leaves me cold. There aren't even any rips in the vinyl upholstery of our booth. The menu isn't tacky to the touch. When our waitress arrives with spot-free water glasses, I frown, which only invites Cavallo to observe there are 59 Diners all over the place. On Interstate 10, for example.

"Across from IKEA," she adds.

"Yeah, thanks. Listen. I'm sorry for leaving you to go it alone on the task force."

"What are you talking about? We have enough dead weight as it is."

"So you didn't take a sick day when you heard the news?"

"Sick with relief, you mean?" She gazes into the distance. "It's just this case catching up with me. You heard the Fontaine kid's parents got a lawyer? They're talking about suing the city now, which means the DA wants to put a charge on the boy after all. If they would just let it drop, they'd be home free. But you can't expect people to skip a potential payday anymore, even if their kid's slinging."

I could point out my misgivings about the way Fontaine was treated, but that would only get her wound up. And besides, I see her point.

"How's Donna Mayhew holding up?" I ask.

She shrugs. "Doing a lot of media now. You saw her on cable last night?"

"I didn't even know she was on."

"Now she's expressing concerns about the way the case has been handled. I think she's mad they're dragging Hannah's name through the mud. That stuff about the drugs, the restraining order." She slaps her laminated menu shut. "I'd be mad, too—but it's not our fault."

She goes on like this for a while, venting about task force woes. With the media pressure intensifying, more effort at the top seems to be going into damage control than finding Hannah Mayhew. The rumors are getting out of control, too.

"The team's so porous," she says. "Whatever you put into it leaks out by the end of the day."

In the latest gaffe, some bored detectives who'd seen a documentary about forced prostitution started jawing on the topic of white slavery. By that afternoon the news wires were running a story, anonymously sourced, suggesting the task force was looking at this as a probable theory. Blindsided by the question during his cable call-in debut, the chief had responded that "every avenue was being investigated," which had the unintended consequence of validating the rumor.

"So now, in spite of the fact that there's absolutely no evidence, we have half our team suddenly playing catch-up on the white slavery angle. It's ridiculous. I told Wanda I'm sick of playing this game."

"And what did she say?"

"She told me to go to lunch."

I crack a smile. "It sounds to me like you took off sick and ended up watching the news coverage all day."

She nods. "And reading the Hannah blogs."

The Hannah blogs? I don't even want to ask. The life this circus has taken on makes my head spin. "This is the closest I've ever been to a case like this."

"A missing persons case," she asks, "or a media blender?"

"The blender. I worked Missing Persons awhile, remember?"

"The Fauk case," she says. "That was pretty big at the time."

I shake my head. "Not like this."

The waitress, looking clean and wholesome, stuns us both with her high-wattage smile, then jots our selections down with a satisfied nod, like they reveal something deeply good in our respective characters. As soon as she's gone, I roll my eyes, but Cavallo doesn't respond. She's glancing out the window at the lovely view of the parking lot and Highway 249, a lot of concrete washed in searing sunlight.

"What are you thinking?" I ask.

She doesn't answer at first. Her gaze has a soft and sightless quality, as if her eyes were the back of a silvered mirror. When she responds, it's not with words. She digs in her purse and puts her warped copy of

The Kingwood Killing on the table between us. The cover curls upward toward the ceiling. She's not as conscientious with her books as Joe Thomson was.

"I finished," she says.

What does she expect, congratulations? My collar tightens up all the sudden. That book to me is like a crucifix to a vampire. I can't seem to look at it without a cringe.

"You should have told me," she says, her tone pure grief counselor, her eyes piercingly sincere. If my hand was on the table, she'd no doubt give it a compassionate squeeze. "It makes sense now, your obsession with the case. Trying to make all the pieces fit. I'm sorry I wasn't more understanding, March. You should have said something."

I pick up the book, flipping the pages with disdain, then slide it back across the table.

"It must have been so terrible," she says.

"I don't know what you mean."

"You know," she says. "About your girl."

A twitch under the skin of my cheek, an involuntary tic I try smoothing away. She sees it and leans over the table with a pained smile on her lips. I glance away, ignoring her words.

But she won't stop. The woman just won't stop.

"This may sound strange, but now that I know, I feel like I get you. Before, I'll be honest, you always seemed a little cold to me. I knew from Wanda you had a reputation, you used to be an up-and-comer, and I just thought, you know, your whole demeanor, it was bitterness. Angry at life. And that thing you said about God, wanting to kick him . . . now I understand."

You don't understand. You couldn't possibly. You sit there with that book at your elbow and you think that because of those words, you somehow know me, that there's a bond running deeper now between us than anything we could have established through mere contact. You think my soul is in there, my key, the pattern hidden underneath the seeming randomness of my actions. But you know nothing at all. Nothing. And if you would just stop speaking—

"I'll be honest," she says. "It really broke my heart when I realized. Hannah, what she means for you, what they all must mean for you . . ." Her bottom lip swells. "And that girl tied to the bed, the missing body."

I'm going to say something, Theresa, if you don't shut your mouth. You won't like it, the words hitting you like a slap in the face.

"I thought, when they pulled you off, you'd be relieved to get back to Homicide. But now I see what you must be going through—"

My mouth opens, the words lined up like the staggered cartridges in Thomson's magazine, but before I let them off, before I give Cavallo what the drunk in the Paragon parking lot got, my hand snatches the book off the table and flings it, pages fluttering, across the glossy floor. She jumps. The guy in the opposite booth, reading the *Chronicle* in solitude, glances down at the book near his feet, then adjusts the paper so he doesn't have to witness what's developing next door.

Cavallo's eyes flare. "What the—"

"You don't know what you're talking about," I say. "Don't smother me in this cheap psychobabble of yours, telling me what Hannah Mayhew represents for a person like me. Don't even talk about . . ." I can't even form it on my lips, the feminine pronoun. "Don't even. That book," I say, "what's in there," I say, "the whole stinking," I say, "you can't . . . I don't even . . ."

Now her hand reaches for mine, pulls it halfway across the table, and even though she has to know what's at risk, she leans closer.

"I know it's hard," she says.

"You don't know—"

"March, listen to me. You lost your daughter. I get that. But the way you're reacting, it's not right. What it's done to you, it's not right."

"I lost . . . ?" I still can't say it. "Lost isn't the word. Lost is really not what happened. I didn't lose anything. Taken, that's what you should say. 'I know what was taken from you.'"

"And that's why you're angry at the world," she says, stroking my hand. "Angry at God."

"God? I'm not angry at God, Theresa. What does God have to do with anything? I'm angry with the guy who decided to open the Paragon early that day, and I'm angry with all the people who decided to get drunk watching the national tragedy unfold on TV, and I'm really angry—I'm furious—at the woman they let leave there, they let get behind the wheel, and she wasn't even paying attention when she hit them, and there wasn't a scratch on her, Theresa—can you believe that? Nothing but bruises from the air bags. She walked away. I'd kill her now if I could, but—"

"March," she says.

"I'd kill her now, I really would. But she already saved me the trouble. With pills. Now you know what I've always wondered? If she was gonna do that, why'd she have to wait until after, huh? She could have done it the day before and saved us all a lot of trouble. And saved us all. A lot . . ."

"I'm sorry," she says. "I didn't realize how painful this would be for you, or I wouldn't have said a word."

Not good enough, Theresa. You opened this can of worms. "And you think because you read about it in a book—"

"The book has nothing to do with it," she says. "I just didn't know. The book is just how I found out."

"Wanda never told you?"

She shrugs. "It's been six years."

"So what, I shouldn't be so upset about it? I shouldn't be struggling still, or having such a hard time?"

"That's not what I said, March. Don't put words in my mouth."

"And it's seven. Seven years as of next week, remember? The big anniversary."

Cavallo falls silent, gives me a look of pity. My forehead's clammy. The small of my back, too. The people around us are making a point of not paying attention, which is good of them really. Indulgent. I start to wilt a little with embarrassment. Better to say nothing than to pour out all this raw, unedited self-revelation, especially in front of

Cavallo, who doesn't deserve it, and who still has to be convinced to do me an after-hours favor.

"I'm sorry," I say.

"You don't have to apologize."

"I'm sorry. The thing is, it's not something I like to talk about. There's no point dwelling on things. And this time of year . . ." Across the table she's nodding encouragingly, and I know something more is owed to her, some compensating confession. I've told her off, and to make up for that, I have to trust her with some confidence.

"March," she says, "I completely understand."

"The hardest part . . ."

Her eyebrows lift. "Yes?"

"It was Charlotte driving," I say, my voice distant, "and she was injured, too. In the crash. The car, it hit them like this." I form a T with my hands, like a coach calling a time-out from the sidelines. "So the passenger side . . ." My twitch comes back. I can't say more about that. "But Charlotte, her head hit the window hard, and there had to be surgery, you know? I wasn't there. I was still somewhere in Louisiana. They grounded all the planes, you remember, and so me and Wilcox arranged with this detective there, Fontenot, to get a car we could drive back to Houston. We put Fauk in the back in cuffs, then hit the road."

She nods the whole time, the details fresh on her mind from Templeton's account.

"What's not in the book is this . . ."

The doctor had offered to tell her for me, but this was my job, the one I took on without realizing the moment we married, the moment our daughter was born. Charlotte's eyelids fluttered and then opened. She blinked at the gathered onlookers, family and friends from the four corners of Houston, bewildered by their presence. Then the surroundings dawned on her. She glanced anxiously at the tubes running into her arm, at the blinking, hissing machines over each shoulder. Finally, with a hint of panic in her eyes, she noticed me sitting at the foot of the bed. Her intubated arm reached forward.

"Roland?"

I didn't tell the others to leave. I didn't have to. At the sound of her voice they began to file out, all except her sister, Ann, who lingered at the doorway, thinking she might be needed, until Bridger urged her out into the corridor. She disappeared with a suppressed sob.

"What's wrong?" Charlotte asked. "What am I doing in here?"

"You don't remember?"

She bit her lip, eyes darting toward the door. "How long have I been like this?"

"A few hours," I said, checking my watch. "About eight."

"Eight? What happened to me?"

I took a deep breath and tried to start, but lost my grasp of vocabulary. All the words in my head suddenly gone.

"Roland," she says, "am I . . . sick?"

"You were in an accident. You really don't remember?"

Her eyes grew wide. "If I remembered, I wouldn't have to ask. Why did everyone just leave? What's wrong, Roland? It's something terrible, isn't it?"

I nodded my head, unable to do more.

She gazed around the room in frustration, casting back in her mind. Putting the pieces together, I suspected. Working out what must have occurred. Exhaling, her body grew small under the covers, her chin trembling.

"Why wasn't Jessica here? I didn't see her. Where is she?"

"She's . . ." I willed myself to say it, but still nothing came. "She's—"

"Is she all right? Is Jessica all right? Roland, did something happen to her? You have to look at me and tell me. Tell me what happened."

I tried, but couldn't even bring myself to look at her, or even imagine the expression on her face. Begging me, imploring me to do the most terrible thing, to wound her in the deepest way I could. Suddenly, I didn't want to be the one.

"Baby, she's . . ." But no. I couldn't.

"There was an accident." Her voice matter-of-fact. "Was she in it? Was she hurt in the accident?"

I nodded.

Charlotte sucked in her breath, and the tethered hand went to her mouth. I glanced up to see her eyes welling with shock.

"A car came," I said. "The driver ran the light. A drunk driver. She ran into you, into your car." My throat tightened. I began to cough. "She hit . . . She hit the passenger side."

"I was driving?" she asked. "I was behind the wheel? Who was the passenger? Was it Jessica?"

I nodded again.

Her breathing took on a voice, each gasp an unknown word sighed into the air, a glossolalia of grief.

"She's all right, though," Charlotte said. "She's all right." She imbued the pronouncement with a confidence she surely couldn't feel. The intervals between each sentence, each word, punctuated by the strange sibilance of her breathing. She's all right, the words said. No she's not, the breath answered. "Tell me, Roland. Tell me she's all right."

My head shook.

"She's . . . hurt?"

My head shook again.

Charlotte's lip trembled. "She's—?"

"I'm sorry," I said, choking on the syllables.

Her face opened utterly, the eyes wide, the mouth a twisted gash, even the tear ducts began to burst and stream, as if a prophet had struck a rock. The moaning breath came quicker and quicker, hyperventilating, and her arms thrashed at the bedclothes, twisting the plastic tubing against her skin. I moved up the bed, my arms circling, holding her down, squeezing gently.

"I'm sorry. I'm sorry."

"It's my fault," she whispered. "I did it."

"No, it's not your fault."

The door opened and I turned to find Ann there, hands over her mouth. I waved her back and she retreated, letting the wood slam against the doorframe.

Charlotte shrank in my arms, emptied herself out. The sigh from her lips was like a soul departing. Her eyes fluttered again, then closed. She rested her head against the pillow, going slack.

I stood, feeling so drained, so completely flayed open and raw. But it was done. The unthinkable deed. I shrank back, edging alongside the bed, resuming my seat near the footboard. The room grew quiet apart from the occasional beep and hiss of the monitors. I felt my own eyes closing, though there was no relief.

"Roland?" she said.

"I'm here."

I opened my eyes and she was sitting up in bed, examining the tubes in her forearm. She smiled wanly, preternaturally calm, glancing around the room in mild dismay.

"What's wrong?" she said. "What am I doing here?"

"What do you mean?"

She bit her lip. "How long have I been like this?"

"Charlotte, I already told you this. It's been eight hours—"

"Eight?"

"I told you—"

"What happened, Roland? Tell me what happened?"

My fist closed around the blanket. "Are you serious?"

"Am I . . . sick?"

"You were in an accident, remember?"

"An accident?" Her hand went to her mouth again, tugging the tubes taut. "What's wrong, Roland? It's something terrible, isn't it?"

"You don't remember?" I heard myself saying. "You don't remember what I just told you? About Jessica?"

"She's all right, isn't she? Tell me she's all right."

Her hand reached toward me, eyes pleading, the bruises on her cheek glowing with lividity, and I . . . I recoiled, retreated into my chair, glancing to the floor in confusion, the gears of my mind seizing up and grinding.

"She's hurt, isn't she?"

I choked back a sob.

"But she's not—?"

"She is," I said.

Again, the strange breathing, the primal keening grief, as fresh as the first time. Her cheeks flowed with tears, her mouth gaped, and then her arms, so recently still, flailed with renewed violence, slapping the intravenous cable against its pole. I forced myself forward, wrapping her again in my arms.

"It's all right," I told her. "It's okay." Not even listening to what I said, the words running contrary to all reality and sense.

But they calmed her. Just like before, she subsided. The tide of pain went out, leaving her adrift, her head lolling on the pillow. I got up again, weary and disoriented and a little freaked out. The chair was just a few steps away, but I barely reached it before sinking down.

Jessica. Her body was just a few doors down, unless they'd already moved her. I wanted to be with her, to stay at her side, her small cold hand clutched in mine. If I kept holding it, she would have to stay, and the doctor, sensing my state, had offered to tell Charlotte for me, to break the news. He'd volunteered reluctantly, stoically, the way a man steps forward for a thankless task, to do his duty to God and country, and I was tempted. But this was my job, not his, so I had unclasped my hand and let my daughter go.

Now Charlotte's breathing was steady and deep, like she'd gone to sleep. I glanced at the doorway, wishing someone would come through, too tired to get up and open it.

"Roland?"

At the sound of my name, a shiver ran through me.

"What am I doing here?"

She sat up in bed, glancing dreamily at her surroundings, smiling with her chewed lip, the bruises purple and bright, like she thought someone was playing a trick on her. Like she'd been transported to the hospital in her sleep so we could all have a good laugh.

"What's wrong?" she said, the shine leaving her eyes. "It's something terrible, isn't it?"

"You don't remember."

Her hand reached out. "Tell me what happened."

I pushed myself out of the chair, then went to the door.

"Roland?" she called. The note of ignorant alarm, the terrible suspicion alloyed with hope, was the same as before, her memory resetting to the moment she woke up.

"Because of her head injury," I tell Cavallo, "my wife suffered memory loss. Short term. She'd keep forgetting things, and you'd have to tell her all over again. Not who she was or anything like that, but the immediate past. The crash. She'd ask about it. She'd ask about . . . her," I say, finally getting the pronoun out. "And at first I kept telling her, and her reaction every time was pretty much word for word like she was reading from the same script, her head playing the moment over and over again."

Cavallo covers her mouth, peering at me over her fingertips. "That's awful."

"The repetition," I say, "I couldn't keep doing it. So for two days almost, until she finally got her memory back, I kept it to myself. She'd ask what had happened, and I'd lie to her. Our daughter's death, it became my secret. And when she finally did remember, when I knew she wouldn't ask again, God help me I was actually glad. Because I'd never have to tell her again, your daughter is dead. And I hated myself for feeling that."

The bill paid and the story told, I stagger outside, dazed by emotion and blinded by the light, fumbling for the sunglasses I must have forgotten in the car.

On the curb, after a long pause, I ask for the favor I mentioned before. I need help digging some dirt on Tony Salazar.

"If you don't want to help," I tell her, "I'll understand."

"It's not that." She brushes a stray curl from her eyes. "I'm just a little overwhelmed. And to be honest, it makes me uncomfortable not doing things by the book."

"Wanda said you were a little uptight."

"I'm not. But keeping tabs on a fellow cop . . ."

"These guys aren't fellow anything. And listen, I still believe there's some kind of link."

She puts her arm up between us, like she's checking the distance. "You don't have to say that, March. I already told you I'd do it. It's that or waste my time sitting through briefings on white slavery. I'll do what I can."

"In your free time?" I ask, cracking a smile. "Your fiancé won't be too happy about that."

She looks wanly at the engagement ring, its sparkle washed out by the sun. "My fiancé's in Iraq, March. He doesn't care what hours I work."

"I didn't know."

"What can I say?" She starts toward her car, shrugging in profile. "Noboby's written a book about it yet."

I'm still sitting behind the wheel of my own vehicle, soaking up air-conditioning and pondering the turn of events with Cavallo, when my phone starts ringing. Brad Templeton sounds breathless on the other end of the line.

"I don't want to talk to you right now," I say. "Your book is a thorn in my side."

"That's fine. I'm just touching base with all the dirt I dug up on those names you gave me, but if you're not interested—"

"I'm interested. Forgive my uncharacteristic rudeness."

He chuckles. "It wasn't easy, my friend, because you had me looking in the wrong direction with all that Internal Affairs stuff. There's nothing there. But what I did find is a lot juicier. Did you know your friend Keller filed incorporation papers for a private security firm earlier this year?"

"Do tell."

"He's connected, I'll give him that. The corporate officers are a who's who. Looks like he had some backers with deep pockets."

"Had? As in, doesn't have anymore?"

"That's where it gets interesting," he says. "Remember that guy Chad Macneil?"

The name is familiar, but I have to reach back all the way to last week's headlines to make the connection. "The financial planner?"

"The guy who went missing, that's right. Sunning himself on the beaches of South America, or so the story goes."

"What about him?"

"He's on the papers, too. The treasurer."

"You're kidding."

"I'm not. And the crazy thing is, I'm not so sure the investors realize it. I had a chat with one by phone—don't worry, I didn't tip my hand—and he seemed oblivious."

"Are you saying Macneil stole the money out of the corporation?"

He laughs. "It's a private company, March. I don't know how I'd find something like that out. But don't you think it's an intriguing possibility?"

Yes, I do. Thomson reached out with the promise he could name shooters in the Morales case. Morales was, among other things, a money man—Lorenz even floated the ludicrous idea that since there were no drugs in the house, maybe the crew that hit it had come for the money. Now that notion doesn't seem quite so ludicrous anymore. Not if Keller's treasurer, when he absconded, took the company's capital with him.

In fact, a lot of things suddenly start looking like they might connect. Mitch Geiger's rogue crew jacking dealers left and right, showing no respect for the territorial boundaries. The tactical know-how of the shooters at the Morales scene, with Castro's theory about the flanking maneuver outside the bathroom window. It would explain how Thomson could be so certain about naming the bad guys. Maybe he knew them. Maybe he was there. Something like that, it could easily eat away at the conscience of a supposedly reformed man.

"Anything else for me?" I ask.

"That's it. Now, what have you got for me?"

"All in good time, Brad. Just keep digging for now."

After I get him off the phone, I check my messages and find that the elusive Vance Balinski has gotten in touch. He sounds nervous, either because he's not accustomed to leaving voicemail for a homicide detective, or because he knows what's in the box Thomson gave him. According to the message, he's on his way to the Morgan St. Café right now, dropping the package off at the counter. I can pick it up there anytime.

I check my watch. If I drive recklessly, I might just get there before he leaves.

CHAPTER 21

Just inside the door, Vance Balinski crouches on a café chair, head ducked between his knees, attended by a semicircle of alarmed women including the one who'd worked the counter on my last visit. Everyone turns when I call his name, a few even jump. He straightens, casting around blindly for the sound of my voice, eyes clenched tight, a wadded towel pressed to his nose. When he takes it away, the fabric glistens with fresh blood. Blond curls frame his punching bag of a face, perfect as a wig fitted after the fact. One eye opens, the blue cornea bright in a red sea of burst vessels.

"You cops," he says, choking on the words. "Never around when you're needed."

After confirming with the shell-shocked women that the police have been called, I crouch down for a closer look at Balinski's injuries. In addition to the facial trauma, his rib cage has been kicked to shards, so bad that he winces with every labored breath.

"Who did this to you?" I ask.

"Some Mexicans."

"What did they look like?"

He coughs a plug of bile into the towel. "They looked like Mexicans."

"What about the box," I ask, already knowing the answer.

He shakes his head. "That's what they wanted."

Between coughing fits and interruptions from well-intentioned bystanders trying to get him to lie down or drink some water, he manages to communicate the gist of the story. He pulled up outside the Morgan St. Café, popped his trunk to retrieve the box Thomson had given him, then heard footsteps rushing up. Before he could turn, they were already on him, hammering away with their tattooed fists. He flailed defensively, slipping backward into the trunk, only to be pulled out by the ankles. Twisting on the concrete, balled in the fetal position, he endured a flurry of bootheels until a stray steel-capped toe connected with his chin, knocking him out. He awakened in the hot dark confines of his own trunk, using the glow-in-the-dark release lever to get out.

"Funny," he says, showing me what could pass for a child's juice-stained teeth. "I never thought that release lever would actually come in handy."

The Mexicans were gone, and so was the box. He tipped himself onto the pavement and managed to get inside, where his mangled appearance rendered him momentarily unrecognizable in spite of his being a regular.

Losing that box is enough to make me want to kick Balinski, too. Given his injuries, I'm forced to restrain myself in the questioning, keeping the tone civil if not solicitous, but I can't seem to keep the incredulity out of my voice.

"You couldn't just give me the box?" I ask. "What was the point of bringing it back here?"

He studies his bloody towel, looking for a clean patch, then reapplies pressure to his swelling nose. "When Joe first gave it to me, I just stuck it in the trunk and forgot. But then you called, and I got all curious and took a look inside. The moment I did, I panicked. I didn't want anything to do with this."

"So you saw what was in there?"

"Cocaine," he says. "Just like the movies. Plastic bags full of powder, stacked like gold bricks at the bottom of the box." He uses his free hand to sketch the size of the box in the air. "And I'd been driving around with this stuff the whole time, not even realizing."

"The box was full of drugs?"

He nods. "And these blowups. Big pictures, I mean, output from a color printer or something, big tabloid-sized sheets folded over."

"Pictures of what?"

"Some woman. Not the best resolution, but a naked woman kind of laid out on a couch or some kind of seat, with sort of a sheet, some kind of fabric wrapped around her."

"With her eyes closed?" I ask, thinking of the repeated portraits in Thomson's sketchbook. "It was Jill Fanning in the picture, right?"

"Jill?" His red eye blinks. "It wasn't her. The image was jagged, you know? Pixelated. But definitely not Jill. He wouldn't have a naked picture of Jill, anyway."

"They weren't—?"

He dismisses all possibility of an illicit relationship with a wet huff, setting off another coughing fit. Someone hands me a fresh towel. I wait until he regains his equilibrium, then gingerly switch it out.

Then a couple of uniformed officers enter, followed closely by an EMT. I back off, giving them space to do their job, my mind busy making the necessary connections. If what he's saying is right, maybe in losing the box I haven't lost everything. First, using Thomson's studio keys, I retrieve the sketchbook, tucking it under my arm. That done, I get Edgar Castro on the phone, figuring there's no point in swearing somebody else to secrecy when I already have a willing accomplice in the crime lab. I explain about the photo on Thomson's cell phone, asking him to extract it discreetly and make me a couple of prints.

"Should I try and up the resolution?" he asks, his voice trembling with excitement.

A mental image of Castro clicking away in front of a computer screen for the next twenty-four hours, burning time in pursuit of near-invisible photographic enhancements gives me pause. I tell him not to bother with anything fancy. I just want to see the same thing Joe Thomson did.

The dim lighting makes her white skin gray, and all the details punctuating the monochrome bareness are rendered indistinct, a blurred lip, a smudged eye, the vague shadow of an exposed breast. And like a classical nude, some kind of winding cloth envelops her. Not the casual disarray of bedsheets as I'd first assumed, glancing at the photo on the tiny phone screen, but a more deliberate wrapping, a makeshift hammock for quick transport, an improvised shroud.

And although the sketches still resemble Jill Fanning and the photo resembles the sketches, somehow the photo does not resemble the woman herself. For Balinski, who knows her, that much would have been obvious. It takes some back-and-forth scrutiny for me to arrive at the same conclusion.

She is not sleeping, either, as I had supposed. Her eyes are closed, but there's a pallor to the face, a slackness to the expression. Perhaps I'm seeing what isn't there, reading details into the pixels, but I have no doubt the woman in the photo is dead.

Try as I might, I can't match the image to Hannah Mayhew's features. The cheeks are rounder, the skin pale, the hair apparently raven black, though the darkness might be the result of poor lighting.

"What are we looking at here?" Castro asks.

He's been sitting so quietly at my elbow that I'd forgotten his presence. I place the photo facedown on my desk, overtaken suddenly by an impulse of modesty, not wanting her to be exposed to eyes other than my own, to anything but a clinical gaze.

"I think this is the missing victim from the Morales scene, the woman who was strapped to the bed."

"Then what's her picture doing on Detective Thomson's phone?"

I give him a chilly stare. "I assume Thomson took the photo. After they removed her body from the scene."

His lips part, but he doesn't speak. I can hear his breathing, suddenly coming fast and heavy, like he's just finished a sprint. After glancing through the cubicle entrance to make sure no one else is watching, he leans forward, flipping the photo faceup, and traces his finger along a series of vertical lines on the dark background, just over the woman's bare shoulder.

"See that?" he whispers. "You know what I think that is? It looks like a leather car seat, doesn't it? Those stitched seams right there. She was lying in the back seat."

I examine the photo, then nod. He might just be right.

"Only why would they take the body?" he asks.

That's the question. Assuming Keller led the crew and Thomson was there, assuming they'd come for drugs or money, what purpose was served by taking the dead woman with them? If she was dead before they arrived, assaulted and killed by Morales and his entourage, removing her body would make no difference. Same thing if she'd been killed during the shooting, either by Morales or by someone on Keller's team. Only one scenario makes sense to me.

"She must not have been dead when they took her," I say.

"So, what, they were bringing her to the emergency room?" He chews over the possibility, shaking his head. "Then again, maybe she's the reason they were there in the first place. Maybe they were trying to rescue her."

"Maybe," I say, not believing it.

I doubt this photo, grainy as it is, will be enough for a positive identification. The sketches attest to that. Thomson must have been trying to reconstruct the woman's features from memory, using the cell-phone photo as a prompt. Looking at the successive attempts, there's almost a desperation in the pencil strokes, a despairing black frenzy in the haphazard shading. He would have done the series in quick succession, frustrated at his inability to get the face right, perhaps unconsciously substituting the features of Jill Fanning, who might have been at work across the hallway as he drew. An HPD sketch artist might have been capable of doing the job, but of course Thomson couldn't take this to any of his colleagues, not if they'd hustled the woman out of the house after lighting up the other occupants, rushing into the night as she bled out in the back seat.

"She died in the car, that's my guess. He must have taken the picture afterward."

Castro rubs his hands together. "Why?"

All I can do is shrug.

To remember her, maybe. The moment he leaned between the front seats and snapped her photo, he might not have had a clear intention in mind. Acting on impulse, the body sure to be disposed of somehow, the cop inside him insisted on some kind of documentation. And afterward, eating away at him like a slow-working acid, the logical next step: identification. Putting a name to the face, which required getting the face right first, prompting the futile sketches.

When he'd given up on identification, Thomson couldn't let go. The dead woman must have haunted him, because his next move was irreversible, the kind of thing you don't do if there's any other option. He came to me, willing to give evidence against the people who'd been with him in that house, knowing that after that he could never go back.

To get her face out of his mind, he'd risked everything. It worked, I suppose, though not in the way he'd intended. He was dead now, too, his mind blank, erased by a fellow officer's bullet. Either that or, lying in the bowels of eternity, his final sin inexpiable, her image tormented him still.

The seventh anniversary of the September 11 attacks, though solemnly anticipated, lacks the necessary immediacy to eclipse Hannah Mayhew's ongoing plight, especially once the story of the missing girl metastasizes into that of a botched task force investigation. Stoked by rumors of a Fontaine lawsuit and steady leaks from the Sheriff's Department, the story grows more legs than a caterpillar, forcing a series of awkward press conferences in which Mosser and Villanueva stand awkwardly behind a cluster of microphones, fielding increasingly strident accusations from both the local and national press.

If not for Charlotte, I would remain blissfully ignorant of these developments. While I quietly labor away on the Thomson case, hoping the lack of closure will be taken by my colleagues as a sign that I'm overly thorough or perhaps a bit rusty, she spends each night in front of the television, switching from the local broadcasts over to cable, then back to the local stations when they wrap up for the evening. On the rare occasions I'm home, nothing I do can wean her off the remote control.

"There's hardly anything about it," she says, meaning the anniversary. "It's like they've all forgotten and don't want to be reminded."

"It's Hannah Mayhew's fault."

She frowns. "Don't blame her."

We sit together in silence, bathed in the screen's flickering blue light, not speaking of the anniversary's private significance because we almost never do. Not that we've forgotten. Our omission signals many things, but not that.

On the day itself, we will keep our annual vigil, returning together to the graveside, leaving behind fresh flowers and tears and knee prints in the soft grass. Our grief will feel especially acute because it will be ours alone, unobserved by a world whose attention will be rightly fixed on commemorating the day's larger tragedy. The Pearl Harbor of our generation will swallow up all the rest, including the random passing of a ten-year-old Houston girl, killed instantly when a drunk driver T-boned her mother's car.

"Dying that day," Charlotte once said, when the event was still fresh enough to talk about, "it's like being born on Christmas, isn't it?"

Meaning people have bigger things on their minds. There's only so much room in the ledger, and some entries require it all, leaving no space for smaller tragedies, even as footnotes.

Tonight something has changed, though. As Charlotte flips through the channels, instead of Hannah, everyone's talking about the latest hurricane brewing out in the Gulf, picking up speed as it approaches.

Since Katrina, every swirl of clouds on the Doppler screen merits reverent attention, and the weathercasters speak almost hopefully about the potential for a Category 5 landfall, putting the New Orleans debacle to shame.

"It'll fizzle out like all the others," Charlotte says.

"Maybe."

Deep down, I find myself rooting for the storm, or at least for the breathing space it will afford people like Wanda Mosser and Theresa Cavallo. Fewer press conferences would mean more time for investigation, not that I hold out hope that any amount of extra effort will produce Hannah Mayhew, safe and sound or otherwise.

To my surprise, Cavallo's pledge to devote her free time to spadework on Salazar pays quick dividends. He rents a thirty-foot slip at the Kemah Boardwalk Marina, housing an old but well-maintained cabin cruiser, a more substantial and significantly pricier boat than I'd imagined. A call to the marina confirms the whole place is monitored by video cameras. After explaining who I am to the head of security, who has his hands full preparing for the impending hurricane, I get an open-ended invitation to review the footage.

"You have Labor Day weekend on tape?"

"I'll spool it up for you," he says. "But do me a favor and leave it till next week, huh? We've got our hands full at the moment."

"I wish I could oblige, but . . . How about tonight?"

He pauses long enough for me to consider the various ways he could make my life difficult, like demanding a warrant or hitting the delete key to save himself the inconvenience. But some people will bend over backward to cooperate with the police, and he happens to be one of them. We agree on a time and I drive down to Kemah full of hope, imagining a video image of Keller and Salazar hoisting a shrouded corpse aboard the boat.

The fantasy is dashed the moment the security chief, a gray-haired man in white shorts and a potbellied polo shirt, cues up the appropriate footage. Like the surveillance tape from the Willowbrook Mall parking lot, like Joe Thomson's cell-phone snap, the image is grainy and indistinct.

"Is there a particular slip you're interested in?" he asks, stroking his chin.

"I'll know it when I see it."

He's disappointed, but in spite of the man's willingness to help, I don't want to single out Salazar's boat. There's always the chance they know each other, and the last thing I want to do is put my suspect any more on guard than he already is.

We buzz through the footage, which is displayed in split screens on a computer monitor, starting midday on Thursday even though the shooting off West Bellfort didn't go down until later. Approaching ten, the chief pauses.

"The marina lights go off at ten," he says, and sure enough the screens go black.

After that, the only usable footage is of the well-lit parking lot. We fast-forward through a whole lot of nothing, and then he stops just after three in the morning, running the tape back a bit.

"Look at that."

A black extended-cab pickup rolls into the parking lot, the truck bed enclosed by an aftermarket hardtop, turning into an empty space. Two figures get out, moving around to the tailgate. They're too far from the camera to identify, but I'm certain the truck is Salazar's, and there's nothing about the figures to suggest they aren't Keller and Salazar.

"What're they doing?" he asks.

I lean closer to the screen. They reach into the bed, sliding out a long white form. I don't say anything to the security chief, but it looks like a body bag to me. Between them, the two men heft the bag, carrying it off-screen in the direction of the marina. They return hours later, just before daybreak, and drive away, no sign of the body bag they'd been carrying before.

After burning the relevant footage onto a DVD, he hands it over wide-eyed, under no illusions about what he's just witnessed.

"If you talk about this," I tell him, "you'll be jeopardizing an ongoing investigation."

He promises not to, punctuating the words with a dazzled gulp.

The temptation to board Salazar's boat is strong, but for that I really will need a warrant, otherwise anything I find will be inadmissible. Still, I gaze out over the marina awhile, the bobbing boats illuminated by strong stadium lights, thinking about how easily I could slip through for a little preview, just to make sure the search warrant is worth the effort. The only thing stopping me is my conscience. That and the thought of the security cameras overhead.

"Seven years," the captain says, shaking his head at the muted television on the credenza, where a platform of politicians take turns reading memorial speeches before a gathered crowd and the ubiquitous media. The ticker crawling across the bottom of the screen recaps a National Weather Service warning that Galveston, just south of us, is where the hurricane will make landfall, whipping up a catastrophic storm surge.

He turns his chair to face me, momentarily uncertain why I'm here. Then he remembers.

"About Thomson's body," he says. "You haven't released it yet."

"No."

"Any particular reason? The man's wife wants to bury him. It's hard enough on everyone, a brother officer going out like that. No need to prolong the suffering, March."

"Maybe there is," I say.

I take a deep breath, then lay it all out. I start with Chad Macneil, who disappeared, presumably with Keller's money, and then Mitch Geiger's rumor about the string of drug heists, perhaps an attempt to make up the loss. He listens impassively with an occasional lizard-like blink of the eyes. When I mention Thomson's offer and how I took it to Wilcox for help, he raises an eyebrow, nothing more.

The ballistics business, Castro's theory about the tactics at the Morales scene and later the switched barrels, gets no reaction, but at least he doesn't interrupt. I explain the photo on Thomson's phone and end with the footage of Keller and Salazar—I make the identification sound a little more solid than it is—carrying a body bag out to the boat.

"So they dumped this woman's body out in the Gulf?" he asks. "And then they shot Thomson to keep him from rolling over?"

"I think so. Yes."

"And you're just bringing this to me now?"

I answer with an apologetic shrug.

"You wouldn't have said a thing if I hadn't asked about releasing the body."

"I wanted to be sure first," I say.

"Because you were afraid I'd take you off the case?"

I nod.

"Well," he says, leaning forward, "you were right. That's exactly what I'm going to do—"

"But, sir."

He consults the calendar on his desk blotter. "As of . . . let's say next Thursday, the eighteenth. On that date you will conclude your investigation, release the body, and move on. Unless of course something more concrete develops, in which case . . ." His voice trails off and he turns back to the television, dismissing me by unmuting the volume just as a stern-faced woman in red says why we must never, will never, forget, to a ripple of sober applause.

I stumble outside his office with another week on the clock, though it is much more than that, I start to realize. Hedges knows, he knows and approves, willing to give me enough time to develop something solid, assuming I work quickly. There's an understanding between us now, a faint flicker of the dimly remembered bond. Something akin to trust.

There's no time to consider the ramifications, though, because Charlotte is waiting.

I clock out early and head home, pausing at the curb with the engine running until she comes out, unsteady on her heels, fixing an earring in place. She wears a black linen skirt and a black cardigan, her hair pulled back in an elegant chignon, as if it's a dinner date we're headed to and not a graveside.

Stopping on the steps, she remembers suddenly, ducking inside again and reappearing with the plastic-wrapped flowers. I go around to the passenger door, opening it for her, snapping it shut once she's safely inside. Circling back, I get behind the wheel. Next to me, the flowers on the floor mat rising up between her knees, my wife covers her face in her hands and sobs.

"It's all right," I say, flattening a hand on her back, feeling the gaps between the vertebrae.

She motions for me to drive.

So I drive.

At the headstone of our daughter, kneeling down with our hands clasped, we unwrap the flowers and lay them down, and then we water them with tears. On this day seven years ago, something was taken from us all. What we lost, in the overall scheme, may pale in comparison. But to Charlotte and me, it was everything. She was everything. And on the days, the infrequent days, when my heart clings to a belief in the afterlife, she is the reason, the fragile thought that the small, cold hand I let go of once will be warm once more, warm and with the power not only to be clung to but to cling. What faith I have, and it isn't much, resides in the grip of that tiny hand.

CHAPTER 22

After Hurricane Rita, the sequel to Katrina, left the neighborhood without power and thus without air-conditioning, I stopped talking about getting a generator and actually bought one, storing it in the garage along with some sticky, dust-covered jerry cans of gasoline and gallons of drinking water. Now, instructions in hand, I try to work out how to operate the thing. Never much good with engines or anything mechanical, the challenge soon stumps me, but not enough to summon Tommy down to assist. His repertoire of life skills, augmented by the time he spent in Africa, no doubt includes the function of generators. But I'd better wait at least until Charlotte is gone.

Along with Ann, she plans to weather the storm in style at a Dallas hotel, returning once everything's back to normal. Her overnight bag is packed, waiting by the front door for her sister's arrival. She finds me in the garage, frowning at the inscrutable little machine.

"I feel like I'm abandoning you," she says.

"Don't. I'll be happier knowing you're all right. Besides, if I don't figure this thing out, it'll be like an oven inside. You don't want to go through that again."

She takes the instructions out of my grease-stained fingers and attempts for a few minutes to make sense of them. Just as she grasps the basic idea and starts explaining, Ann's Toyota hums quietly up the driveway, a Prius hybrid just like the ones we pretended to be giving away in the cars-for-criminals scam.

"Gotta go," Charlotte says, pecking me on the lips.

Since the grave visit, she's been more relaxed. All the static building in her atmosphere suddenly discharged in a flow of quiet tears, and now it's like the tension never existed. We haven't had an argument in twenty-four hours. Last night, she stayed up with me instead of going to bed early. Even the sleeping pills have disappeared into the nightstand.

"Be safe," I call after her.

"You, too."

The silence following her departure lasts a half minute before Tommy creaks down the side stairs, poking his head through the open garage door. Seeing the coast is clear, he bounds forward with a look of relief.

"Hey, it's supposed to make landfall sometime tonight," he says. "Got any big plans?"

"I've got to work." The instructions hang limp in my hand. "You don't happen to know how to run one of these things, do you?"

He hunches over the generator, a gleam in his eye. "Not exactly. But, hey, we can figure it out, right?"

"You figure it out. I'll be out to check on you in a minute."

I leave him to it, going back inside to change. The house in Charlotte's absence takes on a still, empty air, so I shower and dress quickly, wanting to get back to the case quickly. Hedges gave me a week, which isn't much to begin with, but if the hurricane proves as disastrous as they're saying on the news, with massive flooding and power outages, then my week could contract into a day. So I'd better make the most of it.

Before heading downstairs, I glance inside Charlotte's nightstand to see whether she's taken the pills with her. The bottle rolls against the front of the drawer. I shut it, my idiot grin reflected back from the dresser mirror.

When the phone rings, I answer without checking the caller ID, expecting Charlotte since the image of her in my mind shines so vividly. The voice is male, though, and after a second I recognize it. The youth pastor, Carter Robb, who I haven't seen since my late-night visit to his apartment, when I commissioned him with the task of finding the Dyers.

"I just thought I should touch base," he says. "I managed to get a number from somebody at the church, but it doesn't seem to work anymore. I do have that picture for you, though."

"Picture?"

"Of Hannah and Evey Dyer."

I clear my throat before speaking. "Mr. Robb, I've been reassigned. I'm not working with the task force anymore."

"Oh."

"Have you tried calling Detective Cavallo?"

He sighs. "I have, actually. Donna asked me to, trying to get an update. She feels like, with some of the things she said on the news, there might be some bad feelings. I've left Detective Cavallo a couple of messages, but I was hoping—"

"She's got her hands full," I say. "But I'm sure she'll get back to you as soon as she can. And that's nonsense about bad feelings. The lady's daughter is missing. She can say whatever she wants." I want to get rid of this guy, but I feel like I owe him more than a casual brush-off. "Look, what's the best way to get in touch with you? I can make a couple of calls and let you know what I find out."

"That would be great," he says, giving me his mobile number as well as the number of what he calls a community outreach center. "It's one of the places the youth group did some volunteering. A friend of mine from seminary runs it, and with the storm coming he needs some help down there getting everything secure. I'm planning to spend the night."

"Where is this place?" I ask.

He gives an address in Montrose, just a few blocks away from the Morgan St. Café. I ask if he's ever been to the café before, but he's never even heard of it. It's a small world, but not that small.

"If I find out anything, I'll give you a call."

"Even if you don't," he says. "I'd appreciate hearing something, even if it's nothing."

When I return to the garage, the generator is already running while Tommy stares long and hard at the electrical box, trying to figure out exactly how to achieve a link-up. Maybe he'll electrocute himself, I think, which would solve my tenant problem. Then again, he might burn the house down, which is more solution than I'm really looking for.

"Everything all right?"

"Leave it with me," he says. "I'll have it going in no time."

I study him a moment, trying to decide if what I'm seeing is confidence or foolhardiness.

"Fine." I throw my briefcase in the car and start the engine, rolling the window down to impart some final advice. "Tommy, don't burn the house down."

"Not a chance."

"And don't electrocute yourself, either."

Gene Fontenot answers my call in mid-apology, like he started even before pushing the talk button. "I been meaning to call you, man, really I have. It's right here on my list of things to do." He thumps his finger on what must be the list. "You gotta forgive me for not being quicker on this, but what can I say? We get a little busy around here. You know how it goes—"

"Gene," I say, cutting him off. "It's fine. I've been pretty busy myself. But have you managed to track down this Dyer woman and her daughter?"

"About that . . ." He rustles some papers around. "Here we go. The answer to your question is yes and no. Yes, I found the lady. She got a place over in Kenner, out by the airport. That's the good news.

The bad news is, the daughter Evangeline, she don't stay there no more. The mother says, once they moved back, the girl, she fell into her old ways. They had a lotta problems, and eventually the girl run away with some boy."

"She ran away? When was this?"

More rustling, accompanied by some humming. "That woulda been in July sometime?" He turns the sentence up at the end, uncertain. " 'Bout eight weeks or so ago?"

He gives me the mother's address and phone number, which I copy into my notebook.

"Thanks, Gene. I owe you one."

"Take care of yourself with this storm coming in," he says. "I don't want you turning up on my doorstep, looking for shelter."

"This is Texas, Gene. We don't run."

He chuckles. "Keep telling yourself that."

Once I get him off the phone, I give Cavallo a call. She's surprised to hear that Robb has been leaving messages for her, confessing she's been too busy to empty her inbox. The weary edge in her voice is enough to convince me. I'm almost reluctant to ask about new developments on the Hannah Mayhew case, but I ask anyway, and she replies with a derisive laugh.

"We were planning a big press conference today, announcing a new reward for any information, but now they're arguing about whether to reschedule for after the hurricane blows through. People are 'distracted,' apparently."

"What about the actual casework? Anything there?"

"Let me put it this way. All the tips we've gotten? We're getting down to the bottom. Everything's been followed up. We've interviewed over a hundred drivers of white vans like the one in the surveillance footage, even done physical searches of quite a few, and I don't think we're any closer to finding Hannah than we were on day one."

I pass along the news from Gene Fontenot, which seems to irritate her. She makes me repeat everything, then asks for his number so she can call to confirm.

"Don't worry about Robb," I tell her. "I'll call him back."

"I appreciate that," she says, her tone communicating the exact opposite. Not that I can hold it against her. She's on a dead-end assignment, one of those cases destined to be rehashed for years to come on the unsolved-mystery shows, a future footnote for journalists writing about how media coverage negatively impacts major cases. Cavallo has a right to be difficult.

Before calling the youth pastor, I put in an hour at the typewriter before hunting down Wilcox, who's kept clear of me since his early morning visit to my home. No cubicles for the men and women of Internal Affairs. He has a tiny glass box all to himself, with his name on a plate beside the door. I tap lightly before entering and find him busy typing away, a pair of earphones sealing him off from the outside world. To get his attention, I have to lean across the desk and yank one out.

"What do you want?"

He's dressed in a glossy blue shirt, his tie knot thick as his throat, with his chalk-striped jacket thrown over the back of his chair. Up close, he even smells nice.

"What I want is a favor, Stephen."

"Your case is dead, in case you forgot."

I sit down on the edge of his desk. "The informant may be, but the case sure isn't."

The marina surveillance footage warms him up a little, then I slide the sketchbook and the enlarged cell-phone picture across the desk for his inspection. Wilcox is a sharp enough detective not to need everything explained. He flips through the sketchbook, his expression growing thoughtful.

"There's something I didn't tell you," he says. "The finance guy who skipped to Mexico, Chad Macneil? Guess whose money he took with him."

"Keller's. I already know."

His mouth curls down. "Then you probably also know that Keller's security company rents warehouse space about a block away from where Thomson's body was found."

I blink. "What?"

Satisfied with my reaction, he fishes a file out of his desk, paging through it until he reaches a stack of satellite images courtesy of Google Earth with the street grid superimposed. From the air, the long gray rectangles look nearly identical, set apart only by the placement of HVAC units and natural variations in the color of roofing gravel. One of them is outlined in yellow highlighter.

"That's the warehouse Keller rents."

"What does a security company need warehouse space for?"

"Search me," he says, trailing his finger across the image. "This road along here, that's where Thomson's truck was parked, isn't it?"

I lean down for a closer look. "That looks to be the spot. There's a neighborhood across the street, through these trees, and I figured if there was any geographical connection, it would be to the houses."

"Instead, it's the warehouse. All of these are owned and managed by the same outfit."

The layout comes back to me, a complex of gray corrugated buildings hemmed in by fields of concrete and a tall chain-link fence. "There's a security guard there, a guy by the name of Wendell Cropper. Kind of a strange character, used to be with the department back in the nineties. You know anything about him?"

He shakes his head. "Maybe he saw more than he let on, that's what you're thinking?"

"How likely is it, if Keller's using the facility, that this guy isn't connected with him somehow? It might be worth bringing him in and sweating him a little more. In the meantime, you ever think about getting a warrant for this warehouse?"

"On what grounds? I'd need to show some probable cause. Besides, the feeling on our team is that something like that would only tip our hand. We'd be taking a big risk. If there's nothing in that warehouse that shouldn't be there, Keller would know we're after him and cover his tracks."

"Maybe," I say. "But a warrant is what I'm here for."

"Not for the warehouse—?"

I shake my head. "The boat. If that really was a body they dumped, then maybe there's some trace evidence onboard. Now, if I go through the usual channels, there's no way they won't know what's going on. But you guys, on the other hand, have back doors into the judges' chambers."

"You should have come to me sooner," he says with a laugh. "Trying to find a judge in chambers today is going to be a challenge. They've got mansions to board up and yachts to tie down."

"Maybe we'll find one down at the marina."

His smile fades. "It'll have to wait."

"If we don't get in there before the hurricane hits, we could lose the opportunity. They're talking about Galveston being underwater, Stephen, so I doubt the Kemah Boardwalk is going to be in good shape. I can't have my smoking gun sinking to the bottom of the sea."

"The slips can't be that deep," he says.

"Come on. I know there are strings you can pull. What's the point of having a man inside IAD if he doesn't throw his weight around from time to time?"

After a little token resistance, he gives way. "Fine, March. Whatever you want. But you're writing it up, not me."

I slide the warrant across his desk, typed before my visit. He takes it with a rueful smile, glances over the cover page, then reaches for the phone.

Thanks to the floating docks, the boats in the marina rise and fall as the water does, the waves choppy harbingers of the coming storm, as is the cloudy gunmetal sky. The late afternoon wind is electric, thick with humidity, smelling of salt. Wilcox is with me, along with a couple of handpicked officers from Internal Affairs. We check in with the security chief, who's wearing the same shorts and shirt I remember from before, with a little more stubble around the jowls. He guides us through the network of slips, checking his clipboard from time to time as though he's forgotten which boat we're heading for.

"A homeless shelter would probably be of more use these days, but what can I say?" He shrugs in an outsized, eloquent way. "This is the vision God gave me. 'If you build it, they will come.' "

"Do they?"

He seesaws his hand in the air. "We host some book clubs that are pretty popular."

"There's a lot of that going around," I say, remembering the women gathered at the Morgan St. Café. I pat Robb on the bicep and turn to go.

"Oh, wait," he says, digging in his back pocket. He removes his wallet, shuffles through a wad of folded receipts, and finally produces a folded photograph. "Here you go."

I hold the picture up to the light. Hannah, radiant in the camera's flash, smiles invitingly, her hand thrown lazily around the shoulder of another girl, her face half concealed behind a lump of matte black hair, a bad dye job maybe, her one visible eye rimmed thickly in dark liner. Evey Dyer raises two fingers to the lens, her nails painted black. Whoever snapped the photo probably assumed this was a peace sign, but from my Anglophile ex-partner, I know the gesture she's flashing is rude.

"Thanks," I tell him, tucking the picture away. "So you took your youth group to this place for their summer trip?"

Robb nods. "We helped fix the place up, went out in the community to get the word out, hosted a couple of get-acquainted parties."

"And it was much appreciated," the other man says. "I'm Murray Abernathy, by the way." His handshake has a lot of power behind it. "Resident dreamer."

The three of us stand there in the quickening wind, my jacket whipping around my hips. The sky rumbles overhead, prompting us all to look up momentarily.

"You met Hannah Mayhew, Mr. Abernathy? And her friend Evangeline Dyer?"

"Hard to miss those two," he says, still gazing overhead. "They really helped out a lot here. It's a terrible thing, what's happened to Hannah. We're praying she gets home safe."

The *Rosalita* is tucked between two newer, larger vessels, its hull pearlescent and dingy from the passage of time. We descend from the pier to the cruiser's stern, feeling the roll underfoot, then advance beneath the open-backed enclosure that shelters the wheel. In spite of his portly form, the security chief moves in easy strides. The rest of us, already gloved, reach for the nearest handholds to keep our balance.

"If you think this is bad," he says, "just you wait."

The cabin door is securely locked, but we've brought along an officer who specializes in surreptitious entry. After a couple of minutes crouched at the door, he announces victory, stepping aside to let Wilcox pass. My ex-partner pauses, motioning me forward.

"Ladies first," he says.

A narrow row of steps leads into the cramped cabin, which reminds me more of a fiberglass bathtub insert than the opulently appointed, wood-paneled abode I was imagining. There's a tight banquette molded into one side, complete with folding table, and a set of storage cubbies on the other, lit only by a row of narrow dirty windows that pierce the hull. I fumble along the wall for a light switch, but if there is one, I don't find it.

"I hope nobody's claustrophobic," I say.

The cabin smells damp and a little fishy, but the surfaces gleam cleanly in the dimness. At the far end, behind a tiny door, I find a cleverly compartmentalized shower and toilet small enough to make an airplane restroom seem vast in comparison. The others file in, and somebody finds the lights. Fully illuminated, the cabin reminds me a bit of a camper my uncle used to keep in the driveway when I was a kid. The idea of it seemed cool, but whenever I went inside, I couldn't wait to get out again.

We search slowly, methodically, using flashlights to illuminate every crack and crevice, causing as little disturbance as possible. It doesn't take long, because there's so little ground to cover. A minute or two into the hunt, I begin to lose hope. There won't be anything here. They brought the body—assuming it was a body—already bagged. Salazar's truck, assuming that's where she bled out, might yield a treasure trove of blood evidence, but by the time they reached the boat, the body would have been squared away. At best, this search might allow me to cross another possibility off the list, but there's nothing—

"Sir."

One of the IAD officers kneels at the foot of the built-in cabinets, his arm shoulder-deep inside, cheek flat against the frame. He squints in concentration, then jerks back, pulling something loose with a ripping sound. His hand reappears, clutching a bundle wrapped in layers of thick plastic sheeting, secured by strips of duct tape.

Wilcox takes the package to the folding table, carefully unwinding the plastic. He stops halfway through, once the object's form becomes obvious. I move in, uncoiling the rest of the sheet, removing the final layer aware that no one in the cabin is so much as breathing.

The boat rocks. We sway a little. Our eyes remain fixed on the table. Under the pile of plastic, resting unevenly, lies a blued SIG Sauer P229. On the exposed side of the chamber, visible through the cutout of the ejection port, the barrel is stamped BAR STO .357 SIG.

"Is that what I think it is?" Wilcox asks.

Nobody answers. Nobody even breathes.

Driving home late that evening, I remember Carter Robb. Instead of calling, I flip through my notebook for the address he gave me, stopping by on the way. I find him with a group of other men, all stripped to the waist, nailing plywood sheets across the windows of a two-story brick building that could pass for the scrawny cousin of the one housing the Morgan St. Café. The ground floor is done, and now they've mounted ladders to reach the second, the work illuminated by shop lights in the yard, since the streetlamps are too far away. The boom box is tuned to KTRU, only audible during lulls in the hammering.

I call up to Robb, who shimmies down the ladder and snatches a black T-shirt from a pile on the ground, using it to wipe the sweat from his face.

"I thought you forgot about me," he says.

"I did."

There must be a residual glow on my face, left over from the covery at the marina, because Robb perks up all the sudden.

"Something's happened?"

"Not with Hannah, no. I just happened to be in the neighbor hood so I stopped by. The truth is, the task force is waiting for developments."

He nods slowly. "So we're back where we started."

"There is one thing. I talked to a friend in New Orleans and him track down the Dyer family. According to the mother, Evange Dyer ran away from home again. I know you said she'd done it bef She left eight weeks ago. I haven't spoken to the mother myself, h have her contact information, assuming you'd want it."

"I should call her," he says.

I copy the information onto a blank sheet of my notebook, rip the page out and handing it to him. He studies the writing, tho his eyes don't seem to focus on the numbers. More like he's loo through the page, or seeing something reflected on it.

"I should call her," he says again.

Over his shoulder, the other workers have knocked off for moment, keeping their distance but clearly interested in our conv tion. I glance their way, prompting Robb to turn as if noticing t for the first time. He waves a hand toward the building.

"This is the outreach center."

"And what is that, exactly?"

He cocks his head to one side, smiling faintly. "The idea provide an encounter space. People from the church, people from surrounding community, all coming together to talk. Not just a religion, but life. Everything under the sun."

"I thought it was more of a homeless shelter."

One of the others, a friendly, broad-chested man of about th five, with sunken eyes and a wooden cross around his neck, s forward to join us, chuckling at what I've just said.

"Evey ran away," Robb says under his breath, causing the other man to deflate.

As I turn to go, the first fat drops of rain start to fall. One breaks cool against my neck. Robb knits his eyebrows as another splashes the bridge of his nose. Within seconds the clouds open and the rain drills down on us. Everyone in the yard moves closer to the building, sheltering under the eaves.

Everyone but me.

I reach my car door, glancing back in time to see Robb, his hair plastered against his scalp, ascending the ladder again, rain-battered, his face pointing heavenward.

CHAPTER 23

The dream ends with a crash. I sit up, peeling the damp sheets off my skin, unable to remember a thing. On the nightstand, the glowing numbers on the clock face have disappeared. The fan overhead whirs to a stop. Uncertain whether the collision happened in real life or my head, I move to the window, peering through the rain-washed pane. It's black outside, some shadows darker than others. The sky's accustomed glow—an effect produced by light reflected on the clouds, producing a faint nightlong radiance—is extinguished.

Wind whistles past the house, slapping branches against the walls. I see nothing, and I'm too dog-tired to go out and look. I lie back down on top of the sheets, cocooned in a womb of white noise, and try to get some sleep. My mind races with the last images I saw on television before hitting the sack, newscasters down in Galveston knocked flat on their backsides and skyscrapers downtown popping their windows left and right.

A steady banging starts up not long after. At first I ignore it, but as my head clears and I awaken fully, the sound takes on a panicked intensity. Feeling around in the dark, I grab my flashlight, a tiny Fenix that puts my old Maglite to shame, and head down the stairs. The pounding comes from the kitchen door. As soon as I open it, Tommy pushes through, half-dressed and a little crazy, rivers of water sluicing off him.

"Hey, man," he says, breathless. "You're not gonna believe your eyes, I'm telling you. It's, like, unreal up there."

The door swings wide, propelled by the wind, slamming against a breakfast table chair. I shoulder it closed, then turn to check on him, running the light up and down his chest. His jeans, soaked through, puddle around his bare feet, the cuffs ragged.

"You all right?"

"Nothing hit me, I don't think. But you gotta go look, man. It's like TV."

His mouth twists into a maniacal grin, like he's just bungee-jumped for the first time and is ready to go again. I shine the light along his head, making sure it's water plastering his hair down and not blood and brain tissue.

"What happened to you?"

"You gotta come see," he says, starting for the door. He stops, finger lifted, remembering something. "Oh, yeah. Hey, do you have any plastic bags—you know, like trash bags or something? I need to cover some stuff so it doesn't get any wetter than it already is. I don't know, maybe we should try to carry some things down."

"What are you talking about?" I ask, not waiting for a reply. I bolt through the door, lighting a path up the garage stairs. Everything looks normal to me. He follows me up, panting with excitement. I pass through the door and into the living room, noting nothing.

He leads the way into the bedroom. "In here."

The moment I cross the threshold, my breath catches. My face is a foot away from a shimmering oak branch. Gazing upward, I see the jagged hole in the roof, another thick branch halfway in, and a torrent of rainwater blasting through the opening. A wad of shingles lies on top of Tommy's bed.

At first, I can't say anything. We look at each other, and his manic thrill jumps the divide, setting off a tingle along my spine.

"Cool, huh?" he says.

"You were in bed when this happened?"

His head shakes. "I heard this loud crack—must have been the trunk snapping or something—and my body just took over. I reached the door right when it hit."

I run the light over him again, hardly believing he came through this unscathed, but there's not a scratch on him. He starts jogging in place, like he's cold, or maybe brimming with nervous energy.

"Let's move what we can move," I say, "then you can spend the rest of the night in the house."

"Maybe I'll sack out on the couch. I kind of don't want to leave."

"You're leaving," I say. "Don't even think about staying up here."

We leave the furniture in place—the bed and dresser—just taking the drawers out. Everything from the closet ends up on the living room couch. When we're finished, I go outside for a look at the damage. The tree came from next door, smashing the far side of the garage, which is why I couldn't see anything from my bedroom window.

Seeing a tree like that upended, a hundred years thick, its earth-clotted roots naked to the rain, at first I can't take my eyes off it. It didn't break so much as it was uprooted, leaving a muddy crater rimmed with St. Augustine grass, super green in the Fenix light, as if the storm brought all its chlorophyll to the surface, the way grass might look if it could blush.

Through the roots and down the length of the trunk the whole tree seems intact. Severed power lines crisscross the horizontal canopy as if, once it began to teeter, the tree reached out and tried to steady itself, grabbing hold of the fragile cables, bringing them down with it. I've seen branches break off in high wind and even trunks split by lightning, but never anything like this. One of the lines lies dormant in the neighbor's yard. Another snakes across the garage roof. I'm happy all the sudden that the power's out.

To be on the safe side, I back the cars out of the garage and move the essentials—our rarely used bicycles, the generator, the fuel and water, my tools—onto the back deck. With the weight of that oak still resting on the roof, there's no point in taking chances. Back inside, I throw some sheets on one of the couches, but Tommy's too wired for sleep. He darts through the house, front windows to back, like he's rooting for more damage and doesn't want to miss anything.

Giving up on sleep, I rummage through the fridge, which already feels lukewarm. We'll need to get the generator started pretty soon. But for now I grab a bottle of still-cool water and imagine the phone call I'll have to make later today.

The bad news, Charlotte, is that your garage has a new skylight. The good news is, your tenant's going to need a new place to live.

In her mind, it'll seem like a fair trade.

Just after daybreak, the empty water bottle still resting on my chest, I hear Tommy above me and open my eyes. I installed myself in a chair, not meaning to nod off. He hunches over, speaking in a whisper.

"Hey, Mr. March. The cops are outside."

"The cops?"

"There's one coming up to the door, and another one in the car."

He's talking like we might be in trouble with the law, like maybe it's time to bolt out the back. I pry myself out of the chair, the bottle dropping to the floor. I peer through the front window, then open the door. Sergeant Nix is shaking off his rain poncho on the porch. He looks up, smiling awkwardly.

"How 'bout you get yourself dressed and take a little ride with me?" he says.

"What's the deal?"

He glances back to the patrol cruiser on the curb. "I'm bending the rules as it is, but I figure I owe you after the other day." His eyes drop to the bandage half-exposed by my shorts.

"Yes, you do," I say, patting his arm. "Give me five minutes."

My mind racing with possibilities, I head up the stairs, ignoring Tommy's whispered questions. I pull on a pair of cargo pants, a black T-shirt, and a lightweight raincoat to keep my gear dry, then I'm out the front door, trailing Nix, who opens the back of the cruiser for me, ushering me in with an ironic bow.

"This is Webb." He motions to the uniform behind the wheel.

Webb takes us down Durham, across Interstate 10 and the Allen Parkway, until it becomes Shepherd. Though the storm has passed, the wind gusts remain strong enough to lift the wiper blades off the glass. Condensation spider-webs the edge of the windows. We turn on West Gray, passing between the two Starbucks locations that sit like Scylla and Charybdis on either side of the street. Onto Montrose, heading back to the neighborhood where I left Carter Robb, near Joe Thomson's Morgan Street studio.

Nix gives verbal directions at every intersection, but Webb anticipates most commands, leading me to suspect that we're returning to someplace they've just come from.

We drive the rain-slick streets, avoiding side turns where water's risen higher than the road, and the power lines snapped free and coiled through severed branches. As the sun rises, we see a few people emerging from shelter for their first look at what the hurricane has done.

"Are you going to tell me where we're going?" I ask.

Nix shakes his head. "I'm gonna show you."

Ahead, a side road is blocked off by a parked HPD cruiser. Nix tells Webb to turn and then to pull to the curb. Soon he's out the door, advancing toward some debris strewn across the road, motioning for me to follow. A derelict building off to the right has come apart under the pressure of wind, giving up the scraps of plywood that have long sealed its windows and doors. Out of them poured the structure's long-abandoned contents, mainly soaked boxes and broken-down furniture, a refrigerator door, a lidless cooler with rusty stains inside.

I know these blocks pretty well, and no doubt I've passed this building a thousand times before, never taking any particular notice. On the opposite corner, a sleek modern three-level house is going up, or was until the storm knocked a padlocked trailer sideways against the cantilevered porch.

A long spool of plastic sheeting has unwound, too, running across the derelict's yard and into the street. It snaps like a sail in the wind. As I approach, the plastic glistens, streaked with mud and leaves. Lumps of debris are caught up inside. It makes me think of a distended intestine. The tail end, right across the middle of the road, swells like the body of a python after it's swallowed something whole.

Nix hunches over the unspooled plastic, lifting corners as he edges along its length toward the swollen end.

He grins. "Nothing like a decomp first thing in the morning."

The plastic is opaque, the kind of sheeting used on construction sites to seal openings. I kneel beside the swell in the plastic, which is in fact a swaddled corpse. Discolored clothing, an emaciated and withered shape, a brownish husk of a human being, gender indeterminate, age indeterminate. Small enough that it must be a woman, though, or maybe a child.

My eyes trace the long spool of plastic back to its source, the derelict building, yet another square two-story structure in brown brick, a former business or maybe a duplex but now just a rotted shell waiting to be rehabbed or more likely demolished. Ten blocks or so east of Montrose, ten blocks or so north of Westheimer, tucked into a neighborhood without sidewalks where time-blackened bungalows sit cheek by jowl with the kind of glass and steel architecture projects going up across the street. The yard is overgrown, the windows boarded up, the doors inaccessible, a place so forgotten its plywood coverings aren't even tagged by spray paint.

"Why am I here? You could've just called this in."

"Yeah," Nix says. "But come take a look inside."

We follow the unwound plastic back to its source, the sheet overlapping in vine-like rings. The body must have been tightly wrapped. The wind, knocking through, snatched the bundle up and unraveled it, bringing some long-hidden secret out into the light. Although, in this heat, it wouldn't have to be hidden long to reach such a state.

Glancing through the doorway, I see the interior walls are gone, leaving a vast dark cavity with a feral reek. A stack of wooden pallets is scattered across the floor, more plastic caught up in the slats.

"The body must have been against the far wall," Nix says, "with the pallets stacked in front. Then the wind came through and vomited everything out."

Underneath the pallets I spot something pink and shiny that doesn't belong, a surface too pristine and fresh. Nix stands still, letting me advance alone. Whatever it is, he's already seen it. A faux leather purse almost untouched by the surrounding filth, its surface glinting dully, zippered shut and waiting.

"Everything's just how we found it. Only I did check inside."

I slip on a pair of gloves, then pull the zipper open. A slim wallet nestles up top. I lift it gingerly and place it on the floor, using the edge of my finger to pop the strap. The wallet falls open. Behind the plastic ID window, there's a Texas driver's license.

"No way."

Back at the entrance, Nix smiles grimly. "Murder will out, right? But I've never seen it happen like this before. I thought you'd want to get in on it, all things considered."

I stand up slowly, blinking at the light outside.

"You better put everything back how you found it," he says.

I obey, operating on muscle memory, my thoughts elsewhere. Numb with disbelief. No feeling of accomplishment, certainly no closure. The usual exhilaration a big break induces, utterly absent. Tommy's maniacal grin flashes in my mind. The tree on top of my garage, the translucent winding sheet out on the road. The wound in my thigh starts to throb.

"I've got a call to make," I say.

"I bet you do." He walks forward, gazing down at the purse. "So we're even."

"Right."

Back outside, I'm limping, advancing in tiny increments, stopping to look around. I half expect the sergeant to come after me, laughing, saying it's all some sick joke. Approaching the body once more, I get down on my knees. My hand goes to the plastic shroud, then hesitates, as if my touch had the power to profane. I decide not to look again.

Instead, I put a little distance between myself and the corpse, the object of so much hope on the part of so many people.

After a storm like this, cellular reception is spotty. Houston rain showers have been known to bring a network down. But the line is crystal clear, the ringing so loud I hold the receiver away from my ear.

"March."

Cavallo's voice comes out like a yawn, but I don't apologize for waking her. Instead, I give her the news, flat and detached, and she receives it in the same spirit.

"Are you sure?"

"Not from the body," I say. "It'll have to be tested. But her purse is here, with her identification, so it seems like a safe bet."

"We'll see," she replies. Her words aren't a form of denial, just a professional insistence on checking off the necessary boxes. "If you're right, then I guess it's finally over."

Spoken like a Missing Persons investigator, but I don't correct her. What looks like an ending to her, though, is just a start. We have a body at long last, and a body is not an end but a beginning.

"Just get over here."

"I'm on my way."

After I hang up the phone, I dial another number. I don't have to. I'm under no obligation. And it's doubtful there is anything constructive Carter Robb can do. An identification—even from someone who knew her, even if I was perverse enough to pull back that plastic and ask him for one—isn't going to be very easy, given the state of decomposition. Maybe the clothes would be recognizable, though Cavallo will have an inventory of what she was last seen wearing.

I call anyway, not for the sake of the case, but because I know how I would feel, just blocks away, already consumed with guilt, finding out how close I'd been without realizing. I don't owe it to him, but I can't help feeling that on some level I do, maybe in the way we all owe each other everything, every possible courtesy, on account of what life puts us through.

He arrives first, the officers at the end of the road flagging down his car. He's dressed like he was last night, only he's wearing the wadded T-shirt he used to wipe his sweat. I motion for him to come through, but he approaches slowly, stopping a good distance back, cupping his hand over his mouth, closing his eyes. And then he crumples to the ground.

"What's this?" Nix asks.

I shrug, then start off toward Robb. "I guess we all have favors to pay back."

CHAPTER 24

"This was an act of God in every sense of the word," Cavallo says from behind her mask, speaking to no one in particular. Wanda Mosser glances my way, lifting an eyebrow, but I make no response out of respect for the dead.

We gather around the autopsy table, waiting for Bridger, who enters with a set of X-rays in hand, pegging them up against the light table. The enlarged negative image of a chest cavity, ribs translucent against the black background, and next to it a side view of the skull. He uses a pencil eraser to point out the light-colored blemishes.

"Here and here," he says, indicating two cone-shaped anomalies, one in the chest and one in the abdomen. "And here we have a third." Touching the eraser against another white cone inside the cranium.

Mosser clears her throat. "So that's two to the chest and one to the head? Like an execution?"

A Mozambique Drill is the term she's looking for, but I don't correct her.

"Not exactly," he says, moving to the body. "The angles are very different. Your people will be able to tell you more, but it looks to me like one of these chest shots was fired head-on, and the others at a steep trajectory, like she was on the ground. The head shot, as you can see from this stippling, was a contact wound, probably a coup de grace. But based on the two chest wounds, I'm guessing some time passed before the second shot, at least enough for her to fall to the ground."

I go over to the X-rays for a closer look. "The bullets look small."

"My money's on .22 caliber," Bridger says, "but we'll know for sure in a minute."

The official identification was made this morning using dental records. Wanda and Rick Villanueva prepared the release, but it was the chief who held the actual press conference. Thanks to the power blackouts all over the city, most people in Houston still won't know that the body of Hannah Mayhew, the girl whose disappearance riveted the nation, is now on a slab at the medical examiner's office where, powered by generators, her autopsy is proceeding.

Wanda wanted to be here, as did Cavallo, but by rights I'm the only one obligated. This is a homicide investigation now, and thanks to my captain's dogged insistence on protocol, it belongs to me, the first detective on the scene. Considering my experience on the task force, the decision makes sense. Not that anybody else on the squad sees it that way.

"Time of death?" I ask.

Bridger pauses, then begins the Y-incision, ignoring my question for the moment. A technician steps forward to cut the ribs, lifting the sternum free. Next to me, Cavallo's breath seems to catch.

"I'm only speculating," Bridger says, "but based on the amount of decomposition, it wouldn't surprise me if she's been dead pretty much since the day she disappeared."

Cavallo adjusts her mask. "Sixteen days."

"Give or take. And based on the postmortem lividity, I'd say the body was moved after death. So she wasn't killed in that house, I'm guessing, just dumped there."

The plastic sheeting probably came from the work site across the street, and access to the building itself wouldn't have been difficult.

It was boarded up so long ago that the panels would have been easy enough to shift. The question is, who would think to place a body there? I've already canvassed the neighborhood, interviewing everyone I could find, and the contractor from the house across the street has promised me a list of employees as soon as he can find a way to charge his laptop. Of course, the killer could have driven by on a whim, noticed the location, and taken advantage of it.

By the end of the autopsy, Bridger confirms what the X-rays suggested. Hannah was killed by a .22 caliber gunshot to the head. The bullet entered at the temple. She'd already been shot twice before, once in the chest, collapsing a lung, and once in the abdomen, the second shot probably fired while she was in a prone position or possibly propping herself up.

"There's no indication of a sexual assault?" Wanda asks.

He shakes his head.

"Well, thank God for that."

It's hard to muster much gratitude in the face of the desiccated husk of Hannah Mayhew, but somehow I find myself agreeing.

Out in the corridor I peel off my mask, happy to breathe freely again. Cavallo leans against the wall, then sinks down on her haunches, clenched arms extended over her knees. Wanda pats her absently on the head, then starts to go.

"I want to be in on this," Cavallo calls after her.

"In on what, honey?"

She jabs her thumb in my direction. "This. If he can horn in on my case, then I can horn in on his."

"Fine with me," I say.

Wanda snaps back, "Well, it's not up to you." She's done so much wrangling over the past two weeks it's become second nature, but the flash of anger dissipates like smoke. "Suit yourself. I guess it makes sense for one of my people to keep an eye on things."

She leaves us in the hallway. I start to say something, then stop. Cavallo gets back to her feet, peeling the scrubs off.

"I could do without this part of the job," she says.

"So could we all."

"What I said before, though, I think it's true. This is an act of God. We might have never found that girl if it wasn't for the hurricane."

"That's what the insurance people call it, an act of God. I had an act of God on my garage, too, and I don't think they're going to pay for it. Not that I'm complaining."

She gives me a sideways look. "I don't want to know."

When Bridger emerges for a smoke break, we follow him out, standing on the wet curb in case he has any further observations to make. He's silent, though, absorbed in his own thoughts. After a while, we leave him to it.

The contents of Hannah's purse are spread out on the table between us. Nothing remarkable, really. The wallet I opened at the scene, a zippered cosmetics bag, tissues, a pack of gum, some barrettes and ponytail holders, a stray earring, the usual things. But there are two cell phones, both powered off. The pink Motorola RAZR is Hannah's. The other, a cheap brick of black plastic, is a mystery, at least until Cavallo switches it on and checks the number.

"This is it," she says. "The phone she was getting calls from the day she disappeared."

"If he left it behind, then there probably won't be any prints."

She opens an evidence bag. "We'll check anyway."

"Yes, we will," I reply, dropping the phone in.

Brad Templeton tracks me down not long after, his voice brimming with excitement, like he thinks the Hannah Mayhew murder investigation is something I personally engineered to help with his book deal. He keeps pumping me for information until he finally realizes I'm about as responsive as a CPR dummy.

"You are gonna give me something, right? We do have an understanding, don't we?"

"This isn't the time, Brad."

I have to give him something, though, so I pass along Wilcox's name, suggesting he cozy up to my ex-partner, who's now taking the lead on Keller and Salazar. I'm trying to keep a hand in there, but IAD is a clannish outfit and since their search yielded the potential murder weapon—at least, the part of it that wasn't swapped with Thomson's pistol—they call the shots. For now, anyway. I haven't given up on that one, though anything I do at this point will have to be very discreet.

"You're pawning me off on Wilcox," Brad says.

"I'm leading you to water," I tell him. "It's up to you whether you drink."

As soon as I'm off the phone I grab my things and tell Cavallo we're going back to the scene. Now that the immediate aftermath of the storm is behind us, people might remember things they didn't before, and the ones who weren't around during the initial canvass might turn up. We're almost to the door when Jerry Lorenz steps through, blocking the path.

He looks Cavallo up and down, giving me an approving nod.

"Congratulations," he says. "You sure landed on your feet."

I'm not sure if he's referring to my pretty new partner or to my case. Judging from his smile, a little of both. The strange thing is, he's utterly genuine, offering apparently heartfelt congratulations, no hard feelings in spite of our run-in on the still-unsolved Morales case. He has no idea, since I never briefed him, on how much further I took that case, or how close Wilcox now is to busting it open.

I expect Cavallo to recoil from him, or at least to steer clear, but she pats him on the shoulder as she passes. "Congratulations yourself."

Out in the hallway, I ask, "You know that guy?"

"Who, Jerry?"

"Jerry Lorenz, right. He's the one I had so much trouble with."

"Who, Jerry?" she says again, unaware of how annoying this repetition is.

"Lorenz. I know I told you his name."

She shakes her head. "I never put it together. You don't get along with Jerry, huh? Everybody gets along with Jerry."

"He's an idiot."

"He's not so bad."

"How do you know him?"

She starts to answer, then stops herself, so I repeat the question. Reluctantly, she says, "He's in my Bible study."

"Your what? Jerry Lorenz is in a Bible study? You're jerking my chain—"

"No, really. He is. There's a group of us that meets about once a month. You should come sometime." She frowns. "Or maybe not."

"Why were you congratulating him?"

"What do you mean?"

"Just now, you said 'congratulations yourself.' "

"Oh that. I meant the baby, obviously." She stops in her tracks, realizing I have no idea what she's talking about. "His wife just had a baby. A little boy. Don't tell me you work with the guy and you don't know that?"

I shrug. "I guess it never came up."

We drive back to the derelict house, Cavallo taking advantage of the time to theorize on what it means that I take so little interest in my colleagues' personal lives. Ignorant of Lorenz's baby, unaware that her fiancé is overseas. She wonders aloud what else I don't know, and how with so little curiosity I can honestly call myself a trained observer.

"I'm only interested in people when they're dead."

I mean it as a joke, but it doesn't come out funny. She grows serious, remembering whose death sparked my interest in the current investigation.

The fresh canvass yields nothing, but we do find a small crew of construction workers across the street, trying to square away the damage left by the hurricane. The toppled trailer has been righted and now awaits replacement. In the interest of thoroughness, we have a chat with them, only to discover that half the men present aren't on the list the contractor finally handed over.

"They might not be on any lists," Cavallo says afterward, meaning like so many in the industry, they might be illegals.

When we're done, I take her over to the Morgan St. Café, where the power's finally back on, treating her over iced coffee to the story of Vance Balinski's curbside assault. I show her Thomson's sketchbook and the enlarged cell-phone photo, and seeing her interest is piqued, I take her back to the studio for a look at his intimidating series of busts. Locking up, I'm surprised to find Balinski himself in residence next door, a fat bandage on his nose, a line of stitches running along his bottom lip.

"I'm clearing my place out," he says. "I can't get any work done here now, not after what happened."

His own studio is a tidy, squared-away affair, a couple of large abstract paintings along the wall, a table and stool, an easel for work in progress, and at the back an assortment of finished pieces. I can only see the one in front, which looks to me like a solid field of orange with two fuzzy reddish lines running vertically, dividing it into thirds. It doesn't look too hard to do, but I refrain from saying so.

"When Thomson gave you that box," I ask, "did he explain why?"

Balinski moves the paintings on the wall over to the stack in back. "Honestly, we were both pretty baked at the time. He'd been kind of morbid recently, I don't know how else to describe it, even more obsessive than usual about things. Something had set him off, but I don't know what. We'd been to a couple of bars, and on the way back over here he said he wanted to give me something. I thought it was a gift at first, and I was telling him he didn't have to do that, but he said if he didn't, they might find it. He said they were keeping tabs on him now, because he wasn't reliable."

"Who was keeping tabs?"

Balinski shrugs. "Joe never talked about things, and when he did, you couldn't really ask for more detail, you know? He just said what he said and you listened. That's what I did, anyway."

"So he never said who was keeping tabs on him?"

"Well . . ." He glances around the studio as though he's misplaced something. "That night he was kind of tripping. He said he'd gotten into something, and they started out dirty but went in clean. He kept repeating it, like he thought I was arguing with him. 'No, we were dirty at the beginning, but not going in. Going in, we were clean.' And he was really proud of it, too, whatever it was."

"Did he say what he was going into?"

"I don't know what he said, man. It's not like I was paying close attention or anything. It was all kind of confusing. He was dirty but really he was clean. Whatever. The guy handed me a box full of blow. Then he shot his own head off. It's not like he was sane or anything."

We leave him to do his work. Back in the car, Cavallo asks for the sketchbook again, flipping absently through the pages.

"He meant the Morales house, right?" she asks.

"Going in clean? I guess so. They went into the house clean, whatever that means."

"They went in for the woman. For a righteous cause."

I nod. "Maybe."

"But that's not why they went in the first place."

"They started out dirty, going for the money or maybe drugs, but they were clean when they went in, meaning their aims changed." Castro's computer-generated crime-scene sketches come back to me, the abstract figures transected by red lines. "According to one of the crime-scene investigators, the guys who hit the Morales house showed some tactical sophistication. Maybe they did a little recon first, got the lay of the land—"

"And saw the woman tied to the bed."

"Right," I say.

"And instead of scrubbing the mission, they went in anyway. Not for the loot, but to rescue the victim."

"Something like that." I shake my head. "Only it's quite a coincidence, isn't it? The place they decide to stick up just happens to be the one where this woman's being assaulted? They interrupt the crime in progress, decide to intervene. Seems like a long shot. Besides, these guys aren't the type. We're not talking about heroes here. Just the opposite."

"Yeah, but isn't that the point of the whole dirty-clean thing?"

There's something to it, I realize, but Cavallo's already put a human face on Lorenz. I'm not going to let her humanize Keller and Salazar the same day.

"The point is," I say, "she's dead. Whoever she is. And maybe she wouldn't be if they hadn't gotten involved. Maybe they're the ones who put the bullet in her."

The last time I was at Cypress Community Church, the parking lot was near empty. Now every space marked out on the vast plane of blacktop appears to be filled, with overflow lining the street. Cavallo, dressed head to toe in black, sits beside me in the passenger seat, rubbing her hands nervously against her thighs.

"I don't think I can face her," she says.

Maybe she means Hannah. Maybe the mother. I don't know and I don't ask.

"If what Bridger says is right," I say, "there was nothing you could have done. Hannah was dead before you even started to look."

She nods, but it's one thing to see the sense in an argument and another to really believe it. The girl's death has hit her hard, and Cavallo's not the type to let herself off the hook. I can relate. I feel the same. For me, though, the territory is more familiar. To loved ones, the only promise I can fulfill is to deliver up a suspect. Cavallo works a job where it's still conceivable to bring the runaways home and set the captives free.

We hike across the boiling pavement, blending in with the other mourners streaming between the rows of cars and trucks, of station wagons, minivans, and sport-utility vehicles, each one gleaming hot in the sun. In parts of the city, the power is back, though more for a visit than a permanent stay. It still flickers back and forth, forcing me to run my generator most nights, though it's never enough to get the house truly cool. I've grown accustomed the past few days to always sweating, always feeling dirty, none of us being quite as presentable as we are when the electricity's on. I am not as impervious to heat as I've always assumed.

As the entrance gets closer, I remember the blanket of cold air that descended the first time I was here. Pulling the glass door open, I can almost feel it. But no, as I pass over the threshold in Cavallo's wake, the air is only marginally cooler inside. No respite awaits us inside the church, not even this.

The crowd carries us along through the soaring atrium, and I find myself wondering how many of these people actually knew Hannah. There are surely too many. Glancing around, I observe what I always do at funerals, a throng of people behaving only marginally more sober-minded than usual, most of them dressed for comfort in everyday clothes, a few dressed more formally—usually older, usually present in some quasi-official capacity. The teenage kids in front of us wear jeans and striped rugby shirts, while the women behind us, chatting among themselves, are in blouses and khaki capri pants and sensible flats.

I feel a hand on my elbow and, turning, find Gina Robb staring up at me through her cat-eye glasses. She tugs me out of the crowd and beckons Cavallo to follow, guiding us through the side exit toward the church offices. Her demeanor is grave, her eyes raw from crying, and whenever she tries to explain herself, her throat seizes up. So she relies on hand gestures to convey the fact that someone wants to see us.

Donna Mayhew's office door stands open, but the entrance is blocked by a throng of attendants. Gina parts them wordlessly, conducting us inside until we are face-to-face with the bereaved mother. She stands, austerely composed, at the very corner of her desk, draped in swathes of black, with black netting over her face. In contrast to the casual mourners in the atrium, she's like a figure from the distant past. Her hands, clasped tightly in front of her, are also gloved, prompting me to wonder where this funeral regalia comes from. I keep a black suit in the closet for funerals, but then I attend them with a fair amount of regularity. Of course, this is not her first bereavement. The woman has lost her husband and now her daughter, too. She is alone in the world, a feeling I can relate to only in part.

"Detective," she says, extending a hand to me. "They tell me it was you who found her body."

An awkward cough at the back of my throat. Do I correct her or let the error stand? Glancing around, I see men in dark suits, women with clenched tissue pressed to their eyes, a murmur of grief passing between them.

Cavallo tries to say something. I turn, and find her face wet with tears, her lips trembling. Donna Mayhew opens her arms and the two women embrace. I glance away. In the corner, Carter Robb stares glumly back at me. We haven't spoken since the day I summoned him to the scene. Then, I'd been unable to coax him anywhere close to the body, and he'd only agreed reluctantly to enter the derelict building for a look at the purse. Trying to confirm it was hers, he couldn't stop choking on his words. He'd wanted to help, to do something, but that wasn't what he'd had in mind.

"You have nothing to apologize for," Mrs. Mayhew is saying. "This was not your doing. We all have to be brave in the face of it. The Lord gives and he takes away."

The words seem empty to me, and desolate, but her voice is anything but. There is a strength in her that wasn't here before, back when there was still some chance of a happier outcome. She no longer agonizes over whether she's meant to drink from the cup. Now she knows, and the effect of the knowledge is heartbreaking to witness. Some people, when they suffer, derive power from the ordeal, a certain dignity, and along with it the grace to bestow benediction, as potent as it is unlooked for. In response, the usual hollow assurances about bringing the killer to justice die on my lips, and sensing my inability, she nods, as if she wouldn't want me to say such things, to commit myself to the impossible.

"I wanted to see you both," she says, "because I know some of the things I've said to the media must have sounded like criticism, and I want to say I'm sorry. It was not directed at you."

Cavallo tries to silence her with a lifted hand.

"It's all right," I say. "You don't need to justify yourself to us."

"I also wanted you to know that I'm done. I won't talk to them anymore. I didn't want to at first, and I only did it in the off chance it might help bring my baby home. But now there's no reason, and I won't talk to them again. I wanted you to know."

She speaks quietly, with a determination that doesn't seem congruent with the subject, as if the decision she's referring to runs much deeper than the one her words avow. An embrace of silence encompassing much more than television interviews, as if she's sworn off saying anything ever again.

Her gloved hand closes around mine briefly, squeezing, her eyes gazing at me through the netted veil. "I know you'll do everything you can. Thank you."

I step back. She gives Cavallo a similar blessing, and then we both retreat out into the hallway, joined by Gina Robb and her silent husband. He comes close to me, leaning almost to my ear, speaking in a harsh whisper.

"I want to talk to you later. I want to do more this time."

This time, as if there's a second round to play and everything might still come right.

We leave them, rejoining the other mourners. Cavallo wipes her eyes with the back of her hand, pretending I'm not beside her, probably embarrassed by her show of emotion. We file into a wide, soaring auditorium, a stadium of worship with a semicircle of seats around a raised platform. Behind it, a multi-tiered choir loft and a backstop of abstract stained glass, but I'm not looking past the platform. My eyes get no further than the casket at its base. The lid is closed, and a large portrait of Hannah is erected on an easel behind it. A hush descends on everyone who sees it, the crowd growing still, struck by the reality of that small wooden box.

Another casket flashes in my mind, another body. I see Charlotte pale with grief, the vein in her forehead throbbing, the bruises from the car accident still evident under a layer of makeup. My eyes sting.

"I can't stay," I say, turning back, not waiting for any reply, hoping she won't come after me, hoping she won't try to follow.

CHAPTER 25

Hedges casts a disapproving eye over my cubicle, staring the way he might at a spelling error in the first line of a report. I weather the scrutiny. There's nothing I can do about the mess. Casework grows like weeds all around me. My cup overruns, and so does my murder book. In addition to evidence recovered with Hannah's body, the copious lab work that's been trickling in all morning, and the first wave of file boxes couriered over from the former task force HQ in the Northwest, there's also a layer left over from the Thomson investigation, things I haven't had time to box up for Wilcox. Aguilar has been detailed to help, and Bascombe checks in every half hour or so, looking at me the way a kid looks at a magician, wondering what'll happen next time I reach into my hat. So I haven't had a lot of time for tidying up.

"Everything all right, sir?" I ask, hoping to move him along.

He can't bring himself to give the order—Clean up around here, all right?—but I can see how bad he wants to.

"You have everything you need?"

"Yes, sir."

He nods, clears his throat. "You've been doing good work, March. Keep it up. If I didn't know any better, I'd say you're back on form."

"Thank you, sir."

As he leaves, a little ember of pride burns in my chest. It means something, coming from him.

Lorenz drops by, too, blowing on a steaming cup of coffee, and I notice some kind of encrustation on his collar, a speck of dried milk maybe, though I imagine it's baby spit. I recall having seen something similar before, only I didn't appreciate the significance. I try to picture him cradling a newborn on the bridge of his belly, bouncing back and forth. I put baby talk in his mouth, trying to conceive of the sound.

"You were lucky to get out from under the Morales shooting when you did," he says. "If that thing goes down now, it'll be a miracle. No hard feelings, huh? If I overplayed my hand, I'm sorry. I got a talking to from Terry Cavallo yesterday, telling me you were good people. I shouldn't have come down so hard. What can I say? It was a big break for me, and I kind of blew it."

He cocks his round head, smiling anxiously, practically willing me to accept his apology. But I'm too stunned to react all at once. I buy myself some time by nodding and shrugging, a song and dance of body language meant to convey something like it happens to us all and don't sweat the small stuff. It's easy to be gracious in the ascendant.

"Forget about it," I say, hoping the words don't sound as hollow to him as they do to me.

Lorenz takes me literally, blinking a couple of times, smiling, and generally acting as though he doesn't know who he is or how he got here. He tips his cup in salute and walks away.

When she arrives a while later, Cavallo turns a number of middle-aged heads, but if she notices the stir, she gives no sign. Aguilar grows attentive all the sudden, abandoning his own desk and pulling a chair up to mine. The crowding seems too ridiculous not to comment on, but Cavallo says nothing so I keep quiet, too. Every time I glance his way, he gives a subtle, conspiratorial grin. My desk phone rings.

"Can you come up here?" Wilcox says. "There's something I want you to see."

I grab my jacket and leave the field to Aguilar, who seems grateful for the uninterrupted view.

"You need me?" Cavallo asks.

Over her shoulder, Aguilar's eyebrows rise slightly in alarm.

"I can handle this one on my own."

For the first time in more than a year, Wilcox's lips curl upward at my approach, though his smile is charged not with friendship but triumph. He pulls me into the office, then closes the door.

"We got him."

I turn. "Who?"

"Have a seat," he says. "All will be revealed."

My heart's already racing as I sit down. He circles the desk, grabs a thin folder, and slaps it down in front of me, the same way a poker player throws down a winning hand. The paper trembles in my hand. Inside the folder are test results on the handgun recovered from Salazar's boat.

"First off, there was dried blood on the muzzle and slide, which had been wiped down but not too carefully. The samples match Joe Thomson."

A long breath escapes me. "This is it."

"There's more. The drop-in barrel and the rounds in the magazine both had prints all over them, also Thomson's."

"And the frame?"

His smile's as wide as a crocodile's, showing just as many teeth. "That's where it gets really good. Like I said, the gun was wiped down. The lab had a hard time lifting prints from the frame and slide. But they pulled a partial off the hammer, another partial off the front of the trigger, and a thumb that wasn't Thomson's on the magazine."

"Are you going to tell me whose it was?"

"Look and see."

I flip the page over, scanning the lines, until my eye rests on the name. REGINALD ALLAN KELLER. I let out another breath. "The man himself."

"And it gets better. That particular P229, the serial number traces back to Keller, too."

"So it's airtight."

"Exactly."

We observe a moment of silence. This was a long time coming, and now that it's here, now that my old nemesis is literally in my hands, it doesn't seem real. The feeling's very different from the sense I had kneeling next to Hannah Mayhew's corpse, the numbness at the end of what I knew all along would be an unfulfilled quest. There's nothing conflicted or ambiguous about this. If anything, I'm giddy, and Wilcox must be, too, the way he's grinning ear to ear, the way he insisted on us sharing this moment together.

I start to laugh.

He laughs, too, slapping his hand on the desk. "You got him."

"I got him," I say. "No, we got him."

He shrugs the honor off. "It was all you, March."

"It was Thomson," I say. "If his conscience hadn't gotten to him—"

"It was you."

He comes around the desk, clasps my hand in his, shaking, stoking the ember inside me into a full-blown flame. Whatever came between us before, whatever drove Wilcox away, it's not there anymore, or at least it's abated for now. I rise out of the chair and he gives me a manly, one-armed hug, beating my shoulder blade with his open hand.

"Now what?" I ask, reeling back.

"What do you mean, now what? We're gonna frog-march him out of here. The man killed a cop. He's going down."

"When?"

"I've got people on him now. He's holed up in his apartment as we speak. As soon as I can get the team together, we're taking him. The warrant's in process now."

"I'm in."

"I know you are."

"And what about Salazar?"

"We don't have eyes on him, but we will." His smile fades. "To be honest, I'm not sure we can make as strong a case there—"

"It was Salazar who tried to have me killed," I say, my voice thick.

"I realize that, but tying it to him is another matter."

"We have him on video carrying the body. It's his boat the gun was on."

"Right," he says. "Now, think about that. Why would Salazar hold on to that gun? I'm assuming Keller didn't intend him to. If you ask me, he kept it so he'd have some leverage over his boss, just in case. Which means Salazar might be willing to pull a Thomson. He might be willing to roll over on Keller. Would you be okay with that?"

"I don't know. I don't think so."

"You might want to prepare yourself."

So the guy who dirtied up my shooting years back will go down, but the one who undoubtedly arranged to take me off the board gets a walk? It's hard to wrap my mind around. So I don't even try. There's no point admitting clouds on what ought to be a sunshine moment. Keller's done, that's what's important.

My head's still swimming as I exit the elevator on the sixth floor, punching the keypad code to admit myself into Homicide. When I return to my desk, Aguilar's gone, replaced by an unexpected visitor. Carter Robb sits across from Cavallo, elbows on his knees, talking earnestly in a subdued voice.

"What's the deal?" I ask.

They both look up. Cavallo speaks first. "Carter came by to talk. He's got some interesting ideas about the case."

"Really."

He gazes up at me with haunted eyes, an expression I recognize all too well from the mirror. I know this man is carrying a load of guilt, floundering for some way to slough it off, but I also know he's not going to find deliverance here, not through talking. And anything helpful he might have been able to give is already in our hands. Cavallo is too compassionate to tell him so, and if I didn't have somewhere to be, an old enemy to slap the cuffs on, I might even play along. I like the guy, after all. But Wilcox is going to give the signal any second, and I don't have time to mess around.

"It can't be a coincidence her body was found so close to the outreach center," Robb says. He rubs at his face the whole time he speaks, probably not aware of what he's doing, running his fingers so hard across the stubble on his cheeks that I can hear the friction. "There's some kind of connection, isn't there? And that's when all the trouble in Hannah's life began, when I took the kids to the outreach center. That's where everything started going wrong."

I check my watch. "Mr. Robb, I'm going to have Detective Cavallo take another statement from you, all right? I've got to be somewhere, otherwise—"

Cavallo's eyes harden. "Where are you going?"

I don't have time for the statement, I don't have time to explain, and the way they're both looking at me, one despairing and the other expectant, both thinking they have a claim on my attention—

"Has something happened with the case?" Robb asks.

"Not this one."

Cavallo stands. I take a step back, only to bump into Aguilar, who extends two coffee cups out at arm's length, trying to avoid spilling on his shoes.

"Hold your horses," Aguilar says.

My desk phone starts to bleep. I squeeze forward, nudging Robb's chair aside. Since I can't push these people out of the way, I push the contents of the cramped cubicle instead, accidentally toppling the topmost box from the nearest stack. Cavallo dives for it, pushing a pile of paper off the edge of the desk, half of it landing in Robb's lap while the other half hits the floor. Aguilar jumps back for no reason, splashing more coffee on himself.

I lift the receiver.

"Be up here in ten," Wilcox says. "And grab a vest on the way."

"Will do."

I put the phone down, surveying the scene. While Cavallo reaches across Robb to wrestle the box back in place, he's on his knees retrieving overturned files from the floor. Aguilar curses his spattered shoes, saying something under his breath about ruined calfskin. It's ridiculous enough to laugh at, if only I hadn't set the comedy in motion.

"Sorry," I say.

My fellow detectives glare, while Robb reappears from under the desk with an armload of now intermingled paperwork, which is going to require some organizing. Later. I take it from him, drop it on the desk, and turn to go.

"Where are you going?" Cavallo asks.

"I've got to grab a vest."

"A vest? For what?"

I glance around, making sure no one's near enough to overhear apart from Aguilar.

"Keller," I whisper. "We're about to kick his door."

"That's not our case."

"It's not yours."

Robb steps closer, holding Thomson's sketchbook open in his hands. "What is this?"

"Nothing to do with you," I say, snapping it away.

He ignores my reaction, his brows knitted. "No, really. What are those pictures?"

I sigh, glancing again at my watch, then flip to the back of the sketchbook, producing the cell-phone photo enlargement. "They're an artist's representation of that."

The photo is weightless, but he reacts like I've handed him an anvil, slumping back against the desktop, letting the image drag his arms down.

Cavallo bends down. "What's wrong, Carter?"

"Where did this come from?" he whispers.

Suddenly, the clock doesn't seem to matter anymore. I take the photo from him. "We believe this woman was killed during a shooting in southwest Houston. Her body was dumped in the Gulf."

"What?" he croaks.

"Do you recognize her?"

316

He reaches for the picture again. "I think . . . I'm not sure. It looks like it could be Evey."

Aguilar puts the coffee mugs down. "Who's Evey?"

"Evangeline Dyer," I say.

I slip the photo he gave me out of my notebook and make a comparison. Maybe he's right. It's hard to tell, given the quality of the cell-phone snap, and the way Evey Dyer's hair hides her face in the candid picture.

I've broken men down in the interview room before, had them crying like babies for their mamas, and at moments like that there's a satisfaction you get, a sense of psychological power. But Carter Robb isn't broken by any power of mine, and when he hunches over the chair, one knee on the seat, his body across the back cushion like a seasick man leaning over water, I can't help but pity him. Aguilar backs off, baffled by what's happening, and Cavallo puts her hand on Robb's back, stroking methodically.

"I've got to make a call," I say.

It takes the rest of my ten minutes to get Gene Fontenot on the line, and as I enlist yet another colleague to obtain yet another DNA swab from yet another mother, Cavallo shakes her head, either at the irony or just the weight of the moment. There's no way Robb could have made a positive identification from that photo, not objectively, but I know in my bones he's right.

Fontenot bucks a little. "You want me to get a swab from this lady? And what am I supposed to tell her, that you've got a body in the Houston morgue you want to check it against?"

"I don't have a body, Gene. Just some blood on a sheet."

"You're a piece of work, you know that?"

I put the phone down, head spinning, the raid all but forgotten. Cavallo gazes at me, eyes shining. "You were right."

"About?"

"The two cases," she says. "They really are connected."

It's true. If the woman on the bed—just a girl, really—was Evangeline Dyer, then that means the Morales shooting and Hannah Mayhew's disappearance are truly tethered, just as I'd suspected at the beginning. Only I still can't fathom how.

"I've got to get out of here," Robb says.

He struggles to his feet, shrugging off Cavallo's touch, and starts loping toward the exit, his shoulders hunched, like Atlas in a T-shirt and jeans. She tries to follow, but I motion her back.

"Let him go. He needs to lick his wounds."

As Robb passes through the door, Wilcox squeezes in, wearing a Kevlar vest over his shirt and tie and a blue HPD jacket over the vest. He bounds over, drawing a lot of attention from the detectives in the squad room, most of them former colleagues, though his move to IAD dampens any impulse they might otherwise have to welcome him.

"Are you coming or what?" he asks.

"I'm coming."

Cavallo grabs her jacket. "Me, too."

Wilcox turns on her, none too pleased. "Do we know each other? Because I don't remember issuing an open invitation."

"The cases are connected," she tells me, ignoring Wilcox entirely. "This is my case, too. Don't even think about leaving me behind."

"What does she mean, the cases are connected?" Wilcox asks. "What cases?"

"Come on." I take each one by the arm and start for the door. "I'll explain everything in the car. Let's not keep our man waiting."

CHAPTER 26

The tenants in Keller's apartment building, a vintage tower on Memorial Drive that was updated a few years back, converted into swanky mid-century pads, react to our shotguns and drawn side arms with a surprising sangfroid, as if they're accustomed to armed police raids. More likely, the scenario is too foreign for immediate processing, the stuff of television rather than real life, more a product of stunned excitement than alarm.

We stack up in the hallway outside his door, first Wilcox, then me, with Cavallo on my elbow clutching a shiny-looking Beretta, barrel down. Her vest doubles her width, like she's wearing a life jacket. Behind her, a couple of IAD detectives, one with a pump shotgun and the other with a portable battering ram, and the surveillance boys we picked up out on the curb, who reported that Keller went in and still hasn't come out and his car's parked in his reserved space.

Still no sign, they said, of Salazar.

Advancing to the edge of the door, Wilcox rings the bell. He waits a moment, then knocks.

"Houston Police Department," he growls.

Nothing. He waves the ram forward and a thrill goes through

me. No matter what anyone says, taking a door down is exhilarating work, a pure adrenaline rush, the law enforcement equivalent of an extreme sport. Anything could be on the opposite side of that door. Keller could be sitting in his underwear in front of the TV, or deafened by the roar of the shower. Or he could be hunkered down behind a makeshift barricade with an illegally converted automatic rifle leveled at the entrance.

The detective rears back, then lets the ram do its work. The metal cylinder coasts forward, seeming to move too slowly to do any real damage. But when it connects, the door crunches open, splintering at the dead bolt. He lets go and the ram thuds to the ground.

We rush the entrance with a frenzy of shouting, advancing into the apartment, making sure no corner goes unswept by the barrel of a gun. My feet thunder through the hardwood entry, breaking right into a wide-open living space with floor to ceiling windows at the far end, and a balcony that overlooks Memorial. Cavallo fans out beside me, circling a white leather sectional. The bedroom is at the far side. I'm the first one there, my gun sights resting just below my plane of vision, ready to snap off a round if necessary.

Over my shoulder I hear the others calling out.

"Clear!"

"It's clear."

"Everything clear."

A low platform bed with bookcases rising on either side. Another window, its light baffled by shades. No sign of him. The bathroom door is open, the light on, casting a golden glow into the room. I step toward it, hugging the wall for cover, canting my barrel into space. Getting closer, I use the mirror to scan the room. The glassed-in shower is empty. No sound of running taps or movement of any kind. Taking a deep breath, I push through.

"Clear," I say.

The team regroups in the living room, where the surveillance guys exchange a shrug.

"Maybe he went down to do some laundry?" one of them says.

"Or walked across the street to the Starbucks?"

I go to the balcony, pulling the sliding door open. Glancing down to the parking lot, I see the reserved spot is now empty.

"His car's gone."

There's nothing more ridiculous than a roomful of drawn weapons and no one to point them at. A spate of dejected re-holstering ensues, then we have a look around the place. The desk in the living room corner has a faint dust line where a laptop computer used to sit—the power cable is still plugged into the wall. A chunk of clothes seems to be missing from the closet, exposing a recessed safe, its door ajar.

"We didn't just miss him," Wilcox says. "He skedaddled."

He gets on the phone, putting the word out to patrol to keep an eye out for Keller's car. It isn't much, certainly not enough to soften the collective adrenaline crash.

"What now?" I ask.

He pauses to consider. "Okay, we need to keep some people here, and we'd better send some to Salazar's place, too."

"Got it," one of the IAD detectives says.

"And that warehouse they're renting—"

"We'll take that," I say, heading for the door, motioning Cavallo to follow.

"I'll send some backup to join you," he calls after us. "Meanwhile, we need to tear this place apart."

I wait until we're in the elevator to say anything, and then I slam my fist against the wall instead. The ringing in my knuckles feels better somehow.

"I knew that was too easy."

Cavallo nods, leaning back against the railing. "Why'd you choose the warehouse?"

"Instinct. I figure they rent that place for a reason, and if he's split in a hurry, maybe he'll need to drop by there first. It's better than chasing our tails back there. I want to keep moving."

When we reach the car, I remember Cavallo's lead foot and toss her the keys. She doesn't miss a beat, sliding behind the wheel and starting the engine. Out on Memorial, as we race past Starbucks, I glance over just to make sure Keller's not in there, slurping on a Frappuccino.

No such luck.

A feeling builds inside, a fear really, that I'll never catch up to him. He's flown for good, escaped the net, cheating me one last time.

We pull up outside the padlocked gate, the block of gray warehouses almost indistinguishable from one another. I knock on the security booth's shuttered window, but there's no response from inside. The sun beats down. Behind the glare on the windshield I see Cavallo thumping her fingers on the steering wheel.

With a pair of bolt cutters we'd be inside in two shakes, but as far as I know we don't have a search warrant on this place, and even if we did, we don't have the cutters. I dial Wilcox for further instructions. Before he picks up, Cavallo starts pointing to the fence. When I turn, Wendell Cropper is standing halfway between the nearest warehouse and the gate, frozen in place.

"Come on over here," I call out.

He advances, stopping about twenty feet off, blading his body sideways, his pistol on the far hip.

"Can I help you with something?" he asks.

"Open the gate."

Cropper lifts one foot, then hesitates, like he's not sure whether to move forward or back. If I tell him it's the warehouse we want to see, he might make a stink about seeing a warrant, so I try a different tack.

"We need to have a talk with you, Mr. Cropper. Open up."

He squints at me, feigning recognition. "Oh, it's you. I didn't recognize you at first, Detective." But he still doesn't move toward the gate.

I grab the padlock and give it a shake. "If you don't mind, we've got other stops to make, so I'd like to get through this pretty quick."

"Well," he says, digging through his pocket. "All right, then."

His hands shake so bad that he has trouble sliding the key into the lock.

"You nervous about something, Mr. Cropper?"

Once he pulls the padlock free, I walk through, pushing the gate wide as I advance, motioning Cavallo to drive through. As she does, Cropper moves to block her path. I take him gently by the arm.

"Don't get yourself run over," I say.

She parks just inside the gate, then gets out. The security guard backpedals, positioning himself between the car and the warehouses. I follow. When Cavallo joins us, she stands on his opposite side, forcing him to backpedal some more just to keep an eye on us both.

"Is something wrong?" I ask him. He's got that wide-eyed fight-or-flight look, and he's still blading his strong side away from us. I flick my jacket back, revealing my holstered gun, just to test his reaction. His hand twitches slightly, then relaxes. Cavallo catches the movement, too.

"Put your hands on your head," she says, resting hers on the butt of her pistol.

Cropper looks at her, aghast. He doesn't move.

Over his shoulder, the metal warehouse door trundles upward. As it rises I glimpse the back end of a black Ford pickup, an enclosure covering the bed. On the opposite side of the entrance a pair of legs advances toward the vehicle. The door lifts and I see a box held in two hands, a lidded file box like we use in the office. Then a muscled torso and the tanned face of Tony Salazar. He glances over, casually surveying the scene, then sees us and stops in his tracks. The box hits the ground.

"It's him," I say.

As soon as the words are out, Cropper makes his move. His hand flashes to his side arm, the gun clearing leather, the muzzle coming up. Cavallo's nearest, so he points her way.

Training takes over, years of muscle memory. I draw in a smooth, single motion, not waiting for the sights to come online. Instead, I let the first round go at his belt line and the second, aided by recoil, hits just below the sternum. The third is in the upper chest, and then the empty brass lands at my feet and Cropper's staggering backward, his Glock in midair.

Next to me, Cavallo stands flatfooted with her hand still on her holstered gun, shoulders hunched by the loud reports.

"Get back to the car!" I yell.

She draws and turns toward the fallen security guard, kicking his gun clear. But Cropper's not a threat anymore. I grab her sleeve with my free hand, yanking her back, just as the first muzzle flash erupts from the warehouse. The shot whistles through the air at head level, a near miss. After a pause, Salazar keeps shooting, and I fire back while beating the retreat, hoping to throw off his aim.

A gouge opens up in the hood of the car as I'm pushing Cavallo down behind the tire. I hit the pavement in a slide, skinning my elbows and knees. My pistol's slide is locked back, meaning I've burned through thirteen rounds already. Three in Cropper and ten downrange at Salazar. As I reload, Cavallo returns fire. I'd rather she stayed behind cover. I grab her arm again and pull her back.

"Don't give him a target."

She shrugs free. "If somebody shoots at me, I'm shooting back."

"You won't hit anything at this range," I say, but she's not listening. As she fires I try to pinpoint Salazar's position. He's tucked alongside the truck bed, using the vehicle for cover. All I can see is the muzzle flash from around the enclosure.

It's hard to think clearly when you're taking fire. Either you go to ground or you keep pulling the trigger. It says something about Cavallo that she chooses the latter, but that kind of bravery won't turn her side arm into a rifle. I open the passenger door and crawl over the seats, fumbling for the button that pops the trunk. When I hear the dull *thunk*, I slide out, grabbing the keys from Cavallo and moving around back. Inside a locked box in the truck, there's a shotgun and an AR-15. With the latter, I can reach out and touch him, something I've been itching to do.

"March!" she yells, her voice shrill. "He's starting the truck."

I raise myself into a crouching position in time to see the reverse lights illuminate. It took him a while, but he's done the arithmetic. All we have to do is keep him pinned. Backup is on the way. But he has to fight his way out, which means the sooner he moves the better.

"Keep shooting!" I say, grabbing for the rifle. I fumble with the charging handle, chambering a round of 5.56 NATO. I've manipulated the controls a thousand times on the range, but now it's like my fingers are disarticulated, one clumsy mass of flesh.

I hear the squeal of tires, smell the rubber burning, and when I look up again the Ford is out in the sunlight. Salazar accelerates backward, cuts the wheel, then rocks to a stop. I lift the rifle, hunting for his silhouette with the iron sights. The truck accelerates, picking up speed, heading straight for us. He would have been better off going the other way.

The front post lines up over his head. I take a deep breath and squeeze off a round. The windshield shatters into a spider web of glass, but the truck bears down on us.

"Move, move, move!"

I jump clear just as the Ford hits, smashing the front of the car, dragging its crumpled shell into the street before slinging it aside. My sights come up again, but before I can fire, the truck hauls across the road, rumbling over the curb, heading straight into the curtain of trees separating us from the houses on the other side. It crunches into a thick oak, sending up a cloud of smoke and steam.

Cavallo limps up beside me, clutching her elbow.

"Are you okay?"

She nods quietly, advancing across the street. I follow, ready to fire. We reach the far curb just as the backup units roll up.

"Stop." I put a hand on her arm. "Let them take it from here."

I toss the AR-15 to the ground and pull my badge out, just so we're clear on who's who. Cavallo holsters her Beretta and sits down on the curb, burying her head in her hands. The uniforms rush up to us, then creep steadily across the grass toward Salazar's mushroomed truck, weapons drawn. They haul him out of the cab. I hear him screaming as they push him to the ground, twisting his wrists back for cuffing. I slump down beside Cavallo and try to catch my breath.

★

I tell the story a dozen times, first to strangers and then to friends. Amazingly, when they haul Salazar to the road on a backboard, he's still breathing in spite of the hole in his upper chest. Wendell Cropper isn't so fortunate. His body, covered by a tarp, lies where he fell. Numbered markers sit next to my shell casings and his unfired Glock. Inside the box Salazar dropped, Lieutenant Bascombe, one of the first detectives on the scene, discovers the cocaine and the printed photos described by Balinski. The bed of Salazar's Ford is full of more boxes, some stacked to the brim with coke, some with dog-eared bundles of cash.

Mitch Geiger, the narcotics intel guru, arrives in time to catalog everything, speculating that the truck's contents represent the haul from at least five stash-house heists.

"They couldn't move this much," he says, "so they just sat on it for the time being. If you hadn't shown up, he'd have disappeared with it all."

When he finishes with me, Bascombe turns to Cavallo for her account of the action. As she's speaking, he stops her with an exclamation of surprise, then bends over, scratching at her chest. She swats his hand away.

"Just look," he says, laughing incredulously.

She glances down. There's a pancaked bullet lodged in her vest. She panics as soon as she sees it, flailing with the Velcro straps. I help her take the Kevlar off, then inspect the damage.

"You didn't feel that?" I ask.

She presses a hand to her sternum. "I didn't realize—"

Bascombe puts an arm over her shoulder, bares his gleaming teeth. "The boss told me March got his luck back. Looks like it rubbed off on you."

Instead of basking in the sense of relief, Cavallo sits down again, the reality of the situation crashing down on her. "I could've been killed."

"But you weren't."

She doesn't look reassured.

Before we're released from the scene, I get a call from Wilcox, who's been camped out at the hospital since the ambulance transported Salazar.

"He's still in surgery," he says, "but they're telling me he's going to pull through."

"Good for him."

"Good for us, March. I was right about what I said before. On the ride over, he kept taking the oxygen mask off and saying one word. Want to take a guess? *Immunity*. I've got a lawyer coming now. I'm pretty sure he's going to talk."

When I hang up, part of me wishes I'd aimed better, putting the round through his head instead of his chest. But then I remember Cropper lying dead on the pavement, and figure I've got enough blood on my hands for one day. There's a burden that goes along with killing, even when you're justified in taking a life. So being spared that is something, even if it means a deal for Salazar, the man who tried to get me killed.

CHAPTER 27

Donna Mayhew reaches her hands out, one toward Cavallo and the other toward me. Without thinking, I clasp the hand, cool and small. She seems smaller since the funeral, diminished, a wan light in her eyes.

"We're here to talk to Mr. Robb," I say.

She nods, as if she'd known this already. "He's upstairs, doing the high school Bible study."

The double doors leading through to the stairwell are at the end of the hall, but we don't move. The three of us stand in the office corridor, exchanging no words, no eye contact. After a moment, Hannah's mother sighs.

"Evey, too," she says. "And in that terrible place."

So Robb told her. Of course he did.

"I tried calling her mom, but I couldn't bring myself to . . ." She blinks at me, smiles weakly, and folds her arms tight around her frame. "I don't know this world. I don't recognize it anymore."

Cavallo's arm goes to her shoulder.

"It's all right. I just, there's a connection, isn't there? The two of them, what happened to them. Something was happening and I didn't see it."

"You couldn't have," Cavallo says.

But Mrs. Mayhew cocks her head toward me, like she's just noticed something that should have been obvious all along. "You knew, isn't that right? When you came here that first time, that thing with the Q-tip. You thought—what? That Evey was Hannah?"

"More or less." My mouth is so dry, the words come out in a whisper. "I got it wrong."

"Maybe we all did. For a long time now I've had this feeling I don't know my daughter anymore." Her tear ducts open, her eyes shine with damp. "And now, I can't really explain it, but it's like I got her back."

At the top of the stairs, my leg throbs and I lean against the wall for a breather, grateful to have the bullet wound as an excuse so Cavallo can't make any cracks about my being an old man. She waits patiently, chin tucked, preoccupied by our encounter with Donna Mayhew.

"Ready?"

I'm not ready, not after that. Mrs. Mayhew has something to work through, a mystery of her own, much deeper than ours. A solitary question that can never be adjudicated, any answers she might find in this life impossible to validate. I know something about that, and what it can do to a person.

So I push on with a nod. This wing of the church is new to me, a long linoleum-lined hallway with classroom doors on either side. It could pass for a high school except for the Bible verses painted on the walls and the framed portraits of robed and bearded men, heroes of the faith presented in a sentimental neo-Victorian soft focus. I glance into a couple of empty classrooms, noting folding tables and stackable chairs, the space flooded by afternoon light.

At the end of the hallway, Cavallo pushes through a set of double doors, holding one open for me. We pass into a larger classroom, where the office-building suspended ceiling has been torn out, the exposed trusses painted black. Past a sea of now-empty couches, a group of thirty or forty teenagers sits in a semicircle around a raised stage. Carter

Robb is up there, a tiny book dangling from one hand, a trap set and amplifiers and a couple of guitars on stands behind him.

"Let's wait back here," Cavallo whispers, motioning toward one of the couches. Glancing around, I spot a table in back stacked with empty pizza boxes and two-liter bottles of Coke and Sprite. We take our seats, and a couple of kids turn to see who's come in. Robb gives no sign of noticing us, though we're hard to miss.

Judging from the tone of his voice, the lingering pauses between the words, the way he makes pointed eye contact with first one student then another, his talk has reached its climactic finale. Robb's style is very different from, say, Rick Villanueva's, making up for what it lacks in polish with an extra dose of intensity. But then he's not coaxing ex-convicts with outstanding warrants into a state of mental paralysis; he's telling a bunch of slouching, dough-faced teens that all God wants from them is justice, mercy, and humility. Justice must be the greatest of these, because it's justice Robb lingers on—not only justice for ourselves, he insists, but for the strangers among us, for the outcasts.

"If God, the judge of everything, does what is right, then will he expect anything less from you? Or you?" He points his finger into the audience, then turns it on himself. "Or me? We look out for ourselves, but it's not enough. We look out for our friends, but that isn't enough, either. Justice for all, that's our calling. We can talk about mercy for the undeserving—and we're all undeserving—but here in the fallen world, living life under the sun, we have to talk about justice for the undeserving, too. And at the end of the day, it has to be more than just talk."

As I listen, our conversation in the church van comes to mind, the conflict in his head between the safe and the good. If it's still there, he's not sharing it with his disciples. If he blames himself for Hannah Mayhew's fate, or Evangeline Dyer's, he hasn't tempered his message as a result.

He ends suddenly, dropping his head, clenching his eyes tight in prayer. Next to me, Cavallo does the same. I shift in my chair, looking around. At the back table, a woman in an apron and baggy jeans starts taking foil off a tray of brownies, cringing at each metallic ripple.

The gravity of the moment ends as soon as the prayer does, with the teens rushing back to the table for dessert, casting a curious glance or two our way. Three or four gather around Robb, who tries to edge toward us while some more wander onstage to pack up instruments. These kids would have known Hannah. They would have known Evey Dyer. Of all people they'd have a right to be shocked by what happened to the girls, to be traumatized. If they are, I see no sign. The resiliency of youth? Maybe. Or it could be that some wounds go too deep to be casually observed. I know something about that, too.

"I'll be with you in just a second," Robb says, slipping past us to confer with the brownie lady.

"Hard to believe he's the same guy from the other day."

Cavallo shrugs. "Life goes on."

He rejoins us, holding on to the last remnants of the stage persona until we get to the hallway, where he sighs and hunches his shoulders, taking up his burden again.

"We can talk back in my office," he says.

"Just so you know, you were right about the photograph. The mother's DNA was a match. Which means it really was Evey Dyer in that house. The question is, how'd she get there? And what does it have to do with Hannah's death?"

He runs his hand over his head, raising a jagged clump of hair. "It's all I think about."

Pausing near the stairway, he points out one of the framed pictures on the wall. Unlike the smiling ancients, this one is abstract, random primary-colored dots swirling on a white background. He walks over, telling us to look.

"Seems like nothing at first," he says, "but if you stare long enough, you can see the face."

Cavallo cocks her head. "It's Jesus."

"Yeah." He gives an embarrassed grin. "It's corny, I know. Not my kind of thing, believe me. But that's how I feel all the sudden, ever since

I saw that picture in your office. Like I've been staring at something that doesn't make sense, and suddenly I recognize the pattern. There turns out to be a design in it all."

She nods and we descend the stairs. It must come easily to him by now, turning everyday things into object lessons.

"So what's the pattern here?" I ask, trying to keep the annoyance out of my voice.

"Have you talked to Murray? The guy I introduced you to the other day?"

"The resident dreamer?"

He pushes through the ground floor doorway, taking us back to the office wing. "I guess he's a little corny, too, but a great guy. Not very many people would leave their high-powered corporate jobs to go to seminary and then do the kind of mission work he does."

"So why should we be talking to him?"

"When I took the youth group there that first time, Hannah and Evey were really good about going out into the community and talking to people, inviting them to the center, that kind of thing. Hannah was being altruistic, but unfortunately Evey had other ideas." He reaches his office door, then pauses. "No, I shouldn't say that. It's not fair. I don't know what was in her mind, but afterward I found out she'd met a boy. The other kids were talking about it. After that week, she saw a lot of him. I didn't worry too much—girls that age want boyfriends, right? But then Murray told me this guy was older, and maybe even a little bit dangerous."

"When you're sixteen, that's the appeal," Cavallo says.

In the office, Robb perches on his desk, motioning us to the couch. I gaze up at the sagging bookcases all around, hoping they don't choose this moment to collapse.

"When I say dangerous, though, I really mean it. Like, drugs dangerous. And Mrs. Dyer got concerned, too, because of Evey's past. She'd run away before, been on the streets awhile, and everybody was afraid of some kind of relapse, only you couldn't say that to Evey because she was sensitive. Touchy about being judged."

"So what happened?" I ask.

"Her mom put an end to it. There was a big fight. I remember Hannah coming to me, because she felt like she was in the middle. Anyway, after a week or two, everything seemed fine. Evey was back to normal, as normal as she ever was. But ever since I saw that picture, I've been thinking. Remember those youth-group girls who said Evey and James Fontaine were going to run away together? Well, I always thought there could've been a kernel of truth to that. Maybe it wasn't Fontaine, though. Maybe it was this other guy, the one she'd met before."

"Does this guy have a name?"

He shrugs. "I'm drawing a blank. That's why you should talk to Murray. He talked to the guy a few times when he'd come into the center. Some deep conversations supposedly."

"Why don't we call your friend Murray now?"

Robb lights up as if the possibility never occurred to him. He goes around the desk, punching the number into the phone.

"I'll put him on speaker."

Murray Abernathy answers, but asks if he can call back later. "I'm with somebody."

"I've got the police here, Murray. It's really important."

"Oh." He pauses. "Give me a sec." When he comes back, Murray settles into some kind of stuffed chair, the air hissing out as he applies weight. "All righty then. What's up?"

Robb explains, then asks for the mysterious boyfriend's name.

"His name? It was Frank."

"Frank what?" I ask.

"Hold on," he says. "It'll come to me." Another pause. "Frank was a Latino guy, in his early twenties I think, handsome and well-spoken. I was excited when he first showed up, because he was interested in all the big questions—life, the universe, the whole shebang. But I could see right off I wasn't gonna make a convert. For him, it was like a test of wits. He always wanted to prove he knew more than I did. Frank was an autodidact, one of those guys who acts like he knows everything—and then surprises you with how much he really does know."

"His last name?" I ask again.

"I'm trying to think of it. He had a cousin doing construction work around here. Somebody would drop him off, and he'd hang out at the center while he waited for the cousin to get off work."

"The cousin worked construction?" Cavallo and I exchange a glance. The site across the street from where Hannah's body was found is just one of many in the neighborhood. "Did you ever get the cousin's name?"

"Wait a second." He starts humming over the line, drowning out all distractions. "I got it. Frank was short for Francisco—" He pronounces it *Frahn-see-sco*, reproducing the sound from memory. "Francisco . . . Rio? Rios? Something like that."

"Francisco Rios?" The name is familiar. I quiz Cavallo with a raised eyebrow, but she just shrugs. "I've heard that somewhere."

"I have no idea what the cousin's name was," Murray says. "But he'd pull his van out front and blow the horn, and Frank would drop everything and go."

Cavallo leans forward. "You told Carter this guy was dangerous. Why was that?"

"He talked a lot of nonsense, but I started thinking maybe it wasn't nonsense after all. Because he presented himself so well, I kind of assumed he was . . . normal. Like everybody else, you know? A little stuck up, but basically a decent guy. But some people in the neighborhood told me he'd offered to sell them drugs, and once he got in a fight out on the street and pulled a knife on somebody. Said he was gonna come back that night and shoot the guy. Around here, you've got yuppies living next door to dealers, you've got people walking designer dogs past muggers. Frank kind of fit the vibe, I guess, but when I heard one of those girls was running around with him, well . . ."

I lean over to Cavallo. "I know that name."

She keeps asking questions and Murray keeps talking, but I tune it all out, focusing on those syllables, picturing the letters in my mind.

I write them out in my notebook, underlining the words. Why is Francisco Rios so familiar?

And then it comes to me.

"Where are you going?" Cavallo asks.

But I'm off the couch and halfway through the door, leaving her to make apologies to Robb and come running after me. She catches up in the atrium—I make a point of not glancing toward the auditorium doors, where the coffin of Hannah Mayhew so recently stood—grabbing at my arm to slow me down.

"Come on," I say.

"What's the rush?"

"That guy, Francisco Rios? I know him. We scooped him up at the George R. Brown, and he handed me Salazar's business card. He's a confidential informant. I called to check, then cut him loose."

"If he was Salazar's snitch—"

"It's him. He's the one we want."

"So maybe Salazar will give him up."

Out in the parking lot, the sun blazing overhead, I stop in my tracks, one hand on my hip, the other pressed to my forehead, trying to pull the memories free. "There was somebody with him. A guy named Coleman who had a warrant out. When we let Rios go, he blew up. He kept yelling he was going to tell everybody, that Rios was going to be dead."

"Tell them he was an informant?"

I nod. "We need to talk to Coleman. I got the feeling they knew each other pretty well."

Robb wasn't wrong, not about the pattern. You stare long enough and nothing's random anymore. The pieces fit.

Sometimes all too well.

I'd had him. Zip-tied and all to myself, alone in the restroom at the end of the corridor, Saturday morning on Labor Day weekend, within forty-eight hours of Hannah's disappearance and Evey Dyer's death. I'd had him and I let him go, not realizing who it was I was letting walk out into the sunlight. All I wanted was to get out of there, to bag the assignment and move on to real police work, to get my teetering career back on two feet. His fear comes back to me, how desperate he was not to be locked up, to the point he'd even out himself as an informant in front of Coleman. I'd even given him advice, telling him to play it cool next time, never wondering why he panicked in the first place.

And Salazar, when I'd offered to take the kid downtown, had suddenly changed his tune about wanting to see him. Neither one of them wanted Rios in custody. Now it made sense. Rios knew he had blood on his hands. Salazar didn't want his informant, who'd been tipping him to the location of stash houses, to spend a moment inside, either, afraid he'd start talking.

"I didn't see it."

"See what?" Cavallo asks.

But I don't answer. All the mistakes of the past couple of weeks come back to me. Getting kicked out of Homicide for ditching Lorenz. Spooking Thomson's wife to the point that she outed him to his killers. Cutting Tommy slack when I should have come down on him, when for all I knew Charlotte was right and something bad had happened to Marta, the girl who spent the night in the garage apartment. It all pales in comparison to letting Frank Rios walk. The trouble is, in a case like mine, mistakes are irreversible. You can't always work your way back. You can't bring the dead back to life. And the man you let go might never be caught again.

There's nothing left but the guilty knowledge of what you might have done, how brave or selfless or good you could have been, if only you'd known then what you do now.

Salazar's willing to talk, but not with me in the room, the guy who put him in the hospital. His attorney does the complaining, and before Wilcox can lodge a halfhearted protest I throw my hands up and head for the door. Glancing back, I take little comfort in Salazar's condition, the wheezing pumps and dripping tubes, the oxygen feed, the inert lump of flesh beneath the sheets. Partial paralysis, the doctors told us, the loss of control on his right side. In spite of the successful surgery, Salazar is anything but okay. I reached out and touched him all right, with a hand that's never going to let up.

I wait in the hallway awhile, until Cavallo comes out to report.

"He's putting it all on Keller," she says. "He dragged the others into the business, he orchestrated the raids. It was him who killed Thomson and forced Salazar to cover it up."

"And Evangeline Dyer?"

"He had no idea she'd be there. When they looked through the window and saw her, Keller wanted to abort, but Thomson insisted on going in. He says it was Keller who shot her, accidentally, firing blind through the door. They were taking her to the emergency room, he says, and then she died."

"What was she doing there in the first place?"

"Says he doesn't know. Rios told him it was another stash house, and afterward the informant disappeared, so he never got a chance to ask."

"What about Rafael Ortiz, the gangbanger who shot me?"

"Says he's never heard of the guy." She shakes her head. "He's not going to cop to that, March."

I take off down the corridor in a rage. "So basically, he's not giving us anything we don't already have?"

"He'll testify against Keller."

"In case you didn't notice, we don't have Keller. At this rate, there's not going to be a trial for Salazar to testify at."

"It's better than nothing."

"Not by much." My frustration is the sort that only grows when it gets an airing. A host of dead-end possibilities flood my mind. "Think about it: he's been trying to find Rios since day one. When I let the kid go, he was already gunning for him. Why? Because he wanted to put a bullet in him. Believe me, he wasn't going to ask what went wrong, why the informant suddenly sent them to the wrong house. If he'd have been able to find Rios, somebody like Ortiz would have finished the kid off, like he almost did me. Or maybe Salazar would have done it himself and dumped the body alongside the Dyer girl's." I slap the wall, drawing a glare from a passing nurse. "You know what? Maybe he did. That would be perfect. The Rios kid might already be at the bottom of the Gulf. We'll never find him because there's nothing left to find."

"Calm down, March," she says. "It's not your fault you didn't arrest Rios when you had him. You had no way of knowing . . ."

"I'm not stupid. I realize that."

"Then stop beating yourself up and get on with the job."

That's good advice, and I decide to take it. Leaving Cavallo to hold Wilcox's hand for the remainder of the interview, I bug out, heading back to Montrose with my list of construction workers in hand. Nobody by the name of Rios, but that doesn't mean the cousin isn't on the list. I park in front of the site, where some damaged framing is being slowly repaired by a skeleton crew of helmeted workers, stripping my jacket off and leaving it in the car, not a concession to the heat but a psychological tactic. I want these men to notice that the approaching hombre wears a gleaming shield, and more than that, a dull black, well-worn gun.

"Francisco Rios," I say, motioning them over. "Which one of you knows the guy? He's got a cousin here, right?"

The workers shrug and exchange glances, one of them asking me to repeat the name. I do better, whipping out the driver's license photo off the system, along with the picture Salazar took when he registered Rios as a confidential informant. They gather round, squinting and shaking their heads. One of them leans forward, though, tapping a hard brown finger on the page, his eyes drifting upward in recollection.

"Yeah," he says. "I seen him. You know who this is?" He turns to one of the others. "That's Tito's cousin, the one with the big attitude."

The man next to him looks again, then nods. "I think you right."

"Who's this Tito?" I ask.

"Tito the Painter." He brushes his hand back and forth in the air, like I might not be familiar with the term. "He don't work here. We got nothing to paint yet. But he's always around, you know, at the various sites, 'cause he's working so cheap."

"What's his last name?"

He scratches his chin, then murmurs something in Spanish to the other man, who shrugs. "Everybody just call him Tito the Painter. But I can tell you where he stays." He rattles off an address over on the West side, an apartment complex off Hammerly.

I thank him, then turn to go. Instead of heading straight to the address, I drive around the area looking for other sites, asking workers and foremen alike whether they've seen Tito the Painter around, or know his full name. Everybody seems to be familiar with the guy, some even recognize the photo of Rios, but no one can add to what I already know.

Passing by the outreach center, I see Abernathy out on the front steps talking to two slender white guys in retro sunglasses and snap-front shirts. He comes out to the curb for a quick chat, but he's already told me everything he knows about Rios.

"What about the van?" I ask. "You said his cousin would pick him up in a van."

"It was white. It had ladders on the side, I remember that."

"He's a painter, apparently."

"Makes sense. It was that kind without windows, you know? Sliding door on the side. I can't remember if there was a company name. I don't think so."

"You didn't write down the license number or anything?"

He smiles. "I'll remember for next time."

Back downtown I go through the boxes of task force paperwork, hunting for the Willowbrook Mall surveillance footage, or at least some stills. Aguilar, sensing my excitement, wanders over and dives in. A minute later, Lorenz joins him, and then Bascombe and Ordway walk by wondering what's going on. Before long, we're all digging through boxes side by side, stacking the contents on the floor, my chair, and any empty space we can find.

"Got it," Bascombe says, lifting a sheaf of paper from the bottom of his box.

We spread the stills out on the conference table, scrutinizing the grainy images.

"Does that look like a ladder to you?" I ask, pointing to a pixely shadow alongside the van.

They all take turns looking. The consensus is that it might be, though Ordway has to spoil the moment by pointing out it could also be a long dent, a streak of paint, or even a missile—basically anything. Look long enough and you see what you want to.

"You have the address," Bascombe says. "Why don't we go check it out?"

"All of us?" I ask.

He smiles. "Why not? You want to keep the glory all to yourself?"

"Let's roll."

On the drive over, convoying in three cars, I can't help remembering my last outing in force, the pointless kick-down of Keller's door. Hopefully this one will turn out better. We pass the apartment complex and then circle around, cruising slowly through the parking lot. At the front of the line, Bascombe sticks his arm out the driver's window, pointing up ahead. I crane my neck, gazing along the length of vehicles parked under the complex's corrugated shelter.

At the end of the row, a white van sits, with a long, paint-spattered ladder knotted to the roof rack. The lieutenant parks right behind it, leaving me to pull ahead while Aguilar takes up a spot behind. We all get out at once, donning sunglasses, adjusting gear.

"You know what to do, ladies," Bascombe calls out.

We're detectives, so we do what we always do. Knock on doors. Ask questions. Throw our weight around. It's not hard to find out which door belongs to Tito the Painter, or that his real name is Tito Jiménez, and he has a little cousin who sometimes stays with him. We congregate in front of his door, ready for anything.

"March," the lieutenant says. "You do the honors."

Jiménez opens right away, throwing the door wide, no apprehension. He shields his eyes from the sunlight, confused by the sudden appearance of so many HPD detectives on his doorstep, but he doesn't panic or run, doesn't try to slam the door on our faces. He's older than I expected, in his early forties, with a salt-and-pepper goatee, a belly that strains against his white T-shirt, and skin the same shade of yellow-tan as a shade-grown Connecticut cigar wrapper.

"Is this your van out here?" I ask.

He nods.

"Is your cousin here?"

"Frank? He don't stay here no more."

"No?"

He pushes his bottom lip out. "I told him to leave. He had this girl here living with him, and I said, 'If you're man enough for a live-in girlfriend, you're man enough to pay your own rent.' I didn't like her here, always messing everything up."

A glance over his shoulder suggests the standards of tidiness haven't improved. I flip through my notebook, pulling a photo of Evangeline Dyer—not the postmortem snap Thomson took, but one Robb provided, Evey and Hannah in happier times, before the Dyers returned to Louisiana. It's folded over so only Evangeline's face shows, the part not obscured by her hair.

"Is that the girlfriend?" I ask.

He pauses to study the picture. The silence is so intense over my shoulder I know I'm not the only one holding his breath. Jiménez hands the photo back, nostrils flaring.

"Yeah," he says. "That's her."

I ask him where Rios and the girl went after he kicked them out, but he claims to have no idea. According to him, they aren't that close, him and his cousin. Rios showed up one day saying some dudes he owed money to had taken his car and ransacked his old apartment, stealing a lot of his stuff. Before that, they hadn't had anything to do with each other.

"Who did he owe money to?" I ask.

He shrugs, not because he doesn't know, but because he doesn't want to say the name, afraid of getting involved. I push him, and when that doesn't focus the man's attention, Bascombe steps forward, all six foot four of him, lowering his sunglasses in slow motion.

"Dude by the name of Octavio Morales," Jiménez says. "Bad dude, but not anymore."

"He's dead now."

Jiménez nods uncomfortably.

"What do you know about that?"

Up to now, he's been forthcoming, but the painter suddenly loses all interest in talking. I can't tell if he knows something and doesn't want to say, or if he's just afraid of being dragged into a court case, running the risk of having to testify. Either way, he's obstinate, so Bascombe decides to wrap things up.

"Mr. Jiménez, we're gonna have to ask you to come downtown. We're seizing the van, too. Detective Lorenz, you wanna call us a tow truck, son?"

"On it, sir."

Before he knows what hit him, Jiménez is cuffed for his own safety and baking in the back seat of my parked car. We take a quick look inside—we'll be back soon enough with a warrant for a more thorough search—and then gather at the van, not opening the doors or even touching the handles, leaving everything for the forensics team to go over in detail. But we can't help peering through the glass. Ordway goes around back, using his flashlight to peer inside.

"Boys," he says.

We join him, taking turns glancing through. A sheet of plywood lies in back, a makeshift floor, with ladders and buckets and rollers stacked high. Along the side, though, near the sliding door, there's a crawl space cleared from front to back. The white metal between the plywood and the door is marked with specks of dried liquid that look black from here.

"That could be paint," Aguilar says.

"Yeah." Bascombe adjusts his sunglasses. "It might also be blood. Anybody want to bet?"

Nobody does. We're all thinking the same thing. We might not have found our killer yet, but we're standing just outside the crime scene.

CHAPTER 28

"You look good in orange, Coleman. It suits you."

He responds to my jibe with a tug of the wrist, drawing the hand-cuffs securing him to the interview table taut.

"At least loosen them a little bit," he sighs.

"Sorry about that, but last time we met, you got pretty rowdy. It's for your own good. I don't want all those deputies outside to have to come in here. They didn't look too fond of you, to be honest. Here I was thinking you were a trusty, some kind of model prisoner."

"You the one who put me back in here," he says. "Don't expect a man to make your life easier when all you do is make his harder."

"I'm not asking you to make my life easier. I just want you to make it harder for Frank Rios. Remember him?"

Coleman's brow lowers and his cheeks puff up. He remembers.

"Looked to me like you knew him pretty good," I say. "Where's he stay, huh?"

He smiles at the question, shakes his head. "Hey, send that other cop back in here, man. At least she's pretty to look at."

"I would, but she's sensitive. I don't think she appreciated what you said."

"It was a compliment, man." He gives a one-handed shrug, jiggling the handcuff again. "You can't lock a man up like this and expect him not to say nothing when a piece of *that* walks through the door."

"Oh, I'm sure she was flattered."

It's been five minutes since Cavallo walked out, either feigning offense or really feeling it. Either way, we'd been getting nowhere and he was using her presence as an excuse. Things needed a little shaking up.

"The way it's supposed to work," he says, "is I have something you want, so you give me something I want in return. Like a trade, man. Why I gotta explain all this?"

"I thought I had something you want. Revenge. You told Rios he'd be dead, so as long as he's out there enjoying life, he's making a fool of you. Now, if I knew where he stays, then he'd be in here, too, and maybe the two of you could work out your issues."

"Our issues? You mean, like therapy?"

"Something like that."

"So let me get this straight. The trade you're offering is, I tell you where to find him, and you'll send him to jail so I can shank him? They gettin' all this on tape, man?" He laughs at his joke. "Here's what I don't get, though. When they made it a crime to snitch out your homeboys? You ain't gonna send a man to jail for that. So what he done, man? You at least gotta tell me that."

"You want to know what he did?"

"Man, how many times I gotta say it? Yeah, I wanna know."

"You want me to tell you?"

He throws up his free hand, slumping back in his chair. "Mr. March, you didn't used to be this slow. What happened, you have a stroke or something? Can't you understand plain English no more?"

"Murder," I say.

He sits forward, eyes narrowing. "Who he killed?"

"Nobody you know."

"That boy Octavio? I heard about that."

"No, not him."

"Who then?"

"A girl, Coleman. He killed a teenage girl."

His eyebrows raise. "He killed her? You talking literal or meta-phorical? 'Cause I don't think literally he killed nobody. It's Little Evey you talking about, right? The one always followin' him around." He shakes his head. "I mean, what he done, it's bad, but it ain't the same as killin'."

The hair on the back of my neck stands up. I want to pounce on him, dragging out everything he knows, reaching down his throat with my fist if I have to, but the worst thing I can do is let on that I'm excited, or even interested.

"So you're sticking up for him now, Coleman?"

"I ain't stickin' up for nobody, but if you was in the same kind of bind, you might see it different. You say he didn't kill Octavio, but if anybody had a reason, it's him. Man, he loved that girl for real. Drove all the way to New Orleans to get her back, that's how much. Some-body take your woman like that, like she just another installment on the payment plan, what you gonna do then? Yeah, he killed him."

"He didn't," I say.

Now he looks confused. "He told me he was gonna. I talked to him right after he left Octavio. He said he gave over the money—not all he owed, but a nice chunk he got from moving some product—and Octavio, he goes, 'That's a pretty little thing. She can stay here and work some debt off, too.' And I go, 'What you gonna do?' I thought maybe he was wanting me to back his play, only that's not my thing, right? But he's all like, 'I got it handled already. I got it taken care of.'"

"You thought he meant he was going to kill Octavio?"

He looks at me like I'm wearing a dunce cap. "What else you think he meant? Like I said, you'd do the same thing."

"Where's he stay, Coleman?"

"Listen," he says. "Since I been in here, I been thinking. So what if he's snitching to the police, huh? He's all right. What I said, that was words spoken in anger, without due consideration. I don't wish nobody no ill. There ain't no hate in me at all, not no more.

It's wrong to be a snitch, and it's for sure wrong to leave that girl behind instead of throwin' down right there, but what's he gonna do? Answer me that. He said there's, like, four or five of 'em, and they got guns."

"Coleman, I'm going to tell you something and I want you to listen good. I'm not talking about Octavio Morales, and I'm not talking about Little Evey, either. The girl he killed was somebody else, a friend of hers. He shot her. He shot her three times with a .22. Right here"—I mark the spot on my own body with a fingertip—"and right here. And then he put the barrel against her temple and put the last one right here. In cold blood, Coleman. Now, are you going to sit here and try to defend that, or are you going to tell me where he stays?"

But he's not ready to roll over yet. "Why he done it?"

"Does it matter why?"

He clamps a hand over his mouth, looking down at the table through slitted eyelids. I sit there and let him stew. Whatever I can say, I've said it already. The rest is up to him. If Cavallo were back at the table, she could try to work on his sympathies. She could whip out that cross of hers and tell him if he wants to get right with Jesus, it's time to talk. But all I can do is level with him man to man and hope it's enough. Part of me wishes she would walk back in so the burden wouldn't rest on me alone. But she's not going to sit here and be spoken to like that any more than I could sit through Hannah Mayhew's funeral, thinking of my own girl in the casket the whole time.

"Listen," he says, then lets out that sweet long sigh every interrogator will tell you is music to the ears, the sound that means he's about to give it all up. "The thing is, there ain't no one place he stays. But I know a couple you can check. He's got this cousin named Tito—"

"We know about that. He isn't there."

"All right. Did that cousin tell you he's gotta van? Frank borrows it sometimes, and when they was looking for him that's what he'd do, just pull over somewhere and sleep in the van."

"We've got the van," I say."

He nods. "Before he start paying him again. That's why he went, to get clear of the man. He was like, 'I'll pay you, but you gotta leave me be.' Only that ain't how it worked out, I guess."

"Besides the van, where would he stay?"

"There's some motels he'd go when he had money. And a couple of people he might stay with sometimes—including me, before this happened." He jerks the cuffs again. "Give me that notepad and I'll write some things down."

I slide the legal pad across to him along with a pen. He hunches over and starts writing. I should feel relief, even optimism, but the longer it takes the less likely it is that Rios will be holed up at any of the locations. I was hoping he'd have a fixed abode, some kind of hideout known only to him and Coleman where we were sure to find him.

He hands the pad back.

"Now, Mr. March, on account of all this cooperation here, you gotta do something for me, right?"

I stand and head for the door. "I can put in a good word—"

He laughs. "Whatever. That ain't what I mean. Listen here. My grandma, every Saturday morning she walks over to Emancipation Park and sits on a bench there. She reads her psalm and she prays, probably for me. She can't come up here, and me . . . well, I don't like to call from here, neither. But you could tell her a message for me."

"What message?"

"That everything's all right," he says. "Tell her it's okay. Tell her I go to church every Sunday and sing in the choir."

"Do you?" I ask.

He rolls his eyes. "You can tell her that, man. I helped you out."

"Fine," I say, tapping the edge of the pad against the table. "I'll tell her."

Cavallo waits outside, arms crossed, still steaming from Coleman's earlier baiting. She asks what I got out of him and I tell her. When she hears I'm supposed to assure the grandmother that he's a choirboy, she snorts in derision.

"There must be a different definition inside."

★

While detectives from my squad work Coleman's list, trying to bring Frank Rios to heel, and Lieutenant Bascombe sweats Jiménez personally in Interview Room 1, I pay a visit to the crime lab garage, where the white panel van has been carefully gone over, every surface scrutinized, every fascia removed for testing. The technician walks me through the results. The dried specks we saw through the window are indeed blood, and Luminol tests show smears all over the interior, especially under the plywood.

"He scrubbed it out pretty good," the tech says, "but when I shined the black light on it, the floor just lit up."

Removing the plywood, he also recovered a single spent shell, a tiny, crimped .22 caliber casing. Rios knew to collect them, but missed one in the rush.

"When we unloaded the painting supplies, we also found rolls of plastic they use as drop cloths. We're seeing if we can match the ragged edge up with the sheet her body was rolled in. Might not work, but it's worth a try."

I nod in agreement. "What about the gun?"

"No sign of it."

Back upstairs, a group of spectators is camped out in the monitor room, watching Bascombe's performance.

"How's he doing?" I ask.

Ordway sits up front, paws folded over his belly. "He's just staring at the poor man. It's unbelievable. Tito talks and the lieutenant just stares him down, so Tito talks some more."

"Anything good?"

"He's admitted to keeping a Ruger .22 under the seat of the van."

"It's not there now."

He nods. "He says it's got to be Rios who took it."

"Does he know where Rios is staying?"

"Naw, but he offered to go undercover and find him."

"For real?"

"The man's desperate at this point. He also says Rios might have hightailed it back to Old Mexico."

"I doubt that. Remember, I spoke to him. The kid's got no accent. If he wasn't born here, he definitely grew up here. It's not like he just crossed the border. I saw his driver's license."

"And illegals can't get those." Ordway smiles at my naiveté.

"Well, if he is south of the border, Mack, we're sending you down to get him."

"Be my guest. I'm overdue for a vacation."

Back at my desk, I stare at the computer awhile, then find myself flipping through Joe Thomson's sketchbook, tracing the lines of the now-familiar face with my fingertip. While I'm daydreaming, Aguilar taps me on the shoulder and says the captain wants to see me. I knock on the boss's door and he summons me inside.

"March, we've had our differences. You haven't always made things easy for yourself around here, not recently. But I've had a good feeling about you the past couple of weeks. Kicking you down to the task force was probably the best thing I ever did."

"Thank you, sir."

"I've talked to Bascombe about this, and we're on the same page."

I nod uncertainly.

"To make a long story short," he says, "I'm putting you back on the board. Starting tomorrow, you're on rotation like everybody else. No more special assignments. No more loaning you out. You've proven yourself."

He reaches across the desk to shake my hand.

"No more suicide cop?" I ask.

He hesitates at first, then smiles. "Right. No more."

The heavens haven't exactly opened up and no choirs of angels sing, but the firm pressure of the captain's handshake goes a long way. Light-headed, I turn toward the door.

"Sir," I say, pausing on the threshold. "My cases aren't down yet. We don't have Keller. We don't have Rios. The way Wilcox is handing out immunity, Salazar will walk."

"It's a matter of time, that's all. Your work on this . . . everything before pales in comparison." He glances around, retrieving his copy of *The Kingwood Killing* from the shelf behind him. "This pales in comparison. Really. Good work."

"Thank you."

The door closes behind me. The farther I get from it, the less his confidence reassures me. We know what happened and we can pretty much prove it, and by some standards that's enough, even if no one spends a day behind bars. The detective work is the same, either way. But there are things you can live with and things you can't.

If Rios left his girlfriend behind as part of a payment to Octavio Morales, and then he put three bullets into Hannah Mayhew for trying to help her friend, the idea of him walking away, growing old somewhere in Mexico or under another name here in the States, in this very city where a man can walk in plain sight for decades without being recognized for who he is, that concept is unacceptable. If the world works that way, I want no part of it.

But it does work that way.

The guilty walk, it happens all the time, either because people like me can't make the charges stick, or we can't even find the suspect to stick them to.

Cavallo comes through the squad room door, flicking a strand of hair behind her ear, not yet noticing me. I fall in behind her, overtaking, prompting a surprised smile.

"I've just been patted on the back," I say, "but I don't feel like a good boy."

"Maybe this will make you feel better. I just saw Wilcox in the elevator. The case against Keller lost one of its legs. The hospital called. Salazar flatlined this morning."

"He's dead?"

"Some kind of blood clot," she says. "It got in the lungs."

"I need to sit down." I slump into the nearest chair, pulling my tie loose.

"Are you all right?"

"Let's see. I've been shot. I got a bad cop with a conscience mur-dered. I killed a rent-a-cop and just found out I killed a real one, too, even if he was dirty. And I'm still missing both of my murder suspects. But I'm doing a great job, and they're putting me back on rotation—"

"Which is what you wanted, right?"

"What I wanted," I say, "though I was never foolish enough to think it could happen, what I wanted was to find that girl alive. And instead I've found two of them dead."

But that's not right. I know it's not. I never wanted to find her alive. All along I wanted her dead, I wanted to be the one who made the connection, the one to point the finger and say, The girl you're looking for? She was here all along. And in a way, that's exactly what I've gotten. I'm only whining because, having gotten it, I find I don't want it anymore.

"Hollow victories are still victories, at least on paper, but I find them a little hard to celebrate."

"You were almost killed," she says, pointing to my leg. "And if you hadn't shot the rent-a-cop, he'd have killed you—or worse, me. The same goes for Salazar. He dealt the hand, not you. Tonight you're going home alive, and you get to sleep in your own bed. Tomorrow, you can get up and hunt the bad guys again. In my book, there's nothing hollow about any of that. So if you're done feeling sorry for yourself, why don't we get back to work?"

She charges down the aisle, heading for the crowd near the inter-view room. I climb off the chair, brush my pant leg off, and follow.

CHAPTER 29

Days have passed, Coleman's list of haunts is long exhausted, and the hunt for Frank Rios continues. His face is plastered all over the news. The tip lines are flooded with dead-end sighting reports, pinpointing him all over Houston, in Mexico, and as far away as California. Patrol drags in a young illegal who more or less fits the description, then another, but it's all for nothing. Rios is in the wind.

At first, Bascombe lets me slide. This isn't homicide work, after all. He ignores my riding out with the surveillance teams, knocking the same doors I knocked yesterday and the day before. He doesn't raise an eyebrow at Cavallo, who's still camped in my cubicle even though our case is technically down.

Then he appears at my desk, coffee mug in hand, and says, "All good things come to an end."

We troop down to the captain's office, where chairs are already set out, and I'm congratulated again for the good work. Hedges gives Cavallo a sideways glance, like he wants to check her out without seeming to. She's busy tracing her fingertip along her pant leg, following the course of a pinstripe. Not looking up, just waiting for the inevitable heave-ho.

"I think Wanda wants her detective back," Hedges says. "And I'm feeling the same way about you."

I clear my throat. "Finding Rios is a top priority. The chief said so himself on the news."

"Which is why there's a full-court press out there. But let's face it, your talents can be put to better use. It's time. Right, Lieutenant?"

Bascombe's grunt is open to interpretation, but the captain takes no notice. Later, outside the office, he puts a big hand on my shoulder, shaking his head in commiseration but not saying a word.

Cavallo perches on the edge of my desk, arms crossed, blowing a stray hair out of her eyes. She blinks a lot, then tries to smile.

"Oh well."

"I'll talk to Wanda," I say.

"And tell her what?"

"She's closer to this thing. She'll understand."

"No," she says with a resigned sigh. "Hedges is right. We've done all we can do for now. When Rios comes up for air, they'll grab him, and then we'll take this thing to trial. In the meantime—"

"We'll keep working it, you and me. After hours. They can't dictate what we do on our free time."

But Cavallo's not buying it. She gets up, twists her purse over her shoulder, and gives me what's meant as a reassuring smile.

"You should transfer out of there," I say. "Come to Homicide. You could hack it up here, Theresa."

"You think I don't know that?" She heads for the door. "I'll be honest. I think I'd rather be hunting for the victims, not the killers. It's better for the soul."

Aguilar sees her going and stands. Lorenz does, too. By the time she makes it out, the whole squad is on its feet, even Bascombe leans through his open door.

"I'll miss that one," the lieutenant says.

Aguilar nods. "She's a good one."

But I don't have time for sentiment. I grab the phone, start dialing the number, slumping in my chair as it rings and rings.

"Hello?"

"You're a patient kind of man," I say, "the kind who likes to sit and watch a place for hours on end. Isn't that right?"

After a pause, Carter Robb answers in the affirmative. He's already proven himself, staking out James Fontaine like he did.

"You said you wanted to do something this time."

"I do," he says.

He knows Rios, has seen him up close. He won't mistake someone else for him, the way a uniform working from a photo and a physical description might. "Well I have something, assuming you're still interested."

"I am."

"We aren't giving up," I tell him. "That's the main thing."

And just like that, I set Robb loose on the street, another set of eyes. I give him the list from Coleman, give him my home number, and tell him that in the unlikely event he catches sight of Rios, he should call me right away.

"It's a wild goose chase, I realize that. But it's better than nothing."

"I'm on it," he says, then hangs up.

When I put the phone down, there's a warmth running through me. I like this kid. I haven't misjudged him. Just like that, he's taking up the task. What I've just done, it's wrong. It's outside the bounds. But I don't regret it, not even a little.

Charlotte returns from Dallas looking tan and rested, with a canvas tote full of new clothes and a determination to see the last of our tenant. While he's out in the suburbs winging his way through one of the many community college classes he teaches for extra money, she and Ann pack up the sleeping bag and dirty clothes and men's magazines he's littered around the living room in her absence, boxing everything neatly, then climb the stairs and do the same thing in the garage apartment. Thanks to the neighbor's chain saw, the roof is free of tree limbs, so they work in the heat beneath the rustling blue tarp, so focused they barely speak. My offers of help are uniformly rejected. Clearly the sisters cooked up a strategy on the drive home.

"I'm not sure this is entirely kosher," I say. "Tommy has rights here as a tenant."

Charlotte hardly glances up. "Don't worry."

She's gotten tired of waiting for me and has taken matters into her own hands.

Just as they finish carrying all the boxes down to the driveway, leaving nothing upstairs but the furniture, a moving van pulls up to the front curb. Ann gives instructions while Charlotte watches, a contented smile on her lips.

"It wouldn't be right," she says, "to expect a tenant to live in conditions like this, and there's no telling when the insurance will pay up. Finding him another place is the decent thing to do, Roland. Anything else would be irresponsible."

"Shouldn't he get a say, though?"

"His dad pays the rent, and I've already talked to him."

"You have? When?"

Her smile widens. She has been busy, very busy during her absence. The thought of Tommy's reaction worries me a bit, but it's a relief to have the old Charlotte back, in control of her life once more, the refractive, toxic influence of the anniversary finally in abeyance. I put my arm around her bare shoulders, squeezing her tight, as the movers head up the stairs to do the heavy lifting.

"Go up and change," she says, brushing her hand on my suit jacket. "We're all going out to dinner when Tommy gets home."

"Dinner? All right then."

In the bedroom I peel off my work clothes, changing into jeans and a short-sleeved pullover, leaving it untucked over my backup gun, a slim Kahr K40. My mobile phone rings, a number I don't recognize.

"Mr. March? It's Gina Robb. I'm sorry to bother you, but—"

"What can I do for you?"

"I was wondering . . . have you seen my husband? It's just, he's been out looking, you know, and he didn't come home last night—"

"Out looking for what?" I ask, pretending I don't know.

"That man. The one who killed Hannah."

"He's up to his old tricks," I say, trying to make light of the situation. "I told him when he staked out James Fontaine's house to leave it alone. I figured he'd learn his lesson."

"Well, he hasn't. He thinks he has to do something. No matter how many times I tell him it's not his fault, no matter how much he's already done—and he's done a lot. No offense, but I don't think anyone's done more than him. But it doesn't matter. Nothing he does can bring her back—either of them, Hannah or Evey."

"And he's not answering your calls?"

"I'm afraid. Either something's happened to him or . . . he's done something."

"Don't worry," I say. "I'm sure he'll get in touch."

"If you hear from him—"

"I'll make sure he calls you."

Once she hangs up, I dial Robb's number. Charlotte, who's come inside with Ann, interrupts her conversation to call up the stairs. As the phone rings I tell her I'll be down in just a second. Robb answers.

"I just got a call from your wife," I say. "She's worried that you didn't come home last night, and you're not answering her calls."

He doesn't say anything.

"Listen, Carter. I wouldn't have given you that list if I didn't think you'd be cool. You're freaking out, and that makes me worry."

"I'm not freaking out," he says.

"It's going to take more than that to reassure me."

"I'll call her. I was stupid. I wasn't thinking."

"You were out all night?"

"I couldn't leave. I had a feeling he was gonna show up. Every time I'd put the key in the ignition, I'd know the moment I left he was gonna be there. So I couldn't do it."

"Maybe this wasn't such a good idea," I say. "I've made a string of bad calls lately, so I guess this is just the latest. It's not your fault, it's mine. But look, it's time to pull the plug."

"Not yet."

"It's time," I say. "You've spooked your wife, and you're starting to spook me, too. So let's put an end to it, all right? I appreciate your help. You made a real difference. Without you, we wouldn't have put this case down. You've done good work, okay? It's time to let yourself off the hook."

"Not yet."

"I understand you feel responsible. Get over it. This isn't your load to carry. You're absolved, all right? So go home to your wife."

He's quiet a long while, long enough for me to picture him. Not in a church van but in his own car—I've already lectured him about that—a mess of fast food wrappers and water bottles on the floor, his worn out little Bible on the dashboard or across his lap, so he can read and pray and watch all at once, convincing himself his freelance surveillance has some kind of religious significance. I recall his eagerness when I first made the offer, like a starving man invited into the bakery. I should have known right then what I was doing was wrong.

"Carter?"

"Fine," he says. "I'll go home."

"You promise? I'm going to call Gina later, so if you don't—"

"I said I would."

Charlotte calls up the stairs again. Apparently Tommy has arrived home. I want to press Robb harder, but I don't have time. I'll have to assume his promise is good. And I will be making that call to Gina sooner rather than later. Trust but verify.

When I join them in the kitchen, Tommy seems baffled by the sudden goodwill coming from Charlotte, but he's sufficiently in love with himself to imagine that, given time, anyone could share the feeling, so he doesn't peer too deeply into the matter.

"Hey, I just need to run up to the apartment before we go."

"No time," Charlotte insists, tapping her watch face. "We've got reservations."

Ann loops an arm through his. "Besides, you look perfectly fine. Don't go changing on our account."

On the way out, he glances toward the living room, but if he notices all his things are gone, he doesn't let on. We crowd into Ann's car, the sisters in front, and accelerate into the early evening traffic. As we cruise past the Paragon, Tommy and I exchange a look. But our table is booked at a trattoria on Morningside in Rice Village, not far from the Bridgers' West University home, where the manager seems to be on friendly terms with Ann. This is all, I realize, her doing. In spite of her bleeding heart when it comes to humanity in general, she can conjure up a ruthless streak for one-on-one dealings.

My hunch is borne out by the way my sister-in-law plays hostess, an unaccustomed role for her, offering a running commentary on the menu, drawing Tommy out about his teaching, the intangibles of his dissertation, and what he calls his activism, which consists mainly of attending various coffeehouse meet and greets and dropping in on the occasional protest. The funny thing is, I can tell she likes him. They have a good bit in common, really.

She gets him talking about West Africa, no doubt having learned from Charlotte that his summer in Ghana is such a touchstone. He can talk about it for hours. I relax and sneak a look in Charlotte's direction. She still wears the contented smile, as if she's reclining poolside in the sun, her eyes hidden behind big round sunglasses, her fingers trailing in the water.

By the time the bill arrives, we're all good friends. The wine has flowed on Tommy's side of the table, and now he glows with a damp-skinned sense of social triumph. In the car he talks at length about what's wrong with the world, using words like bourgeois, consumerism, and globalization to great effect. Ann and Charlotte smile encouragingly, the car heading amiably down Kirby past Dryden, making a left onto Swift. We cruise the vehicle-lined street, block by block, until Ann pulls to a stop in front of a white brick duplex with black shutters, a hulking structure from the 1940s that looks part Tara and part art deco.

"Here you go," Ann says.

The car is silent. Tommy glances toward me in confusion, noticing the keys dangling from Charlotte's hand as she reaches between the seats.

"What are we doing here?" he asks, a baffled smile on his lips.

Charlotte puts the keys in his open palm. "Dropping you off."

"I don't get it."

"This is your new place," Ann says, adjusting the rearview mirror for a better look.

"I'm afraid the insurance isn't going to come through anytime soon," Charlotte says, "so I had a talk with your father, and he thought it was best for you to relocate. You'll like this place."

"It's great," Ann agrees. "Original fixtures and tile. And plenty of space out back for entertaining. The old lady downstairs is charming."

He turns to me. "Is this a joke?"

In spite of everything, I feel for him. The occasion calls for a quip of some kind, but I have a hard time mustering anything, so an anticlimactic shrug has to suffice. Tommy sputters a few objections, only to find the sisters ready, swatting him down with ramrod charm. His things are already in the new apartment waiting for him. The first month's deposit has been made. Charlotte digs through her purse, producing an envelope from the bank with his prorated rent refund in cash. That seems to clinch things. Fingering the stiff bills, he pops the door open and climbs onto the curb, waiting for the rest of us to get out.

He seems to think we're all going upstairs to have a look at the place, but Ann quickly disappoints him. Her foot punches the accelerator, slamming the passenger door shut.

"Hey—"

I turn in my seat, watching Tommy watch us, the keys drooping from one hand and the envelope from the other. Charlotte bursts out laughing, her feet drawn up onto the seat like a girl's, and Ann grins, proud at her achievement. She rights the mirror, then glances over her shoulder at me.

"That's how you solve a problem," she says.

The sisters exchange a high five. I sit quietly in back, reflecting on how differently problems are solved when you're a lawyer instead of a cop. Tommy, impervious to hints and even subtle intimidation, has been a conundrum to me, a first-class irritation. Even after the hurricane offered deliverance, I allowed him to install himself on the couch. It never occurred to me to buy him off. Charlotte has spent no telling how much to bring about her long-awaited eviction, but now she has it and she's utterly pleased.

Not that Tommy was ever the real problem. It's just that the real problem couldn't be solved and never can be. This time next year, there will be another Tommy, because there always is. To move on, even temporarily, we need a sacrifice on the altar; we need to shed some metaphorical blood. Again, a hollow victory, but a necessary one. Yet another means to an end.

Or maybe I'm talking nonsense. My wife is happy, laughing like she used to when we first met. Instead of overanalyzing, maybe it's time to simply enjoy. I pass my hand between the seats, finding hers. She clasps it, drawing it onto her lap, sitting back with a heavy, satisfied sigh.

It's dark when Ann drops us off. Charlotte starts through the back door, dragging me by the hand, but I notice a light still burning in the garage apartment window.

"You left a light on," I say, peeling my hand free.

"Leave it."

"It's people like you causing the energy crisis. Go on in, I'll be back in a minute."

She goes inside, leaving me to bound up the stairs, fumble with my keys, and shoulder my way through the door. Already there's a musty, outdoors stench to the apartment, conjuring fears of the dreaded black mold. Now that Tommy's out, we'll have to see to this.

The neglected light is in the kitchen, reminding me of my conversation with Marta, the waitress from the Paragon. I pause with my hand on the switch, making myself a commitment not to return to that place, one I'll probably break in time, though perhaps I won't. To seal the promise, I turn off the light.

"March."

The voice, coming suddenly out of the depths of the pitch-black living room, makes me jump. My hand slides under my shirt, reaching automatically for my off-duty piece.

"Don't do it. You can't see me, but I can see you."

A pinpoint flashlight switches on at shoulder height, maybe fifteen feet away, blinding me, the kind of light usually affixed to a tactical firearm. Blinking, I struggle to make out the silhouetted figure behind the halo. But not because I haven't identified the voice.

"It's not too bright of you, coming here," I say.

"That's funny, under the circumstances. I never figured you for a wisecracker, so that's good to know. Just keep in mind, if you go for that gun, it'll be the last thing you do. And it won't be hard for me, putting you down. I'd enjoy it."

"Then go ahead. If you're expecting me to beg, you've got another think coming."

The bravado in my words surprises me, but I'm pleased, too. You fantasize about this situation—when the time comes, how will you go? On your feet or on your knees, that kind of thing. And I've always wanted to think of myself as defiant right to the end, a man who won't snivel when the time comes to take his bullet, who'll fight if the opportunity presents itself, not clinging too tightly to life.

"I hope you're proud of yourself," he says.

"Good. I am."

He snorts with derision, the light dipping slightly. "I'll bet you are. You know something? I've never understood you, March. From the very beginning. It's like you picked me out of the air, picked me at random, and decided to do everything in your power to ruin my life."

"You started it. You made me look dirty."

"What, snatching that gun? Your shooting was clean and we both knew it. What I did, it didn't harm you. I wouldn't have let that happen. If you think that, then you don't know me at all."

"I know you, Reg. Believe me, I do."

"You don't know a thing."

"I know you popped Joe Thomson. What kind of cop—what kind of friend—does a thing like that? You worked with that guy for years. That's cold-blooded. Don't say I don't know you, man, because I know your type. I always have."

"I never could figure you out," he says. "Back in the day, I saw some real promise in you. The way you handled yourself under fire, I was impressed. And even later, after you had me in your crosshairs, I still used to think you could be salvaged. When I heard what happened to your kid, March, I was genuinely sorry. And then the way you used it, wringing a confession out of that wife murderer. Man, that knocked me over. You want to talk cold-blooded—"

"I didn't use anything. That's not how it happened."

He whistles impatiently, unimpressed. "Thomson? He was as dirty as they come, and you would've let him walk just for testifying against me. Isn't that right? The irony is pretty rich when you consider it was him that lit up that girl."

"The girl on the bed? Salazar said that was you."

"No doubt. He also said I pulled the trigger on Joe, which is a lie. He was the one. He's your rogue cop. If I'd had any idea what was going on under my nose, I would've done something about it, but instead of coming to me—"

"Is that your story? That's why you're here? You're holding a gun on me to tell me you didn't do it? Get a lawyer then and let's go to court. I'd love to see you try to wiggle out of this."

He tries to laugh, but it comes out as more of a hiss. "He stitched me up good, him and you. There's nothing a lawyer can do . . ." His voice trails off, like even he's losing confidence in the innocence ploy. Whatever his reason for being here, it's not to enter a plea. "And I was almost out, March. All you had to do was wait and I would've handed over my badge and gone into retirement. Nobody had to die . . ."

"Tell that to the girl."

"We tried to save that girl," he sniffs. "That's the crazy thing. It was all running fine until we put the white hat on."

The tactical light lowers a bit more. I can almost see him, at least that's what I tell myself. My body breaks out in a cold sweat, my hands tremble, my thoughts race. Do I stand here and banter until he decides to pull the trigger, or do I draw, risking an early demise? There's a chance, there's always a chance, that he'll miss and I won't. Or I'll be wounded but still able to get off a shot. If the roles were reversed, though, I wouldn't fancy the other guy's chances.

"I have to tell you," he says, his voice different, talking more to himself than me, "a turn of events like this, it's enough to make you think. As long as we did our thing, you wouldn't believe how easy it was. Everything went like clockwork. Believe me, we're only losing the war on drugs because we aren't fighting it, not on their level anyway. It was beautiful. Candy from a baby. But the moment we try to be the good guys, it all blows up. I should have left her there. I knew that. We should have stuck to our thing. We hadn't planned for that, so we should've walked away. But we didn't. Instead, we went in there, guns blazing, like the cavalry coming to the rescue, and that one . . . pure . . . instinct, that's what destroyed us."

The room grows quiet. In a moment, wondering where I am, Charlotte will venture outside. She'll call up the stairs, or even ascend them, and I'm not going to let that happen. My hand is damp. I wipe it against my pant leg. I don't want anything to ruin my move, no glitch in the cycle of muscle memory, my hand flashing, pistoning forward, firing blindly into the light.

"March," he says. "Don't be stupid."

I relax my hand, biding my time.

"I'm not here to punch your ticket, man. Not yet. It'll happen one day, believe me. When you least expect it. Blah, blah, blah—you know the speech. But I'll do it now if you want, and I'll go down there and put a bullet in your wife, too. It's your call."

"Then why are you here?" I ask.

"Good question." He laughs dryly. "Call it pride. Arrogance, maybe. But I wanted you to know I could do it. I wanted you to know you didn't win. Trust me, March, I'm gonna land on my feet. I have other irons in the fire, my friend. There are people in this world who will pay gladly for the kind of skills I have to offer. You got lucky, sure, but it wasn't your great detective work that brought me down."

"I realize that. It was your own people, Reg. Thomson's conscience. Salazar keeping that gun around to use against you."

"No," he says, the light bobbing. "It wasn't that. It wasn't you. It was fate."

Before he finishes, the light disappears, leaving a ghost image behind on my retinas. I hear him moving. I shuffle backward, deep into the kitchen, drawing my pistol as I slip on the linoleum floor. Steadying myself, I raise the muzzle, but there's nothing but darkness to focus on. My vision adjusts and I see the lighter darkness of the open door. I edge forward, gun at the ready, peering around the doorframe and down the stairs. The back door of the house, illuminated by a mosquito-swarmed bulb, is shut tight. Outside the cone of golden lamplight, nothing stirs.

I edge my way down, puzzling over the rapid exit. The stairs creak under me. When Keller left, I didn't even hear the descending footfalls. Wait a second . . .

Back in the apartment, I switch on the overhead light. The bedroom door stands open, the tarp flapping gently in the night breeze. Moving slowly, leading with my weapon, I approach the threshold, sweeping the room until I'm sure it's clear. I feel around for the bedroom light, but nothing happens when I flip the switch. The closet light works, though. Once it's on, I can see the gaping hole in the bedroom wall where the roof and window collapsed under the tree's weight. The tarp is folded back, revealing a stretch of windowsill.

As I advance, the top of a ladder is visible. It leads from the bedroom window down to the neighbor's yard. On the far side of his property, the wooden gate stands open. Tires squeal on distant pavement, the sound of a nemesis making good his escape.

Arrogance, he said, and he must be right. What else would drive him to put everything at risk like this, just to let me know he's not finished with me? Just to issue an empty threat. The funny thing is, I could see myself taking the same risk for the same pointless gesture. That's rivalry for you.

I let myself into the house, shutting the back door and locking the dead bolt. The stairs give off an odd glow. Investigating, my gun still in hand, I find a row of candles flickering upward, one every couple of steps.

At the top, Charlotte stands, her legs bare, her body swathed in one of my white dress shirts, the collar turned. Her eyes sparkle in the candlelight.

"I thought you'd never get back," she says. "What took so long?"

I slide my off-duty gun back in the holster, slump down on the bottom step, and bury my head in my hands. Behind me, I hear her weight on the steps, her bare feet padding down, and then her hand touches the back of my neck, cool and dry, her fingers sliding upward through my hair.

CHAPTER 30

The sheets drag away from me, Charlotte rolling in her sleep, and I wake up, staring into the dark, feeling the fan's cool breeze on my skin, listening to the blades revolve. A thought surfaces, a memory, a yellow string knotted around my imaginary finger, and I turn to the nightstand in dismay, where the clock reads a little past midnight. I was supposed to phone the Robbs. Is it too late to bother them?

My mobile, still in my pants pocket on the floor, displays a string of missed calls. At dinner I'd turned off the ringer and never switched it back. Gina Robb is listed, and so is Carter, calling from his cell. He left a message just a minute ago—it was the buzz of notification, not Charlotte's movement, that must have wakened me—speaking in a breathy whisper, mentioning an apartment complex in Sharpstown and giving me a unit number, telling me to meet him there right away. I redial his number, but the call goes straight to voicemail.

"What are you doing?" Charlotte asks as I pull my clothes on.

"I've gotta go."

She's been married to a homicide detective long enough to accept sudden departures. She rolls back over, then grabs my pillow to shore her head up.

"Since you're leaving," she says.

Past midnight the landscape of Houston changes, which is another way of saying there's a lot less traffic. I roll the window down, letting in a blast of humid air, my foot heavy on the accelerator, my heart tight in my chest. The blocks fly past and I'm racing down Interstate 10 until it melts into the Loop, the lighted glass and steel buildings along Post Oak and the towers hedging the Galleria all shimmering in the hazy night. I exit onto Highway 59, impatient in spite of the brisk driving, a sense building inside me that I've overstepped. That the error I planted by enlisting Carter Robb will reap a black harvest.

When I reach the address—a modest, drive-up affair with tiny fenced balconies on both levels, perhaps a dozen units in all—I find to my surprise a red logo-covered van from Cypress Community Church parked on the curb just a block away. The man knows nothing of subtlety, but then who would suspect a church van of containing a set of watching eyes?

The complex is not one of the access-controlled empires favored by the gangs, but just a brown, run-down and rusted rental property dating from the 1970s, the kind of place I would have driven past without notice if I hadn't been looking for it. And if there wasn't a church van out front. One thing I'm sure of: this address was not on our list.

The number Robb gave me is upstairs, so I ascend the metal steps, keeping my footfalls light, not knowing what to expect. A dusty, spider-webbed grill sits next to the door. The bulb in the fixture beside the entrance is burned out, but the peephole glows dimly, letting me know somebody's home. I draw my pistol, tucking it down beside my hip, then give the door a light rap.

It opens slightly, straining against a security chain, and I get a glimpse of Carter Robb's face, pale, damp with sweat, eyes bulging a bit, before the door slams shut. He releases the chain and throws it open wide. His skin has a noticeable pallor, as if he hasn't eaten in a long time and might be feverish. He wears dark jeans and a black T-shirt that reads VIVA LA REFORMACION in red letters, with a posterized man dressed like he's going to the Renaissance Festival taking the place of Che Guevara.

"You called," I say, casting a wary glance over the apartment.

The living room is filled with matched furniture straight out of a thrift shop, upholstered in nubby, synthetic-looking blue tweed. A stack of magazines, mostly checkout counter fare, is centered on the coffee table with the TV remote on top. Posters tacked on the wall. In an armchair, a basket of laundry consisting of towels and socks and T-shirts and women's underwear, still waiting to be folded. Plastic cups are discarded everywhere, some of them empty, others still with liquid stagnant inside.

Robb wobbles on his feet, taking a step back to steady himself. I reach out, then notice what's hanging from his left hand.

"You want to give me that?"

He blinks, then glances down at the Ruger .22 caliber pistol, almost as if he didn't realize it was there. With the barrel down he hands it over. I strip the magazine out, ejecting a round from the chamber, then tuck it into my waistband for safekeeping.

"Now, why don't you tell me what's going on?"

"I better show you," he says.

He points down the hallway, toward the bedroom presumably, and I see there's blood on his hand, and more wetting his dark shirt. His knuckles have the bruised and scuffed look of a man who's thrown some punches without knowing how. We walk toward the hallway, Robb pausing over the laundry basket. He lifts a wadded shirt, leaving a smear of blood on the fabric.

"This was Evey's." He turns it this way and that, then lets it drop. "I was just about to leave, like you said, and as soon as I turned the engine on, there he was. He knocked on a door—not the one from your list—and talked to some guy. They exchanged something. I think he sold the guy drugs, because he had a wad of cash in his pocket. I followed him, and this is where he went."

He leads the way to the back bedroom, with me trailing a few feet behind, dreading what I'll find on the other side of the door. I remember the saintly spasm of Octavio Morales's death agony, the startled expression on Joe Thomson's face in his final gasp. The security guard, Cropper, coiled up in a pool of blood, dead by my hand on the warehouse pavement. And Salazar, his body small and crumpled under the hospital sheets, that death also down to me.

And this one is, too. Even if Robb pulled the trigger, it's my sin to carry, just as much as if I'd put the gun in his hand and told him to shoot. I'd deputized him, appointed him an instrument of vengeance, and probably destroyed the man in the process. I can tell by the way he's moving, the jerking, twisting shuffle, the thousand-mile stare. He's been gutted, his soul carved out, astonished to find himself capable of such bestiality.

I pause in the dark hallway, just outside the light spilling through the bedroom door, imagining Frank Rios as I last saw him, picturing him spread out on the bed like Morales, hands lifted stiffly heavenward, the blood cooling, settling in his extremities. But when I enter, it isn't a beatific corpse waiting for me.

Rios sits on the edge of the bed, his wrists lashed together with an extension cord, its opposite end secured to the bedpost beneath him, between his legs, forcing him to hunch forward, to tilt his battered head up in order to see. He looks at me through one eye, the lid swollen, his face puffy and scratched, blood dripping from his mouth and nose. It takes a moment for him to recognize me, and then he tugs on the cord violently. He spits to clear his mouth.

"You gotta help me, man," he whispers.

Robb goes to the mirrored closet, leaning back against the door, his knees buckling under him. As he slides down, he leaves a wet trail on the glass. I kneel beside him, pulling at the T-shirt. A seeping washrag is duct-taped to his side. Underneath, a tiny hole oozes blood.

"Put pressure on this." I replace the rag, moving his hands to cover it. "I'm calling an ambulance."

"Wait," he says, reaching toward my hand. "Make him tell you what he told me."

"You've been shot, Carter. We've gotta get you to the hospital."

"It doesn't matter. Make him tell you."

I pull free, walking out into the hallway. There's no way I'm going to let him bleed to death on the carpet while I chat with Frank Rios. The emergency operator scrambles ambulance and police and then it's back into the bedroom, where both men look up, both appealing to me. From the bathroom I grab fresh towels, then bend over Robb to try and staunch the flow of blood. Over my shoulder, Rios coughs sloppily and spits some more.

"You don't get it," he hisses, addressing Robb, not me, continuing a conversation I must have interrupted with my arrival. "Not you, not that other one—Murray. You talk, but it's not inside you like it was in her."

"Shut up," I say.

Robb shakes his head weakly. "Let him talk."

"I knew," Rios says. "I could tell looking at you. Talking. That Murray thinks he's so smart, quoting all these philosophers he's never read. But he's not. You're not. This"—he shrugs against the cable—"it means nothing."

I don't want him to talk. I don't want to hear his side of the story. Some killers, when they realize it's over, they want to tell their life story. They have pronouncements to make, as though taking life gives them some heightened insight into living it. I've sat through enough of these lectures, even been entertained by a few, but not this time. Not him.

"You murdered Hannah Mayhew," I say.

"It wasn't like that."

"What was it like, then?"

He drops his head, showing me the top of his skull, his matted hair, a target to lash out at, to crush. I feel it in me, that desire to hurt him, to make him suffer, to put him down like a rabid dog. The lives he's destroyed, the anguish, the senseless brutality—no one would begrudge me doing it, and there are plenty who'd consider it my duty. There are some men not worth bringing in alive, not if you can help it. I have the means, and coursing through me like a high, like a toxin in my system, I have the motive, too.

"I loved her," he says. He does more than say it. He wails the words, filling them with a repellent self-pity. "I tried to stop them from hurting her."

"Evey, you mean. You abandoned her. I know what happened to Evey. I saw the aftermath firsthand."

His head shakes. "I sent them to save her, but they didn't. You know what they did? He told me. Tony told me. They dumped her, man. They put her in the water like she was just garbage. And they were gonna do that to me, too, if they ever caught me."

I can hardly stand it. "So you're the victim here."

"Everybody's the victim. I work for the police, man. The good guys. I pass along whatever they need to know. And they supposed to help me. That's what he says. Tony. They gonna help me with the money I owe. They gonna square everything in time. Only they don't, so then I gotta do it. Except . . . Except . . ."

The emotion in his voice is real enough. I can believe, in his own sick and self-centered way, that he loved Evangeline Dyer, just like Coleman said. But hearing him say so, hearing his words thicken with grief, pollutes her memory. I see her face in Thomson's photo, on the many pages of his sketchbook, in the picture folded over and tucked in my notebook, Evey and Hannah saying goodbye before the Dyers left for Louisiana. Even though I never knew her, even though I pursued her blindly, just a body tied to a bed, I feel she belongs to me in some way she doesn't to him, the man she ran away with, the man who left her to her fate.

Something Donna Mayhew said comes back to me. I didn't know her, but now I feel like I've found her. Only I'll never find Evey, down at the bottom of the Gulf. She's lost for good, and this is as close as I'll ever get.

"You left her," I say.

"I sent help."

"And what about Hannah? She didn't deserve to die. She didn't deserve to have her body dumped, either, but that's what you did."

At the mention of her name, his demeanor shifts. He twists his head up, looking at me through the hooded eye. "That girl, she wouldn't stop calling. She had to talk to Evey, wouldn't stop until I put her on the phone. But how could I do that? I tried putting her off, but she knew something wasn't right. She wouldn't let go of it. And I thought, this girl could get me in a lot of trouble—or maybe I wasn't thinking. I was afraid." He spits again. "Afraid of them finding me, afraid of anyone knowing."

"So, what, you kidnapped her?"

"I agreed to meet her. Told her Evey and me would be at the mall. That's where we used to meet, before Evey went home to the Big Easy. Hannah, when she showed up, I told her she had to stop calling me. I said Evey went back again, but she could tell it was a lie. And I went, 'This has gotta end.' "

"Then you killed her."

He shakes his head. "I was just trying to scare her, man. But she got real angry and was like, 'What you done to her?' And she says she's gonna call the police. Under the seat, my cousin Tito, he keeps a loaded gun." He turns sideways to look at Robb, who hasn't moved in a while. "He's got the gun, man. You better watch out."

"I have the gun," I say, then hunching over Robb: "You okay? Help's coming, so just hang on."

"Is he okay?" Rios says. "What about me? Look what he done to me!"

"He could've done worse."

A sticky laugh escapes his red lips. "No, he couldn't. Not after what I told him."

He stops talking, now that I want him to. But there's no way he can keep it up. Not everybody talks, but everybody wants to, I'm convinced of that. The hard men, the professionals, they know to keep their mouths shut. But it doesn't come naturally. Like killing, you have to overcome a lot of instinct to stay quiet, whether you're guilty or not. The effort on its own is sometimes enough to give the game away. So I know he's going to open up.

"Told him what?"

Under the circumstances, though, he could admit to anything and get away with it. It won't take much of a lawyer to argue any confession made in this room is coerced. But I don't need him to confess to anything. All I need him to do is exist; all I need is his body so that justice can be executed upon it.

"Told him what?" I ask again, giving him a nudge.

"Don't touch me, man."

I push him again, and he rears back.

"What did you tell him that was so important?"

"Go on," Robb says.

Rios starts nodding, a nod like a train coming over the horizon, slow at first, hardly perceptible, then it gains momentum, quickening to the point that his head bobs back and forth, his intention arriving. "It was her fault. She saw the gun and the stupid girl reached for it. It went off, and she's sitting there in the passenger seat, looking surprised, like she never saw that coming."

He looks up at me, gauging my reaction, then he chuckles. Telling the story is like committing the crime again, only this time with an audience. We're helpless bystanders, Robb and I, witnesses. Forced to hear, powerless to stop him.

"She was trying to save her friend," I say, because I can't say nothing. "A girl you supposedly loved. And you killed her."

My anger leaves him unfazed. "She didn't react at first, but then she kind of cried out. I dragged her back between the seats, put her on the floor of the van, you know." He closes his eyes, remembering. "I never did that before, never shot someone, and it kind of surprised me she didn't die right there. Maybe the bullets were too small. She started crying then, laying in back. I started driving, 'cause I was afraid somebody heard the shot."

I recall the parking lot, standing in the space where Hannah's car was found. He'd shot her, and when she didn't die, he threw her in back and drove around, waiting for her to bleed out.

"So I'm driving," he says, "and I look back and there she is, crawling up to the front again."

The more he speaks, the calmer he gets, like his energy is channeled entirely into the story and he's almost proud to tell it. There's a pleasure he takes in describing the scene, like a kid at a campfire describing the weirdest thing that ever happened to him.

"She was kind of clawing herself toward me, you know? Her hair was hanging over her face, like in a horror movie or something. And it was scary, man, scary to see her coming."

Behind me, Robb shifts his weight. "She didn't give up. She was brave."

The interruption trips him up, and for a second Rios can't remember where he was. Maybe the emotion in the youth pastor's voice has thrown him off. It's not anguish. It's not the choking, soul-eating rage that I'm feeling. What it sounds like is love.

"I had to shoot her again," Rios says, his voice rising an octave, "while I'm still driving. That time she got quiet. And I thought, Wow, I think she's finally dead. I drove like that awhile and then I look in the mirror and she's right there, staring at me all pale like a ghost. I almost crashed, man. I had to pull into the driveway of somebody's house, and I turn around and she's holding her stomach, and she's got these tears streaming down her face, and she keeps going, 'What did you do to her? What did you do?' And I keep telling her, 'It wasn't me. It wasn't me.'"

He shakes his head, laughing incredulously at the thought.

"There I was. I got the gun, and it's like I'm the one who's afraid, you know? Trying to make an excuse or something, so she don't get mad at me. Well, she kinda fell over then, up against the side of the van, and she started making this noise . . . I can't even describe it. It was loud, though, and I thought somebody was gonna come outside and see what was going on. I climbed in the back and told her, 'You gotta shut up now, you gotta shut up.' And I put the gun against her head . . ." He makes a pistol of his fingers, inching it forward in the air, drawing the cord along. "I put it against her head just the way he put it against mine." He cocks his head toward Robb. "And she looked at me just how I looked at him, and she said just what I said. Only she meant it."

"What do you mean? What did she say?"

"She said it twice, like she wanted to make sure I understood. What she said was, 'I forgive you.' She said it two times, maybe for her and Evey both. 'I forgive you, I forgive you.' "

When he speaks the words, something goes out of me. I turn to Robb, who's looking up, expectant, making sure I understand what I've just heard. We are witnesses together, yes, but not helpless. He looks feverish from the gunshot wound. His eyes burn into me.

"She forgave me." He whistles under his breath. "You believe that? If I'd known she could be like that, I don't think I coulda shot."

He leans back a little, tugging on the cord, offering up his wrists like he expects me to free him, like he thinks I'll whip out my lockback knife and cut him loose, the way I did last time, when Hannah Mayhew's blood was still fresh on his hands, though I couldn't see it. I straighten up, feeling tired and spent.

Seven years ago, on that awful day, while I transported a knife murderer across the state line, my little girl's heart was so full of empathy, so sad for all those strangers and their families, that she made Charlotte take her to a church vigil. They held hands, sitting on the hard pews, and they prayed for those people, and when they left, the car hit them and Jessica died.

And it was for nothing, I always thought. But I was wrong.

Against the mirrored closet door, Robb winces at the wound in his side, which is good. It shows he's not too far gone to feel. He catches my eye, smiles grimly against the pain, and tries to get up. I move to stop him, but change my mind. I help him to his feet.

We edge down the hallway, leaving Rios behind, and I clear the basket of clean white laundry out of the way so he can sit.

"It wasn't true what he said," Robb whispers. "About me putting the gun to his head. Maybe he thought I was going to shoot him, but I never would."

"It doesn't matter to me."

"It does to me," he says.

I go into the kitchen, find a fresh plastic cup, and pour a measure of tap water out. Then, uncertain whether he should drink anything, given the position of the bullet, I dip a fresh towel in the water and use it to wipe his brow.

"You did good," I tell him. "Hannah would be proud."

He shakes his head, but not in denial. "I'm the one who's proud. Proud of her."

The metal steps rattle outside with the weight of uniformed officers and EMTs, the knock at the door filling me with relief. I step away from him, letting the responders do their work, taking Robb's vitals and freeing Frank Rios, then cuffing his hands behind his back. I slip the Ruger from my waistband and put it on the kitchen counter along with the magazine and the bullet from the chamber, alerting the uniforms to its presence.

Then I step outside into the warm night, gazing up into the thick, radiant blanket that in this city always hides the stars.

ONE YEAR LATER

More than time has passed. The last time I drove by, the place seemed packed, with crowds spilling out into the lot. Election night, beer bottles raised in salute, the dawn of a new age. Now my wheels crunch over gravel and my headlights cast cones across the darkness. The facade is stripped bare, only a shadow left where the sign once hung, the plate-glass windows covered in a film of dirt. I sit a moment, gazing at the sight, wondering when this could have happened and how I of all people could have missed it.

I throw the car in reverse and drive home.

The house glows in the night, every chandelier and lamp, every fixture radiating, a sparkling stone set among the glimmering neighbors. I park in the driveway, popping the trunk, hoisting two bags of ice over my shoulder, saving the rest for another trip. Out of the shadows, Carter Robb pads over, flip-flops smacking against his heels. He reaches in to grab the rest of the ice, then slams the lid shut with his elbow.

"She's been wondering where you were," he says. "People are gonna start showing up."

I smile. "Let her wonder."

We let ourselves in through the back, hoisting the ice onto an empty section of countertop, one of the few gaps left that isn't occupied already by dishes or glasses or finger foods ready either for cooking or plating. Charlotte tosses her apron aside, counting the bags of ice like she suspects me of holding some back. Satisfied, she gives me a kiss on the cheek. Over her shoulder I see Gina Robb peering into the oven, her cat eyes steaming, an oversized quilted mitt on her hand. Ann comes through from the dining room, silverware bristling from each fist, looking pinched as always but excited.

"He's back," Charlotte says.

Robb makes his excuses and retreats outside, taking the garage stairs two at a time. When he returns five minutes later, the flip-flops have been replaced by lace-up shoes, and he's changed into clothes without any holes, without any ironic messages printed on them. For the past six months or so, ever since he finally resigned his position out in the suburbs, after much soul searching, to join Murray Abernathy at the outreach center, he and Gina have been living in the apartment over the garage. A temporary arrangement that, as far as I'm concerned, can remain permanent. Charlotte's warmed to the couple, too, grateful at last to have tenants who never throw parties and never leave bottles strewn across the yard. She's even talking about going back to church regularly, and dragging me along, kicking and screaming or otherwise.

The doorbell rings and I switch into host mode, but it's only Bridger arriving as a harbinger.

"How did it go?" Ann asks.

"Brilliant. There were more people than seats, so I guess that's a good sign."

"Is he on his way?"

"He's coming. They all are."

Brad Templeton's article about the case, when it ran in the *Texas Monthly*, set off another firestorm of interest, and is set to be anthologized with the rest of the year's best crime reporting. His full-length account is fresh off the presses, another fat paperback. I fulfilled my promise to him, and this time, instead of dreading the publication, I feel relieved. I only left the signing at Murder by the Book early to fulfill Charlotte's last-minute request for ice, dawdling pensively along the way.

The final chapter in the book is the only one I've actually read. Going further might spoil my reconciled equanimity. A few days after Christmas, in the bathroom of a Buenos Aires luxury hotel, a man who was later identified as Chad Macneil, the missing financial wizard, was found dead, his head submerged in a half-full bathtub. There was no sign of the missing fortune, but Brad made much of his theory that it was Reg Keller who did the deed before vanishing once again. Something tells me he's right, but I haven't admitted it to anyone. Sometimes, in the dead of night, I find myself hoping that restored wealth will keep him from ever coming back to fulfill his threat of revenge. And then I feel like a coward and tell him to bring it on.

After describing the book signing for the benefit of the ladies, Bridger slips out the back for a cigarette. I join him under the moonlight, grateful for the break. He tells me he's still thinking about quitting, or at least cutting back.

"I just had a bit of a shock," I say. "Did you know the Paragon closed down?"

He regards me thoughtfully through a cloud of smoke, then shakes his head.

"It's all gone."

"You make it sound like such a tragedy," he says.

We stand there quietly, a couple of loners steeling themselves for a night of mandatory entertaining. Bridger exhales, then chuckles on the smoke.

"Something funny happened today." His eyes light up in the dimness. "Just before heading out to the bookstore, I was in line getting coffee. I guess I looked impatient, because the lady behind the counter asks me why the rush. So I tell her about the book signing, and I have to explain what it's all about, of course. I mention Hannah's name, and she starts nodding. 'What a tragedy,' she says, 'and she was just ten years old.' "

"She was seventeen."

"Right. But this lady had her confused with that other kid, the one they found in League City."

"The Bonham girl?"

He shakes his head. "You're thinking of the other one, but she was older. This lady meant the little Latina girl, the one who disappeared from the playground."

"They never found that one's body, I thought."

He shrugs. "She was confused. The point is, I tell her, 'No, this is the one they found during the hurricane, the one that died trying to find her friend.' And she gets this vague look in her eye, like she kind of remembers, then she just gives up. 'There's been so many,' she says, waving her hand in the air. I couldn't believe it. This was all over the news, twenty-four seven, and she couldn't even remember. I told Templeton at the signing and he looked disappointed, like that was one less person to buy his book."

The door opens behind us and Carter Robb slips out. Bridger drops his cigarette and covers it with his foot, exaggerating the move so that Robb can't miss it, his way of razzing the new tenant, even though Robb has never said a word about his smoking, or any other vice. The faults Robb occupies himself with tend to be his own.

"Everybody's showing up," he says.

But he makes no move to go back inside, and neither do we. Instead, we all stand there, shuffling our feet, taking final breaths, preparing mentally for the inevitable.

"Then there's the appeal," Bridger says, picking up on his theme. "That's going to put the story back in the headlines, I bet. Assuming it gets that far. Templeton's gotta be hoping it does."

Frank Rios would be sitting on death row today if Donna Mayhew hadn't made her appeal at the sentencing, asking for mercy on behalf of her daughter. Not many people understood that gesture, and she declined all opportunities the media offered her to explain. Now he's in the Walls Unit up at Huntsville, working on an appeal. His defense team reached out to Ann, hoping she'd do some pro bono agitating on their behalf, but she had the good sense to decline.

"Whatever happens," I say, "he's not going anywhere."

Before we can go inside to fulfill our duty, the door opens again and Theresa Cavallo slips out, shutting it firmly behind her.

"I thought so."

"Pull up a chair," I say, though nobody's sitting.

"You got out of there early, I noticed."

"Charlotte told me to come back with a bag of ice or on it."

"Great." She takes up a position beside me, arms crossed, and I glance down at her ring finger, where a wedding band is finally coupled to the engagement rock. Her fiancé came back from Iraq long enough to tie the knot, then he shipped out again for Afghanistan. I was there for the ceremony. She made a beautiful bride. It was hard to believe that in all that foamy white silk, I'd ever watched her exchange gunfire with Tony Salazar, or ever seen the blunted bullet embedded harmlessly in her vest. Her new husband kept shaking my hand, as if he owed me something.

"Bridger was just telling me something strange," I say, shaking off the thoughts. "He met a woman today who couldn't remember who Hannah was. She got her confused with some other kid. It's hard to believe, don't you think?"

Nobody replies. Nobody has to. We ponder the way of the world, the object of so much searching eventually forgotten, relegated to the dustbin of missing daughters. None of us will ever forget, or ever confuse her with anyone else.

"All right," Cavallo says. "It's probably time to go inside."

We exchange looks, but none of us go. We're all waiting to see who will make the first move.

ABOUT THE AUTHOR

J. Mark Bertrand has an MFA in Creative Writing from the University of Houston. After one hurricane too many, he left Houston and relocated with his wife, Laurie, to the plains of South Dakota. Find out more about Mark and the ROLAND MARCH series at:

www.backonmurder.com